KT-440-922

Gallachers

Margaret Thomson Davis

ARROW

Published by Arrow Books in 1999

1 3 5 7 9 10 8 6 4 2

Copyright © Margaret Thomson Davis 1998

First published in the United Kingdom in 1998 by Century

Arrow Books Limited
20 Vauxhall Bridge Road, London, SWIV 2SA

Random House Australia (Pty) Limited
20 Alfred Street, Milsons Point, Sydney,
New South Wales 2061, Australia

Random House New Zealand Limited
18 Poland Road, Glenfield
Auckland 10, New Zealand

Random House South Africa (Pty) Limited
Endulini, 5a Jubilee Road, Parktown 2193, South Africa

Random House UK Limited Reg. No. 954009

A CIP catalogue record for this book
is available from the British Library

Papers used by Random House UK Limited
are natural, recyclable products made from wood grown in
sustainable forests. The manufacturing processes conform to
the environmental regulations of the country of origin

ISBN 0 09 925529 4

Printed and bound in Great Britain by
Bookmarque Ltd, Croydon, Surrey

GALLACHERS

Margaret Thomson Davis has lived in Glasgow since the age of three. She is the author of twenty previous novels, an autobiography and over two hundred short stories. Two of her novels have been adapted for the stage; *The Breadmakers* won a Festival Award for drama.

This book is dedicated to
my dear friend and super-cook,
Catherine Brown

Acknowledgements

I would like to thank everyone who assisted me with my research.

First of all, Catherine Brown who allowed me to use recipes from her books on Scottish cooking.

The librarians and the security guard at Possilpark Library in Glasgow were real founts of knowledge about the area.

Hugh McGuiness, the manager of the City Housing Department gave me a fascinating guided tour.

Then there was the manager of the Community Centre who put me in touch with lots of people, including the wonderful old lady who told me all about her happy days as a fancy box maker.

Ian Ryder who owns the ladies and gentswear shop in Saracen Street, and the many other kindly Possilpark folk were a great source of local information.

Ena Baxter of Baxters and Sons was so kind and generous in her help, I can never thank her enough.

Sheriff Andrew Lothian was very helpful. (He treated me to a couple of good lunches as well!)

Professor Ross Harper, CBE was extremely generous with his time and advice.

I must make special mention of the lady CID detective at Saracen Police Office and all her uniformed colleagues there.

Also, many thanks to Detective Inspector Robert Barrowman of Strathclyde Police CID Divisional Headquarters, Glasgow who gave unstintingly of his time.

Talking of time, I mustn't forget Alan Hamilton, TD, Management Support Officer of Her Majesty's Cornton Vale Prison at Stirling, who was so patient in showing me around the prison, explaining procedures, and allowing me to pester everyone with innumerable questions.

Many thanks also to George Boyd who entertained me with anecdotes about his marvellous granny.

I always find people kind and helpful but never more so than while I was researching this book.

THE CREDIT BELONGS

The Credit belongs to those
who are actually in the arena,
who strive valiantly,
who know the great enthusiasms,
the great devotions,
and spend themselves in a worthy cause;
who at the best,
know the triumph of high achievement;
and who, at the worst,
if they fail,
fail while daring greatly,
so that their place shall never be with
those cold and timid souls
who know neither victory nor defeat.

Theodore Roosevelt

Quote hanging on the office wall of the Staff Support Officer in Her Majesty's Prison at Cornton Vale

Chapter One

Kate Gallacher was stubborn. Or so her mother never tired of saying. Occasionally the words were delivered as a compliment. More often than not, however, her mother was complaining about her. Kate could remember as a wee girl – before she was even old enough to go to school – standing on a stool at the kitchen table, in deep concentration, watching Mary making bread or biscuits or pastry. She'd copy the process. If she failed the first time, it never put her off trying again. That was the kind of occasion when her stubbornness was held up as something to be admired.

Her brother Joe often said that getting all that practice in cooking when she was little was a mistake because since then she had been landed with most of it to do.

Now her mother tended to say, 'Och, Kate's better than me at aw the fancy stuff.'

The trouble was as she got older, Kate longed to get out more with her pal, Dorothy. Now there were her secret meetings with Pete Brodie.

She'd put forward tentative objections about having to stay in for precious hours at a time to make meals for weekly family gatherings, visits from her mother's friends, special occasions like Christmas, New Year, Hallowe'en, Easter or anybody's birthday, to mention but a few. Her mother had quickly squashed her.

'Don't be bloody selfish. An' thrawn. Ye know fine ye enjoy footerin' aboot doin' aw that fancy stuff.'

Instead of vigorously fighting her corner as she should, Kate's anger and resentment burned inwards. She had been conditioned, like Pavlov's dogs, to recognise that outward cheek or mutiny towards her mother meant immediate violence in the form of a punch in the eye or a blow on the

1

ear. Her mother possessed amazing reflex speed, as well as wiry strength, for someone so tiny. She was nicknamed 'Wee Willie Winkie' or sometimes 'Shorty' but always behind her back. No one had the nerve to call her either of these names to her face.

Kate hated her outward weakness in not speaking up more but sometimes she couldn't help it. She had even become a bit shy and timorous in other situations with other people. At primary school, she'd been bullied mercilessly. It was even worse than being bullied at home.

Of course, even their dog Rajah, who was a German Shepherd the size of a lion, was only too well aware of her mother's toughness. Rajah was terrified of Mary. Kate's only consolation was that she could make up for her weakness with an inner strength of sorts. For instance, she had sat at the front room table, her long hair curtaining her face as she slowly struggled to make sense of geometry and algebra. She hated it but she was determined not to be beaten by it. In the end she got a first-class pass in Maths. Her mother had been proud of that.

But mostly Mary spoke to Kate in a bitter and complaining tone. Just last week, for instance, Kate had stubbornly insisted on leaving school. It wasn't long after her sixteenth birthday and Mary had looked forward to her daughter staying on, then eventually 'doing the family proud' by going to university. No one in the Gallacher family, or in Mary's family, had ever made it to university. Or even stayed on at school. Kate's father was known locally as 'Gentleman George'. He was clever and had done well. But it was by working his way up from office boy to Provident man. He was important in the area because so many families depended on him for supplying their Provident Club cheques.

Her two brothers, Tommy and Joe, had left school as soon as possible. Tommy, the eldest at twenty-five, always called her his wee sister but in fact she was taller than him and not nearly as skinny. Tommy was working his way up in

Minnie's Mini-Market. Twenty-year-old Joe was a motor mechanic. He was Mary's favourite because, as she always said, 'He takes after ma George.' This could only be because of his considerable height and hefty build, and despite his red hair and freckles.

'We couldnae afford tae keep the boys on in them days,' her mother explained, 'but you could huv yer chance if ye'd jist take it. But no, no' you!'

Then, to make things a hundred times worse, Kate now announced that she wanted to get married to Pete Brodie.

'Whit?' her mother screeched, venting her anger by giving Rajah a kick when he approached hoping for a pat on the head. 'That chancer? That layabout? Anyway ye're far too young tae marry anybody. Forget it!'

'He's not a layabout,' Kate protested. 'He works just as hard as Tommy and Joe.'

Wee Mary started peeling the potatoes for their tea. She still referred to their evening meal as tea, and their midday meal as dinner. Although snobby Aunty Bec kept reminding her, 'It's lunch in the middle of the day now, Mary, and dinner in the evening.'

Aunty Bec had been born and bred in Possilpark like the rest of them but she had moved to Queen's Park after marrying Uncle Willie Murray. She and Uncle Willie now voted Conservative and spoke as if they alone had been responsible for getting Margaret Thatcher into power. They had enough common sense, and instinct for survival of course, not to boast of this in Possilpark.

'Work? Work?' Mary tossed sarcastic words over her shoulder at Kate as she viciously attacked a basinful of potatoes. 'It would be easier to get Pete Brodie into a strait-jacket than a work jacket.'

Kate was far more afraid of her mother than of Aunty Bec, who was twice wee Mary's size and double her bulk. Now she felt both afraid and furious. Afraid because she'd still to confess that she was pregnant and furious because she couldn't fathom what her mother could possibly have

3

against Pete. It was her love for Pete that gave her courage. She thought he was so handsome, so different from the other young men she knew. He had such glossy black eyes and hair, and deeply tanned skin, he could pass for a gypsy. Or some foreign romantic stranger like a Spaniard. She'd never met any Spaniards but she could just imagine Pete as a matador or a flamenco dancer. Lots of guys wore a gold earring nowadays but Pete looked as if he was born for one.

And he did work. As a young child he worked on the fairground with his mother and father. He had lived in a caravan in those days. Then they'd moved into the house in Byshott Street when Pete was about fifteen. Not long after that his mother had been murdered coming home from the fairground one night on her own. Pete's father had never forgiven himself for letting her walk home through Possil alone like that. After all, Possilpark wasn't Queen's Park. The place was hotching with junkies who'd rob their grannies for a fix.

Pete's father had lost the place after that. He'd become depressed and got drunk as often as he could. He'd given up his roundabout at the fair. Sold it and squandered every penny on drink. Poor Pete had had to fend for himself for the past nine years, working at this, that and the other. Now he'd got a job with a minicab firm.

So what was her mother blethering about?

'That's not fair,' Kate cried out. 'You know fine he works. He's always worked. I can't understand what you have against him.'

'He's a nutter.'

'He is not.' Kate flushed at her temerity. 'You don't know him.'

'And ah dinnae want tae know him. From what ah've heard an' what ah've seen, he's a bloody nutter. An' dinnae jist hing aboot at ma back. Ah thought ye said ye were goin' tae make some sort o' fancy fish for the tea.' She turned to snarl at the dog. 'You get tae yer bed oot the road.'

Kate said, 'Well, I do know him and he's . . . he's . . .'

4

She stared at the back of her mother's head piled a foot high with red curls and rolls. Like the ridiculous high heels Mary teetered about on, her hairstyle was meant to give the impression that she was as tall as the next person. Kate struggled for something suitable to say. She couldn't very well blurt out 'He's so sexy, he makes me throb inside until I could burst, makes me nearly swoon at the sight of him.'

'Good looks won't feed the wean,' Mary said. 'He disnae even look like a Glasgow man. He's a right dago.'

Kate felt suddenly faint and had to sit down, even though she realised what her mother had just said was quite a common expression. Her mother couldn't be referring to 'the wean' that her daughter and the hated Pete had so recently created. Rajah whined in sympathy from the safety of his basket in the corner.

'Shut it!' Mary bawled at him. Then to Kate, noticing the pallor of her daughter's face, 'Whit's up wi' you now?'

She banged the pot of potatoes on to the cooker.

'I want to marry Pete.'

'You must be a nutter as well. Ah'm tellin' ye, ye cannae an' that's that. Ye're hardly out o' school. Hardly out o' nappies, for God's sake. Get on wi' yer fancy stuff an' stop yer nonsense. Yer daddy'll be here in half an hour an' he likes his tea on the table.'

Kate's mouth tightened in frustration. Everything she had ever made, her mother referred to scathingly as 'yer fancy stuff'. But Mary enjoyed it as much as, if not more than anybody else. Of course, it was part of the Glasgow tradition not to be over-lavish with praise. To mention casually that something was 'no' bad' was a compliment of the highest order.

'It's only poached fillets of sole with grapes and cream.'

'Fish wi' grapes an' cream,' her mother cried heavenwards as if sharing the ridiculousness of it with God. 'Whit next?' She began to gather up dishes and cutlery to take through to the living room. The kitchen had a small scrubbed table where a coal bunker used to be but Mary wouldn't dream

5

of having 'Gentleman George' crush in there and eat in the kitchen. She treated her man like royalty. Nothing was too good for him. Every day it was a nicely set table in the living room with a table cover and paper serviettes. The serviettes, like a few other niceties, had been copied after visits to Aunty Bec's posh flat in Queen's Drive.

'Mammy.' Kate's voice loudened in desperation. 'Will you sit down for a minute. Please! This is serious. The fish won't take a minute.' Actually it would take a bit longer by the time she poached the fillets of sole and added the cream and grapes and arranged the whole thing nicely in a serving dish.

Mary glared at her.

'Is there something wrong wi' yer ears as well as yer brain? Ah said – no.'

'But Mammy . . .' Kate burst out, 'I'm pregnant.'

'Whit?'

Quick as a serpent's tongue, Mary's fist flashed out and punched Kate hard on the eye.

'You stupit wee cow!'

Kate began to howl and cry, not because of the insult but because she felt as if her left eye had burst and was pouring down her cheek.

'You stupit wee cow!' her mother repeated with a smack to each side of Kate's face in time with her words.

Kate was gasping for breath now but her fury was returning. She struggled to her feet, giving herself an immediate advantage. She wasn't very tall but she was still five or six inches taller than her mother (even with her mother's mountain of hair).

'No, I'm not. I want to marry him. And he wants to marry me. There's no problem.'

'Nae problem?' Mary shouted. 'Ye're barely sixteen. Ye're jist a wean an' that oily bastard's taken advantage of ye.'

'Pete wants to take care of me.'

'God!' Mary gazed heavenwards again. 'The innocence o' the wean! That bastard couldnae take care o' a budgie.'

6

'OK,' Kate half sobbed but she was still on her wave of fury. 'OK, I'll go and stay with him and his da in Byshott Street. Forget about a wedding. Pete and I can go to Gretna Green by ourselves.'

'Whit huv ah done tae deserve this?' Mary asked the kitchen in general. 'Whit heinous crime huv ah committed?' Then straight at her daughter in an unusually polite tone, 'You will not disgrace me or your respectable daddy by doing any such thing.'

'Well then,' Kate said, suddenly not angry any more, just tired. She'd hardly slept a wink the night before with worrying about it all. She knew about the birds and bees, and where babies came from but she was still a bit in the dark about childbirth. In fact, she felt she had entered a scary black tunnel and was totally ignorant about what awaited her at the end of it.

She'd heard her mother and her mother's cronies swap too many dramatic and horrific tales about childbirth. She loved Pete, it was true, but she had come to realise that he didn't understand her fears. He had laughed when she'd nervously repeated some of the stories she'd heard.

'Rubbish! It's nothing,' he'd assured her. 'Women are having babies all the time. It's a natural thing, just like having a shite. Native women just crouch down at the side of the road and instead of having a shite, they have a kid.'

She hadn't argued with him but it did occur to her that there were differences. What could happen (if indeed it ever had happened) with native women in the jungles of Africa or wherever, wasn't the same as what happened in Glasgow. The diet was different, the lifestyle was different. The women out there could even be *made* differently, for all she knew.

Anyway, talking to Pete hadn't helped. She was still frightened. But of course she wouldn't admit such a weakness to anybody else. She'd brazen it out.

'Ah'll have tae talk tae yer daddy,' Mary said. 'He's no gonnae be pleased. Pete Brodie of aw folk. An' Byshott

Street of aw places. Ah mean, even if ye did get merrit, ye'd still huv tae go there. Yer daddy would never huv that trash stayin' here under his respectable roof. An' my God,' she suddenly remembered, 'yer Aunty Bec an' yer Uncle Willie are coming for their tea tonight!'

'He is *not* trash.'

'Aw, shut up, ye idiot,' Mary bawled.

Kate was trembling violently as well as sobbing now but she still managed to stand up straight.

'No, I will *not* shut up. I'm *not* an idiot. Pete is *not* trash and there's no "even ifs" about it. I am going to marry him. I don't care what you or Daddy or Aunty Bec or Uncle Willie says. I'm going to marry Pete.'

Her mother shook her head.

'Ah've always said it an' ah'll say it again, there's a stubborn bit aboot ye.'

Chapter Two

Neither Kate nor wee Mary got a chance to tell Kate's daddy before Aunty Bec and Uncle Willie, and their daughter Sandra, arrived for their tea. The conversation took its usual turn. After Mary announced apologetically that Kate had made one of her fancy things and the Murray family had accepted it with good grace, Aunty Bec said,

'We could hardly get in the close for those awful junkies, or whatever they're called.'

'Och, they must huv been jist passin',' Mary protested. 'There's nae drug dealers or junkies up oor stair.'

'Killearn Street's notorious, so it is.' Bec's eyes bulged dramatically. 'It's even too much for the police. They just turn a blind eye, so they do.'

'Aye, but no' at oor end,' Mary said. 'It's aw up the Byshott Street end.' She lapsed into sudden tragic silence, obviously remembering the other Byshott connection.

'Is something up?' Bec could sniff out trouble like a professional bloodhound.

Kate rose.

'Does anybody want any more fish *véronique?*'

Sandra spluttered and doubled forward over her plate with giggles. She was fat like Bec. Or as Bec liked to put it, 'Sandra favours her mother.' The only attractive thing about Sandra as far as Kate was concerned was her long curly lashes and blonde hair with its silky fringe hanging down to her eyebrows. Sandra was conceited about her eyebrows and hair.

Kate snapped.

'What's so funny?'

'Well . . . fish *véronique.*' Sandra tittered and slid a sly glance up through her fringe at her mother.

9

'I know,' Bec said. 'It doesn't seem to fit a place like this.'
It was wee Mary's turn to snap.

'Whit's wrang wi' the place?'

She was always ready to hotly defend her home but secretly she accepted that, despite all her efforts to keep it like a new pin, it could never be in the same class as the huge, high-ceilinged flat in Queen's Drive, in the leafy district of Queen's Park.

'Nothing, nothing,' Bec said, 'it's a very nice place . . . for Possil.'

'There's nothin' wrang wi' Possil either. Ah've got good neighbours an' friends here. Ye were born an' brought up here yersel', Bec.'

'Yes, but it's gone sadly down the hill since then, hasn't it, George?'

George had been tucking into his fish *véronique*. He enjoyed his food and consumed a great deal of it. As his wife always said, 'He's a big man, he needs more than most.'

'Yes indeed,' George said. 'Changed days, Bec. Changed days. Possilpark had a proud history before it all went down the drain.'

'Had it?' Bec was surprised. She had never been as well read as her brother. Their mother always said, 'George keeps that library going.'

'Oh yes. Did you know,' he aimed his fork around the table, 'that Charles Dickens once visited Possilpark?'

There was a general gasp of astonished disbelief.

'It's true. He stayed with Sheriff Alison in Possil House. And he was only one of many important visitors down through the ages.'

'Fancy,' Mary said. 'Fancy you knowing that.' She gazed at him with pride. What a fine-looking big man he was, with his thick mane of black hair and the distinguished touches of grey at each temple. Those bushy black brows with their streaks of grey were dramatic as well. And what a luxurious moustache! He took such good care of it too. He even had a special brush for his moustache. Compared with Bec's wee skinny Willie, with his skimpy, sandy hair, her George was a noble giant of a man. Willie looked like a wax candle that had begun to melt down.

'There's puddin',' Mary told her man. 'Rice. Ah made it masel'. None o' yer tinned stuff. Good auld baked rice wi' a skin on it the same as ma mammy makes.'

Her mother, at eighty-three, was still going strong in her wee room and kitchen above the shops round in Saracen Street. She still made her rice puddings on an old black range. No modern cookers for her.

'How is your mother these days, Mary?' Bec asked politely.

'Och fine, fine. She's still able tae stomp around the house but she disnae get out much. It's the stairs she cannae manage. She cannae get doon the stairs tae the lavvy. She uses a pail in the room cupboard for a pee an' I go round an' empty it every day or two.'

Bec's large face took on an expression of acute suffering but she struggled through her pained sensibilities to say, 'Of course we were never used to an outside toilet, were we, George? Mother's four-in-the-block has a bathroom.'

Mary and Kate were very well aware of this and also that Walnut Crescent was the best part of Possilpark.

'Well,' Mary said defensively, 'it's never done either ma mammy nor me any harm.'

Bec looked extremely doubtful about this.

'And ma brother Jack has done awfy well in Australia,' Mary added for good measure.

'How's business, Willie?' George asked, dabbing at his moustache with one of the pink paper serviettes.

'Oh I have my loyal regulars, George.' Willie was manager of a shoe shop in Victoria Road practically round the corner from where he lived. 'Ladies and gentlemen who like a bit of advice about a comfortable fit. People with problem feet are my speciality. I find bunions my biggest worry. Although corns can cause me a great deal of concern as well. And I get some dreadful ones. I had an elderly lady the other day . . . You've never seen such feet.' Willie was obviously enjoying himself. He loved his work. He had an almost Christ-like dedication. He spent most of every day on his knees religiously caring for people's feet.

'Is Sandra gonnae join ye in the shop when she leaves the school?' Mary interrupted a vivid description of a fungal infection between somebody's toes.

'What?' Bec's brows shot up. Thick eyebrows she had; not as thick as George's but still too thick for a woman. Mary never said to George but she often thought to herself that fifty-five-year-old Bec was as ugly as an old hippo. She'd said to Bec once, 'Why don't you give your eyebrows a wee pluck, hen?' Bec had been offended. 'I'm as the good Lord made me and I'm perfectly content with His handiwork, so I am.'

It must have been one of God's bad days. 'Well,' Mary said, 'ah don't mind givin' the good Lord a wee helping hand. Ah pluck ma brows an' dye ma hair an' plaster on as much make-up as ah can.'

'Yes,' Bec said, 'there's no need to tell us, Mary. Your efforts are only too obvious.'

Now she said, 'Our Sandra's at Hutcheson's Grammar. The best school in Glasgow.'

Mary said, 'Ah know, hen, but she's – what – past seventeen now? She surely cannae stay in Hutchies for ever.'

'She's just sat her Highers. She'll be leaving after the holidays.'

'And *is* she gonnae go into the shoe trade?'

Sandra peeked up through her fringe in amusement and her mother's voice acquired a note of pride.

'Of course not! Our Sandra's going to university, aren't you, pet?'

Mary cast a tragic look in Kate's direction. For Sandra to be the one to go to university was adding insult to injury. In fact, it wasn't easy for Kate either. She was thoroughly fed up with Auntie Bec and cousin Sandra boasting, and looking down their noses at the Gallacher family. Every Gallacher that is, except 'Gentleman George'. Of course he was a 'collar and tie man' like Uncle Willie. Even Tommy didn't wear a collar and tie at his work. The uniform in the mini-market was a navy T-shirt and trousers and a light blue nylon jacket with M.M. embroidered in navy on the top pocket. Joe of course was always in greasy overalls.

'She's looking forward to it, aren't you, Sandra pet?'

'Oh yes,' Sandra sighed with utter contentment. 'Edinburgh Uni as well.'

'Of course, we'll miss her.' Bec's mountainous chest heaved out a sigh. Kate nearly said 'We'll not', but controlled herself in time.

'Aye, so ye will,' Mary said, rising. 'Ah'll fetch the puddin'.' She escaped into the kitchen. Probably to kick the dog. She loved the animal dearly but confused it by alternating between violent hugs and kisses and equally violent kicks.

'So,' George beamed and patted his broad belly, or his 'corporation', as he was fond of calling it. 'You're emigrating to the Far East, eh?'

Everybody laughed except Kate.

'The capital city.' Bec savoured the words. 'It's a lovely place, so it is. Willie and I went through with her the other day. We had a grand time, didn't we, Willie?'

'We did indeed. After visiting the university, we did so much walking and exploring around the city, I was glad I was wearing Dr Semple's insoles in my black Oxfords. They're like miniature water beds, they cushion your feet so well. I recommend them to a lot of my customers.'

'Remember the view we had from the castle, Willie?' Bec said. 'Wasn't that spectacular?'

'It was indeed.'

Bec waited until Mary bustled back into the room wearing oven gloves and carrying a large ashet of steaming rice before asking. 'And what's your Kate going to do, Mary? Staying on, is she?'

Kate groaned inside. Oh God. Is she going to blurt it out now, in front of everybody? Her mother had always been like a tiger in her protectiveness towards her sons. But for

13

some reason, within the family at least, she did not have the same sense of loyalty towards her daughter.

'Ye might as well aw know at once,' Mary said, dishing up the rice and practically throwing each plate across the table.

Oh God!

'Naw, she's no' stayin' on. She cannae stay on. The stupit cow's got hersel' pregnant.'

For a long minute there was shocked silence mixed, Kate felt sure, with a perverted sense of triumph in the broad bosoms of Aunty Bec and cousin Sandra. How dreadful, they'd be thinking. But of course we always knew she would come to a bad end one day.

'Pregnant?' It was her father who spoke first. The tone of his voice reminded her of Lady Bracknell in Oscar Wilde's play, *The Importance of Being Earnest*, when she was told her nephew had been found in a handbag. 'A *handbag*?'

'Oh,' Bec managed in a more funereal tone. 'Is that not terrible!'

'Who's the father?' Sandra was wide-eyed with enjoyment. Callous cow!

'Pete Brodie,' Kate burst out defiantly.

'*Pete Brodie?*' Her father repeated his Lady Bracknell act.

Bec said, 'Not that awful showground character with the gallus swaggering walk?' Half the male characters in Possilpark, if not Glasgow, had the same mixture of cocky swagger and sailor's roll. In Bec's opinion however Pete Brodie's swagger was more aggressive than most.

'Dead gallus,' Mary said. 'Ah told her. Ah told her right from the start. But would she listen? Naw . . .' Kate mentally mouthed the words along with her. 'There's a stubborn bit aboot her.'

'Well, I never . . .' Bec gasped.

I could believe that, Kate thought. Sandra's arrival in the world must have been a virgin birth.

'What are you going to do, Mary? And poor George.' She turned to her brother, bulbous eyes brimming over with sympathy. 'Oh George, the shame of it!'

Kate spoke up, still defiant.

'I'm going to marry Pete. There's no problem.'

'Would ye listen tae the stupit cow?' her mother asked everybody at the table.

'But dear,' Bec turned to Kate, solicitous now, 'you're under age. In fact,' her eyes lit up, 'it's a crime.'

'What's a crime?' Kate asked.

'A crime?' Mary echoed.

'Yes, he's had sexual intercourse with a child. He could be flung in jail.'

'I'm not a child.'

'You must have had ... you know ... when you were under age, dear. That's a crime.'

Kate felt sick with fear. She struggled valiantly not to show it.

'I know that it's all right for us to be married now that I am sixteen. That's Scots law, in case you didn't know.'

She got up from the table with as much dignity as she could muster.

'You can talk about me as much as you like, I don't care. I'm away to see Pete. He's *happy* about the baby. And what's more,' she added, lying through her teeth, '*I'm* happy about it too.'

Chapter Three

Killearn Street, Stoneyhurst Street and Allander Street ran uphill and parallel to one another like a three-sided ladder with Saracen Street at one end and Byshott Street at the other. The three rungs of the ladder between Saracen and Byshott were Barloch Street, Rednock Street and Kinbuck Street. It was said that this area was the drug capital of Europe. But in Kate's opinion, the other side of Saracen, Sunnielaw Street for instance, was worse, the absolute pits.

Still, around here was bad enough. She passed queues stretching all the way down two or three flights of stairs from houses that were selling heroin and temazepam. The queues were mostly of young people with asthmatic breath and scabby faces, hands plunged deep in anoraks, eyes wild and staring or with a dazed faraway expression. If they hadn't cash, they'd beg for tick, for a share, or for a needle. If they couldn't get anything, they'd go and rob or burgle or mug to get the money for what they needed. What puzzled Kate was where the men or women in the houses got the drugs to sell. Who dealt with the dealers?

As her mother said, their end of Killearn Street wasn't so bad (and it was so handy for the shops in Saracen Street). Dealers and druggies passed, often very noisily, to and fro but they never came in their close or up their stair. They never even hung about in the street outside. They knew wee Mary would set the dog on them: she always seemed to be on guard at her top-storey window. Even if they just stopped for a minute to light a fag, she'd haul the window up and bawl down at them, 'Move it, you. If ye dinnae piss off pronto, ah'll open ma door fur the dug.'

Her voice had an amazing power for the size of her. Like a Clyde hooter, it was. There used to be plenty of hooters heard in Glasgow when the River Clyde was chock-a-block with ships and boats of all kinds. Not any more.

Mary's dog had a bark like an elephant's trumpet. If undesirables didn't get off their mark immediately and put a wide enough space between them and Mary's close, the brown monster would come charging and trumpeting down the stair, desperate to sink its fangs into them. Even when she was walking the dog along Saracen Street to Granny McWhirter's place and they were at the shops where they had a perfect right to be, everyone hastily gave wee Mary a wide berth. Only somebody stoned out of their mind dared take wee Mary on. And they always got the worst of it. She had a tongue like a plumber's mate as well, except when she was with 'Gentleman George' in the pub or the café. She always tried to act the lady when she was out with him.

There had been nobody hanging about outside the close when Kate emerged to walk up Killearn Street with its dismal grey houses and dusty swirls of litter. As well as the queues in the closes, knots of people were buying and selling drugs in the street. Some were having a snort there and then. But injecting was the worst. It still made Kate wince to see anybody sticking a needle into themselves. She had a horror of needles. But it was difficult to avoid the sight of them. She'd even seen girls not much older than herself crouched behind the bookshelves in the library, injecting. There was a full-time security guard in the library now but, as he said himself, he hadn't eyes in the back of his head. The guard had told Kate's father that when some of them were high they didn't know what they were doing. One girl had even relieved her bowels in the library and the poor librarian had to clean it up.

Kate had never touched any kind of drug. One reason was that her mother had warned her, 'You touch any o' that stuff an' I'll leather ye black an' blue.' And she would have.

Another reason was she never felt the need of an artificial buzz. She got enough of a buzz without drugs. Her relationship with Pete Brodie, for instance. He'd been standing at the corner at Saracen Cross when she'd first seen him. She had been strolling along with her pal, Dorothy McKinlay, secretly hoping to meet a boyfriend. They'd passed the group of boys at the corner and giggled together at the bevy of wolf whistles aimed at them. Not that they'd been surprised at the admiration they provoked, even from older guys like them. After all, Dorothy had been wearing her new jeans and ankle boots and Kate her belted jacket that accentuated her neat waist. Dorothy had recently had her curly hair cut short and had tried unsuccessfully to persuade Kate to get hers cut too.

Later Kate had been glad she'd resisted the temptation because since their first encounter, Pete had fingered and stroked her long chestnut-brown hair and said it was what he liked most about her.

Dorothy had laughed when Kate had confided this to her.

'That'll be the day! With his sexy eyes it's not your hair he's after.'

Right enough, as soon as they'd started going out together, Pete had tried to have sex. Kate had been hesitant, secretly frightened. At first he'd been quite nice about her shrinking away physically and mentally.

'Everybody does it,' he'd whispered. 'What's the problem?'

Part of the problem was they were standing in the dark and draughty back close. It stank of cats' pee despite her mother's efforts with disinfectant and pails of water. Not that her mother cleaned the close so often now. After all, they lived upstairs and the close was supposed to be the responsibility of Mrs McKay and Mrs Dooley who had the bottom flats. It was Mrs Dooley's cats that were to blame, of course.

'Such a nice wee soul in other ways,' Mary always insisted. 'An' she wis that good when Rajah bit wan o' Fluffy's ears aff. Ye've got tae come an' go wi' folk.'

At least the top flat stairs and landing were kept spotless.

It didn't seem right, and certainly was not very romantic, to make love in a stinking, draughty back close. She'd felt too shy to explain to Pete that she nursed a dream of getting married first and losing her virginity on her honeymoon on a lovely comfortable bed in some posh hotel. He'd probably have laughed at her. He would have tossed back his dark head and shown his perfect white teeth in that strange grimacing way he had. Eventually she'd blurted out as an excuse,

'My mother might come down looking for me.'

This was a real danger, right enough.

'She'd murder me,' she added for good measure.

Eventually Pete had taken her to his home. She'd never forget the shock of that first visit. The place was manky. It looked as if the Corporation cleansing department had tipped most of Possil's rubbish into the four-apartment house.

'My da never lifts a hand these days,' Pete explained. 'And I haven't the time.' At least Pete's bedroom wasn't so bad, although the bed sheets didn't look too fresh. Kate began to regard it as a miracle that Pete could emerge from a place like this looking as clean and smart as he did.

'How do you do your washing?' she asked, really wanting to know despite Pete's efforts to kiss her neck and be romantic.

'For fuck's sake!' he mumbled from inside her collar. At the same time he manoeuvred her over to the bed. It wasn't made, Kate noticed, and there was a pile of crumpled underwear, a couple of shirts and some socks at the foot of it. Obviously, he hadn't done this week's washing.

Her shock and fascination at the enormity of the place helped her overcome her apprehension. She'd been shaking, nearly collapsing with fear, until the moment Pete swung open the outside door and revealed a sea of litter almost as bad as she'd waded through coming up Killearn Street.

'Jesus!' she'd gasped. An expletive for which she would

have received a vicious belt on the ear from Mary, despite the fact that Mary often swore herself.

She couldn't get over the sight of the place and the state it was in. Her mother's house was spotless. Granny McWhirter's wee room and kitchen were equally neat and clean. Aunty Bec and Granny Gallacher's place was posh, as well. All of them would have died if they'd seen the inside of this house. Her mind was still reeling with it all as Pete tried to made love to her. She was still reluctant. It wasn't her idea of a romantic alternative. In fact, it was worse than the back close.

'Come on,' Pete cajoled. 'Relax.' But she couldn't relax. When he did eventually persuade her, she cried out in pain and wouldn't hear of a repetition of the intimacy for some time. It took much persuasion and many assurances that he'd be gentle and not cause her any more pain before she would join him in the same bed again. She began to almost enjoy it except, at the back of her mind, always spoiling everything, was the state of the place. There was the awful thought too that Pete's father might burst in. She began to think quite a lot about Budd Brodie. His name, she'd discovered, wasn't a traditional showground one, but in fact an old Celtic name. She'd often seen Budd staggering up Killearn Street, baggy trousered, his thin sallow face unshaven, singing at the top of his voice. She'd never seen him speak to anybody though. She'd heard that he used to be full of the patter when he worked in the fairground. Now, when he was sober, he'd just give a nod of greeting to anybody in the street who said hello. He looked shabby and neglected with buttons missing from his shirt. He never wore a pullover or a tie or a scarf. Or even a coat on cold days.

One thing was for sure: if she was to come and live in Budd's house, she'd have to clean it up. Of course she'd only ever be here on a temporary basis. She had wonderful dreams of Pete and her having a lovely place of their own. She'd keep it like a wee palace. The job of tackling the tip didn't bother her. She discovered she enjoyed a challenge. Already she'd made a start. Practically every day after school, she'd gone and attacked the place with a brush and shovel and made innumerable trips out to the bin in the back court. No wonder she was knackered every night and nearly fell asleep over her homework. Her mother thought she must be getting anaemic and began forcing an iron tonic down her throat.

Reaching Byshott Street, Kate rang the doorbell, then stood gazing at the green-tinged brass name plate. B. BRODIE it said, but you could barely read it. She would have to clean that as well.

'The old man' as Pete sometimes called him (although he couldn't be more than fifty if he was a day) opened the door.

'Is Pete there, Mr Brodie?'

He shook his head.

'Oh.'

'Come in if you want.' He turned back into the house. Kate followed him.

'Have you any idea where he is?'

'Working.'

'I thought he was going to take tonight off.'

Mr Brodie shrugged and lit a cigarette.

'He told me,' she said.

'The cab office phoned.'

Since Pete got a job with Possil Cabs, he'd had the phone installed. He seemed to make very good money. She didn't know exactly how much, but Pete never seemed short. Even though he spent a lot on clothes and had recently treated himself to a stunner of a gold watch. Big and chunky and fashionable, you couldn't miss it. He'd promised her a diamond engagement ring. Real diamonds. They planned to start looking in jewellers' shops as soon as she'd told her parents.

Now where was he? Of course, with all the extra expense of a wedding and a baby, he needed to work all the hours he could, she supposed. There was also the deposit for their dream house to save up for. She would have to find a job, and keep working so that she could start saving as well. That wouldn't be easy, especially after the baby came. Still, she determined she would manage.

'I wonder if he'll be late?'

Mr Brodie shrugged again, sat down in his armchair and lifted his *Daily Record.*

'I might as well do a wee bit while I'm here.' She took off her coat and began rolling up her sleeves.

'You're a good girl,' Mr Brodie's voice was muffled behind his paper. 'He doesn't deserve you.'

Why was it that no one seemed to appreciate Pete except her? Not even his own father. Although Mr Brodie and Pete seemed to rub along OK. At least she'd never heard them argue or fight. Pete gave the impression of being the boss, right enough. Poor Mr Brodie alternated between sick benefit and the 'buroo'. He wouldn't get much money either for being depressed or unemployed. It must be Pete who was paying the rent and feeding them both. Or near enough.

'I'll make you a cup of tea once I get organised.'

'Thanks, hen.'

Eventually she sat down and drank a cup along with him. There was silence for a long minute or two. Then Mr Brodie put down his cup, stared at her with those sad droopy eyes of his, and said,

'You don't know him very well, do you?'

She grinned.

'Well enough. I'm going to have his baby.'

'Christ!' The word dragged his mouth down, even seemed to drop an extra weight on his shoulders. The defeated, hopeless kind of look of him even made her feel depressed.

'He's going to marry me,' she informed him in case he was thinking the opposite. 'There's no problem.'

Mr Brodie just sat hunched in his chair, staring down at the linoleum.

Chapter Four

There was a family conference. Immediate family, that is. Aunty Bec and Uncle Willie weren't invited. Nor were the two grannies or the boys' wives. Only Mary and George, and brothers Joe and Tommy, and of course Kate (not forgetting Rajah, who lay as usual at Mary's feet), gathered in the front room to discuss the problem. They ignored Kate's protests that there wasn't a problem. It was decided that because of the baby, she must get married. Everybody would just have to make the best of it and do what they could for her. Although Joe's freckled face did take on a look of anxiety at one point and he asked,

'Do you really want to marry him, Kate?'

'Yes, I do.'

'OK. That's the main thing as far as I'm concerned.'

Kate smiled her gratitude. Of course it wasn't so long ago that wee Mary had been slagging off Joe's wife, Marilyn. When Joe had announced his intention of marrying her, Mary cried out, 'For pity's sake, Joe, you could dae better than that stupit wee blonde. Aw she can dae is kid hersel' she's the double o' Marilyn Monroe. An' she's no'.'

Marilyn wasn't all that bright and she did make a bit of a fool of herself pouting and widening her baby-blue eyes and wiggling her bum so much. That's what most women thought. But the men seemed to like it. Especially Joe. Nobody could deny Marilyn was a good-natured girl. There was no badness in her and she made a good wife for Joe. Not most folk's idea of a good wife, right enough. It looked like Joe did most of the cooking and a lot of other things as well. But he was happy. That's all that mattered. Maybe that was the reason Mary had come to accept her. She didn't slag Marilyn off any more. Indeed, she often helped the girl and was always giving her advice. Marilyn hung on Mary's every word with gratitude and affection. Kate often thought that Marilyn was closer to Mary (and to Gentleman George) than she was nowadays. Indeed, she sometimes wondered if Marilyn was as stupid and empty-headed as she looked.

It was decided that the wedding had better take place as quickly as possible. 'Before she shows,' as her mother said.

Whether or not they should brazen it out with a white wedding was discussed at some length.

'What do you want, hen?' Joe asked.

'A white wedding,' Kate said, glaring around. 'Why shouldn't I?' It was a silly question not worthy of an answer. Nobody gave one.

'It's nearly Easter,' Tommy said. 'Would that be too quick?'

'It'll huv tae be nae longer than a month, two at the most, or she'll show. We'll have to go like the clappers. We could hire a dress an' she could make her own cake an' we could get the invites out right away. We could huv it jist as a family affair an' the reception here. She could make some o' her fancy stuff.'

'Oh, thanks a bunch,' Kate said.

'You think yersel' lucky' – her mother pushed a beaky, aggressive face forward – 'that ah'm no beatin' ye black an' blue instead o' givin' ye a weddin'.'

Kate rolled her eyes, thinking, Giving me a wedding? She'll probably expect me to be up half the night cleaning the house as well as doing all the cooking.

Her father said, 'Yes, your mother's been very good to you. So just you remember your manners.'

God!

'Yer Daddy an' I expected great things o' ye an' now look whit's happened,' Mary said. Tragic unspoken words hung in the air: Sandra's the one who's going to the university.

Kate kept her mouth firmly shut. She refused to say she was sorry. She wasn't sorry. At least, not about marrying Pete.

Her mother went to make a cup of tea and bring more cans of beer for the men. After they all settled down again, Kate said, 'Pete should be here just now. He should have been invited.'

'Aw, shut yer stupit face,' her mother said. 'Is it no' enough that we'll have tae put up wi' him at the bloody weddin'?'

They now had pen and paper out and were intent on calculating cost. She could have told them that Pete had offered to chip in but if that was their attitude, to hell with them. She told Pete afterwards,

'Let them pay for everything. We'll need all the money we can get, what with the baby and saving up for a place of our own.'

Pete had just shrugged, and went on chewing his spearmint gum. She regarded him as a very laid-back man. Sometimes she wished she could have the same easygoing nature. There was something restless about her. She was always looking ahead to getting something better. Working for it, not dreaming about it (although she did have lots of dreams as well). She had a real capacity for hard work. This had been amply proved by the work she did and was still doing at the Brodie place. To the point so far beyond exhaustion that it was becoming an obsession. The wedding proved what she was capable of in the work stakes. All right, her mother did pitch in and do a lot of the cleaning. She even decorated the place. In fact, Kate had to say eventually, 'For goodness sake, Mammy, we haven't invited the sanitary inspector. The place is beginning to stink of disinfectant as well as furniture polish.'

'Yer Aunty Bec, or Granny Gallacher, or anybody else,' Mary said, 'is no' goin' tae accuse me of havin' wan dirty corner, wan speck o' dust, in this place.'

'Everybody in the family knows that there never has been a dirty corner or a speck of dust in this place.'

As it turned out, it wasn't just the family who were invited. The neighbours, according to Mary, had to come as well.

Kate's heart sank at the thought of Mrs Dooley. The two old bachelors, one a big teuchter who always insisted on singing doleful Highland songs, were bad enough. The other old bachelor was a wee bauchle whose Glasgow songs were at least a lot cheerier. Then there was Dorothy as the best maid and Dougie, a friend of Pete's, for best man.

Kate had never worked so hard in her sixteen years of life. After bringing the Brodie house up to normal standards, she had baked the wedding cake and prepared the food. As much as possible had been made in advance so that on the actual wedding day all she had to do was put all the dishes and cutlery on the sideboard. (Half of them had been borrowed from the neighbours.)

As if all that wasn't enough and before she'd even got started on the wedding day jobs, before she'd even got out of bed, her mother appeared in the bedroom doorway with Rajah and announced,

'Come on, ye'll huv tae wash the stairs. Ah've the bathroom still tae dae an' the windows.'

'Wash the stairs,' Kate echoed incredulously. 'It's my wedding day.'

'Ye're no' gettin' married until this afternoon. Dinnae jist lie there. Ye'll huv tae wash right doon from top to bottom an' oot the back close. An' mind ye use plenty o' disinfectant. The minister's comin' back for his tea, don't forget.'

'Right down from top to bottom?'

'Whit dae ye think ye are? A ventriloquist's dummy? You heard me.'

'Why can't everybody else take their turn?'

'Ye know fine we've two auld bachelors on the stair an' there's Mrs Lipton's arthritis an' Mrs McKay's no' aw there at times an' Mrs Dooley's goin' to be too busy keepin' her cats oot the road.'

There was bloody murder in Kate's heart. It was just terrible: down on her knees getting them all red and sore and probably putting her back out carrying a heavy pail of water.

'An' you do nice squiggles on each side wi' the pipe clay, remember. Like ah always do. An' ah'll have none o' yer dark looks either, m'lady.'

With that she was gone.

She's enjoying herself, Kate thought bitterly. She's in her element with all this cleaning and polishing. Well, I'm not. She knew better, however, than to refuse to do the stairs. A black eye would not look good with her white dress. But she made a pad for her knees and went easy on the amount of water in the pail. She had to keep changing it though. It became dirty so quickly. The trouble was that an awful lot of people used the stairs. There were the neighbours and families who came to visit. (Friends and families of the cats as well, it seemed.) Not forgetting Rajah and his dirty big paws. There were people who came to sell things or deliver things and God knows all what else. She burned with fury and frustration with every splash and slosh of the cloth on each and every stair. Her wedding day! She'd be lucky if she had time to have a bath and wash her hair.

By some miracle she did manage it, despite Aunty Bec arriving far too early and banging on the bathroom door. She could have forgiven Granny McWhirter for a desperate need to get in for a pee. She, after all, was in her eighties and had to get up to her pail in the cupboard a dozen times or more during every night. Kate knew this for a fact, having slept with Granny McWhirter on occasions and heard the all-night tinkling. There was no excuse for Aunty Bec, so Kate kept her waiting as long as she dared. Until, in fact, wee Mary came banging and bawling at the bathroom door. The dog joined in with the most earsplitting barking and yowling.

'All right. All right,' Kate shouted. 'Keep your hair on. I'm coming.'

'Ah'll keep yer hair on, ye cheeky bisom. Yer poor Aunty Bec's in agony oot here. She'll be wettin' her good silk knickers any minute.'

Aunty Bec had long ago boasted that she always wore 'good silk knickers'.

As soon as Kate opened the door, Aunty Bec burst in like a stampeding rhino, nearly knocking Kate over and her stumble sideways was helped along by the cuff on the ear her mother delivered.

'Whit dae ye think ye're playin' at? Loafin' aboot in there aw this time. Ye're no' even dressed yet. An' dinnae you mumble at me in that tone o' voice.'

'I never said a word.'

She was thinking plenty though. Mainly how glad she'd be to get away from this place and her mother. Even going to stay in Byshott Street would be better than this. Budd Brodie wasn't so bad. Quite nice in fact once you got to know him. And the house was all right now. She'd even washed the bedclothes and ironed the sheets. She'd be her own boss there. She'd be able to do whatever she liked with no one like her mother to bully her or batter her. Sheer heaven. She couldn't wait!

Tommy's lot arrived next. Too early as well, of course. The children, five-year-old Linda, four-year-old Ella and one-year-old Mungo were, it seemed to Kate, seriously hyperactive. And never more so than today. They couldn't sit still (or keep quiet) for one minute. They were running about the house as if the devil himself was at their heels. Even Mungo was crawling at full speed. Twice she tripped over him. She was so harassed she almost succumbed to the temptation of kicking him out the window. Normally she adored the baby and was always cuddling and kissing him.

How she got all the food made and set out and got herself made up and dressed on time, she never knew. She guessed it was one occasion where her famous stubbornness stood her in extra good stead. She wasn't going to be beaten. No way. Not by Aunty Bec's silent condemnation. Nor Uncle Willie's lecture on how her narrow high-heeled shoes would be the ruination of her feet. (He kept following her around like a prophet of doom. It was terrible.) Nor screaming kids. Nothing.

Eventually she stood in front of the dressing-table mirror and studied her reflection. She was flushed with all the exertion but the pink glow to her normally pale skin was quite flattering. The shampoo Dorothy had given her (Dorothy used to work in Cut Price Toiletries and still got some wonderful bargains) had made her hair even more glossy than usual. A coronet of artificial flowers and flowing veil set it off quite nicely. Kate would have preferred real flowers – spring flowers – but there weren't any growing in Possil that she'd noticed. Probably they'd died with depression at the look of the place. She was feeling depressed herself all of a sudden. It wasn't anything to do with how she looked. The plain white dress flattered her slim figure. She had managed to stand her ground against the frilly-fancy dresses that were her mother's choice.

She didn't know why she was depressed. It surely could be nothing to do with leaving home and her mother and father. After all, she could still see them as often as she wanted to. She was only moving up the road, not to Australia. She took a deep breath and concentrated on Pete Brodie. She closed her eyes and imagined being held in his arms.

'Is that you ready, Kate?' Dorothy burst into the room, scarlet with sweaty excitement. 'Oh, you look great! How do I look? Do you think this lavender really suits me?'

'It really does.' Kate picked up her bouquet. 'Especially with your fair hair.'

Behind her appeared 'Gentleman George', resplendent in his hired grey suit and high stiff collar. He looked courtly, big shoulders back, head up, carrying before him with pride his corporation, decorated with the gold watch and fob that had belonged to his late father.

'Ready, hen?'

'Yes, Daddy.'

'Now I want you to know,' her father said, sternly, importantly, 'that no matter what has happened or will happen, you'll always be welcome in this house.'

'Thanks, Daddy.'

She was really very lucky. But even that thought didn't totally lift her depression.

Chapter Five

'Let's slip away early,' Kate whispered to Pete. 'I'm so tired I can hardly keep my eyes open.'

She'd come to the conclusion that it was her fatigue that had lowered her spirits.

'You'd better keep them and everything else open tonight,' Pete laughed.

'I've been hard at it all day.'

'Not with me you haven't.'

She punched him.

'You know what I mean. Yesterday as well. It was me who made all that food. Honestly, Pete. I'm so knackered now I can hardly stand up.'

'I'll have you on your back in no time, don't you worry.'

She could have wept. She really was exhausted. Perhaps it was something to do with being pregnant as well. She didn't know. She didn't care. All she could think about was divine bed, blessed sleep.

The car that Pete drove for the private company was parked at the close.

'Do you think you should drive tonight?' Kate asked, clutching up her white skirts. She'd have to remember to pack the dress and veil and return them to the hire shop next day so that they wouldn't charge any extra. 'After so much drinking?' (He'd stumbled a couple of times coming down the stairs.)

'For Christ's sake, it's only a few yards up the street.'

The street was busy with people despite the late hour – late for normal nights but early for a wedding celebration. The party would still go riotously on until about three or four in the morning. God was with the drunks and druggies, it seemed: they just staggered out of the way of Pete's erratic driving without coming to any harm. Kate struggled wearily out of the car in Byshott Street and stood half-asleep, waiting for Pete to lock the car door, come round and take her arm to support her into the close. The window of the house next door to Budd's was boarded up and somebody had scrawled on one of the boards in large chalk letters: HELP THE POLIS — BEAT YOURSELF UP.

She'd chuckled the first time she'd seen it. Now she just stared at it blankly.

'Come on.' Pete came swaggering round, passed her and went into the dark tunnel of the close. She trailed after him, struggling not to trip on the dress and worried about it getting dirtied. Once in the bedroom she carefully stripped it off and hung it with the veil in the old-fashioned wardrobe with its mirror the length of the door and the deep drawer underneath. For a few seconds she watched in the mirror as Pete undressed. He was ripping his clothes off with such speed, he was lurching about the room. Flash Harry, wee Mary had called him when she'd seen him earlier. And she wasn't referring to speed. Kate had never seen Pete drunk before. None of her family ever got drunk. They enjoyed a few drinks, mostly on Saturdays or at special celebrations, but she'd never seen any of them drunk. Her mother went to the pub every Saturday with Gentleman George and had what she called 'a wee refreshment'. Joe used to go out with his pals but now he only went out with Marilyn. Tommy had kept up with his old mates though, despite, or maybe because of, having such boisterous children.

'Stop admiring yourself and get into bed,' Pete ordered.

She hadn't even seen herself. She'd been lost in thought, in a daze, more asleep than awake.

The mattress was hard and lumpy but Kate didn't care. She was so tired she would have collapsed on to a bed of nails and been grateful. No sooner was she on her back than Pete bumped on top of her, making her gasp for breath so much she was unable to speak. She wanted to cry out but all that she managed eventually were half-moans, half-sobs.

He was treating her like a rag doll, something not human. Totally obsessed with his own pleasure and gratification, he thumped on top of her, entering between her legs, tossed her over and forced himself into her anus, then in her mouth, making her gag and choke.

In her fatigue, in her physical and emotional pain, she thought she would die. After what seemed hours, Pete rolled over and lay loudly snoring. She *wanted* to die. Yet she was frightened to close her eyes in case she would sink helplessly down into the pit. She struggled to keep awake, determined to hang on, no matter what.

She must have slept at last because she awoke to see Pete standing over her. He was holding a steaming mug of tea and grinning down at her. He looked startlingly handsome.

'Don't say I'm not good to you.'

'Oh thanks, Pete.' She struggled into a sitting position, accepted the tea and took a grateful gulp of it.

'I'm having to go out. The boss phoned. I'm wanted on a job.'

'Now? Today? I thought you had at least today off. What about the pictures?'

They had planned to take it easy during the day – maybe go for a drive out to the country, then have a slap-up meal in a restaurant in town and go to the pictures afterwards. She'd been looking forward to it. Later on, during the summer, they hoped to go on a holiday that would serve as a honeymoon. But today was special, the first day of their married life.

'I'll be finished in time for us going into town.'

'Surely one of the other drivers could have taken the job.'

'Just mind your own business, and let me see to mine.' He winked at her. 'What you don't know won't do you any harm, eh?'

She stared back at him, puzzled, uncomprehending.

He bent down and planted a kiss on her brow. 'Have a nice day.'

Then she was left in the deep pool of silence inside the

room. Outside children were shouting and quarrelling. A ball was thumping against concrete. As she drank her tea she became aware of pain all over her body. She remembered how rough Pete had been in his love-making the previous night. Love didn't seem to have come into it. She couldn't hide from the fact that he hadn't just been rough, he had been brutal. Now, in the cool light of day and enjoying the tea that Pete had given her, she began to think differently.

Pete had been drunk and like most people when drunk, he didn't know what he was doing. He probably didn't remember what had happened during the night. She hoped he didn't because he would be so upset and sorry. Poor Pete, he obviously couldn't take too much alcohol. It made him go berserk, become an entirely different person.

The day stretched before her like a lifetime of loneliness. She wondered what she could do with the time until Pete returned. She thought of going to visit her mother. But her mother might think it odd that she was on her own today – of all days.

'Where's Flash Harry?' she'd say. And Kate would reply, 'He was called out on a job.' Then her mother would say, 'Surely one of the other drivers could have taken the job.' And she wouldn't know what to reply.

Pete must be the best and most dependable driver that Possil Cabs had. Yes, that would be it. Kate felt proud and happy at the thought. She could tell her mother that. Yet, still she hesitated. She could hear her father-in-law up and around now. Quickly she finished her tea, dressed and went through to the kitchen where an unshaven, bleary-eyed Budd was pouring himself a mug of black coffee.

'Will I make you some breakfast, Budd?'

'No, it's all right, hen. I think I'll go back to bed. It was near four in the morning when I got in.'

'You enjoyed the party then?'

'Och aye. It brought me out of myself. You've a nice family there.'

'I know.'

'Joe was telling me he's worried about his job.'

Kate was surprised.

'Is he?'

'McPherson's going bust. Of course, the old guy looks as if he'd be due to retire soon anyway. He's been losing the place for a while.'

'You mean the garage is going to close and Joe'll lose his job?'

Budd nodded. 'McPherson told Joe he'd better start looking around.'

'Oh dear. It's not easy to get a job nowadays.'

'Don't I know it!'

'I've started to try myself.'

'It'll be easier for you – a young lassie. They can pay young lassies less. In shops and places like that. Bosses are taking on part-time lassies so that they can even save paying insurance.'

'I've had no luck so far. Poor Joe. He must be worried sick. He probably hasn't said anything to Mammy or Daddy so as not to worry them.'

Budd sighed and shook his head.

'Aye.'

Silence stretched between them, something that Kate had got used to. Budd's long silences no longer made her feel uncomfortable. Eventually she said, 'I think I'll go down to Joe's place and have a word. I think he's got today off.'

'Oh aye. Everybody's got the day off except our Pete.'

She couldn't tell by his tone if he was being sarcastic or sympathetic. His voice always had that half-hopeless, half-cynical tone.

'Well, it is Saturday,' Kate said. 'The busiest day for taxis. I suppose they have to take the work when it's there, to make up for the quiet times.'

Budd said nothing.

'I'll get back in time to make you a bite of lunch.'

'No, you have the day off, hen.'

'I don't mind . . .'

'I'd rather just have the day in bed. I've got a hell of a hangover.'

'Well, if you're sure . . .'

'On you go and visit your brother.'

'OK. See you later then.'

Joe and Marilyn lived in a room and kitchen flat above the shops in Saracen Street, just a couple of closes along from Granny McWhirter. But their house had an inside toilet, a long thin room that had been a walk-in cupboard. They were terribly proud of it. A plumber friend of Joe's had installed a shower, Marilyn had bought a pretty plastic shower curtain and Joe had fixed up a rail for it. Like a couple of kids with a new toy, they were always having showers. As wee Mary said,

'A cleaner couple ye couldnae meet.'

Joe's red hair was squeaky clean and his freckled face shone like a polished apple.

Marilyn answered the door to Kate's knock. She was wearing a satin dressing-gown and nothing else, by the look of her.

'Oh Kate! Come in. Where's Pete? You can't have fallen out already. Oh dear, have you?'

She followed Kate along the windowless lobby brightening the shadows with her blonde hair and shining pink satin. 'But don't worry, dear. We're on your side. Aren't we, Joe?'

'Aren't we what?'

Joe rose from the kitchen table, dwarfing the room.

'No, it's nothing like that,' Kate said. 'The taxi place is so busy, Pete had to go out on a job. I came as soon as I heard about the garage, Joe.'

'Oh.' Joe sat down again.

'Is it true?'

'Aye, worse luck. Old McPherson's told me to look around.' He shrugged. 'But where?'

Marilyn put her arm around his shoulders. 'You'll think of some place, Joe.'

Joe sighed and leaned his head against Marilyn's soft body.

'The trouble is there's just not enough jobs to go around.'

Suddenly Kate had a brilliant idea.

'You can drive.'

'Aye.'

'Well, maybe Pete can help you. Maybe you can get a job as a cabbie with Possil Cabs. Pete does well with them.'

Joe's eyes brightened with hope.

'Do you think so?'

'Definitely. I don't know why I didn't think of it right away.'

'When will he knock off? I'll come round and have a word with him. Or maybe I should go direct to the Possil Cabs office?'

'No, let me speak to Pete first. He's one of their best workers and if he puts a word in on your behalf, I'm sure it'll do the trick.'

Joe nearly knocked his chair over in his rush to hug Kate and joyously toss her into the air.

'My smashin' wee sister. You've saved my life, hen.'

Marilyn was dancing up and down and clapping her hands like an excited two-year-old.

'Hang on, the pair of you,' Kate laughed. 'You haven't got the job yet.'

But all three of them were sure it was, as wee Mary would have said, 'as good as in the bag'.

Chapter Six

'But I don't understand.' Kate stared at Pete in astonishment. 'You know Joe's not only a good driver, he's great at fixing cars. You know he's honest and straight . . .'

'I told you to mind your own business.' Pete continued to shovel food into his mouth. She'd taken great care in cooking a special meal just in case they weren't able to go into town after all. Sirloin *chasseur* was the butcher's best Aberdeen Angus sirloin steak served in a sauce of wine, spring onions, tomatoes and mushrooms. Budd had warned her when he'd heard about the proposed restaurant and cinema plan, 'If he comes in at all, it'll be to grab something to eat and bomb out again.'

Oh well, she'd thought resignedly, such was a taxi driver's life. And she'd known about his job before she married him.

'But it is my business,' she protested. 'Joe's my brother and he's needing a job. The least you can do is put in a good word for him.'

'Forget it.'

Pete finished his lemon meringue pie and smacked his lips.

'I'll give you this. You're a fuckin' good cook.' He rose, hitching his shoulders and jerking his tie straight. 'I'm away. See you later.'

She couldn't believe it. After the front door banged shut, she sat staring at Budd for a long time, stunned.

'Joe's better out of it!' Budd was the first to break the silence.

'How do you mean?'

'Possil Cabs is owned by one of them drug barons. The cabs are just a front. They move drugs and launder money.'

'Launder money?' Kate echoed stupidly.

'Make it legit. These guys make so much money they don't know what to do with it all. Some of the betting shops have been taken over. And pubs. God knows what else. They're into everything these days.'

She shook her head, trying to make sense of it.

'Pete doesn't take drugs.'

'No. He always takes good care of number one.'

'I still don't . . . I can't . . .'

'Ask him. I can't tell you all the details. But it's about drugs. My guess is Joe might end up a spanner in the works. Joe's too straight. That's his trouble. He's better, and safer, out of it, that's what I think, hen.'

'What'll I tell him? He was over the moon. We all took it for granted there wouldn't be any problem.'

'Well, you'd better be careful. Pete might not be pleased if you let on to Joe or anybody else about what he's up to. It would get him into trouble with his boss. These guys don't play around. I know Pete is a shite at times, but I'm still his father. I don't want to see his head get kicked in.'

This awful vision was too much for Kate. She burst into tears.

'Aw, come on, hen.' Budd was embarrassed. 'None of that.'

Hastily Kate dried her face and fought for control.

'It's just the thought of Pete and drugs. I can't believe it somehow. It's too . . . Oh no, Budd. You must have got it wrong.'

Budd shrugged. 'Please yourself, hen. It's your funeral.'

'I don't know what to do. What can I tell Joe?' she repeated.

'Say Pete wouldn't co-operate. Say Possil Cabs aren't taking anybody on. You'll think of something.'

'I'd better go right away before him and Marilyn make any more plans.' They had been like a couple of children looking forward to Christmas. Joe had been talking about chauffeuring Marilyn around. 'No charge for you, hen. You'd be like the Queen. No, a princess. You're my wee

39

princess.' He'd given Marilyn a cuddle and they'd both laughed.

Kate would rather have done anything than deflate their happiness. She felt terrible – raising their hopes one minute and dashing them the next.

Slowly she returned down Stoneyhurst Street to Saracen Street, oblivious of the seedy grey tenements and hordes of children. She passed the building in which Tommy, Liz and their children lived without giving it a glance.

'Gosh!' Marilyn greeted her. 'Twice in one day. What have we done to deserve this?'

Kate didn't share her laughter and Marilyn called out,

'Joe, it's Kate again.'

Joe had been sitting by the living-room fire enjoying a read at the *Evening Times*.

'Hello, hen.'

'Will I put the kettle on?' Marilyn asked.

'Not just now,' Kate said. 'There's something I want to tell you.'

She avoided Joe's eyes and twisted miserably at the strap of her shoulder bag.

Joe put down the paper.

'It's no go,' he said quietly.

'What do you mean, pet?' Marilyn asked.

'It was him, wasn't it?' Joe said. 'I might have known.'

'It wasn't his fault,' Kate said. 'I mean, he just couldn't do anything. It's more complicated than I thought, Joe. Oh, I'm so sorry. I should have checked with him first . . .'

Marilyn let out a wail.

'What are you talking about? Is Joe not getting the job?'

'I'm so sorry,' Kate repeated. 'There isn't any job. It's all my fault. With Pete being so busy, I thought . . . I didn't realise. I should have spoken to Pete before I said anything. Pete is sorry too.'

Joe gave a mirthless laugh.

'And the band played – believe it if you like.'

Marilyn was now reduced to hiccupy sobs and Joe pulled

40

her on to his knee and nursed her like a baby. She cast a tragic look round at Kate.

'You said . . .'

'I know. I shouldn't have.'

'Ssh, ssh,' Joe comforted. 'It was as much our fault as Kate's. She meant well and we all just got carried away.'

'There's folk round here who've been years without a job,' Marilyn wailed. 'I don't want us to get like them. No money, no hope, no nothing.'

'I promise you,' Joe said, 'I'll turn my hand to anything. Even if it's something with that old van McPherson offered me. He said I could have it to make up for losing my job. He can't pay me any redundancy money.'

'What van?' Kate asked.

Joe sighed.

'Oh, a customer took ill. An old bachelor. He's dead now. But anyway, he couldn't pay the bill for work on the van. So he told old McPherson to keep it. He wasn't able to work it any more so it was no use to him.'

'What kind of van?'

'Ice cream. He sold ice cream, crisps, sweeties, bottles of ginger. That sort of thing.'

'Here!' Kate began to see a light shining in the darkness. 'That's your answer!'

'I suppose it'll have to be,' Joe agreed but without enthusiasm.

'Why not?' Kate said. 'I bet you you could make a good living at that. We've all seen how busy ice-cream vans can be.'

'I wouldn't know where to start,' Joe said. 'I'm a motor mechanic. Tommy's always been the salesman in the family.'

'Och, I shouldn't think there's anything difficult about selling ice cream and sweeties. You'd probably enjoy it. Getting out and around and meeting folk instead of being stuck under a car all the time.'

Marilyn was speedily becoming bright-eyed and bushy-tailed again.

'And I could help you, Joe. I used to love playing at shops when I was wee. Oh, it would be great fun and I could wear my nice frilly pinny . . .'

Joe laughed and shook his head.

'Oh, Marilyn.'

'Well, I could. I could help. Couldn't I, Kate?'

'Do you know, I believe you could, Marilyn!' Kate felt like dancing with joyful relief. 'You'd be the star attraction. People would come from miles around to be served by somebody who looked as gorgeous as you.'

'I'm not so sure about that.' Joe half laughed but his eyes were anxious. 'Of course Marilyn's gorgeous,' he hastily added, 'but folk around here wouldn't pass another van just to look at who's serving in ours. They'd want value for money. I mean, they'd want better ice cream than the next van.'

'Well, you could give them better ice cream.'

'Our ice cream could be the talk of Possilpark.' Marilyn clapped her hands. 'We'd become famous.'

Joe laughed again but still retained a seriously worried expression. Kate didn't blame him. After all, they'd gone through much the same excitement and wonderful plans for the future today already.

'Look Joe,' she said, 'earlier on you were dependent on someone else for helping you to get a job. This is different. It's all up to you. I mean, it'll be your van, your business. You'll be your own boss.'

'Yes,' Marilyn cried out. 'Oh Joe, let's do it. Oh, please Joe.'

'It's different all right,' Joe said. 'I'll need capital. Money to buy the ice cream and everything.'

'Yes,' Kate agreed. 'You'd have to look into that. But surely you could get some credit to start you off? And the family would help all they could. Marilyn's already offered so that would save on having to pay a stranger. Mammy would give you her last penny, you know that. You've always been her favourite.'

'I couldn't take Mammy's savings – she can't have more than a few pounds in her Post Office book anyway. And that's for her holidays. As far as having better ice cream, it's all the same, isn't it? I mean, all the vans around here'll get their supplies from the same place, I would think.'

Something else suddenly occurred to him. 'What do you bet they'll have their own runs as well.'

'Hang on,' Kate said, 'I can understand you being cautious, Joe, but don't try to sink the ship before we've even got it on the water. The guy that had that van must have had his pitch. Where was it? Do you know?'

Silence for a minute while Joe tried to remember.

'Well, he was never up our way,' Joe said at last. 'I mean, before I got this place. Up Killearn Street, I mean.'

'There's Luigi now. I think he goes to Byshott and round to Stoneyhurst Street. At least the top end.'

'I think I remember Rab – that was the guy's name, Rab Donaldson – I remember now Rab talking about the other side, Bardowie, Sunnylaw, down that way.'

Kate's heart sank.

'Well,' she managed, 'you could start there anyway. And later spread out a bit. Even try Ruchill or Maryhill or Springburn. There's no law about where you can sell ice cream as far as I'm aware. You ever heard of an ice-cream man being arrested by the police?'

'No,' Joe agreed uncertainly. 'I suppose it must be some kind of unwritten agreement. Two vans don't stand in the same street at the same time, that sort of thing. I suppose it's just common sense when you think of it.'

'OK. So we could easily sort that one out. Now, about the ice cream . . .'

She had been hit by another brilliant idea. Absolutely, joyously brilliant. 'How about if I make it?'

'You make it?' Joe echoed incredulously. 'Don't be daft.'

'Why not? You've always said what a great cook I was. Even as a wee girl I could do it. You once said I must be like these music prodigies. Only I was a food prodigy.'

'I know.' Joe laughed with embarrassment. 'But ice cream's not cooking, or baking like you're used to. And there would have to be so much of it. No, Kate. But thanks all the same, I appreciate you wanting to help.'

'Now, wait a minute. You're being negative again, Joe. I *could* make ice cream. I *know* how to make ice cream. I made it not that long ago when Tommy and Liz and the kids came for their tea.'

'But Kate, it's one thing to make a wee drop of the stuff for Tommy's kids – '

'Is the van equipped?' Kate interrupted. 'Or is it just an empty shell?'

'Oh no, it's still got all Rab's gear in it. Even a wee sink.'

'And a big freezer?'

Joe nodded.

'Well then!'

Still he hesitated.

'But do you think . . . Do you really think you could do it? It seems an awful lot for you to take on. And there's the baby to consider. You're pregnant, don't forget.'

'No problem,' Kate said with new-found confidence. 'No problem at all.'

Chapter Seven

Instinctively, Kate hesitated to tell Pete about the plan. She and Pete were getting on quite well, on the surface at least. Underneath though, as far as she was concerned, a lot had changed. She could still look at his handsome face and feel her pulse quicken. When they made love, she could still feel stabs of physical pleasure. These things however were momentary, superficial and fast becoming less important compared with her growing disillusionment. The suspicion that he was mixed up in the drugs scene had become a certainty. Nobody made the kind of money he did by just driving a cab. It didn't help that he had never told her about his involvement and what it actually meant in practical terms. Did he drive one of the cars that were always creeping back and forward in front of schools plying the stuff to schoolchildren? The knowledge of where the money he earned might be coming from took away any pleasure and enjoyment it had previously given her. Even when she looked at her diamond engagement ring now, she experienced both distaste and guilt. She had grown up with the reality of what drugs could do to people's lives. The results were all around her. Not long ago, several young boys that she'd gone to school with had died in one of the nearby tenements as a result of injecting heroin. It wasn't the first time this had happened. Last year, Anne, the daughter of Mrs Chambers, one of her mother's pals, had died as a result of taking an overdose of temazepam. A lovely girl Anne had been, and clever too. She'd passed seven O levels and five Highers. Mrs Chambers had still never got over it. And her a widow with no other family. The whole street had tried and were still trying to do what they could to comfort and support her, especially wee Mary.

'See them evil bastards that sell drugs to weans,' Mary said, 'they should be shut away in Barlinnie for the rest o' their days. They're far worse than ordinary murderers.'

It had been one thing about which Kate had always agreed with her mother. Apart from ruining people's lives and actually killing them, it led them into crime to feed their habit. Her father said that most of the crime in Glasgow now was drug related.

Over Possilpark there hung a pall of fear. Whether it was real or imaginary was another question. One thing was certain, though. Old people like Granny Gallacher wouldn't put a foot out of doors after dark. Even during the day, quiet back streets and lanes, or pieces of waste ground, were nervously avoided.

The community centre bus was the lifeline of the local elderly. Twice a week it called for them and ferried them to the community centre to the lunch club where they enjoyed a cheap meal. Afterwards the bus delivered them safely back home. A couple of nights there was the bingo and the same thing happened.

'God knows,' Mary said, 'whit this place would dae withoot that community centre. One thing ah *know* would happen – a lot o' old folk would get depressed an' die o' loneliness.'

It had been a good place for young people like Kate too. All sorts of things went on to suit all ages. Yet so many folk were tempted into drugs. Cars cruised outside the centre as well as the schools, openly supplying young people. Several children barely out of – or sometimes still in – primary school were hooked. So many folk being unemployed didn't help. They were without any purpose or direction in life.

Sometimes into the second and even third generations in Possilpark had never experienced work or any hope of work. If she hadn't got married straight from school, she probably wouldn't have found a job herself and who knows how depressed she might have become.

Joe was lucky he'd fallen heir to the ice-cream van. Already he'd done it all up and it was now sparkling clean and ready to go. Actually, apart from the need of a good clean and polish, it had been in excellent condition. Tommy had been very good at advising and helping Joe to get credit at the cash and carry place for the sweets and crisps and bottles of ginger. Packets of biscuits and nuts as well. Kate had been searching out and studying all sorts of books about ice cream. She'd been experimenting and testing recipes on Budd and Pete without them knowing it. She had never realised that there were so many different types of ice cream.

She decided on an Italian method eventually. There were two distinguishing features, she learned, that set Italian ice cream apart. Full-cream milk, and not cream, was used and a low percentage of air was beaten into it during freezing. She read that Stephano Boni, of Mr Boni's excellent ice-cream parlours in Edinburgh, had said that there were three ways to make cheap ice cream. 'Firstly by using cheap ingredients such as artificial flavourings and whey powder instead of milk, secondly by making it in a large-scale industrial plant which reduces labour costs, and thirdly by beating huge amounts of air into it.'

She remembered tasting Boni's ice cream when her mother and father had taken her on a visit to Edinburgh, and she now determined to aim at its delicious taste and high quality. She made some and took it to Joe and Marilyn for their verdict. They were over the moon.

'I always said you were a genius,' Joe laughed delightedly. 'That's bloody marvellous, Kate. The best ice cream I've ever tasted.' His eyes bulged with excitement. 'That's what we'll call it – the best ice cream in Glasgow. I'll paint that on the van.'

Marilyn closed her eyes and smacked full scarlet lips.

'Mmm. Really and truly wonderful.' Her eyes widened again. 'Darling Joe, we'll make a fortune. I know it. I know it. We're going to be rich!'

Joe laughed.

'Hang on. We haven't even started selling the stuff yet.

And Kate's pregnant, don't forget. We can't expect her to go doing this for ever.'

Kate had almost forgotten about her pregnancy, she'd been so busy. This was something she was truly thankful for. She was also grateful for the fact that all the prophecies she'd heard about ghastly morning sickness had not come to pass. She felt as fit as she'd ever been. Maybe this meant that all the horror stories she'd heard about childbirth wouldn't come to anything either.

'I'm as fit as a fiddle,' she told Joe and Marilyn. 'Don't worry about me. After all, I'm doing my bit in the comfort of my own home. As long as you two get out and around in the van and sell the stuff, everything'll work out fine.'

'As soon as we start selling, we'll pay you for your work, Kate. That goes without saying.'

'Och, don't worry about that. As long as you pay for the materials.'

'No, no, we want to be fair,' Joe insisted. 'You and I will be equal partners. Yes, that's how I want it to be. Isn't that right, Marilyn?'

Marilyn nodded enthusiastically.

'Yes, we've talked it over, Kate.'

Kate smiled. 'OK, if you're sure. Thanks.'

She would have to tell Pete about the van and her involvement some time. Surely he wouldn't mind. Nothing was coming out of his pocket.

Probably Pete would be pleased. She couldn't explain to herself why she felt so reluctant, a little nervous even. Maybe it was because this drug business made him seem such a different person. Not the young man she'd married at all. Still, they had a better marriage than most as far as she could see. Or hear. Up their close in Byshott Street was bedlam at times with the sound of couples quarrelling and bawling at each other. Sometimes there were screams as a husband gave his wife 'a doing'.

She supposed she had nothing too serious to complain about as far as Pete was concerned – except of course how he was earning a living. They made love. Or rather, they had sex. (Neither of them ever mentioned the word love.) Pete had never become much gentler than he'd been on the first night. She now excused this roughness in him as passion. He was a very passionate man, she kept assuring herself. Probably all passionate men were like that. She'd never had any exposure to other men, so she didn't really know. She and Pete went out together occasionally. Sometimes it was just to his 'local', sometimes it was to a cinema in town. They never went out for a meal now.

'Listen, hen,' he told her, 'none of these chefs in town are a patch on you.'

He enjoyed the meals she gave him. (So did Budd.) The food was always on the table on time and she was always there to serve it. She had learned from her mother how to be a good wife and to 'look after her man'.

Although she thought her mother went unnecessarily far at times. Her mother brushed her father's shoes and even peeled and cut up his apple. If Pete wanted to eat an apple, he could peel it and cut it up himself. But she was sure Pete would never expect her to perform such a task for him. He had never expected her to brush his shoes either.

The more she thought about it, the more she convinced herself of what a good husband she had. Of course, she didn't see as much of Pete as she'd expected she would once they were married. As well as working long and anti-social hours, he went out with his mates, his fellow drivers. Quite often, he brought some of them home to, as he said, 'try out her grub'.

Kate felt shy with these men. They weren't in the least like her brothers and certainly nothing like Gentleman George or her Uncle Willie. There was an aggressiveness about Pete's mates. They had cold, bullet-hard eyes that frightened her. But she couldn't deny they spoke to her in a friendly enough way. They were enthusiastic and complimentary about any meals she gave them. She had no reason at all to complain about them. Except of course their foul language when they spoke among themselves. Every other word seemed to be cunt or fuck. But they had never used the offensive words directly to her. That didn't stop her feeling frightened and worrying about whether or not they too were involved in the drugs scene. She kept her fears and worries to herself, however. But now she wasn't at all happy about the idea of confessing to Pete about making the ice cream for Joe's van. She'd have to tell him some time: even though he wasn't in the house all that much and seldom, if ever, in the kitchen, there was still the chance of him spotting a most unusual amount of milk and eggs and sugar piled up in every cupboard. He'd surely want to know why and what for.

Budd was the first one to ask and she'd not worried about telling him. He laughed.

'Great, hen. We'll never be short of a wafer, eh?'

'Do you think Pete will mind?'

'Why should he? So long as it doesn't cost him anything.'

'I won't neglect either of you, I promise. I'm able to do it at home. I don't need to go out at all. Marilyn's going to help Joe with the selling.'

'Well then. Best of luck to you, hen.'

She'd felt a bit relieved after that, more courageous.

The very next day, she blurted it out to Pete. She'd been gearing herself up for it for hours until just before he left for work she said, 'Pete, I've got a wee job. Only helping Joe out,' she added hastily. 'I'll be doing it at home. You won't even notice the difference. And you know how I like cooking and messing about in the kitchen.'

Pete was intent on brushing his hair in front of the wardrobe mirror. He didn't show the faintest interest in her important announcement.

'After he gets the business going and starts selling lots of ice cream, he's going to pay me a wage as well as the materials, the milk and eggs and all that I'll need . . .'

'Aye, OK, hen.' Pete tugged at his tie after his hair had

met with his careful scrutiny. 'Anything that keeps you happy.'

'Oh thanks, Pete.' She rushed at him to give him a hug but he pushed her aside. 'Watch what you're doing.' He smoothed his hair again before glancing at his watch. 'It's time I was off.'

She could hardly believe her luck after he'd gone. And even when he returned in the middle of the night and wakened her up to have sex, she still felt grateful enough to respond with warmth. In the morning, she gave him a splendid breakfast, or brunch as it could more accurately be called, because it was nearer lunchtime than breakfast when Pete got up. He went off to spend a few hours at the bookie's, a happy man. She was happy too, although she soon discovered it was hard work making the ice cream in such large quantities, even with the use of the late Rab Donaldson's churn and freezer. Still, she managed it.

Kate organised herself into a routine. She never had a minute from morning till night. But she was young and strong and, for the first time in her life, she began to realise what fulfilment meant. She had always found a strange satisfaction in hard work. The harder it was, the more triumphantly satisfied she felt. Long ago she had come to the conclusion she must be a masochist. Now, however, there was a purpose to it all. She was making money. She was helping Joe and Marilyn make a decent living as well. Joe had soon got his side of things organised. Even the run. He was a pleasant, likeable big chap and customers took to him. They liked Marilyn as well. But most of all, the customers kept coming back for the ice cream. And they passed the word around about how good it was.

Kate felt happy about that, deeply, sweetly happy. She felt happy too about the baby growing inside her. Despite the fact that she became so large and clumsy, she experienced a sense of achievement. Her mother shook her head at her when Kate said that pregnancy was creative and satisfying in the same way as cooking and baking and making the ice cream.

'God, wid ye listen tae her?' She tossed the words up to the kitchen ceiling. 'Did ye ever hear anythin' sae stupit?'

It was a challenge to keep up the same level of hard work that was necessary both to keep Pete and Budd well fed and happy and also to fulfil her commitment to Joe. Kate was determined however not to be beaten, either by her physical condition or anything else.

Budd tried his best to help in the house. Joe pleaded with her to give up working for the van – at least for a time. In fact, she hardly took any time off to have the baby. Even that went to plan. She'd hardly felt a thing.

It was a girl. A lovely, healthy, adorable little girl. Her mother immediately offered to babysit.

'Jist bring her up tae me, hen. Ah'll take her aff yer hands, especially durin' the day when ye're busy.'

'Oh no, Mammy.' Kate shrank from parting with her baby. 'I'd worry about the dog.'

'Whit dae ye mean?' her mother cried out. 'Worry about ma Rajah?'

'Well, he might be jealous and harm her. You never know with animals.'

'Ah know this animal.' She bent down and hugged and kissed Rajah's enormous lion's mane. 'He's as gentle as a wee lamb. Aren't ye, son?'

Kate recalled the 'gentle wee lamb' bounding in pursuit of many a person, tearing the seat out of their trousers, and on many an occasion drawing blood. Rajah was the most feared animal in Possilpark. People said he was mad. Even the local police gave him a wide berth.

'Mammy, the whole of Possil knows what Rajah's capable of. He's no gentle wee lamb.'

'Listen, you,' Mary waggled a warning finger. 'Dinnae you say a word aboot ma dug. Ye know fine how good that dug wis when ye were wee. There's no' a jealous bone in that dug's body.'

'He was only a puppy then.'

'Ye're only making excuses tae hang on tae the wean.'

'Well, what's wrong with that?'

'Ye've got tae help Joe an' ye cannae help him if ye're lookin' after wee Chrissie full time. Joe needs aw oor support.' Her voice melted. 'He's such a good boy.'

'I can manage,' Kate said stubbornly.

'Ah always knew he'd do well. An' he's that good tae his mammy. Always has been.'

'I know, Mammy,' Kate said patiently.

If it had been anyone else but Joe, she might have been jealous, never mind the dog. Her mother doted on and never tired of raving about her favourite child. She had never got over being able to produce an offspring of over six feet in height. 'Look at the size o' that boy,' she'd say.

Kate didn't think Tommy was jealous either, although poor Tommy was about as wee as their mother and seldom one word of praise was ever aimed at him. Both Tommy and Kate were glad Joe was doing well and the business was so successful.

The only cloud on the otherwise rosy horizon was the rumours they began to hear about some ice-cream vans being attacked.

'Why would anyone want to attack an ice-cream van?' Kate said to Joe.

He shrugged.

'Nothing's happened on my run. I expect it's mostly kids. Vandals throwing stones because they enjoy the sound of breaking glass. Could be to try and pinch the takings, of course. Or the occasional driver trying to muscle in on somebody else's run. But I've had no trouble.'

'Gosh.' Marilyn gave a delicate little shudder. 'I hope we never do. I'd die. I'd just die.'

Chapter Eight

Kate was determined not to part with Christine, or wee Chrissie as her mother kept calling her. At first she was able to keep an eye on her in her cot or pram every now and again while she worked in the kitchen. She'd keep running through to the bedroom to check she was all right, to gaze down at her with love and pride, or to give her a quick kiss. But her mother never stopped nagging at her about the baby's welfare.

'That wean needs fresh air. It's a disgrace the way ye keep her in that place every minute o' the night an' day.'

'I can't put the pram out the back,' Kate protested. 'You've seen what it's like.'

'Bloody tip,' Mary said. 'Movin' wi' rats as well. They'd eat the wean for their tea.'

Kate shuddered.

'Don't say things like that, Mammy. Anyway, I take the pram down to Saracen Street when I've to do the messages. That reminds me,' Kate smiled, 'I bumped into Maisie Dempster yesterday when I was down at the shops. Remember her that came from England when her daddy got a job up here. She was in my class at school. The first time I said I was going for the messages, she said, "What's that?" And when I told her it was for your potatoes and meat and things for the dinner, she said, "Oh, you mean shopping" in that funny accent of hers and we all laughed like anything. It was the same when I spoke about our house and she said, "Oh, you mean your *flat*."'

'Don't change the subject,' Mary said. 'That wean's goin' tae go intae decline for lack o' fresh air.'

'What fresh air is there around here anyway?' Kate said.

'Better outside than inside. You give the wean tae me

54

durin' the day an' ah'll take her for walks. Ah've plenty o' time tae push the pram aroon'. You huvnae.'

'Maybe I shouldn't do so much,' Kate said worriedly. 'I'm making scones now as well as ice cream for the van. I tend to do that. Take on too much. I think I'd better speak to Joe.'

'Ye'll do no such thing.' Mary was outraged. 'Ye'll no' pull the plug on ma Joe while ah've got wan breath left in ma body. Yer brother's workin' all hours that God gives in that van – Marilyn as well. I always knew that wee lassie had more in her than met the eye. She's supportin' Joe one hundred per cent an' so will you, m'lady, or ye'll huv me tae answer tae. I'm warnin' ye.'

'But Mammy, I've my baby to think about. I can't neglect Christine. Not for anybody. Not even Joe.'

'There's no question of neglectin' wee Chrissie, if ye jist stop bein' a stupit cow an' listen tae whit ah'm sayin'. Ah'll take the wean while ye're workin' durin' the day. She'll be fine wi' me. She's no' fine here. Ye jist need tae look at her wee white face.'

Kate hesitated miserably.

'Well, maybe just for an hour or two in the mornings. So that I can get the baking done.'

'Come first thing an' leave her wi' me until after ye've given Budd an' yer man their dinner. Ah cannae stand yer pig o' a man but he's still yer man an' ye should be there tae give him his dinner. Have wee Chrissie at ma door at nine sharp an' come back for her at two or three in the afternoon.'

'Och Mammy . . .'

'Never mind yer och Mammys. Jist dae as ye're told. It's the best thing for the wean.'

It was physically painful handing the baby over and going back to the empty house without her. It was as good as empty because Budd was such a quiet man when he was in. Although he was more talkative now than he'd been when she'd first met him. And he'd never come in drunk since the baby was born; a bit unsteady on his feet perhaps, but never noisy or difficult. He'd point towards the baby, put his finger to his lips and stagger, on tiptoe if he could manage it, into his room. He'd even got his long straggle of hair cut and smartened himself up all round. She had helped by pressing his jacket and trousers and keeping him supplied with clean, ironed shirts with all the buttons sewed on.

It was a help having her mother take the baby for most of the day, of course, painful though it felt. And, as Mary reminded her, lots of women had to work nowadays. She was lucky she could be at home: no travelling, no boss, and safe in the knowledge that her baby was being well looked after.

'The dug loves that wean,' Mary kept insisting. 'Don't ye, son?' she added, giving the dog one of her enthusiastic hugs.

Kate still felt a bit worried and also guilty. After all, she had to admit to herself, it wasn't as if she *needed* to work. She didn't need the money. Pete gave her enough for the housekeeping. Joe was making such a good living, despite generously sharing it with her, that he was talking about buying another van.

'We'll make a fortune!' he told her excitedly. 'One day we'll have a fleet of vans, you'll see. The way things are going, it's not just a pipe dream, Kate. It really could happen.'

She believed him and was glad for him. Joe needed the money – to buy a nice house. He and Marilyn planned to start a family but not in a room and kitchen in Saracen Street.

'A place with a garden, that's what a baby needs. And a room of its own. Marilyn and I have even planned how we'll decorate it.'

They had so many plans. She too had planned for a nice house with a garden. Pete had promised to see to that. He boasted that he was going to buy a really 'top class' place.

'None of your mortgages though,' he'd said. 'I'm waiting until I can pay cash down. I'm not lumbering myself with a whole lot of debt to some fuckin' building society and end up paying double what I've borrowed.'

The thought of Pete having the huge sum of cash needed to buy a house at any time was staggering. Somehow, because surely it must be coming from the sale of drugs, she had lost the pleasure of one day having her dream house. But, as her mother so often told her, 'Ye've made yer bed, m'lady, an' now ye'll just have to lie on it.'

It looked as though any money she made would be nothing to Pete. He didn't need it any more than she did. But an instinct she couldn't pin down or explain made her feel as if her earnings were some sort of survival kit. She never spent a penny of what Joe gave her. Instead she opened a bank account and stashed it away. She grew more and more secretive, although Pete had never shown the slightest interest either in what she did or what she earned. She even gave Joe's address to the bank so that her statements and any other correspondence would be sent care of him.

Pete might be surprised at how quickly that bank account was growing but still she hesitated to mention anything about it. She often asked herself why but could never give a satisfactory answer. Except perhaps that on the occasions when Pete brought a crowd of his fellow drivers in for a bite to eat, she felt acutely vulnerable among them. They were Pete's world and it was a world in which she was an outsider, a stranger. Nor did she want to be part of whatever they were all mixed up in.

She moved around the periphery of their deep, male voices and coarse laughter, serving food, clearing away plates, trying to feel that everything was perfectly normal, but knowing it wasn't.

Her mother had arrived one afternoon when these men were in. The baby's bottle had been left behind in her house and she had brought it in case Kate didn't have a spare.

'My God,' she'd exclaimed to Kate in the kitchen, 'what a shower o' bloody gangsters.'

'Ssh!' Kate warned. 'They might hear you.'

'Ah dinnae care tuppence if they do hear me. It's the truth. Especially that scarface Dougie character. No' that any o' the others are liable tae win any beauty contests. Has he been slashed by a razor?'

'I don't know. Anyway, looks don't necessarily mean anything,' Kate said unconvincingly. 'None of them have done me any harm.'

'They didnae get eyes like alligators wi' being kind tae their grannies. They're Glasgow hard men an' you'd better be careful, especially wi' an innocent wee wean lying through there.'

The mention of the baby in connection with the men caused Kate's heart to race in panic. But she took a deep calming breath and told herself not to be stupid. There was no connection. She made her mother a cup of tea and they sat in the kitchen, with Kate trying to divert her mother to other things.

'Do you like the scones, Mammy?'

'They're no' bad. Whit's the recipe?'

'It's one pound of self-raising flour . . .'

'Hang on till ah get a pencil.' Mary rummaged in her handbag and produced a pen. Kate passed her a notepad.

'A teaspoon of salt, two ounces of butter, one egg and three-quarters of a pint of milk. Or you can use plain flour with a teaspoon of cream of tartar and a teaspoon of bicarb of soda for a sharper-tasting, moister scone. Of course, I double up the ingredients now because Joe has such a demand for them.'

'Och, that's much the same as ma scones.'

'Do you sift the flour and salt twice, rub in the butter, then make a well in the centre and add the egg and milk?'

'Aye.'

'Mix to a soft elastic dough. Turn out on to a floured board and dust with flour?'

'Aye.'

'Handling as lightly and as quickly as possible. That's the secret, Mammy.'

'Ah huv made scones before.'

'You asked me for the recipe.'

'Aye OK. Ah jist wondered if you were doing them any different from me. Then what?'

'I just make small pieces into balls, put them on to a greased baking sheet, press down lightly on top and bake them in a very hot over for about eight to ten minutes.'

'No' that much different from mine then. Dis Joe sells a lot o' them?'

As usual the mere mention of Joe's name acted like a beacon, lighting up Mary's small, beaky face.

'Dozens!'

'For all he's so busy,' Mary said, 'he's never missed his usual weekly visit tae me. When ah told him ah'd understand if he didnae manage – ah know Sunday's bound to be one o' his busiest times on the van – "No, Mammy," he says, "You'll always come first with me".' She sighed with pleasure. 'He's always been the same, that boy. That affectionate right back even before he went to school.'

She laughed, slightly embarrassed. 'Always kissin' an' cuddlin' at me. An' he still gives his mammy a cuddle. Ah tell him he's daft but he just says tae me, "You know you like it, auld yin." Ah'll auld yin ye, ah tell him. Ah'm no' too auld tae give ye a clip on the ear. But of course – '

Just then she was interrupted by the thunder of heavy feet going along the lobby as the men made their way out. One of them shouted into the kitchen, 'See you later.'

'No' if ah see you first,' Mary bawled back at him.

They disappeared in a gale of laughter. The front door banged.

'Is that yer man away wi' them?' Mary asked incredulously.

'I expect so.'

'Without even sayin' cheerio to ye?'

Kate shrugged.

'He's not working tonight. He told me. He'll be back in a wee while.'

'Yer daddy would never've done that.'

Kate knew this to be true. When she was younger she had been secretly amused, even sometimes derisive about her father's rather pompous ways and his unusually good manners. Gentleman George certainly got plenty of attention from his wife but it had to be said that he also gave plenty of attention to her.

Now Kate could truly admire her father and look back with yearning at the polite and respectful way he'd treated his wife. Sometimes she felt she was only a convenience for Pete, something in the background he hardly noticed. A non-person. As long as he was well fed and well sexed, everything was great as far as Pete was concerned. He never bothered about anybody except himself.

'An' did ye see him?' her mother asked. 'Talk about Flash Harry!' It had become her mother's favourite name for Pete, surpassing even 'oily dago'. Nowadays, Pete sported a very stylish haircut. He often wore smart suits and silk ties. Even his more casual wear was designer labelled. Kate had been shocked when she'd discovered the cost of his trainers. Although he always gave her as much, probably more, for housekeeping than the next woman, he'd never given her enough money to cover the cost of anything so expensive for herself.

Nearly every penny he gave her went on food, soap powder, disinfectant, toilet rolls, etc. Now that she came to think of it, she'd never had a new dress or a pair of shoes since she'd been married. Her mother was always buying clothes and things for Christine so she hadn't needed to worry about that. The more she thought about it, the more she realised how selfish Pete was. He obviously spent a fortune on himself. She couldn't resist tackling him about it eventually.

'Mind your own fuckin' business,' he told her.

That was always his response. It was as if she wasn't his

wife at all, as if she had nothing to do with him. She wanted to argue, to tell him what she thought, but instead she swallowed her resentment. For one thing, she didn't want to end up like so many other couples around them. She knew too many unhappy and abused wives. For another thing, she had always shrunk from violence. It was then she realised that deep down she was afraid of Pete. He had never raised a fist to her but she knew instinctively that he would have no scruples about doing so. He was violent enough in bed. She had begun to dread sex with him. He had hurt her terribly by having too much sex too early after she'd given birth. She'd lost all pleasure in it since then.

'Ah'm sorry fur ye,' her mother said in between mouthfuls of tea. 'That pig o' a man disnae care tuppence fur ye.'

It was then Joe and Marilyn came to collect the baking and the ice cream. It was obvious Marilyn had been crying.

'Whit's up wi' you, hen?' Mary asked.

'Oh, Mrs Gallacher,' Marilyn burst into tears. 'It was awful. I was so frightened.'

'Whit wis awful, hen?'

'Two men attacked our van with basketball bats, broke one of the windows. Battered all over the van. It was rocking about. I thought it was going to crash right over. And the noise was terrible.'

Kate looked over at Joe.

'Thank God one of my customers, Bert McGlone, was just over the road,' he said, 'Bert's a big hefty guy, afraid of nothing. Came racing over to help us. I got out of the van and me and Bert chased after these guys but they got away.'

'Who were they?' Kate asked.

Marilyn said, 'They wore black balaclava things with just slits for their mouth and eyes. They looked terrifying, Kate. I'm sure they meant to kill us.'

'No, no, love,' Joe soothed. 'It would be the takings they were after. Or,' he turned thoughtful, 'maybe they want to run us off our pitch. I've been hearing of a lot of incidents . . .' His mouth hardened. 'But nobody's going to

61

frighten me. I've built up a good business and I've no intention of allowing anyone to ruin it or take it over. On the contrary. I plan to have another van on the road before next summer.'

Marilyn was sobbing broken-heartedly now.

'I just don't know how I'll be able to go out again tonight. I'm really dreading it. I mean, they did that in broad daylight. What might they do in the dark?'

Joe hushed her.

'The window's been fixed so there's nothing to stop me going out tonight on my own.'

'No,' Marilyn wailed. 'I'd feel worse. I'd be so worried about you. No, I'll come with you, Joe.'

'Oh my,' Mary said, 'isn't she the rare wee wife, Joe?'

'Yes, Mammy, she is. But I can't have her upset. First thing tomorrow, I'm going to see about taking on a man to help in the van. I can afford it now.'

'That's a great idea, son. An' tonight Kate can go out wi' ye. Marilyn can stay here an' watch the wean.'

Kate glared at her mother. Wasn't that just typical, she thought bitterly. It didn't matter if *she* got murdered.

Joe shook his head.

'Kate does enough for me already. I couldn't ask her to do any more.'

'Nobody's askin',' Mary said. 'Ah'm tellin'.'

Kate couldn't get out quick enough. The only thing she feared was that if a murder was going to be committed, it would be her mother that was the victim.

Chapter Nine

It was a blustery night and rain was slanting across the window of the van. It soaked the swooping, flapping newspapers and other litter that roamed the dark streets. Half the lights had been vandalised and only an occasional lamp spread a dismal grey sheet around its base, darkening the shadows.

'I think we should pack it in now,' Joe said. 'We've done not bad. Especially considering what a bloody awful night it is.'

'I'm surprised anybody put a foot out of their doors.' Kate was hugging herself and stamping her feet in her efforts to keep warm. 'Especially to buy ice cream.'

'I think it was your scones that tempted them more than anything else.'

'Even so.'

Just then a car drew up behind them. They could barely make it out in the dark, but it looked like a navy or black Volvo.

'Customers?' Kate asked uncertainly. The van was parked in Balgair Street and it didn't seem too likely that the car belonged to any of the residents.

'I think we should be ready to shoot off, just in case . . .' Joe went to squeeze behind the wheel but at the same time the doors of the car flew open and several men burst out. It all happened so quickly that Kate wasn't sure how many men there were or what happened. There was a crash of glass and she felt a sharp pain rip down her arm, followed by a stunning blow to her head. There was a crescendo of thumping and crashing all around. The van, the whole world it seemed, reeled, convulsed, careered from side to side. She heard someone bawl,

'Yer last fuckin' warnin'. Get aff the road, ye stupit cunts.'

Somehow Joe got the van started. It lurched forward and sped away, knocking Kate off balance and leaving her to scrabble for a hold on the floor, along with loose clattering bottles and a rustle of potato chips.

'You all right?' Joe shouted.

'Just get me home, for God's sake.'

'Nearly there.'

It turned out she wasn't all right, although not quite as bad as she looked. Marilyn fainted when she saw her and Joe got into such a state about his wife, he forgot about his sister. At least for a few minutes, while he ministered comfort and drinks of water to Marilyn. It was Budd who got a hold of Kate and led her to a seat, wrapped a towel round her arm and held another to her head. One sleeve of her white nylon coat had turned completely scarlet and there was blood matting her hair and pouring down her face.

'Where's Pete?' Kate managed.

'He's snoring his head off through in the room. Dead to the world. He must have had a right skinful. It'll take an earthquake to waken him. You know what he's like after he's had too much. I'll phone for an ambulance.'

She could have wept. Not with the pain of her physical injuries. She was just heart-sore that Pete was never able for any or every reason to be of the slightest support and comfort to her.

'No, I'll be all right.'

'Don't be daft. You're bleedin' like a pig. You're needin' to get to casualty and quick.'

Joe came over to her then, now that Marilyn had recovered.

'My God, Kate. I didn't realise. Come on, I'll drive you to the Royal.'

The casualty department at the Royal Infirmary was absolute bedlam. It was like a scene from hell. Kate allowed Joe to lead her through the drunken rabble of men with knife and other injuries. Many were still intent on continuing the fight, the bloody results of which had brought them there in the first place. Children were screaming. Women who looked as if their faces had been used as a punchbag were slumped hopelessly in chairs. Kate, in a daze, was feeling fainter by the minute. Then suddenly, she slid down into a black pit of silence. When she came to, she was lying on a trolley and a doctor was bending over her.

'Don't worry,' he said, 'you'll live.'

They X-rayed her and there were no broken bones; fortunately no fractured skull either. After some stitches to her head and arm, she was ready to go home with Joe. Her orders were to have a cup of hot sweet tea and then go straight to bed. A date was given for returning to have the stitches removed.

'What a place!' Kate said, after she was propped in the seat beside Joe in the van.

'Yes, I don't envy the doctors and nurses in there. It's like being the first line in a battle. They should be paid danger money. They're always getting attacked, apparently. Can you imagine anybody being so stupid? Attacking the people that are there to help them?'

'Stupid drunk, by the look of things.'

'Aye,' Joe sighed. 'Kate, I'm so sorry about what happened tonight.'

'It wasn't your fault.'

'I shouldn't have allowed you to come out with me.'

'What's it all about, Joe? I mean, why are gangsters like that trying to put you off the road? It doesn't make sense.'

'Yes, it does. There's a lot of cash to be made in ice-cream runs, Kate. You know how well I've been doing. I never dreamt before I started that there was such a good living in it. Where so much cash is involved, you'll get guys like that trying to muscle in.'

'What are you going to do?'

'I told you. I'm not going to let any gangsters frighten me off. I'll get another guy to come on the van with me.

Two if necessary until this gets sorted out. Until these thugs get the message and give up.'

'Is it worth it, Joe?'

'What?' His voice raised angrily. 'Of course it's worth it. I've worked hard, we've all worked hard, to build up a good business. No way are crooks like that going to spoil everything.' He paused and then, in a gentler tone, said, 'We've such dreams, Marilyn and I. A nice house, kids, a good life. We talk about nothing else nowadays. Marilyn has everything planned down to the last detail, posh curtains, carpets, the lot.'

Kate patted his hand.

'I hope all your dreams come true, Joe. And if you're game, then so am I. I'll go on helping you all I can.'

'Thanks, hen. You're a real pal.'

'I'll help you clean up the van when we get back.'

'Don't be daft. You heard what the doctor said. I'll see to the mess. You just get a good night's sleep.'

The painkillers the doctor gave her helped and she felt much better by the next morning.

'What the hell happened to you?' Pete asked after she'd returned from taking Christine to her mother's and he saw the shaved bit on her scalp and the line of stitches.

'Somebody threw a brick at the van and I got in the way.'

'What were you doing in the fuckin' van? Your place is here, not out enjoying yourself driving around the scheme.'

'Enjoying myself?' She laughed but she felt bitter. 'That's rich coming from you. I hardly ever see you, you're out so much enjoying yourself. If it's not boozing, it's the bookie's.' She was getting really worked up. Everything was beginning to spill out. 'You spend a fortune on yourself on clothes and God knows what else and it's a filthy fortune because I know how you make it. You're pushing drugs. It's despicable. You're a – '

'Shut your fuckin' mouth, or I'll shut it for you.' His voice was low and quiet and it frightened her far more than if he'd shouted. But she was surfing on a wave of recklessness ºnd couldn't stop. 'You're a criminal of the worst sort. You deserve to be banged up, not driving around preying on kids, ruining their lives . . .'

She reeled back from the sudden blow to her face. She gasped and choked for air at the second, even more vicious blow to her chest. When she fell and he began kicking her, her screams brought Budd running.

'You fuckin' madman.' Budd struggled with his son and managed to drag him off. 'Do you want to kill her?'

Suddenly Pete was his usual laid-back, cheerful, cocky self. 'Yeah, I do. So what?'

'So you'll end up doin' life. That's what.'

'No way.' He laughed. 'I'm off. See you later.'

After he'd gone, Budd helped Kate up.

'You go back to bed, hen. I'll make you a cup of tea.'

She dabbed at the cut on her lip.

'No, I'll take another painkiller. I'll be all right. I've too much to do.'

'You'll kill yourself if you go on like this.'

'If you mean the baking and the ice-cream making, it's more help than harm. I enjoy doing anything like that. I always have.'

'Well, no more going out in the van then.'

'Yes, OK. I would have but Joe says he's going to try and get a man or better still two men to go out with him at night until all this trouble blows over.'

'Here, how about me?' Budd almost looked cheerful. 'I could go out with Joe. I'm not doing anything else.'

Kate smiled.

'I'm sure Joe would take you on like a flash. When he comes to collect the ice cream, tell him. That's if you're sure you know what you're taking on, Budd.'

'Listen, hen, I've been used to dealing with a few thugs in my time. I used to work nights at the fairground, remember. Can you manage through to the kitchen, then?'

She got the painkillers at the ready.

'Once I get a cup of tea to help me swallow these down, I'll be fine.'

'I'll help you with the ice cream. And anything else. Just tell me.'

Normally she liked to 'do her own thing' in the kitchen. She didn't need or want any help but she was aching in every part of her body. She felt sick with the pain. But even worse, she felt sick at heart.

She saw with sudden horrifying clarity that she was no different from any of the other wives up the close. She, like them, had been sucked into a downward spiral of misery and violence. There was no tender affection and romance, no being adored and respected and looked after, no loving partnership. She had been kidding herself, no doubt as many another girl in the scheme had kidded herself with false hopes and impossible dreams. She saw her future stretch before her as an empty, crushing despair, something only to be endured.

'Drink your tea, hen. It'll make you feel a wee bit better.'

She did as Budd told her and whether it was the tea or something already in herself, she didn't know, but she began to feel a steely determination harden inside her.

No, she thought, that will not be my future. I will not be beaten down and destroyed like all the others. Somehow, some way, I'll show him. By God, I will. I'll show them all!

Chapter Ten

At first she managed to pass off her discoloured eye and cut mouth as the result of the injuries she'd received on the van. Even so, her mother and the two grannies, Granny McWhirter and Granny Gallacher, were shocked. Mary and Kate could pop in to see Granny McWhirter any time. Their visits to Granny Gallacher were more formal and planned. Every Sunday they went there for afternoon tea. It was a regular meeting of the Gallacher clan which included Gentleman George, Aunty Bec, Uncle Willie and Sandra. Kate tried to dodge the visit once she was married but Mary wouldn't hear of it.

'She's an auld widow woman jist like yer Granny McWhirter. Ye'll be auld yersel' some day, dinnae forget.'

Granny McWhirter was tiny and thin like Mary. She was still a tough old stick, although not so active as she used to be. Her room and kitchen were spartan, with a scrubbed kitchen table, four spar-backed chairs, a blackleaded range, and a rocking chair. Scrubbed linoleum covered the floor, and a Brassoed swan-necked tap sparkled at the sink. Over all, hung one light bulb shining from under a white glass cover like a Chinaman's hat. Easy to wipe with a damp cloth, Granny maintained. Nowadays she got Kate to stand up on the table and wipe it and the bulb.

You could see your reflection in the lobby linoleum. It was the same in the room, where a lone rug lay in front of the fire. 'Carpets just harbour dust and fleas,' Granny maintained. 'I've never had any truck with them.'

Furniture was suspect. The enormous room furniture with 'drawers deep enough to keep two weans in' had been replaced by fitted cupboards. Her late husband had been a joiner and kept busy doing jobs in the house. Only a darkly polished table and four matching chairs remained, plus two comfortable sagging leather armchairs, one on each side of the narrow tiled fireplace.

The whole house smelled of Mansion polish and disinfectant, except when Granny was. making her famous soup or baking her delicious cakes. The mouthwatering smell of food always won.

At one time, when there was a bakehouse underneath, the kitchen had been a sea of cockroaches every night. Granny McWhirter and her man had raged a continuous war against them. They had battered them, trampled them, poisoned them, all to no avail. Hordes kept reappearing. Eventually, the bakehouse and bakery had been taken over by a bigger firm who had a factory elsewhere that supplied their many shops all over the city. The bakery shop downstairs had been enlarged but the bakehouse, and with it the cockroaches, had gone. This blessing was no doubt helped by the pest control people the new owners had initially brought in, along with the joiners, glaziers and shop fitters. They'd cleared all the mice out as well.

'The only thing I miss,' Granny McWhirter said, 'is the heat that used to come up from that bakehouse. This kitchen used to be like one of their ovens.'

Granny McWhirter liked to sit in her rocking chair at the kitchen range, reading her *People's Friend*. Or she'd go through to the front room to watch the world go by down in Saracen Street. She particularly enjoyed (if she could manage to get the window up) 'havin' a hing', as she called it. That meant putting a cushion on the windowsill, folding her arms on it and peering down, often shouting to passersby that she knew and having a laugh with them. It was obvious from whom Mary had inherited her powerful voice.

Granny McWhirter had worked in one of the machine rooms of McCellands Rubberworks before she got married. She often reminisced about how, if you went to the toilet, you had to tell your supervisor. It was too bad if your need was desperate. You had to walk to the end of the big machine

70

room, down flights of stairs and across the open yard. Then you had to go through the hydraulic press machine place and up another four flights of stairs away at the other end of the building. A woman stationed outside the toilet asked for your check number. She'd mark it down and order you to hurry up.

'If ye were wan minute over yer time,' Granny shook her head, remembering, 'that wumin wid batter at the door bawlin', "Whit are ye daein' in there? Come oot here at once!"'

Kate liked going to visit Granny McWhirter. She could feel at home there. At Granny Gallacher's she felt claustrophobic. Granny Gallacher wasn't fat and ugly like her daughter, Bec, nor very tall like her son, George. She was medium height and more soft and cuddly than fat. At least that's how she liked to think of herself. The trouble with Granny Gallacher was she didn't know how to stop decorating her three-apartment, upstairs 'four in a block' house. And that didn't mean the painting and papering kind of decorating. She covered everything with frills and bits of lace (including herself) and embroidered cloths. You had practically to wade through the lace in her house. She couldn't leave a thing alone. Even the stairs up to her flat had a fancy plate on each step sitting on top of a frilled, lace-edged doily. The edge of each step was decorated with a bit of lace pinned on to the edge of the stair carpet. Into the tiny hall at the top of the stairs was crowded a chair draped with floral taffeta and a table covered with a white cloth edged with a rainbow of embroidered flowers that trailed voluptuously on to the floor. Another smaller cloth of sage green covered the large one. Granny Gallacher was never content with one tablecloth. There had always to be at least two. On top of the cloths was a clutter of knick-knacks, little figurines whose nakedness was demurely clothed in satin, lace-edged skirts and satin stoles to cover their top halves. Miniature teddy bears (of which there were a great many) wore gauzy, ballerina-type skirts.

The coffin-shaped bathroom, as far as Kate was concerned, was a veritable nightmare. Even when she was a child it had offended her with its fussy clutter. On the lace-edged windowsill was a crush of ornaments and boxes, all covered and frilled. A box of matches sat in a red satin holder. Toilet rolls were hidden under dolls wearing knitted crinolines or knitted hats. Or the favourite satin and lace. The soap dish had a lace frill and the box of Kleenex a satin lace-frilled box, as did the waste bin. The front of the washbasin was draped with a rose-patterned material edged with scarlet binding. The bath was draped with scarlet material edged is gold. The rubber end of the lavatory chain had been replaced by a large gold tassel. The floor was covered in a floral patterned carpet and two shaggy mats.

The only room in the house to surpass the bathroom was Granny Gallacher's spare room. It wasn't much bigger but it lay like something out of *Alice in Wonderland* to ensnare the unsuspecting guest. The modern double bed, bought in a sale at McElvy's in Saracen Street, nearly filled the floor (and ceiling) space. It had been transformed by four poles, a handmade canopy and long and lavish (and frilled) drapery, into a four-poster of indeterminate age. Kate always felt she'd rather die anywhere else than be smothered by all that drapery. (There had been no escape for Grandpa Gallacher, who had a frilly lace pillow and cover in his coffin.)

As with the double- and treble-clothed tables, Granny Gallacher had not been content with one layer, or one colour, or one pattern of drapes. Each generous layer was a garden gone wild. The curtains with their frilled pelmet were no exception and frilly little tables and chairs vied with those in the tiny hall.

Granny Gallacher had worked before her marriage in a fancy box factory. She loved to reminisce about how happy she'd been there.

She and two or three other girls would sit at a large table. Each had a pile of cardboard on the floor beside them.

They'd pick up a sheet at a time and smack it about on the 'glue tray' on the table in front of them, then they'd stick the pieces together.

'We were all so happy,' Granny Gallacher told Kate. 'We sang all day.'

'Silly old cow,' Pete sneered when she told him. 'She was high on glue.'

Kate never had the heart to tell Granny Gallacher.

They had all been sitting drinking afternoon tea from Granny Gallacher's rose-patterned china cups when Joe arrived. The boys and their families came when they could and it was Kate's ill luck that on this particular Sunday, Joe could.

'Thought I'd just pop in for a minute to treat you to a wafer, Gran,' Kate heard him say as he came up the stairs.

'Thank you, son. Your mammy and daddy and the whole family's here. You'll stay and enjoy afternoon tea with us, I hope. I was just about to refill the teapot. You go through to the sitting room. I'll put this in the fridge. It'll make a nice dessert for my dinner.'

'Aye, OK, Gran. Hi,' he greeted everyone. The occupants of the room looked lost in the jungle of frills, flounces, tassels and walls chock-a-block with floral gardens and Patience Strong poems. 'Here. What's happened to your face?' he cried out as soon as he noticed Kate.

Mary said,

'Whit dae ye mean? Ye were there when she got hit wi' the brick an' God knows whit else in the van.'

'It was her head and her arm. There wasn't a mark on her face the last time I saw her.'

All eyes turned towards Kate. Her mother said incredulously, 'Dinnae tell me that pig has lifted his hand tae ye after ye'd suffered all that!'

'No, of course not.' Kate laughed in an attempt to make the denial more believable. 'I was feeling a bit dizzy after getting battered about so much, and I fell.'

Mary peered at her suspiciously.

73

'Are ye sure aboot that?'

'Absolutely.'

'Well, if he ever does raise his hand tae ye, take ma advice. You raise yer foot at him. Get him in the crotch an' before he gets his breath back, batter him wi' yer rollin' pin or yer iron.'

Aunty Bec tutted and Mary whirled on her.

'Well, whit wid ye huv her dae?'

'Call the police.'

'Aye, well, she could dae, if she liked, but *after* she batters him.'

Very few people, at least in the toughest areas of Possilpark, called the police. It was an unwritten law that you sorted out problems for yourself, especially domestic problems.

'As long as you're OK, hen,' Joe said.

'I'm fine, honestly. How are things going now, Joe? Did you speak to Budd?'

'Yes, but I'm not sure about that, Kate. I think I might be better with a young bloke. Somebody more able to handle himself.'

'Fancy!' Aunty Bec's eyes swivelled over the ceiling before resting on Uncle Willie. 'Fighting over ice cream. Anybody would think it was the 1680s instead of the 1980s.'

'It's my living, Aunty Bec,' Joe said, accepting the cup of tea Granny Gallacher offered him. 'Thanks, Gran. I can't just let thugs take it away from me.'

'What's Possil coming to?' Aunty Bec asked herself.

Her brother George said,

'It was never like this when I was a lad starting up in the Provident Mutual Society. It was a respectable place and a man, woman or child could walk the streets at any hour in perfect safety.'

Kate doubted the truth of this but thought it prudent in the circumstances to say nothing. She was only too grateful that the attention had switched from her face.

'But Parkhouse,' Granny Gallacher beamed with pride, 'is

still as it always was, praise the Lord. As you well know, George, and you too, Bec, Parkhouse has always been superior. Most folk have the telephone and if I or any of the neighbours see anyone who doesn't belong, we phone the police immediately and have them removed. It's a comfort to know that there's usually a police car patrolling around. The mere sight of that is enough to put undesirables off.'

Kate suspected that another reason there weren't many excursions into Walnut Crescent and the few streets nearby was the fact that there were so many elderly and long-standing tenants who had no money and little worth stealing. Even Granny Gallacher's treasured Aladdin's cave would be more likely to repel thugs or thieves than entice them. She'd avoid the place like the plague herself if she could.

'Changed days, though, Mother,' George said. 'You used to be able to go out at night, didn't you? Would you go out at night on your own now?'

'Indeed I would not, George. You're quite right. Have another fairy cake, son. And Joe, what are you having, dear. A big lad like you needs his food. Have a sandwich. We're past that stage now and there's plenty left. Tuna mayonnaise and corned beef?'

'Thanks, Gran.' Joe helped himself to two of each variety at once. Granny Gallacher made dainty little fingers of sandwiches for her Sunday afternoon teas. Mary always said after they were away from the house that they ought to be thankful the sandwiches hadn't a lace frill on them. Bad enough that they were served in a blue basket lined with pink, lace-edged cotton.

'Since her man died,' Mary confided to Kate, 'the pour auld soul has nothing better to do but knit and sew. It helps keep her goin'.'

What amazed Kate was the fact that Aunty Bec and Uncle Willie and, as far as she knew, Sandra as well thought the place so 'superior'. In Kate's opinion, it was absolutely ghastly. There was no real harm in Granny Gallacher, of course. She was, as Mary said, a nice enough soul and kind and generous-hearted in her own way. She was very fond of all her family, including her son George's wife. Indeed, she had said much the same about Mary as Mary had said about her.

When Bec groaned about how common-spoken Mary was, Granny Gallacher would say, 'Och well, there's no real harm in her. She's kind and generous-hearted in her own way.'

They were all united in their agreement that Kate had made a terrible mistake getting herself 'into trouble' and having to marry that awful young man.

'Poor Kate won't have her sorrows to seek,' Granny Gallacher prophesied.

The only good thing, they said, that had come of the marriage was 'wee Chrissie'. Granny Gallacher loved to dandle her on her ample lap and nurse her against the soft pillow of her bosom. Kate had quite a struggle to prise the baby away from her.

'How has he been to that wean?' Mary asked Kate unexpectedly as they were leaving Granny Gallacher's.

'Fine,' Kate said. 'Why?'

'You jist watch yer wean,' Mary warned. 'Ah wouldnae put anythin' past that pig.'

Kate felt annoyed at her mother. She was always trying to worry her. If it wasn't about one thing, it was another. The truth was, Pete had little or no interest in the baby. Hardly ever gave her a glance. His daughter meant no more to him than his wife.

Kate impulsively leaned into the pram and spoke silently to her daughter: You'll be all right. Don't worry. We'll both be all right. Despite her determination to think positively, however, anxieties scurried back like Granny McWhirter's cockroaches.

Chapter Eleven

Kate could now look at Pete and know without a doubt that she no longer loved him. Had she ever loved him at all? Maybe it had just been a childish infatuation. She didn't care. All she wanted was to get away from him. She was determined not to remain with a husband who was systematically destroying her. It was a sad situation. Nobody wanted to stop loving or to give up the slightest chance of being loved. She could see the temptation of deluding oneself into believing that when the man promised he'd never again be violent, he really meant it. Wishful thinking. Once was enough for her. She wasn't stupid, she told herself. And she had her pride. No man was going to abuse her and get away with it. He could say what he liked. Pete, of course, had never said anything. It was as if nothing amiss had happened. He swaggered in and out. He enjoyed his food. He took as much sex as he fancied. He didn't even seem to notice that she was blanking out her mind and her feelings, giving him no response whatsoever. She lay like a cold, dead thing. Inside she had been resenting him more and more, until now she absolutely hated him. She couldn't bear him to touch her.

'Look,' she told him eventually. 'We've got to talk.'

He'd just finished a lunch of mince and tatties. She'd chosen the pound of stewing steak herself, and asked the butcher to mince it, keeping an eye on him as he did so, so that he didn't slip lumps of fat or anything else into the mincer as well as the steak. She'd served it with creamed potatoes. It was Budd's favourite. He always smacked his lips over it and said, 'I've never tasted mince and tatties like you make it, hen. I don't know how you do it but you make ordinary Scots food seem special.'

Kate wondered why only foreign food and posh recipes were 'special'. Scottish food was special if it was cooked properly. She cooked with loving care, even for Pete.

'OK,' he said, leaning back in his chair and lighting a cigarette. 'Talk.'

Kate glanced across at Budd. He immediately took the hint and got up.

'I'm away through to my room, hen.' He turned at the door. 'Do you want me to collect Christine later on?' He had grown very fond of his grandchild.

'I'll let you know after I clear away and see what else I've still to do.'

'Right you are, hen.'

He closed the door behind him. Kate looked round at Pete.

'I can't go on like this.'

'Like what?'

'I don't feel anything for you any more. I don't want to have sex with you. I don't want to have anything to do with you. I should never have married you. I realise that now. I feel – '

'Aw, shut up,' Pete interrupted. 'I don't give a fuck what you want or how you feel.'

'Oh, charming!' Kate said bitterly. 'That more or less sums up what's wrong with our marriage.'

'Listen, you.' He grabbed her by the hair and twisted her head back. The pain was excruciating but she managed to keep her mouth clamped shut. She just concentrated on hating him. 'I want none of your fuckin' lip. If I do get any more of it, I'll give you the licking you deserve. OK?'

He flung her back with such force that the chair overturned and she landed on the floor. 'Now get me a mug of coffee.'

Silently she went through to the kitchen, her mind working overtime. She had to get away but it had to be for good. She would have to be clever about it. She had to think everything through. She mustn't dissipate her energies by shouting or fighting. Later, on the way to collect Christine, instead of just going down Killearn Street, she slowly walked down the hill of Stoneyhurst Street. Dorothy was married and lived here now but there was no use going to speak to her. Dorothy had enough problems of her own with an unemployed husband who had become addicted to heroin. Dorothy was struggling to keep herself and her twin babies alive. As if that wasn't enough, she had been forced to look after her husband's whippet. He regularly entered the dog for events at his favourite racetrack and insisted that the animal had to be well looked after and have the best of food. Her late mother's cat was another burden. Dorothy had promised that she would always take good care of it. Kate suspected that the animals were Dorothy's last straw. She was losing the struggle. She couldn't cope. She had sunk into a morass of hopelessness. Dorothy, who had always taken such a pride in her appearance, now looked like a tramp, with shapeless clothes, a tired, unmade-up face and matted hair.

The last time Kate had gone to see Dorothy, she had had the door shut in her face. Through the door, she heard moaning sobs. There was nothing she could do. She wanted to call out 'It's all right, Dorothy', but they both knew it wasn't.

She passed Dorothy's close. A few of the windows were boarded up. Graffiti covered the walls inside the close from top to bottom: they had been desecrated with paint spray. Tommy's close was the same. Mary had told Tommy and Liz,

'If ah saw any o' the weans – either ma ain or anybody else – makin' a mess like that on the walls, ah'd box their ears fur them.'

Tommy and Liz said they wouldn't dare do such a thing to anyone else's children nowadays.

'Why not?' Mary asked.

'We'd get our windows put in, Mammy,' Tommy said. 'The kids' mothers or fathers or big brothers would come and take a brick to our window or an axe to our door.'

'That's terrible!' Mary was outraged. 'Weans need tae be taught whit's right an' whit isnae. That's whit's wrang wi' the world today. Weans get taught aw the wrang things. Or nothin' at aw. By God, if ah see them, ah'll set the dug on them.'

Rajah barked enthusiastically and Mary gave him a hug and a kiss. 'Aye, you'd soon sort them out, son, eh?'

'No, please,' Tommy and Liz cried out in unison. 'Don't cause any trouble.'

'Me, cause trouble!' Mary looked as if she was about to pounce on them and strangle them. 'A milder, more peace-lovin' wumin ye couldnae meet.'

Kate reached Saracen Street and went into the Sari Café. She ordered a cup of tea and sat staring sightlessly at the notice pinned up on the wall opposite.

ANYBODY THE WORSE OF BOOZE OR DRUGS WILL BE
FORCIBLY EJECTED.

Kate sipped at the tea and tried to think. Her scalp still ached and she had a throbbing pain in her hip and shoulder from her fall. Thank God she had some money in the bank. It wouldn't last long, though, if she had a rent to pay and herself and Christine to keep. If she remained in the area, her mother would no doubt look after Christine during the day if she got a job. But could she get a job? Would Pete just do nothing if she walked out on him? Would she get the chance to live in peace and safety even if she could find work and a place to live?

She thought of her mother and father's house, but to go there would be such a terrible admission of failure and defeat. She didn't know if her pride could stand it. Far better to be independent. Anyway, she doubted if her mother would be willing to have her back.

'Ah told ye so,' she'd say. 'Ah warned ye but would ye listen? No, ye would not. There's always been a stubborn bit aboot you, Well, ye've made yer bed, m'lady. Now ye'll jist huv tae lie on it.'

What about the DHSS? Would they be able to help? Kate wondered. If only she could go somewhere else, far away from Possilpark. If only she could get a mortgage and a place of her own. Or even a council house in her name. Private rents were so high they were out of the question. If she could wait for another month or two she might have enough in the bank for a decent down payment for a wee flat. A one room and kitchen would do. Even just one room. As long as it was away from here. It wasn't that she minded Possilpark. She was at home here. She knew the people. She had never known anywhere else. She had made excursions into the city centre of course, but that was all. The important thing was, however, to put a safe distance between her and Pete.

How did one go about buying a flat? She was still only seventeen and had no experience of such things. First, she decided, she must get more money. Joe was very generous. Each week the van raked in more and she got her fair share. Soon he would have two vans.

She wasn't stupid, she kept assuring herself. She wasn't going to do anything rash. She would stick it out until she had more money. Money meant security. Then it occurred to her that no job could pay her as much as Joe was paying her. Once she got a place of her own she would have more time to do what she was happiest doing – baking for Joe and making his ice cream. As well as the scones, she could try something else. The one sponge mixture could be divided and made into fairy cakes, chocolate iced cakes, cakes decorated with marzipan. Her imagination was fired with all sorts of possibilities.

She began to feel excited, almost happy. Why hadn't this occurred to her before? Probably because she enjoyed cooking and baking so much, she'd never thought of it as a job. She left the café and with a firm confident step, made her way towards Killearn Street and her mother's close. She ran up the stairs to the top flat. Her mother came to the door nursing the baby. The child's eyes were half closed. One cheek was flushed bright pink and she was feebly hiccuping.

'Ah think the wee soul's havin' another tooth come through. She's been howlin' her heid aff.'

Kate's euphoria immediately dissolved into anxiety. She put out her arms for the child.

'Give her to me, Mammy.'

Her mother turned back into the lobby.

'Ah've nearly got her tae sleep. Away an' put the kettle on. Ma tongue's hangin' oot for a drink o' tea.'

Kate reluctantly went through to the kitchen. She'd have to be careful. She mustn't forget she had her baby to consider. Christine must be her first priority. She had to think things through.

Carefully. Cautiously.

Chapter Twelve

'He's taking me on for two afternoons a week,' Budd told Kate. 'But I bet, once he sees I'm a good man, he'll take me on for longer.'

'Joe knows you're a good man, Budd. It's not that. If it was just serving the customers or even driving the van, there would be no problem. But you know how things are.'

'I told him. I'm maybe not as young as I used to be but I'm still fit and able to handle myself.'

The truth was Budd wasn't fit at all after years of heavy drinking. He was still little more than skin and bone and the brown crêpey bags under his eyes made him look even more gaunt and ill. The good food he now ate and enjoyed seemed to drop to below his waist and just stay there, creating a round football of a belly. But at least his depression seemed to have lifted. He was really happy about Joe giving him a start.

'Joe's going to make it big, Kate. He'll have a fleet of vans one day. That's what he said, and I believe him. He's a decent, hard-working fella. And with the help of your ice cream and home baking, how could he lose?' Budd had never looked so animated. 'Yes, that fella's going to make it and I'm going to make it along with him. You too, hen. We'll be all right.'

For a rash moment, she considered taking Budd along with her when she left Pete for good, but the moment passed. For one thing, it would look very odd running off with her father-in-law. People would get the wrong idea. Anyway, she would have enough to cope with looking after herself and Christine, and working all day making everything for Joe. She had it all planned. If she could just hang on for another couple of months, she'd have enough for a down payment on a small flat. Or if she couldn't find someone who would take a lump sum, then pay the rest up weekly or monthly, then she'd just have to rent a private place. Even a bedsit would be better than staying on here. She kept the lid on her hatred, never quarrelling or contradicting Pete if she could help it. For Christine's sake as well as her own, she must keep physically fit and all her wits about her. She had been tempted to neglect his meals, serve up burnt offerings or other disasters as a form of revenge or an expression of her hatred. However, she thought better of it. The only result of that would be getting herself battered senseless. No, she wouldn't give him the chance. She even continued to cater for his mates, serving them delicious food, smiling her thanks in return for their rough and ready compliments. All the time she wanted to throw the food at them. Sometimes only one would turn up. Sometimes two or three or more would crowd round the table. She loathed the sight of them. She detested their aggressive swaggers, their Neanderthal skulls, their foul mouths. She kept out of the way as much as she could. She stayed in the kitchen or she went through to the bedroom and sat beside Christine's cot. But she could still hear their loud laughter and their f-ing and c-ing. Every second word was f- or c-.

They made her sick.

Just another couple of months, she kept telling herself. You can do it. Then Pete found out that Budd was now working for Joe. This knowledge unfortunately came on the same day that she had got behind with her baking and didn't have Pete's meal ready on time.

'Listen to me, the pair of you,' he shouted. 'I've had enough of fuckin' Joe. This isn't a fuckin' bakehouse or tally's to keep Joe Gallacher's van supplied. It's all I hear about – fuckin' Joe Gallacher!'

'Don't talk nonsense,' Kate couldn't resist saying, 'I hardly ever mention Joe's name to you. Anyway, this is Budd's house. It's his name on the door.'

Pete's eyes narrowed.

'Oh, clever dick, is it now? I think fuckin' clever dick needs to be taught a fuckin' lesson.'

Budd stepped forward, his face anxious. 'Now, wait a minute, son . . .'

'Shut up, you drunken old cunt.'

Suddenly he took a wild swipe at the carefully packed box of scones she had been about to put a lid on, ready for Budd to deliver to Joe. The scones flew around the small kitchen. Some landed on the floor, some in the sink which was full of soapy water. Some splashed into a pot of soup she had been preparing for the dinner. Hours of work wasted. If she hadn't become well practised at keeping her emotions battened down, she would have gone berserk and killed him. As it was, she just looked at him with loathing.

'And you can take that fuckin' look off your face before I change its fuckin' shape.'

Budd spoke up again.

'Listen you, you've done enough harm. Away you go and meet your pals. They're more your sort.'

'I told you to shut up.'

He gave Budd a punch that winded him and knocked him backwards to crash against the sink. Budd quickly regained his balance and made to lunge at Pete. But the younger man caught a grip of Budd's hair and pushed his head down into the water in the sink.

In a panic for Budd's safety, Kate rushed at Pete, clawing and pulling and punching at him.

'Let go of him, you fool.'

'Fool, is it?' Pete let go of his father and turned on her. Budd collapsed, gasping and choking, to the floor. Kate grabbed a towel and wiped at his face.

'Don't panic, Budd. Take slow breaths . . .'

Before she could say or do anything more, Pete had dragged her off and was punching her viciously on the face and body. She tried to hold the towel to her face, to protect it and to stop the blood spurting down over her clothes. She thought she heard Budd shouting but could no longer distinguish words. She was swimming in her own blood, sinking, gurgling, choking on it.

When she recovered her senses, Pete had disappeared and Budd was bending over her, holding a sponge to her face. Ice-cold rivers of water were trickling down her neck.

'I'll have to get an ambulance.' Budd's voice was agitated.

'And report him to the police as well, I suppose?' Kate managed bitterly. 'Pete would be pleased. He'd never touch me again after that. You know what the police always say anyway. It's "just a domestic" to them.'

'You might have broken bones, hen,' Budd said. 'You'd better at least get checked out.'

She rocked a little from side to side, then moved her arms and legs.

'No, I think I'm OK.'

'You need stitches.'

'Help me up till I get a look at myself in the mirror.'

As Budd grasped her under the arms and heaved her up, Kate cried out in pain. She felt bruised from head to toe. The pain was so bad she began to retch. Budd got her to the sink just in time. Vomiting was like somebody jabbing knives into her ribs. Maybe they were broken as well as bruised.

She could hear Christine crying now. The noise must have wakened her.

'Oh God,' she moaned.

'I'll go and give the cot a bit of a shoogle.'

'Thanks, Budd.'

He left her clinging to the sink. She managed to pull out the plug to allow the soapy water to run away. Then she turned on the cold tap. After splashing her face and neck, she felt a lot better. She crept across to the cooker like a bent old woman and plugged in the electric kettle.

The baby had quietened and Budd returned with some paracetamols.

'Take a couple of these, hen.'

'Thanks.' She swallowed them with some water.

'Your face is going to be a right mess. It's swelling up already. And that cut at the side of your mouth's opened up again. Let me phone you a taxi. You'll have to get that stitched up, hen. I'll see to Christine until you get back. She'll be all right.'

Kate had to agree. She couldn't stop the bleeding. So there she was back again. One of them, she thought. One of the regular walking wounded, one of the sad defeated women in the casualty department. Only she was not one of them. She refused to be one of them. She would not be defeated. Her hatred of Pete hardened. She felt grateful for it. She clung to it. She nursed it deep inside her.

She hoped he would die.

Chapter Thirteen

Budd started taking Christine to Killearn Street every day. Kate missed the extra few minutes with her daughter. Each day she felt upset. She kissed the baby and hugged her close as if for the last time. Budd called to collect her as well. Kate pleaded with him not to tell her mother about Pete's latest attack. She hoped she could hide from her family until the bruising – at least on her face – had healed. She didn't know what she would have done without Budd, who also delivered the ice cream and scones to Joe. He had to take a taxi but it was worth it, rather than have Joe come to the house and see the state she was in. Budd had got to know one of the black taxi drivers, which was lucky because as often as not, the taxis licensed by the Glasgow Corporation would refuse to venture into Possilpark.

Kate had confided in Budd that she was going to leave. She couldn't wait the two months she'd originally planned. Not now. Apart from the violence that could erupt again at any minute, it was becoming more and more difficult to do the baking and ice cream as well as the family meals, and keep the whole house immaculate into the bargain. She'd be damned if she'd end up like Dorothy. No way!

She planned everything down to the last detail. Housework and family cooking during the hours while Pete was at home. Then as soon as he went out, she'd tackle the baking and the ice cream. His hours were so irregular and unpredictable, that was part of the problem. On one occasion, she had even got up during the night to bake, then hid the results away in boxes in Budd's wardrobe and under his bed while Pete slept off a night of drinking.

Budd had taken her news about leaving as if it had been a tragic death. All the spirit and energy he'd shown in recent weeks and months vanished and he seemed to shrink before her eyes.

'Don't worry,' she tried to assure him, 'we'll still be in touch and you'll still be working for Joe.'

He nodded.

'Aye, there's that. But I'll miss you and Christine about the house.'

'You'll visit us as often as you like. You can still take her out. I can't go on like this, Budd. You know that.'

'No, of course you can't, hen. You've done marvellous to hang in this long. There's a strong bit about you.'

Kate laughed.

'You sound like my mother. Only she always says, There's a stubborn bit about you.'

He managed a smile.

'Well, both, I suppose. But where will you go, hen? How will you manage?

'I'll ask my Granny McWhirter if I can move in with her until I get a place of my own. I've always got on well with Granny McWhirter. Before I was married, I used to spend the odd night or weekend there. At least she won't keep saying I told you so, or slag me all the time like my mother.'

'You'll have a bit of a tight squeeze at her place. She's just got a room and kitchen and the lavvy outside, hasn't she?'

'Och, she managed to bring up a family there. No, I think she'll enjoy having the company.'

'Well, I wish you luck. But you'll have a bit of a struggle getting the stuff done for Joe there, will you not?'

'Not as bad as what I've had here.

'When are you planning on going, then?'

'I think I'll ask Granny tomorrow and then if she says it's OK, I'll start taking things down to Saracen Street gradually – clothes and personal things – a few bits and pieces every day so that Pete won't notice. I reckon a week or a fortnight at the most.'

'Och well, I suppose Saracen Street's not at the other end of the world. It'll be easy enough to see you both.'

'Of course, every day if you like. I told you.'

She had it all planned. Then, as fate would have it, her mother arrived and everything changed.

Mary had been getting more suspicious by the day.

'Why is she never comin' wi' the wean?' she kept demanding of Budd. 'Whit's she up tae?'

'What do you mean, up to?' Budd asked indignantly. 'She's working hard for Joe. I keep telling you.'

The mention of doing anything for Joe usually worked like a charm. But tension and suspense were in the air and Mary was sniffing it out. Budd could no longer hide how he felt. His anxiety that Pete would find out what was going on was undermining him. His sallow face now looked even more unhealthy. He couldn't eat. He couldn't sleep. He wasn't worried for himself but for Kate and his grandchild.

'There's somethin' goin' on,' Mary said. 'An' ah'm gonnae find oot whit it is.'

Budd hurried anxiously home to warn Kate. She was preparing the evening meal in the kitchen.

'Oh well,' Kate sighed, 'I suppose I'll just have to go to Killearn Street tomorrow morning with Christine and take the consequences. I can just hear her – "I told you, I told you he was a right pig of a man, etc., etc. . . . . But would you listen?"'

'It's just her way,' Budd said. 'She cares about you.'

Kate smiled.

'Och, I suppose she does but sometimes she has a funny way of showing it.'

Budd lowered his voice.

'All I was worried about was in case she says something in front of Pete. Is he in?'

'Through in the room with that Dougie character.'

Budd grimaced.

'That nutter. Well, I hope to God wee Mary doesn't turn up tonight and start anything.' His voice sank to a whisper.

'She doesn't know about you leaving but if she sees the state of you . . .'

'This is Mammy's bingo night.'

Bingo night or not, Mary, accompanied as usual by the giant Rajah, did turn up. Kate was serving the meal to Pete, Dougie and Budd when the doorbell rang.

'I'll go,' Budd said.

In a minute or two Budd and Mary could be heard arguing.

'Whit a bloody nerve!' Mary was shouting indignantly. 'No, ah'll no' come back later. Ah dinnae care a damn if ye *are* in the middle of yer dinner. Or if Kate's busy servin' the bloody royal family. Get oot o' ma way.'

Before Kate could get out to the lobby, Mary had burst into the living room.

On catching sight of Kate, she said,

'Oh aye. Now ah understand. Ah see whit's been goin' on. That pig's been at it again. An' why may ah ask hus he no' got a couple o' black eyes an' a cut mouth? Did ah no tell ye to give back as much, no – mair, than ye got?'

Pete said,

'Mind your own fuckin' business.'

'Oh, big man, is it? Givin' me orders. Well, ah'm no' her. Ah see exactly whit ye are. Ye're scum. Ye always huv been. Ye're slime. Aw the fancy shirts an' ties an' suits cannae hide that . . .'

'Mammy!' Kate warned, but she was too late. Pete's temper had burst into flame. He rushed at Mary to grab her by the back of the neck and run her from the house.

'Get out of here,' he bawled, 'before I – '

He got no further than the living-room door when Rajah pounced. Strong teeth sank into Pete's arm and dragged him down. Pete began to scream.

'Get it off me!'

But the dog's huge body was straddling him now and it was fighting to get at Pete's throat. It was so wild with rage, it couldn't even hear Mary shouting. Suddenly Kate saw

Dougie reach inside his jacket and pull out a gun. It only took one shot to Rajah's head to kill him.

Pete pushed the dog's heavy body aside and struggled up, blood soaking his jacket.

Dougie said, 'You can get poisoned with a fuckin' dog bite.'

Nursing his arm, Pete glared hatred at Mary.

'By Christ, you'll pay for this,' he said. Then to Dougie, 'Don't just stand there. Get me to the fuckin' Royal.'

Mary was staring at the dog in shocked silence. When the two men had gone, she kneeled down and cradled its head in her arms.

'He wis protectin' me,' she managed eventually. 'Like he always does.'

'Kate, take the baby,' Budd said. 'Away you go to your Granny's.'

'He wis protectin' me,' Mary repeated.

'It's Mammy he'll be after. It's Mammy I'm worried about,' Kate told Budd. See her safely home as quick as you can. That Dougie guy was always frightening enough, but my God, with a gun? I've never thought about guns before. Maybe Pete has one as well. Oh please, Budd. Take Mammy home and warn Daddy.'

'Aye, you're right. Come on, hen,' he said to Mary. 'You'd better let me see you safe home.'

'Ah never go anywhere withoot the dug,' Mary said.

'OK, I'll . . .' He looked at the size of the animal and realised he couldn't carry it.

'I tell you what, I'll put it in the pram and wheel it home with you. Then George can help us carry it up the stairs until you decide what else to do.'

It was a hard struggle. It couldn't be made to fit. The best they could do was to drape the dog's massive body across the pram.

Mary still wasn't weeping. Kate had never seen her mother look so lost and helpless. She whispered to Budd,

'Keep an eye on her crossing the road. She looks in a daze.'

'Aye, OK.'

Kate watched them from the front-room window until they turned down Killearn Street. The scene would have been funny if it wasn't so tragic.

Afterwards, clearing the table, dropping things, hardly able to pick them up because she was shaking so much, she struggled to calm the whirlpool of terror in her stomach.

Surely even someone like Pete wouldn't make a serious attack on a tiny creature old enough to be his mother. He couldn't be that stupid either. Mary was too well known and respected in the neighbourhood. It would do Pete's reputation no good if he hurt her. It wouldn't do Pete any good physically either. He'd have Tommy and Joe to contend with for a start.

No, she kept assuring herself over and over again, her mother would be all right. She tried to pray but her mind was too fevered. She just kept on repeating, Mammy's going to be all right.

Chapter Fourteen

Joe buried Rajah in the Killearn Street back green. Mary wept then and said it was a disgrace that he should end up in such a neglected place with a jungle of long grass and the overflow from the bins getting trampled on to him. The Corporation should have a decent graveyard somewhere for dogs. The Corporation didn't care. The Corporation could afford lawn mowers. Why didn't they mow the grass in the back green? Why didn't they empty the bins more often?

'Bloody Corporation,' she sobbed.

They all tried to comfort her, but she'd only listen to Joe.

'Mammy, Rajah would want to stay here in Killearn Street near you. He wouldn't want to be stuck away in some graveyard alongside other dogs. He didn't like other dogs. He just liked you.'

Mary nodded.

'Ye're right, son. Bit doon there in such a place! It's no' nice enough fur him.'

'How about if I put a wee wooden fence round where I buried him. Then you could tend that bit of the green and keep it nice.'

She didn't look too sure but at least she made an effort to control her sobbing. She mopped at her eyes.

'Ye're a good boy, son. Ye've always been a good boy tae me.'

Joe gave her a hug.

'I'll get some fencing right away and come back as soon as I can to fix it up.'

Mary nodded.

Kate said, 'I've brought some of my scones for your tea, Mammy.'

'Away you go back tae that pig o' a man,' Mary said in a

sudden rush of her old spirit. 'There's nae place for ye here any more.'

'Och Mammy,' Joe said, 'you don't mean that. You're just upset. It wasn't Kate's fault.'

'Ah never wanted anythin' tae dae wi' folk like that. Bloody gangsters. Goin' aroon' wi' bloody guns. We've always been a decent family. Until she got mixed up wi' that crowd. Ah warned her. Over an' over again. Ah told her but would she listen? No, she would not. An' now look what's happened.' She burst into tears again, remembering her loss. 'Ah'll never forgive her. Never for as long as ah live.'

Joe said gently to Kate,

'You'd better go. But don't worry. It'll be all right. She's just upset. I'll stay with her until Dad comes home.'

Kate felt like weeping herself but she left without saying anything. She was upset and sad about Rajah too. After all, she'd been brought up with the dog. It had been like one of the family. The previous night she had been too anxious about how Pete would be when he returned from the Infirmary to think about Rajah. If Pete was still in a rage, he might seek her mother out. She visualised terrible and violent scenes in Killearn Street. Nothing happened however. Pete and Dougie had returned, had something to eat then a few whiskies and beers, and that was that. Dougie left and Pete went to bed. He hadn't even bothered with sex.

She thanked God that his anger had burned out. He probably wouldn't allow her mother to set foot in the house again but that would be it. He was only violent when he was in a rage and was provoked.

The next day Joe appeared at the door. She thanked God again. This time because Pete wasn't in. No doubt Joe would be completely banned now as well.

Once through in the kitchen where Kate needed to take a tray of scones out of the oven, Joe said,

'I thought I'd better check if you were OK.'

'There's been no more trouble from Pete, if that's what you mean.'

'It was about what Mammy said as well. She didn't mean it. Give her time.'

'I know.' She couldn't believe that her mother meant to disown her for ever. 'Don't worry, Joe. I'm all right. How about you? No more trouble with the van?'

'No more trouble?' Joe echoed incredulously. 'It's getting worse. I'm going to have to put a stop to it once and for all.'

Kate stared at him in surprise.

'Budd told me things were OK now.'

'He's been lucky. There's been nothing happen on the couple of afternoons he's there. But nearly every other afternoon, there's been something. And nearly every night. It's driving me out of my skull. I didn't say to Budd. He'd be wanting to pitch in and help at night and he's not fit for it, Kate. The other guy who's with me, Jimmy Gardner, he's a fit eighteen-year-old, and he's thinking of packing it in already. They nearly broke his arm the other night with their bloody baseball bats and I was nearly knocked unconscious.'

'I never realised. That's terrible, Joe. For goodness sake, go to the police.'

'I've told the police but I suppose they can't follow me around all the time. Anyway, they've never been there when anything's happened. But by God, I'll be ready for them tonight. They're in for a big surprise.'

'How do you mean?'

'I picked up something in one of them auction sales the other day. I just happened to be passing as it was going on. I paid a bit over the top for it but still . . .' He gave a grim laugh. 'I think it'll be worth it.'

'What'll be worth it?'

'A huge Samurai sword. I'm going to rush out at them, yelling like a Japanese warrior and brandishing the thing. You should see the video I had about these Japanese guys. Frighten the shite out of anybody, they would.'

She laughed along with him.

'I wish I could make a video of you chasing them like that. I can just imagine it. I bet you're bigger than any Samurai warrior as well.'

'Anyway,' Joe said, 'I'm hoping that'll sort them out. Granny McWhirter tells me you're wanting to move in with her, Kate.'

'Just until I get a place of my own.'

'Well,' he hesitated, 'that was another thing I came about. Granny says would you hang on for a wee while. Just until Mammy gets over all this. Granny's worried about Mammy and feels she has to put her first. She's afraid that Mammy might think she was taking sides with you against her. Of course she wouldn't be but Mammy's awful vulnerable just now and she's just not thinking straight.'

'Yes. Of course. Tell Granny not to worry. I'll stay away for a while.'

But she felt depressed after Joe left. She had been looking forward so much to a quick escape from Byshott Street and to settling safely with Granny McWhirter even just for a couple of weeks until she got organised. It was so difficult nowadays to do anything for herself. Even to think clearly and make sensible plans wasn't easy when she was having to cope with so much work and under such stressful circumstances. She could have wept with weakness and disappointment. She fought to control the urge and concentrated instead on making another batch of scones.

'I was trying iced sponge cakes as well,' she told Joe.

'Great, hen,' he'd enthused. 'But how will you manage? Budd tells me the pair of you have a terrible job hiding everything from Pete. And all this having to make everything while he's out and never knowing when he's coming or going. It beats me how you do it.'

'I couldn't do it without Budd. But if only I could get a place of my own, Joe. It wouldn't be all that easy even then, but I think Mammy would still take a turn with Christine no

97

matter what she might think of me. She's really fond of the baby.'

'Of course Mammy would go on helping,' Joe assured her.

'I'd need her help at least until Christine's old enough to get into a nursery,' Kate went on. 'I'd manage. I might not be able to get her into nursery of course, but I'd still manage somehow. If I just could get away from here, Joe.'

Joe's freckled face creased with worry.

'If I'd a bigger place, Kate, you know I'd – '

'Don't be daft,' Kate interrupted him. 'It's different with Granny's room and kitchen. You know what it's like.'

She didn't need to say any more. In both their minds was the contrasting picture of Granny's sparse and spartan quarters compared to Joe and Marilyn's room and kitchen. Marilyn's clothes and perfumes and make-up and God knows what else cluttered and overflowed all over the place.

'I'm hoping to get a bigger house, as you know.'

'Yes, I know but even so, I wouldn't move in with you, Joe. I want to be independent.'

'Quite right,' Joe said. 'And good luck to you, hen.'

'Oh, I don't think luck has much to do with anything,' she told him. 'It's all down to hard work as far as I can see.'

'Aye, hard work and a determination to succeed. We've both got that, hen.'

She gave him a smile and a thumbs-up sign.

'But definitely.'

Chapter Fifteen

The van parked under one of the few street lamps that was working. A queue had formed and snaked raggedly from the light into the darkness. Some older women wore headsquares, aprons and slippers. Others were decently hatted and buttoned up in coats. They all liked an ice-cream wafer to lick while enjoying their favourite programme on television. Later they would savour Joe's home baking with a cup of tea. They were chatting together and having a good laugh. A couple of smart young girls in high heels and short skirts wanted a small tub of ice cream each to spoon while waiting on the bus to take them into town to a disco. Some children skipped impatiently up and down. A couple of teenage boys in denims and Doc Martens puffed nonchalantly at cigarettes. Older men always sent their wives out for the ice cream, the bottles of Irn Bru and the home-baked scones.

'Hey, Joe,' one of the women shouted, 'get yer skates on, son. Ah'm beginnin' tae take root here.'

Another called out, 'If you want tae spend the night wi' me, Joe, come on up tae ma room.'

Joe's big frame topped by his mop of fiery red hair all but filled the opening at the side of the van through which he was serving. Jimmy Gardner who was helping him kept disappearing behind Joe.

'Hold your horses,' Joe called back to the woman. But his voice was good-natured and his freckled face was seldom without a grin.

'We'd rather hold you,' the call came back.

'Hey, Martha.' A window nearby had gone up and a man in shirt sleeves and braces was leaning out. 'Get us a packet of fags as well, hen.' Just as he was about to withdraw into the room again, he suddenly stiffened.

'Joe,' he warned. 'Watch yer back, son.'

Joe knew immediately what the man meant.

A red wash of rage swept through him. The familiar big Volvo was creeping slowly up behind the van with its side-lights on. Before it came to a standstill, Joe sprang into action, scattering customers right, left and centre. He leapt from the van screaming like a demented banshee, the sword held high in a two-handed grip. Lashing out at the front wheel of the Volvo, he burst a tyre with an explosive bang. Damp, rubbery-smelling air gusted past his legs. Still screaming, he booted the driver's door savagely shut into the driver's face. He lashed out again this time at the rear tyre. The car slumped down along one side, resting on torn rubber and rims. Joe leapt on to the bonnet, screaming, 'You fucking bastards, you'll not run off this time!'

Savagely, he swung the sword down against the wind-screen. Black balaclavaed heads drew back, eyes bulging with incredulity and horror. With the first blow the windscreen cobwebbed with spidery cracks. Still screaming, saliva spraying and glistening on his chin, Joe chopped furiously at the screen and roof.

With a crunch of gears, the Volvo shot into reverse. Joe staggered off the bonnet, landing running on the pavement. The car attempted a sluggish handbrake turn on its two good tyres and shot crab-like into the dark maze of dingy streets.

It was the talk of Possilpark. People laughed every time they thought about it. They stopped Joe in the street to shake his hand.

'Good for you, son,' he was told. Those who had not had the good fortune to witness the dramatic event said, 'By Christ, I wish I'd seen you demolishing that lot. It would have made my day, so it would.'

Mary had never been more proud of her son. For the first

time since she'd lost Rajah, she cheered up. She blossomed in the sunshine of everyone's praise.

'Och well,' she said. 'Nae harm tae oor Tommy. He's a nice wee lad. Bit ah've always thought Joe would go places that Tommy wouldnae have the nerve fur. Joe's a big lad an' he does things in a big way. He's got his eye on another van already.' She chuckled with delight. 'That big fella'll end up being a millionaire yet, whit dae ye bet?'

Kate felt proud as well. Too many decent folk's vans had been forced off the road and their livelihoods stolen from them. Too many had been afraid to make a stand against those who used force. Maybe Joe's example would give courage. Maybe courage could be as infectious as fear. Anyway, there had been no more attacks on Joe's van.

Budd kept taking Christine to Mary's every morning and collecting her every afternoon. Then one day, some time after the Samurai incident, Kate tried taking Christine herself. Mary opened the door with a ready smile of welcome. She was wearing a floral wrap-around apron and a mountain of rollers on her head. Seeing Kate, her smile faded, her small face stiffened.

'Oh, it's you, is it.' She moved aside. 'Ah suppose ye'd better come in.'

Kate wanted to hug the older woman, to express her love and gratitude for being forgiven. Well, not quite forgiven but near enough. Mary, to use an expression Kate often heard her mother use about others, had a face like fizz. However, to be allowed back into the house was a step in the right direction. (The door had been slammed in her face on another occasion.)

In the living room, Mary lifted Christine from the baby buggy.

'An' how's Granny's wee Chrissie the day, eh?'

Kate said,

'She's as bright as a button, Mammy. Slept all night without – '

'Ah wisnae talkin' tae you,' Mary said. 'Ah wis talkin' tae

the wean.' This was ridiculous: they both knew that at only one year of age, Christine, bright though she was, could not have answered the question.

Her mother dandled Christine and kissed her before setting her down in the playpen she'd bought. Christine gooed and squealed delightedly at being reunited with the special toys that were kept for her at her granny's.

Mary flicked and tugged at her apron before saying in a stiff, grudging tone,

'Ah suppose ah'll have tae make ye a cup o' tea noo.'

'Thanks, Mammy.'

Mary clattered about in the kitchen while Kate sat in the living room, knowing not to push her luck by following her mother through. Mary reappeared eventually with a tray set with the china cups and saucers usually reserved for visitors instead of the usual chummy mugs the family used. There was also a plate of Penguin chocolate biscuits. In silence, Mary poured the tea.

'Thanks, Mammy.'

'Take wan o' them Penguins if ye huv tae.'

'Thanks, Mammy.'

'They cost a fortune in the Co-Op.'

A piece of biscuit stuck in Kate's throat but she hastily gulped a mouthful of tea to wash it down. Finally she said, 'Joe's doing well, isn't he, Mammy?'

'Nae thanks tae you.'

It was only with very great difficulty that Kate refrained from strangling her mother.

'He tackled them gangsters,' Mary went on. 'Single-handed. He's got the courage o' a lion, that boy.'

'So he has,' Kate managed. 'He's going to have the other van on the road by the beginning of the year. He said he might even manage it for Christmas.'

'Aye, it depends if he can get the right men fur it,' Mary said, warming to the subject. 'Men who could face up tae them gangsters. There's too many weedy wee fellas aroon' here. It's them drugs that's doin' it. There's hardly any big hefty fellas like ma man, an' ma Joe, nowadays.'

'That's true. But he's got his eye on a couple. Do you remember Mrs O'Rourke's son, Jimmy?'

'Him that was in the army?'

'Yes. He's out now and looking for a job. And there's Mike McKay.'

'Mrs McKay's grandson?'

'Yes.'

'Ah'm no' sae sure aboot him. He's been in trouble wi' the polis.'

'Och, but it was just for getting mixed up in fights. He's never been into drugs.'

'Well, Joe needs somebody tough, an' you could call Mike McKay a hard man. Ah suppose he'll serve Joe's purpose. Bit he's no' like Joe. Ah mean, Joe can handle himself. Bit he's no' hard by nature. He's got a good kind heart, has Joe.'

'So he has, Mammy.'

'He's always been good tae me.'

'So he has, Mammy.'

'He'll go far, that fella. Ah've always said it.'

'I know you have, Mammy. He's been good to me too.' She took the risk of going even further and embarrassing her mother who never spoke of love (or anything 'soft' like that) even in connection with Joe. 'I've always loved him.'

'Och, shut up an' huv another bloody Penguin.'

Kate had to laugh. Her mother rolled her eyes, then turned her attention to Christine. She gave her a rusk and patted her head. 'She's gonnae be curly-headed by the looks o' her,' she said.

'I curl up that cockscomb every day with a wee soft brush.'

'Ah dae that as well. It's good tae huv natural curls. Save aw this bother.' She touched her mountain of rollers. 'Me an' yer daddy's goin' oot tae the pub the night an' ah always try tae look ma best.'

103

'You're really good at doing your own hair, Mammy. I've always to go to the hairdresser's.'

'Aye, but you've got mair money than sense.'

Kate felt quite cheered by the time she left. She told Budd afterwards, 'It's great to see Mammy back to her old self again.'

Budd looked dubious.

'I wouldn't be too sure about that, hen.'

'How do you mean?'

'Well, without the dog she seems to have lost a bit of her confidence. She doesn't go out as much. She asked me to go down to the shops with her the other day. The excuse was to help to carry the messages. But I knew it was only an excuse.'

'I suppose it's understandable.'

'Mind you, she's a tough wee bird. I expect she'll get over that problem in time.'

'She never mentioned it.'

'No, of course she wouldn't. She would deny feeling nervous or vulnerable until she was black in the face.'

Kate sighed. 'Yes, you're right. But as you say, she'll probably get over it. She's not getting any younger though.'

'What's that got to do with it? Look at her old mother. She'd face up to any Possil hard man.'

Thinking of Granny McWhirter, Kate laughed. 'True.'

'Now that things are getting better between you and your mother, that should change your granny's feelings as well.'

'I was hoping so. But I don't want to make a mistake by rushing anything. I nearly dashed up to Granny's right away today to tell her that things are more or less back to normal. Then I thought it would be better coming from Mammy than me.'

'Quite right. You've stuck it out this long, hen. A few days or so more won't kill you. You're a tough wee bird yourself. It must be in the Gallacher genes.'

Kate laughed.

'Granny McWhirter isn't a Gallacher.'

'Well, tough genes are definitely in the family, one way or another. You're a bit of a mixture all roads. You've neither your mammy's nor Tommy's nor Joe's fiery red hair, or the black hair of your daddy's side. And you're neither wee like your mammy or Tommy, or as tall as your daddy or Joe. You're just right, so you are.'

'Flattery'll get you everywhere. But it's time we got all this stuff put away in your room before Pete gets back.'

'I might as well take it over to Joe now. I'll be starting work in the van in a couple of hours anyway.'

'OK. If you don't mind starting early.'

'No, I enjoy the van. And Pete might be back by the time I'd be due to leave. I'm glad in a way that Jimmy Gardner's off tonight. Not that I'm glad the poor guy's got the flu but it gives me a chance to show Joe that I can do nights. No problem.'

They packed the boxes and phoned for the usual black taxi to take Budd, the ice-cream freezer and the plastic boxes of scones down the short distance to Joe's house in Saracen Street where it could be transferred into the van. Budd said he could have carried the scones down himself but the freezer defeated him.

Kate waved him goodbye feeling quite cheerful and optimistic. Any day now, thank God, she thought. Any day now!

Chapter Sixteen

'Aren't you working tonight?' Kate asked Pete.

His dark eyes flashed up at her.

'No.'

'Or going out with your mates?'

'No. Why?'

She shrugged.

'I just wondered. It's usually one or the other.'

She looked away from him. It was a mystery to her how she'd ever thought him in the slightest attractive. He was a skinny, razor-faced, mean-eyed, greasy-haired ned. To think she'd once believed he was good-looking. She'd seen him as tall, dark and handsome. She realised now that he wasn't even tall. Joe was a good head and shoulders above him. Always had been.

The television was on, something Pete seldom watched unless it was the horse-racing. Tonight it was a romantic play that she couldn't imagine was of the slightest interest to him.

'Are any of your mates coming here tonight?'

'What is this?' Pete sneered. 'The third degree?'

'I just want to know how much food to prepare for supper, that's all.'

'Nobody's coming. So shut up.'

He'd never done this before. Just sat watching a play, any kind of play, instead of going out for a drink, or out to work, or had one or more of his mates in.

She began to feel uneasy, suspicious. It was impossible to concentrate on the play. She went through to the kitchen but found it equally difficult to think about cooking, despite the fact she had a lot to prepare for next day's meals. She wandered through to the bedroom and stood staring down at the peacefully sleeping Christine. She had been sucking her thumb before she slept. Now the rosebud mouth was slightly open and the small hand, thumb at the ready, rested on the pillow. Kate loved to gaze at the baby roundness of Christine's cheek and the delicate softness of her neck. She kissed the child and quietly left the room. It was too early to go to bed herself but she couldn't sit for a moment longer opposite Pete in the living room. She returned to the kitchen and switched on the electric kettle.

It was while she was standing watching it and waiting for it to boil that she heard Budd's key in the door. She glanced at her watch. He was early. As soon as he entered the kitchen, she knew by his face that something was wrong. She tightened inside in an effort to prepare herself.

'It's Joe,' Budd said. 'He's dead. The police are down at your mammy's just now.'

'Dead?'

Her eyes fixed disbelievingly on Budd's sallow loose-skinned face.

Pete came through.

'What's up?'

Budd didn't answer him and eventually Kate said as if asking a question instead of answering it,

'Joe's dead?'

'What happened?' Pete asked.

'Have we any whisky in the house?' Budd looked at Kate. She nodded towards a cupboard and he brought out a bottle. 'Have some of this to steady you. I need some myself.'

'Poor Mammy. Oh, poor Mammy,' Kate repeated in a daze. 'I'll need to go to her. Was it another attack on the van?'

Budd nodded.

'One of the bastards had a gun.'

'A gun?' Kate echoed.

Pete said,

'What are you looking at me for?'

Kate felt a tremble grow into a shiver until the whole room seemed to violently shake.

'You did this!'

'Don't be stupid. I've been sat here all night.'

She could hardly see him for the red haze in front of her eyes.

'You had Joe shot,' she said slowly. 'You had Dougie shoot Joe. Just as if my brother was another dog.'

'Oh, wait a minute, hen,' Budd appealed. 'We don't know that. There's been other attacks. I didn't realise . . . One of the customers was telling the police . . .'

'Not with guns.' Kate shook her head. 'Joe would have told me.'

Pete said, 'There's hundreds of guns floating around Possil.'

'I don't believe it. Don't think you're going to get away with this. Don't you think that for one minute I'm going to let you get away with this.'

She fuelled her rage so that she would not be able to feel anything else. She could not think about Joe being dead. Such a grief was too much to bear.

Budd handed her a cup with some whisky in it.

'Here, drink this, hen. It's true. There are other folk apart from Dougie who've got guns. It doesn't do any good to jump to conclusions.'

'You know your son as well as I do,' Kate said. 'Better. You *know* it was him that put Dougie up to this.'

Budd swallowed some whisky.

'There's other folk that has guns,' he repeated. 'You're upset, hen. But not half as much as your mammy. She needs you.'

'I'll drive you down,' Pete said.

'Don't you come near me!' Kate shrank back from him.

'I'll walk you back down,' Budd said.

'And I'll watch the baby.'

Kate experienced a sudden panic. She turned to Budd.

'I'd rather walk down on my own. You wait here.'

Budd nodded. Then Pete called after her,
'You'd better keep your fuckin' mouth shut.'

Chapter Seventeen

Tommy answered the door. He looked smaller and thinner than ever, shrinking into the shadow of his mother's lobby like a frightened wee boy. Kate made to push past him. He clutched at her arm.

'Wait, for God's sake. At least let me ask her if she wants to see you.'

Kate hesitated miserably.

'All right.'

Tommy disappeared into the living room. As the door opened she caught a glimpse, in a shaft of yellow light, of a police uniform. A hushed tragic atmosphere filtered out with the light. Kate stood hunched in the darkness twisting at her handkerchief. Tommy came back shaking his head.

'The doctor's given her something', he told her. 'Go into the kitchen. The police want a word.'

Kate did as she was told, blinking when Tommy clicked on the light. Her mind shrank with fear and indecision. She kept thinking of Christine.

Two policemen came and dwarfed the narrow kitchen.

'Mrs Kate Brodie?'

'Yes?'

'We're sorry about what happened to your brother. Can you tell us anything about the incident that might help in our inquiries?'

'Just what Budd – my father-in-law – told me. He was working in the van with Joe tonight.'

'Yes. We've spoken to him and we're going to see him again tomorrow.'

'Somebody shot Joe.'

'Does your husband own a gun?'

'Not that I know of.'

'Do you know anyone who owns a gun?'

'Must I go through this now? My brother . . .' The words choked in her throat. She pressed her handkerchief to her mouth.

'All right. We'll speak to you tomorrow when we call to see your father-in-law and your husband. The doctor had better have a look at you while you're here. I'll send him through.'

It was Doctor Grahame, who'd known her since she was a child.

'Terrible business.' He patted Kate's shoulder. 'Your poor mother. She adored that boy.'

'I know.'

'I've given her a sedative. She'll sleep tonight. I'll come back tomorrow and see what else I can do to help.'

'Thank you, doctor.'

'I'll give you something to calm you. Not a sleeping pill because of the baby.'

'Oh no.' Her panic suddenly spilled over. 'Please!'

'Don't worry. This will just soothe you a bit. Make you feel more calm, help you to cope.'

'It's Mammy, not me. She'll never get over this. She'll never be able to cope.'

'Your mother's an amazing woman. Poor Marilyn is in a state of total collapse through there. But your mother has told the police she knows who shot Joe. The same man who shot her dog. She gave them his name and all the particulars. Anyone else would have been too distraught to be able to think of all that just now. The police have probably picked him up for questioning already. I heard one of them radioing in.'

'If Mammy won't see me, I'd better get back.' Kate stuffed the doctor's prescription into her pocket. 'I'm worried about my baby.'

The policeman opened the outside door for her. She hurried down the stairs hanging on to the banister for support. One of the landing lights had been vandalised and there were signs of graffiti on the close wall, some of it carved deep into the plaster. Kate felt an extra tug of sadness. Her mother had been proud of her close, her stair, her house. She had guarded the whole building with great courage and conscientiousness. It symbolised her battle for decency, her determination to hold back the squalor, hope-lesssness and decay. Now the tide had broken through her defences. It was flooding in.

Some of the street lamps in Killearn Street were also broken. It became darker the nearer she came to the top of the hill and to Byshott Street. Groups of people were barely visible in the shadows, ghosts who had long since been drowned, who now only existed as lifeless vehicles for heroin.

The first thing she did when arriving at the house was to hurry into the bedroom to check that Christine was all right. She was sleeping peacefully. Kate shut the door with care then went through to the living room.

'How is she?' Budd asked.

'She wouldn't see me. The doctor told me he'd given her a sedative.' She turned to Pete. 'He also told me that she'd spoken to the police. She gave them all the particulars about Dougie having a gun and shooting the dog. The police asked me about it but I never said a word. I swear. Not a word.'

'I told you, there's hundreds of guns floating around Possil.'

'Hundreds of guns?' Kate echoed. 'I've lived here all my life and Dougie's gun's the first one I've ever seen or heard of.'

'Thank Christ he had one. Dougie saved my life. That animal was mad. Everyone knew it was mad. The fuckin' animal was notorious.'

'It's not for killing the dog the police will get him. It's for killing my brother.'

'They'll never prove it was Dougie.'

'As I said before, hen,' Budd fixed her with an anxious

pleading gaze, 'it could have been anybody. I don't believe there's hundreds of guns in Possil but there's bound to be a few. I mean, it stands to reason, Dougie won't be the only one to have a gun.'

'Reason?' Kate said bitterly. 'I know about reason.'

'What's that supposed to mean?' Pete queried.

She wanted to scream at him, It's you that's mad. You mad bastard. You had my brother shot as an act of maliciousness, just to hurt my mother. Caution prevented her. She lowered her eyes.

'Nothing. I feel gutted. I'm going to bed.'

She could not believe it when, later, Pete followed and tried to have sex with her. In a desperate whisper so as not to waken the baby in the cot nearby, she said,

'How can you? You must know how I feel. Apart from how I feel about you, I'm . . . I'm . . . Joe being killed . . . For pity's sake, Pete!'

But he had no pity. Sex was a power vehicle and he enjoyed using it. She had hated him before but now her hatred was like knives stabbing her head and chest. Urgent, intense, painful. If she'd had a gun, she would have shot Pete dead without the slightest hesitation.

Next day, two CID detectives and a policewoman arrived. Budd, Pete and Kate were questioned separately.

Kate confirmed what had happened with the dog. Dougie had shot the animal and it was now buried in her mother's back green in Killearn Street. It didn't take a spey wife to prophesy that the police would dig up Rajah and compare the bullets in the two shootings. Realising this gave Kate neither comfort nor hope. Even if Dougie wasn't clever enough or sly enough, Pete was. He would have made sure that Dougie used a different gun.

And that was exactly what happened. It was found that the bullets came from different guns. Of course, no gun was found in Dougie's possession. He'd had a gun for protection at his work, he'd admitted to the police, and he had been going to apply for a licence. He'd used it to save Pete's life.

He had had no choice. Nevertheless, as an animal lover, he'd been so upset about killing the dog, he'd thrown the gun in the River Clyde immediately afterwards.

He got away with it. He even came to the house barely a week afterwards. Kate was in the kitchen when Pete opened the door. She could hear Dougie's coarse laughter once they'd gone through to the living room. Then that high-pitched giggle Pete had when he was excited. She had a kettle of boiling water in her hand. She was going to run through and pour the boiling water over the pair of them, scald them, mark them for life. But when she reached the lobby the sight of the bedroom door and the memory of Christine stopped her in her tracks. They'd see that she wouldn't get away with it. She'd go to prison. Then what would happen to the baby?

She made a cup of tea and allowed her trembling legs to lower her on to the chair beside the sink. The tea slopped over on to her lap as she tried to drink it. Her mind longed to find a method to kill Pete and Dougie, and get away with it. The perfect murder. It occurred to her then that anybody was capable of murder. *Anybody* could kill if they were pushed far enough. She had always shrunk from violence of any kind. She'd been bullied at school because she'd been a quiet, gentle type.

Pete bawled, 'Are you takin' fuckin' root through there? We're starving.'

She couldn't move. Couldn't stand up. Couldn't make a sound. Pete came swaggering through eventually. She could see by his heightened colour and loose jaw that he'd been drinking.

'Don't just sit there, you lazy cunt. Where's our fuckin' supper?'

'I'm sick of your foul tongue,' she said, as if that was the only thing about him she was sick of. 'You can't string one sentence together without using a c . . . or an f . . . It's disgusting.'

He came over, bulging-eyed.

'What did you say?'

Kate got up and turned towards the chopping board where she'd been cutting up beef and vegetables for a casserole.

'The supper's in the oven. It'll be ready in five minutes.'

'It had better be. You've no fuckin' excuse now. No wasting your time baking and God knows what else for your precious brother.' He suddenly erupted with one of his giggles. 'He's in the ice-cream van in the sky now, ringing his stupid wee bell, playing his stupid wee tune.' Sneeringly Pete began to mimic the music Joe had played in the van. It had been one of Joe's favourites, the hauntingly beautiful 'Greensleeves'. At his wedding he had dreamily circled the hall to it, with Marilyn in his arms. Joe had been so full of dreams.

'Come on,' Pete came towards her, his arms outstretched in an invitation to dance. 'Ta-ra-ta-ra-ra-ra . . .'

Somehow the chopping knife got into her hands and before she could think, it was plunging into Pete as if of its own accord. A look of astonishment stretched his eyes wide. He staggered back a few steps, grabbed the side of the cooker, then slid down on to the floor.

She stared at him. Blood was pumping, spurting, out of his neck, soaking his clothes, the side of the cooker, the floor. In a matter of seconds, the whole place was a sticky sea of crimson. She could hear Dougie coming through.

'Hey, Pete,' he was calling. 'Yer beer's getting flat . . .'

He stopped at the kitchen door.

'Christ!'

'Phone the police.' Kate was amazed at how calm and ordinary her voice sounded.

'Fuck that. I'm getting out of here.'

And he ran, not even shutting the outside door behind him.

Chapter Eighteen

Kate didn't know what to do. He was dead. She could see he was dead without needing to touch him. The blood had stopped pumping. She dreaded Budd coming back from the pub and finding Pete like this. Budd had gone to bits after Joe's death and started drinking heavily again. God knows how he'd take the death of his son. And such a dreadful, bloody death. She'd never seen so much blood in her life. She'd have to wade through it to escape from the kitchen. All she wanted was to escape, to get away from the kitchen, the house, the street. She never wanted to see any of it again. It had all been a nightmare that had gone on for too long. She wanted to wake up in her bedroom in the top flat in Killearn Street. She wanted to see her dressing table with its three narrow, hinged mirrors. She wanted the comfort of the tortoiseshell brush and comb set that Aunty Bec had once given her for Christmas neatly displayed on the dressing table. She wanted to lie listening to Rajah padding about beside her mother and her mother chatting to the dog as if it was her best friend, or one of her sons. She always called the dog 'son' when she was talking to it.

Then her mother would bawl at her,

'Kate, are ye gonnae lie there aw day? Ye'll be late fur school. An' dinnae think ye're gonnae rush oot o' here withoot any porridge in yer stomach because ye're no'. Sure she's no', son?'

In fact Kate had never been late for school nor ever rushed out without breakfast. It had been her brothers who'd done that. Her daddy would bid both her mammy and the dog, 'Cheerio, see you later, folks.'

'Aye, OK.' They never kissed but Kate felt secure in the knowledge that they loved each other. She would leave the warm nest of her bed and go over to the window. Hugging herself in her white flannelette nightie, she would wait for her daddy to reach the bottom of the stairs and come out of the close. He always looked up and gave her a wave. She smiled and waved back. Then for a few minutes she'd watch with pride his tall dignified figure in his dark suit and coat and grey trilby hat with its navy petersham band. He was a patient and kindly man who had been a good father to her and her brothers. He'd always made quite a ceremony of giving them pocket money every Saturday. He'd sit behind a small table, empty his pockets and line up his small change in neat piles. What he paid them varied from week to week according to their answers to a questionnaire. Some of his questions made her giggle.

'Have you fell foul of the law this week, Kate Gallacher?'

'Have you been the recipient of corporal punishment from your mammy? And if so, on how many occasions?'

This was a difficult one. Sometimes there had been so many slaps, punches and pushes that had knocked her off balance, she lost count. He pretended to deduct pennies for each punishment but in the end, as often as not, he'd give a surreptitious wink when her mammy wasn't looking and slide the punishment pile of coins across to Kate to hide in her waiting pocket.

Her daddy never kissed her or said he loved her. But she knew he did. The same as her mammy did. It wasn't as much as her brothers, of course. But she understood it was all right. There had been times, she had to admit, when she'd been moody and resentful. But who was perfect?

She edged round the pool of blood and out of the kitchen. In the narrow windowless lobby, she stood twisting her hands. She was more afraid of Budd coming back than anything else. She wanted to run but couldn't. Not without the baby. She went through to the bedroom. There was a smell of Pete about the place. His aftershave, his hair cream, his sweat. She felt like apologising to Chrissie. She was sorry for messing up her daughter's life before it had barely started. She said the words out loud,

'I'm sorry.'

Somehow, hearing her voice, any voice, when the house was so dominated by death, shocked and frightened her. She began to tremble. It was as if she feared that Pete would rise up and be standing at the bedroom door barring her way. She was terrified to turn round. Instead she went over to the cot and carefully lifted Christine and wrapped her in the cot blankets. Then she tucked and strapped the child into the baby buggy. Christine's head lolled forward. Clutching fiercely at the pram's handle Kate forced herself to look towards the door. There was only the shadow of the lobby. Quietly, carefully, on tiptoe as if Pete might hear her, she left the house.

.Out on the street, she quickened her pace and at the same time began to think hysterically – where could she go? Her mother, and even her father now, didn't want anything to do with her. She brought the family nothing but trouble and heartache. Now she'd bring them into disrepute and shame. She was going to be in trouble with the police. Terrible trouble. She reached her mother's close at the foot of the hill and felt confused. The lights of Saracen Street beckoned her from the dark mountain of Killearn Street. But what was for her in Saracen Street now? She couldn't go to Granny McWhirter's. The shock of police coming to the door to arrest her granddaughter would be enough to finish the old woman. The recent death of her grandson had all but killed her.

And there was Christine. Kate's mind kept repeating silent words to the sleeping baby: I'm sorry. I'm sorry. I'm so sorry.

She turned up the close, suddenly realising what she must do. She struggled to carry the buggy up the stone stairs rather than bump it up and risk waking Christine or alerting anyone else. On the top landing, she parked the buggy outside her mother's door. She knelt beside it for a minute or two, looking at the baby until her gaze became blurred with tears. Carefully she kissed the drooping, sleeping head. Then she rang her mother's doorbell and flew down the stairs. In her slippers she didn't make a sound. She stopped on the downstairs landing and pressed herself up against the far wall so that even if her mother or father leaned over the banister and peered down, they would not see her.

She heard the door open and her father cry out,

'Mary! Come here. Look at this!' Then he called down over the banister. 'Kate, is that you? Kate!'

'My God,' her mother said. 'The poor wee wean. Oot at this time o' night. Never mind bloody Kate. Stop yer shoutin', ye'll waken the poor wee soul. Come on, get her in oot the cold.'

The door shut.

Kate was shivering violently. She was only wearing a thin blouse and skirt. Not even a cardigan. A cold wind moaned up the stairs and gathered like ice on the landing.

She didn't know where to run to next. She kept getting glimpses in her mind's eye of Pete staring up from a sea of blood. Then it came to her. She felt relief. She'd be safe there. They'd look after her. With frantic eagerness she hurried round to Barloch Street and to the police station.

Chapter Nineteen

Bec's dark eyes bulged into distress and she clutched at her mountainous bosom.

'This is terrible. Just terrible. There's been newspaper reporters pestering us. In Queen's Park. Fancy! I can't go out to do my messages. I daren't think about what my neighbours must be saying.'

'There's been television cameras here.' George repeated the words, as if he couldn't credit them. 'Television cameras.'

Mary was spooning custard into Christine's mouth but she turned to say, 'It's these reporters diggin' up that stuff about drugs an' exaggeratin' everythin'. Fancy callin' Possilpark the Drugs Capital of Europe. They'd do anything for a sensational story, that crowd.'

Willie said, 'Even my customers are more bothered about the gory details of the murder than about their feet. Even old Mrs Peterson – '

'They didn't need to exaggerate anything, if you ask me,' Bec interrupted. 'The place is hiving with drugs. You only need to look out that window. It's terrible. Just terrible. And now there's the trial to suffer. And all the publicity of that.' She sniffed. 'I don't know how you could go and see her in that prison, Mary. After all the worry and trouble and shame she's brought on this family. I just don't understand it.'

'She's ma wean.'

'You didn't say that when . . . after . . .' Bec hesitated to mention Joe's death. 'I mean, you wouldn't have anything to do with her.'

'Ah never meant her any harm. Ah just couldnae face her. But she could be shut up in that prison fur life, Bec. She disnae deserve that.'

'She killed a man. She's lucky there isn't the death penalty these days.'

'She wis driven tae it. Ah often felt like murderin' that pig masel'. An' jist think o' aw the sufferin' an' death he'll huv caused wi' aw that heroin he wis sellin'. Tae school weans, some o' them. He didnae care. He never cared about anybody except hissel', that pig.'

'That's beside the point.'

'No, it's no'. An' ah can see that the poor soul's grateful for ma visits. She disnae say much. Ye know how quiet she can get. Bit one time she came out wi' it. She said, "You were right, Mammy." Then her face closed in again. God alone knows whit's goin' on inside that lassie's heid. Jist think how you'd feel if it wis your wean.'

Bec was affronted.

'My Sandra's a university student.'

'Oh aye?' Mary raised a pencilled brow. 'Dis that make her a bloody saint?'

'She moves in a different circle. There's no drug takers or drug dealers at Edinburgh University.'

'Ah wouldnae be too sure o' that, hen.'

'You haven't been to the prison, have you, George?' Bec asked her brother.

'Just the once. I couldn't face it again.'

'What a humiliation for you, George. I don't know how you did it. You've always been the sensitive one.'

'I had to let her know that I . . .' – he couldn't face the embarrassment of mentioning the word love – 'that I was on her side.'

Mary said, 'She understood how he felt. She told him no' tae come back. It wis a humiliation right enough. Walkin' intae that place. Ah felt for him masel'. Ah mean, ah'm different.'

'Yes, we know that,' Bec agreed. 'But still, I don't know how even you could do it.'

'Ah hud tae. An' ah'm goin' tae the trial as well. So is George. Sure ye are?'

George nodded.

'I'll never forget that time wee Davie McIvor was murdered. Remember him, Bec? He worked in that grocer's that was there before they built the mini-market.'

'Oh yes,' Bec said. 'He was going to the bank with the takings, wasn't he?'

'I went to the High Court then. Just for curiosity.' He shook his head. 'It makes me furious even now to remember that trial. You could see that poor wee Davie's family were afraid of the man in the dock. If you could call him a man. The first time he looked like something the cat dragged in and was so stoned out of his mind he couldn't string a half-dozen words together. His lawyer must have had a word with him because next time his hair was neatly cut and he was wearing a nice suit, and a shirt and tie. He stood up and apologised for his previous appearance. A right charmer. He got off with it in the end. And he'd done it. Knifed poor wee Davie fifteen times. But he didn't know what he was doing, you see.' George's voice turned sarcastic. 'It wasn't him, you see, it was the drugs. He was sent to a place for treatment. Got every help and consideration. I can still see him smirking at poor Davie's family. And that brasser of a mother of his laughing. Proud as punch of him, she was.'

Bec tutted.

'It's the mothers I blame.'

Mary immediately rounded on her.

'Is that supposed to be a dig at me?'

'No, no. You tried your best, I'm sure.'

'We should all go to the trial,' George said. 'Tommy and Liz are going. Even Marilyn. The whole family should stand behind Kate. She was never a bad girl. As Mary says, she doesn't deserve this.'

His wife looked over at him, eyes brimming with gratitude and pride.

Bec turned to her husband.

'What do you think, Willie?'

'I suppose we should,' Willie said without enthusiasm.

'Yes,' Bec agreed. 'It might look bad if we didn't. But not Sandra, of course.'

Later, after she'd settled herself in their comfortable Ford Maxi, Bec managed a smile as she peered up at the Gallachers' window. Mary was there as usual to give them a wave. Bec dutifully returned the wave before the car moved away and turned along Saracen Street.

'I still say,' she told her husband, 'it's the mothers to blame. I'm not a bit surprised. I mean, what can you expect? I would never say this to anyone else, Willie, but Mary McWhirter is as common as dirt. We both know that.'

Willie sighed.

'I've never known what your George saw in her, Bec. He's a perfect gentleman. You wouldn't be ashamed to take him anywhere.'

Bec shook her head.

'Now she's drinking. It's absolutely terrible. I said to her, on the quiet, in the kitchen, "Have you been drinking, Mary?" And do you know what she said?'

'No.'

'She went all indignant and said, "I swear on the head of the Virgin Mary never a drop has passed my lips." What a liar, I thought. I could smell the whisky off her breath and we'd all had nothing but tea.'

Willie tutted.

'What next?'

'And her supposed to be looking after the poor infant as well.'

Willie sighed.

'I don't know.'

Back in Killearn Street, Mary was saying to George,

'Ye're a good man, so ye are. Stickin' up fur oor Kate like that an' gettin' them tae come tae the court. It'll help Kate tae see aw the family there. Give her a bit o' courage.'

'That time I saw her, I was surprised at how calm she looked. Her face set in that stubborn way of hers.'

'Aye, well, maybe that stubborn bit aboot her will stand her in good stead for once.'

'Maybe determination's a better word. She's determined to get through this. Without cracking up or anything.'

'Ah hardly know how ah'm gonnae get through it masel'.'

'Nonsense, you're as tough as they come, Mary. No, tougher. You'll get through it all right.'

Chapter Twenty

The front entrance to the Barloch Street police station had a mock marble black and white floor and tiled walls. Some policemen in dazzling Persil-white shirts and immaculate black trousers passed through. Kate could see others sitting at desks beyond the front counter. Everyone was perfectly calm. She had expected them to be as distraught as herself. Or at least to appear shocked. Maybe after working in Possilpark for some years, they were beyond being shocked.

'I've killed my husband,' she had told the white-shirted officer at the counter.

'Oh aye? We've heard these stories before.'

He was writing on a pad and he continued writing as he said, 'Just sit over there until we can find out what's happened.'

Not one of the other policemen had given her a second glance. She might as well have said she'd lost her house keys, or had accidentally shut herself out of the house. There had been such a routine, all-in-a-day's-work kind of atmosphere. In a strange way, it had soothed her. She had been able, when spoken to again, to give her name and address and repeat, in a clear and ungarbled way, what she'd done. Then she had to sit and wait again. A policewoman had brought her a cup of tea.

Beat men were dispatched to the house in Byshott Street to find out what had happened. When the men saw Pete and realised that there was no chance at all of doing anything, they immediately secured the area. One policeman remained at the house and wouldn't allow anyone to enter. Even Budd, when he had arrived, was not allowed over the door. He was immediately taken to the police station. People living next door and up the close had to use the back close and the back green to get in or out.

The CID were notified that a serious incident had occurred. It was they who eventually had come to Kate and spoken to her very formally.

'In view of the information you've told us, we have established that a serious crime has been committed. In view of all the circumstances, we'll have to caution you. You don't need to say anything, but anything you do say may be noted, and may be given in evidence.'

She had then been taken to an interview room accompanied by a policewoman. She answered their questions as fully and as honestly as she could. She explained about the previous abuse and how on this occasion she had been provoked. The CID detective was as calm and laid back as the other police officers. She was impressed at how smartly dressed the CID men looked; instead of uniforms, they wore good-quality, well pressed suits. Indeed, the smartness of all the officers against the seedy, shabby and depressing surroundings amazed her. This amazement, although adding to her confusion, overlaid much of her initial hysteria and fear. There was something admirable and dependable about such people. They were keeping up standards against all odds, it seemed to her. She knew only too well how difficult that could be.

Meantime, the routine was continuing. The police had established that there was a death. They had many experiences in the past when a so-called murder had been reported. The police casualty surgeon arrived, found a pulse, the ambulance took the 'victim' to hospital, where it was confirmed he or she wasn't dead at all.

But this time, after the casualty surgeon had made up a written report the CID officer had contacted the Procurator Fiscal who called at the scene. A police photographer had also arrived along with people from the police laboratory.

No one in the street had slept a wink. Everyone had

their windows wide open and leaned on their windowsills, watching what was going on.

The photographer even photographed the close and the outside of the building before the body was removed to the mortuary where it was left intact pending a post-mortem.

The neighbours had been questioned. One said she'd seen a man she knew as Dougie running from the house. No, they hadn't heard any noise of an argument. But then Kate was such a quiet girl. Polite enough in saying hello with a bit of a smile, but not one to stop and enjoy a blether or a gossip. Shy, maybe. They didn't know. But they thought she'd have plenty to bother her with a man like Pete Brodie. Everybody knew what he was like and how he got the money to dress and spend like he did. Not on her, though. They always thought she was a poor wee soul. She'd taken a good battering more than once. They could all swear to that.

At this stage, Kate had been again cautioned and this time charged with murder. A mountain of a man with a cropped grey head spoke slowly and in a clear voice. Kate had tried hard to concentrate on what he was saying while her heart beat feebly and fast.

'Now listen carefully to me. I am going to read out a charge against you. When I have done so, you will have an opportunity of saying anything you may wish to say. You need not say anything, but if you do, it will be noted and may later be used in evidence.'

He cleared his throat and she had waited, gazing up and thinking how the solidity and size of him reminded her of her father.

'You are charged that on the 23rd of August 1982, you did in the dwelling house occupied by you at 17 Byshott Street, Possilpark, Glasgow, assault your husband, namely Pete Brodie, stabbed him on the body with a knife or similar instrument, whereby he died as a result of his injuries and you did murder him . . .'

She had been asked if she wanted the services of a lawyer. When she said, 'I don't know anybody' she had been amazed now at how calm, almost nonchalant, her own voice was. But she was glad that she was managing to retreat deep inside herself, grateful for finding her protective shell.

It had been explained to her that there was a duty roster for lawyers. She was asked if she wanted the duty lawyer called out and she said that she did. Another calm and knowledgeable person to listen to. Someone else to bring comfort. One part of her knew this was a ridiculous, indeed pathetic line of thought. She was clutching at straws. But it was all she could do. She daren't think about the effect this might have on her child, her mother, her father, her brother, her Granny McWhirter, her Granny Gallacher, her Aunty Bec, her Uncle Willie. It was impossible. A nightmare.

To think of Pete was easier. She felt only relief that she was free of him. And from the fear of him.

But oh, her poor mother and father! Then she had remembered Budd. She could have wept for him too, but daren't. The floodgates must be kept shut. It was the only way she could survive the night. She was asked if she wanted her mother or anyone else to bring in a change of clothes because the clothing she wore had to be taken from her and examined as evidence. For a moment, she panicked.

'Don't let my mammy see me. I don't want anyone to see me.'

'All right, we'll collect clothes when we notify your mother what's happened.'

She was asked if she had any children or other dependants that would have to be taken care of.

'Mammy's got the baby. She'll be all right.'

The clothes came eventually and she was taken in a police van to the Divisional Headquarters in Maryhill where, she was told, she would be detained in a cell.

It had been very dark when they arrived in Maryhill Road. But Kate had seen by the light of the street lamps that the Divisional Headquarters was a much bigger place than the police station in Barloch Street, Possilpark. Inside, she was led not to the counter at the front office but to another that they called 'the bar' at the rear of the building. There seemed to be a great many sparkling white shirts around. She began to feel confused again.

She was formally charged at the bar before being taken in a small, claustrophobic lift up to where the cells were situated. It was as she stepped out of the lift that the full realisation hit her. She'd entered another world. She'd always kept the seedy, shabby, neglected Possilpark that she knew – for that was her world – on the outside, at arm's length. Inside her home, whether it had been at her mother's or at Byshott Street, everything had been sparkling clean, brightly polished, well cared for and smelling warmly of lavender or pine furniture polish, and home baking. There had been an atmosphere of fighting spirit and optimism.

Here she had felt, in the stale air, the bitter breath of endless defeats. Lies, evasions, weaknesses, pointless hatreds and resentments clung unresolved to every shabby, comfortless corner. Again she marvelled at the smart appearance of the policemen. But there was an unfriendly suspicious look in every eye. A wide barred gate through which Kate could see the corridor and solid doors of cells on either side was unlocked, and opened with a loud clanking sound. It set up shouts and bangings from the cells. The hollow metallic echo was strangely reminiscent of the public baths. Only here the noise gave Kate the frightening feeling that she was sinking under the water. She was shown into the first cell on the left and told she would be taken to the Sheriff Court the next day.

The first thing she had noticed was that the wall on the left of the door was three-quarters glass. Through it she could see a small cluttered room in which the female turnkey was now settling herself at a table littered with papers, in the middle of which was a computer.

Kate looked around the cell. The other walls looked as if they were made of concrete. So did the floor. Part of the floor opposite the door was raised a few inches. A thin

129

excuse for a mattress lay on top of it. It was dark navy and made of tough material. Later she learned that this was to prevent any potential suicides from tearing off a strip and using it to hang themselves. There was a sleeping bag of the same material, also a depressing dark navy. In the opposite corner, almost up against the glass wall, was a lavatory pan made of what looked like steel or aluminium. It had no seat. The turnkey was watching her. Kate didn't know where to look. She stood motionless in the middle of the dismal, comfortless place with harsh bawls, shouts and obscenities echoing all around her. She shut her eyes and strove with every last ounce of energy to find a safe place deeper and deeper inside herself.

Chapter Twenty-One

'"You'll die facing the monument" used to be a Glasgow insult or warning,' George said, as he perambulated with great dignity in his good pin-striped suit and grey trilby, down the Saltmarket towards Jail Square. That was because all the murderers used to be hanged in public in front of the court facing that monument in Glasgow Green. Not just murderers. Thieves and burglars and forgers. Not just men either. There were plenty of women. They were all hanged in front of the monument.

Mary, tottering miserably along beside him on her high heels, said 'Fancy!', but absentmindedly. She was usually proud of and impressed by her husband's knowledge but for once she wished he'd keep it to himself.

The baby had been left with Granny Gallacher. Granny McWhirter had taken the recent happenings so badly, she had become senile. One minute she'd be perfectly lucid; the next minute she'd forget things, forget even where she was or what year it was. She kept lapsing into the days when her husband was alive. She would suddenly announce that it was time she got her man's dinner ready. She would tie her pinny on and her gnarled bony hands would start fussing with pots and trying to balance them on the small barred fire. It wasn't safe to leave the baby with her. It had ended up that Marilyn couldn't come either. She had to stay at Tommy and Liz's place to look after their children. Mary and George had meant to arrive with Tommy and Liz but Marilyn was late.

'You'd better go on,' Tommy said. 'We'll come as soon as we can.'

Bec and Willie had promised to be there but were going straight to the court from Queen's Park.

131

'It depends when Willie can get away,' Bec explained. 'He's got an assistant but he likes to open up the shop himself and see that everything's properly organised. Keep us a good seat,' she'd added, as if they were going to the pictures.

'There used to be thousands gathered all around here and in the Green to watch the hangings,' George went on mercilessly. He always enjoyed showing off what he'd absorbed in the Possilpark Public Library.

'One of them was beheaded as well as hanged.' They were nearing the court building now with the low-roofed mortuary on one side of it. The court building itself was imposing with its high pillared frontage.

'Of course, this place was opened in 1814. Before that it was the Tolbooth along at Glasgow Cross. It wasn't just hangings there but the jongs, the cock-chair, the head spikes, the pillory. They used to throw rotten eggs and dead cats – '

'George!' Mary wailed.

'What?' George gazed down at her in surprise. 'Is there something wrong?'

Mary thought it must be the understatement of all time.

'We're here. Had we no' better concentrate on gettin' oorsel's in?'

'Right. Hang on to my arm going up these steps.'

They felt intimidated and awestruck by the lofty interior but neither of them would have dreamt of showing it. When a policeman came towards them, Mary stared up at him, giving her high bouffant of curls a confident pat. Her small figure oozed aggressive impertinence.

'Whit way fur the Brodie case?' she demanded before George could make a more civil enquiry.

They were directed to the main Justiciary Court, an even more awesome place. It was circular in shape, its dark polished wood lit by seven huge windows on one side. On the other, the richly decorated judge's bench was elevated high above the floor. It towered over, on one side, the area for the jury, and on the other, the seats for the magistrates. Facing the judge's bench was the 'Panel's Box' where the accused would stand. In the inside part of the circle were all those connected with the business of the court, including men in black robes and grey curled wigs. They sat at separate tables, busying themselves with papers and important-looking folders. The outside of the circle above them was where the public was accommodated. The place was almost full when George and Mary made their way to one side where they'd get a clear view of the box where Kate was due to appear.

'Pit yer hat on wan o' them seats an' ma handbag on the other fur Bec an' Willie,' Mary reminded George. A call had just rung out – 'Court!'

Everyone stood up as the judge entered and took his seat at the bench. They sat down again just as Bec sailed in, followed by Willie. Both were dressed in black as if attending a funeral. They whispered greetings like condolences before settling down. Then Bec announced in a tone tinged with what Mary angrily suspected was satisfaction,

'Oh look, there she is.'

Kate was standing, stiff and straight-backed, with an air of defiance about her. Her face was white and hard, her eyes expressionless.

'That's not going to do her any good,' Bec whispered.

'Whit dae ye mean?'

'Well, she looks as if she *could* commit murder.'

Mary glared round at her sister-in-law.

'Well, she *did*, didn't she?'

'Oh well, if that's how you feel,' Bec said huffily.

'You don't know how ah feel, hen.'

'I was only meaning that it would be in her interest to try to get the sympathy of the judge and jury. Look as if she's sorry or something.'

'She's no' that two-faced. She's no' sorry an' ah wouldnae be either. He was a rotten selfish – '

133

'Ssh, ssh!' George warned. 'You'll have us put out. It's started.'

'Nothing's an excuse for murder,' Bec hissed, determined to have the last word.

The judge looked impressive in his wig. He wore robes of scarlet and a white silk cape and on his cuffs shone small cut-out diamonds. He seemed totally relaxed in his throne-like seat, a plump, luxuriously clad buddha, motionless and benign. Until one noticed his eyes. They were as watchful and alert as a fox.

'Ah don't like the look o' him,' Mary whispered and George hushed her again.

'Her Majesty's Advocate Depute against Kate Brodie,' called the clerk of the court.

John Cunningham, the bewigged and black-gowned Lord Advocate who sat at a table beside the Fiscal, suffered from a stomach ulcer. It had been playing him up with increasing vigour these past few months. He'd had to take another Zantac just before coming to the court. His marriage was going through a bad patch and he suspected his wife Diane was having an affair. This morning, the private detective he'd hired confirmed his worst fears. He nursed his anger to blot out the distress and sense of betrayal.

Diane might as well have stuck a knife in him. Although his Diane was nothing like the hard-faced bitch now standing in the dock, staring up at the golden coat of arms on the wall high above the judge. *His* Diane. That was a laugh, he thought bitterly. He shuffled some papers while struggling to gain control of his emotions. He fought valiantly to superimpose on the burning hell of them a fair and impartial state of mind.

The clerk of the court addressed the prisoner:

'Are you Kate Brodie?'

Kate answered, 'I am' in a clear voice.

Allison Menzies now rose to announce,

'I appear with my friend Edward Smith for the panel who pleads not guilty.'

Bec sucked in her breath through pursed lips and Mary immediately dug the plump cushion of her with a bony elbow.

The clerk of the court then nodded to the judge, the panel, the jury. From a big glass bowl he picked out the first name and called it out.

'Mrs Elizabeth Browntree.'

An elderly woman stood up, wide-eyed and startled, in the body of the hall. She then had to walk all the way down to take her seat in the jury box. One name after another was read out and a motley crew of all ages and sizes joined the first woman. Only two were objected to: one because he lived in Byshott Street, another because he was a school-teacher. School teachers were always objected to because it was considered that they would automatically lead the jury.

The jury was sworn in and then the clerk of the court read out the charge,

' . . . that Kate Brodie on the 23rd of August in the flat at 17 Byshott Street, Possilpark, at 6.30 p.m., did stab Pete Brodie and thus commit murder.'

Then, as was the custom, the judge welcomed them. Everyone shuffled in their seats and nervously avoided his piercing stare.

The first of the string of witnesses was the photographer who had taken photographs of the dead body. Copies of the photos were passed to the judge and jury. One witness was Dougie Gibson.

Mary whispered to Bec,

'That's that wicked gangster that shot ma dug. He should be the wan gettin' tried fur murder.'

'Ssh, ssh!' George warned.

The Advocate Depute rose, with a pained expression on his gaunt, lantern-jawed features. His face was long, making his wig look short.

'You are Mr Douglas Gibson?'

'I am, sir.'

'Can you tell the court where you were on the night of 23rd August?'

'I was at 17 Byshott Street, with my friend Pete Brodie.'

'What were you doing there?'

'Pete had taken me home with him for a meal.'

'And what exactly happened?'

'We were having a laugh in the living room, talking about this and that – things that had happened during the day at our work. We were both starving and there was never any sign of the meal, so Pete went through to the kitchen to see if he could give Kate a helping hand.'

The defence council wasted no time in disputing the 'helping hand' part of this statement.

'As Kate Brodie will testify, my Lord, her husband never once gave her a helping hand in all the days of their married life.'

Once Kate gave her evidence, it was made clear that Pete Brodie had in every way treated her like a slave and expected her to regularly provide and serve meals not just to one but to crowds of his friends and fellow drivers. Her exhausted and stressed state were established and the physical abuse brought out. Then there was the last straw: the final taunt about her brother.

She said in a clear voice in answer to counsel's question that yes, she had been frightened. Yes, she had been in fear of her life many times. She had been afraid for the safety of her baby too.

The Advocate Depute in cross-examination put it to her that she had had a callous disregard for human life. She knew that she was going to kill her husband. She planned to kill him. But she could not just take the law into her own hands. She could not disregard the law.

Kate calmly denied everything. Witnesses were called to vouch for her normally gentle nature. A doctor told of how she'd been in a totally exhausted condition, and of her injuries caused by being beaten by her husband. Council asked in conclusion,

'Did you suffer a terrible life with your husband?'

'Yes, I did,' Kate said, then added, 'but I never planned or meant to kill him.'

The Crown then began its address to the jury.

'This, ladies and gentlemen, is murder pure and simple . . .'

When it came to the turn of the defence QC, Allison Menzies rose, pulled her gown modestly around her slim shoulders, and put the case in a pleasant, reasonable tone. She said that Kate had been very fair and very frank. She had admitted what she'd done but it had to be taken into consideration that she was severely provoked. The QC ended by smiling disarmingly at the jurors and telling them that she felt sure it was the fair and right thing to do to ask for a verdict of culpable homicide, not murder.

There was a silence and then the judge looked over at the jury.

'You are the masters of the fact. The law is this. Criminal homicide is either murder or culpable homicide. Murder consists of the wilful taking away of another's life where there is unlawful and unprovoked intent to kill.'

His Lordship paused to allow his words to sink in. There wasn't a sound or movement to be heard in the court.

'Culpable homicide is distinguished from murder – although sometimes the dividing line is narrow – by the absence of the intent to kill.'

He paused again.

'No killing however can be justified by the circumstances of it. If you think, as a result of the evidence you have heard in this court, that the accused, in killing her husband, did not intend to kill him, then you must bring in a verdict of culpable homicide. If you decide, on the other hand, that the accused wilfully and with intent killed her husband, then you must find her guilty of murder . . .'

Chapter Twenty-Two

This suspense is killin' me,' Mary said. 'How long do ye think they'll take?'

George shook his head. 'There's no telling.'

Bec sighed. 'The trial took long enough. Willie has the shop to think of, haven't you, Willie?'

'Some of my customers have very serious problems...' Willie began.

'Oh aye, it's obvious yer bloody customers an' their bloody corns are more important than ma lassie. A lot you care if she's banged up fur life.'

'Now it won't come to that,' George soothed.

'Oh, I don't know,' Bec said. 'I didn't like the way that judge went on about murder, did you, Willie?'

'No.' Willie sounded, as well as looked, like an undertaker. 'But rest assured, you have our sympathy. And we feel for poor Kate as well. That's why we're here.'

'Aye, well...' Mary was only slightly mollified.

At last the jury was ready to come back in, and the court reassembled. Mary had to cling to George's arm for support.

'Ah feel sick,' she said.

'Oh, for pity's sake,' Bec hissed in outrage. 'Swallow it down. Don't give us all a showing up.'

Mary held her hanky against her mouth with one hand, and clutched hard at George's arm with the other.

The clerk of the court's voice rang out to the jury:

'Who speaks for you?'

A man rose reluctantly from the bench. Absolute silence gripped the court for at least ten seconds.

'What is your verdict?' the clerk of the court asked.

Another agonising silence. Time stood still. Everyone froze as if they would never be able to make another sound.

The juror looked nervously about.

'Guilty . . .' the word sounded so shocking that a gasp exploded from the court before the man was able to go on, 'of culpable homicide.'

'Thank you. Sit down.'

The clerk of the court wrote on a piece of paper before including the whole fifteen members of the jury when he repeated the verdict and asked,

'Is this your verdict?'

They all nodded and the clerk passed the paper up to the judge.

'Dis this mean she'll get aff?' Mary whispered. 'When it's no' murder?'

Willie sighed. 'I'm afraid not, Mary. I'm sorry to say she still could be sentenced to many sad years in Cornton Vale.'

'Oh God,' Mary wailed.

'Ssh,' George admonished.

The judge was addressing the Crown.

'Anything to say?'

'No previous conviction. Your Lordship has heard all there is to say . . .'

The defence then stood up and made a plea of mitigation in which counsel accentuated the fact that the panel had never been in trouble before, that she'd had a horrific life with her husband, and she had been severely provoked.

There was silence once more. Eventually the judge faced Kate with an unwavering stare. 'You cannot take the law into your own hands. You cannot kill. If there had not been provocation here, if you had been found guilty of murder, you could have gone down for life. In the circumstances of the jury's verdict, I am prepared to sentence you to three years' imprisonment.'

George whispered to Mary, 'She won't serve all that. With good behaviour she'll be out in two.'

'Thank God.' Mary suddenly relaxed, slumped like a rag

doll. 'Ah dinnae know about you lot but ah could murder a dram.'

'With good behaviour,' Willie reminded. He was never one to look on the bright side.

'Well?' Mary challenged, suddenly regaining her spunky energy. 'So what?'

'I was just repeating what George said.'

'Come on.' George rose. 'Let's go for a wee refreshment. We've all been under a lot of stress.'

'Nothin' tae whit Kate has been under,' Mary said. 'Ah must find out how soon ah can visit her.'

'I thought she looked amazingly calm throughout,' Willie said, as they made their way from the building.

'Och, that's jist her,' Mary tutted, and shook her head. 'She's never been wan tae make a fuss. Bit did ye no' see her face? White as a sheet, it wis. The poor soul . . .'

'Willie and I,' Bec interrupted, 'never go into pubs. Do we, Willie?'

'No. Never.'

'We do have a drinks cabinet, of course,' Bec informed her brother.

'Oh well,' George said, 'I'll buy a bottle of whisky in the off-licence in Saracen Street on the way home. We can have a drink in the house.'

Mary said, 'Nae need tae stop at the off-licence. Ah'm sure ah've a bottle tucked away somewhere in the house.'

Bec nudged Willie and slid him a meaningful glance. Her suspicions were confirmed.

'Ah'll go an' see her as soon as ah can.' Mary's mind was still on Kate. 'The poor lassie'll be missin' her wean somethin' terrible. Ah wonder if ah'll be allowed tae take wee Chrissie in now?'

Bec raised a surprised brow. 'I thought you said Kate wouldn't hear of you bringing Christine in to see her, even if you were allowed.'

'Och, that's jist her, as ah say. When anythin's too much for Kate, she jist kind o' shuts off. Ah don't know,' Mary became exasperated, 'ah cannae understand her half the time masel'.'

They had a generous glass of whisky each once they arrived in Killearn Street. Then Mary went through to the kitchen to make a meal for her in-laws before they returned to their own place in Queen's Park.

'Did you notice,' Bec said to Willie in the car on the way home, 'that she took the bottle into the kitchen with her? No doubt she helped herself to at least two or three more drams while she was there.'

'Yes,' Willie agreed. 'The meal took a very long time to appear.'

'That girl takes after her.'

'No doubt about it.'

'She maybe doesn't look like her.'

'She's taller.'

'Yes. And when she does talk, she talks more polite. That's my brother's influence, of course. Mary is *so* common.'

'Dreadful!'

'I believe the less contact our Sandra has with women like that, the better. Don't you think, Willie?'

'Sandra is a different type altogether.'

'Mary can say what she likes about Kate but she did commit murder. That jury was just splitting hairs.'

'Playing with words.'

'She did kill somebody.'

'Dreadful business.'

Bec shuddered. 'The shame of it! Never in my worst nightmares . . .'

'I've all my customers still to face.'

'The Women's Guild!'

'The church on Sunday. I wouldn't care if we never went near Killearn Street again.'

'I know, Willie. If it wasn't for George . . .' Bec sighed. 'Poor George. If he'd known when he married Mary McWhirter what he was getting into . . .'

'The trouble is, Bec, you and George are the kind of people who only see the best in folk.'

'You're the very same, Willie.'

Willie sighed in modest agreement.

Chapter Twenty-Three

The police van was full. Kate had been disconcerted to find herself packed into the vehicle with four other women and a couple of police officers. Two of the women could have been ages with herself. The other two were older, although maybe just in their early thirties. It was difficult to tell. They looked so unhealthy, indeed emaciated. They also appeared to be spaced out on drugs. Kate had lived long enough in Possilpark to know a junkie when she saw one.

She'd been to Cornton Vale after her appearance in the Sheriff Court when she'd been on remand before the trial, so it was not so traumatic as it had been when she'd arrived that first time. Although it was even more traumatic in a different way. Before, she might only have been in the place for one week and then released straight from the court after the trial. That's what she'd hoped against hope for. Now she was to be incarcerated here for years. This time, to use the prison slang, she was here to do bird.

The big gates worked electronically. They slid apart, the van crept into a middle section and the gates closed behind them. They were now in a kind of airlock, facing another set of huge gates which would not open until those at the rear had shut. The number of prisoners was counted and checked by prison officers and it was made sure that there were warrants to hold the prisoners. Only then did the gates in front slide open and the van move forward again. The gates clanked shut behind them. They were inside the grounds of Cornton Vale prison and surrounded by a high perimeter fence.

The prison was made up of blocks of two-storey buildings, separated by well-tended green areas. The place looked, at first glance, like quite a pleasant new housing estate, or a university campus. The prisoners were taken to the reception area where they stood in a queue and went through the first phase of the admission procedure. Their name, their date of birth, what their sentence was, the date on which they were sentenced: all of these were noted. Then each of them was put into one of the long line of holding boxes.

Kate felt claustrophobic in the small, windowless box, hardly big enough to turn in. She was stripped and searched. Her clothes were taken away and she was given a white towelling dressing gown to put on. She was asked which she'd prefer, a bath or a shower; everyone had to have one or the other on admission. Also, hair must be washed.

Another much more noisy queue had formed. Obviously these women were only too familiar with the place. They were prisoners who kept reoffending and were easily caught. They were the D-category inmates whose job it was to help the officers with the procedures and who were greeting them like old friends.

The place was literally 'going like a fair'. The noise reverberated, giving Kate a headache.

After her shower, she was given a set of prison clothes consisting of a pair of denims, a T-shirt, a sweatshirt, a pair of shoes, a set of underwear, a nightdress, a dressing-gown and a pair of slippers. Then she was put into a holding room with other prisoners and given a cup of tea and a sandwich.

The prisoners were processed individually and in detail on an admission information sheet. This included Kate's name and number and a note of whether she had been in before. A nurse asked if she was a drug user. A list was made of all her personal clothing and property and her clothing rack number. The clothing rack was where her clothes and handbag and other personal items would be kept. She was not allowed to transfer anything from the reception block into the cell block. Her photograph was taken.

The whole process and medical examination and questioning by the nurse took a very long and dreary time. Kate had not slept well the night before and now she felt utterly drained.

Each block was named from the first letter of the word that described it. Last time she'd been put in the block for remand prisoners. It was called Romeo. The young offenders' block was Yankee. The privilege hall was Pappa. The specialist block where things like the victim support unit and the induction unit were housed was Sierra. And so on. Kate became only too familiar with them all.

Next day she was assessed by a doctor. She was taken into Sierra's modern, well-equipped health centre where the doctor asked her a great many searching questions. More paperwork was completed.

The questions he seemed most interested in were those concerning her child and why she did not want Christine brought in for the allowed 'bonding' visits. They amounted to two hours extra to the usual one hour every other week that her mother or any other member of her family would be allowed.

She didn't want to answer his questions in any detail. Just a brief 'no' was as much as she could manage. To speak about Christine, even to mention her name, was to bring the much-loved little girl to her mind's eye. It triggered off such pain and longing to hold her baby in her arms, that it was unendurable.

How much worse would it be to be allowed to hold her for one short hour and then suffer the agony of parting with her every week. Had Christine been a younger infant, Kate would have been able to keep her with her. There were special cells with a place for a cot. But on a child's first birthday it was taken away from the prison. What anguish that must be! Such trauma did not bear thinking about. At least Christine was older and she would have plenty of loving care and attention from Kate's mother and father, and Liz and Marilyn. She was sure even Uncle Willie and Aunty Bec would be kind to Christine and do what they could to help.

It would not be good for the child, in her opinion, to be brought into the prison, nursed and petted by her mother, only to be snatched away each time. Christine wouldn't understand. She would be upset. Although it would be nothing to the anguish Kate would suffer. Already she had made her decision and said her tearful goodbyes in her mother's close the night of the murder. She couldn't go through it again.

But she couldn't explain all this to the doctor. She just looked beyond him and tried to shut him completely out of her consciousness. As a result – at least she could only surmise that it was as a result of this – she was categorised as a triple S prisoner – Strict Suicide Supervision. She was led to a ligature-free cell, so-called because there was nowhere to tie anything to in order to hang oneself. She was locked up, or dubbed up, as it was called. Once the door clanged shut, Kate felt, the cell was so depressing it would make anyone feel like committing suicide.

The window, with bars on the outside, was high up and had no handles or snibs or anything at all on which anything could be fastened. The sink was a smooth inset on the wall which seemed to work like magic. There were no taps. A long mirror stretched high across the wall under the window, too high to reach. (And there were no chairs in the cell.) When an officer looked through the observation hatch on the door, the prisoner could be seen no matter where she was standing. The slightly raised part of the floor that served as a bed again had a thin, dark navy mattress made of untearable canvas-type cloth and filled with a non-toxic material. The dark sleeping bag which lay on top of it had short strips of Velcro for fastenings and was made of the same tough material, as were the T-shirt and shorts that were supplied. Everything felt rough and coarse against Kate's skin. There was not another thing in the cell. Except of course the call system and the emergency button. All smooth to the wall.

Hunkered down on the low bed area, Kate felt she could,

if she allowed herself, go completely mad in here. For the first time in her life she longed for just a little bit of Granny Gallacher's pretty colours and lacy frills. Only a *little* bit, she thought, remembering how Granny Gallacher's place nearly sent her mad as well. But she hadn't gone mad then and she wouldn't go mad now. She would get through in her own way and with her own strength.

Every fifteen minutes when whoever was on duty opened the observation hatch on the door (if during her waking hours), Kate smiled at the officer. When she came in contact with any of them – at mealtimes or when she got out of her cell to go to the toilet or 'can' – she spoke in a pleasant, calm, well-balanced way to them.

During the day, the cell doors were left open because each section of the block was secure enough. The entrance to every corridor was blocked by a heavy locked door. All doors were electric as well as mechanical. Cell doors that normally opened inwards by a key could, if necessary, be made to open outwards by a special spanner. For instance, if a prisoner had collapsed behind the door, the prison officer could still get into the cell.

After a few days dubbed up as a triple S and becoming desperate, Kate was assessed again. This time she managed to briefly explain why she did not want to have her child brought into the prison. She was then put on to ISS – Intermediate Suicide Supervision. That meant she could discard the dreadful T-shirt and shorts and return to wearing a pair of blue denims and an ordinary white cotton T-shirt. She was now only supervised every half-hour. Then she graduated to being supervised hourly. By the time a couple of weeks or so had passed, she was allowed on BSS – Basic Suicide Supervision and could have books and a radio. She dreaded to think of the prisoners, and there had been a few in the past, who had served all of their sentences on triple S.

Eventually she was moved to another block and soon she was put to work. Kate was truly thankful for this. She dreaded each lonely and useless hour during which she could think about herself, her life and what a mess she'd made of it. Shame would engulf her in a fountain of panic, making her head and her heart thump with pain.

She started work in a room with a line of sewing machines down the middle and was taught how to use one of them. Before long she was adding her work to the children's dresses and other garments that were proudly and colour-fully displayed on shelves and hangers and in glass cases all around the walls. There were knitted toys too that the pris-oners had learned to make. All of the garments and the toys were regularly sent to charity shops, so Kate felt that at least she was doing something worthwhile. But while agreeing it was useful to learn a new skill, she did not have much, if any, interest in either knitting or sewing. Still, the officer assured her she had a definite aptitude for sewing.

Kate asked what other jobs were available. Was there any-thing in the kitchen? No, not at the moment, she was told. The kitchen was regarded as a 'canter' because it was judged as being comparatively easy. (Although prisoners often referred to their sentence as a canter when in fact they were inwardly sick. Kate herself had already acquired an outward nonchalance about her sentence.) There was also a radio in the kitchen so it was a case of continuous music while you worked. She was informed that there was a job in the hairdresser's and the industrial cleaning section. But she wasn't interested in those.

Soon she was transferred to a huge room with many more machines. There, uniforms were made. Everything in the place, Kate noticed, including a metal ladder, was chained up. The number of women working there was much greater and she began to get to know some of them – more by observation than conversation. She preferred to keep herself to herself, determined to progress quietly through the system without getting into any trouble. Some of these women looked like trouble – hard-faced, resentful, defiant-eyed. All Kate wanted was to become what used to be called a 'trusty' but was now known as a 'pass woman'. A pass woman was a D-category prisoner who had access to all sorts of freedoms and benefits within the prison.

Many of the prisoners, she soon discovered, were drug users and were getting drugs passed to them secretly by visitors. The problem was to keep them hidden within the prison. The prison officers knew who the drug users were. Most were persistent offenders, in and out of prison as if attached to the place with elastic. Random searches were made to try and cope with the problem.

One day, a woman called Nita asked Kate to hide some drugs for her. She was a scabby-faced woman with mousy hair thinning at the top with a patch of white scalp showing through.

'You see, tae the beasts ye're clean, hen. They'll no' search you.'

'Yes,' Kate replied, 'and I mean it to stay that way.'

Nita pushed her face close to Kate. 'Whit did ye say?'

'No.'

'If ye know whit's good for ye, ye'll watch yer tongue tae me. If ah say ye've tae dae me a wee favour, ye'll dae it. Or else . . .'

'Or else what?'

'Or else ye'll suddenly no' be sae healthy.'

'Get lost.'

Nita's face took on a look of incredulity. She turned to one of her equally drug-besotted companions.

'Would ye listen tae this mad bastard. They should never have let her out the suicide cell.'

Kate pushed past the desperate-looking knot of women who had gathered. Nita called after her,

'Ye'll be sorry fur this. By God ye will. Dinnae say ah didnae warn ye.'

Chapter Twenty-Four

A pass woman who worked in the garden told Kate there were television men outside the gates. They were filming a crowd of women protesters who were demonstrating on Kate's behalf and making a 'terrible racket'.

'They're hell bent on getting you freed, hen.'

'Well, it's good of them to try but I can't imagine them succeeding. After all, I was guilty. I've never denied what I did.'

'Aye, but they're making out it was your man's fault because he abused you and drove you to it. There's getting more and more cases like yours nowadays. Women used to put up with being used as punchbags, and their lives made one never-ending hell. And never a word from them. But not now. There was a programme about it on the radio last night. Two or three older women who had suffered like that were giving their stories. Did you not hear it?'

'No, I've been writing letters after work and reading my book.'

'They said you were a test case or an example or something. You're getting quite famous.'

Kate felt embarrassed.

'I hardly think so.'

Who wanted to be famous for murder? As if poor Joe's murder hadn't given the Gallacher family enough publicity. Since he'd been gunned down that case had never been out of the papers. Every step of the police inquiry had been repeated and endlessly speculated on. Apparently it had become part of what was called 'The Ice-Cream Wars'.

'Honestly! There are telly men out at the gates. I bet they'll have a thing on the box tonight about how the women are fighting your corner.'

'Oh well, good luck to them,' Kate said. 'But it's what's happening in here that matters most to me while I'm serving my sentence.'

She wished, for instance, that Nita and her cohorts were not in the same block as her. Each block had a number of cells, usually six or seven, with an office for the staff, a common room, a small kitchen, a shower and a toilet. There were seven cells in Kate's block and four of them were occupied by Nita and her friends, all well-known drug users.

A job in the big main kitchen had been advertised and Kate applied for it. She was more than glad when she got the job, and not only because she wanted to work at anything in the food line. It would also mean that she would get out of the area in which Nita worked making uniforms.

She still had to put up with her and her friends in the cell block. It was there that they kept 'accidentally' jostling her and bumping into her. Kate started taking her meals in her cell to avoid them. On one occasion, however, after she'd collected her meal from the heated metal trolley that had arrived from the main kitchen, Nita bumped into her and knocked the plate of food from her hands. The prison officer in charge called to Nita,

'Did you do that on purpose?'

Nita swore on her mother's life that it had been an accident.

Another time, when Kate had ventured into the common room, she was pounced on and man-handled between the women, as if they were playing a noisy game of pass the parcel. Kate struggled furiously and lashed out with her fists. This only made them worse and she was in danger of suffering a serious beating, had she not been saved by a cry of 'Edge up!' from the woman who had been put as a guard on the door. 'Edge up' was a warning that staff were coming. Thankfully Kate was able to escape back to her cell.

Betty, one of the friendlier women, not a member of Nita's group, had whispered to her on one occasion, 'Take ma advice, hen. Jist gie in tae her. It'll dae ye nae good holdin' oot like this. Things'll jist get worse for ye.'

'No way am I going to give in to that weak bully.'

'Oh here, hen, she's no' weak. That's wan dangerous mistake tae make.'

'She's addicted to drugs. That's being weak. I've had enough of folk that are into drugs to last me a lifetime.'

'But she'll make yer life hell,' Betty assured her. 'Believe me, hen, she's done it tae folk before. If ye know whit's good for you, ye'll give up, hen.'

'I don't give up that easily. In fact I never give up at all if I can help it.'

Betty gave a humourless laugh.

'It disnae pay tae be as stubborn as that in here, hen. Especially against the likes o' Nita and her crowd. Maybe she wis right an' ye shouldnae huv been let oot yer suicide cell. Ye're a real danger tae yersel', so ye are.'

Kate felt frustrated and angry. All she wanted was to be left alone, to work hard, not bother anyone, and do her time as best she could. It was becoming increasingly obvious, however, that she was not going to be allowed to have a quiet life 'doing her own thing'.

The aggro from Nita accelerated, and became more dangerous. One day Kate was given a push which sent her tumbling down a flight of stairs. The fall could have killed her. She lay in agony for a few minutes before being attended to by a couple of officers. Everyone else had melted away. Fortunately, she hadn't broken any bones although she had cracked a couple of ribs, pulled a muscle in her back and was bruised all over. She was kept in the health department in Sierra until everything was healed. It was heaven compared with what she was having to suffer in the cell block. The nurses and prison officers were kind but they sighed with frustration when she refused to tell who had pushed her. To grass, or inform on anyone, was a cardinal sin in the prison.

'I tripped and fell,' was all she would say. She was determined, however, that she would deal with the problem of Nita once and for all, and by herself.

Before she had time to do so, no more in fact than ten minutes after she returned to the cell block, another painful incident happened. She was in the kitchen and had just poured a cup of tea when Nita came in, grabbed the cup and flung the contents at her. Kate managed to save her face but in doing so, got her hands and arms burned.

'Right,' Nita said. 'Ye know where tae find me if ye've had enough an' changed yer mind. Ah'll either be in ma cell or the common room. Oh an' by the way, ah see you dinnae smoke so ah'll huv yer fag ration.'

With that she left the kitchen while Kate was frantically splashing cold water on to her burning skin. Later she'd ask the duty officer for a dressing or something to soothe the injury. First she had something more important to do.

She went through to the common room and could hear Nita's laughter ringing out. Kate went right up to her and stood in front of her chair.

Nita smirked at her.

'So ye've come tae yer senses at last, eh?'

'Listen you,' Kate said coldly. 'I killed the last person who tried to get me involved with drugs.' (It wasn't one hundred per cent accurate but in the circumstances, Kate thought, a little embroidery on the truth was not only permissible but advisable.) 'Do you hear me? I might seem a pushover to you. That's because you're stupid. So I'll spell it out. I just like to be left alone to lead a quiet life. And as it happens, I'm quite a patient person. That's why you've been lucky so far. *So far*,' she repeated. 'I can't blame you for getting me wrong. Even my husband made that mistake. He died as a result. I felt good about that. I enjoyed it. Surprising him. I can still see the look on his face. I've never once regretted it.' (At least that was the truth.) 'And I'll regret even less surprising you.'

Absolute silence gripped the room. No one moved a muscle. At last, Nita said with a half-laugh.

'Och, ah wis only havin' a bit o' fun. Ah mean, it's no big deal. If ye want tae dae yer ain thing, well, the best o' luck tae ye. OK?'

'Fine,' Kate said. 'As long as we understand each other.'

She left the common room and went to get her burns properly attended to.

Later, Betty sneaked into her cell to whisper, 'Good for you, hen. Ah wouldnae huv believed that if ah hudnae heard it wi' ma ain ears.'

'Thanks, Betty. Goodnight.'

'Eh? . . . Oh aye, well, goodnight then.'

Kate was glad when Betty left, if somewhat huffily. She'd obviously been expecting to enjoy a good gossip, but the last thing Kate wanted Betty or anyone else to see was her barely controlled trembling. She was in a state of nervous collapse after the ordeal of standing up to her tormentor. She crawled into her sleeping bag, closed her eyes and struggled to take deep calming breaths.

At least after that evening, she was left in peace, and not only by Nita and her lot. Mostly everyone seemed to avoid her, perhaps from fear, she never knew. The prison had a busy grapevine along which things could easily be dramatised and exaggerated.

She didn't care.

She had more important things to concern her. More and more she concentrated on hardening herself, not only so that she could survive, but survive without her baby. Never a day passed that she did not think about and long for Christine.

The only thing that helped keep her sane was the fact that she enjoyed working in the huge main kitchen. The male prison officer, who also had the title of catering officer, explained that she could start by washing the floors and then the dishes. Only the containers that were used in the kitchen were washed in the kitchen. Any that went on the blocks in the trolleys were washed in the blocks.

Soon she graduated to peeling and cleaning the vegetables and eventually to helping with and to doing the cooking under the catering officer's supervision. He very quickly observed her culinary talents. Even the challenge of cooking for a hundred and fifty and more did not throw her for long. She listened with intense concentration to his instructions and advice, thought about it, then worked patiently until she had mastered everything.

The catering officer was glad he had somebody so dependable. He felt confident to leave her to get on with things while he went into his cubby-hole of an office to attend to paperwork. In a daily work book he detailed every diet, for instance. Every day the governor came and sampled the food to make sure it was palatable. Then the book was signed if all was in good order. The doctor came for the same purpose, but less often.

Kate was thankful for the opportunity to concentrate on a job that truly interested her. She found great satisfaction in creating nourishing and tasty dishes. A daily menu gave the prisoners a choice of meal for lunch and dinner.

In fact, it did not take Kate too long to come to the conclusion that a lot of the girls would probably be better off inside prison. She saw emaciated girls arrive who were on drugs and alcohol or both, and who had not been eating. Once in the prison, their health was seen to by doctors and nurses. Their minds were attended to by psychiatrists and psychologists. They were well fed and exercised, and trained in useful skills. As a result they went out in very much better all-round condition than they'd been when they'd arrived.

Unfortunately they went back to the same house, or to homelessness; the same family and friends, the same unemployment, the same hopelessness, the same drugs or alcohol. In a few weeks or months they were back in prison as much of a wreck as they'd been before.

She too had come in as a wreck but, she determined, she would never return here again. Once out, she was going to start a completely new life. She would go all-out to make money. The only kind of independence, the only protection, the only security, the only real freedom was an economic one.

She felt a new excitement and a new courage take root. Come hell or high water, she was going to go for it.

Look out, world!

Chapter Twenty-Five

Kate worked in the kitchen for the rest of her sentence, worked hard in fact, till the sweat was running off her. It was pleasant enough with the radio blaring cheerily in the background. She had never minded hard work and the days flew into weeks, and then months. By the time her two years were up, the prison kitchen had become the routine of her life. Instead of feeling excited about leaving, she felt strangely timid and sad. This anxious feeling, common among prisoners pending their release, was known as 'gate fever'. Kate had got into a safe routine in the prison. She had become friendly with the prison officers. Nothing intrusive, just the odd smile and pleasant exchange or word of encouragement. The catering officer complimented her on her cooking skills. They discussed the menus with genuine interest and care about balanced, nutritional food and special diets. A vegetarian choice was always available. Even the governor had remarked on the quality and tastiness of the meals. In her own strange way, Kate had become happily settled in Cornton Vale. She knew the routine. She knew the people. She knew the work.

What lay in wait for her outside the perimeter fence was not nearly so secure and certain. It would be wonderful to see Christine again, of course. But that too was fraught with difficulties and uncertainties. She would be a stranger to the child. Where would they live and how could she earn a living? The more she thought about stepping outside the prison gates, the more secretly apprehensive she became.

When she did venture outside, it was to be engulfed in a crowd of noisy women with placards, all wanting to pat her on the back and hug her, and shake her by the hand, and be photographed with her. Two or three of the women spoke to reporters but Kate held back, refusing to say anything and feeling more confused by the minute.

Her mother prised her away and got a taxi which took them to the railway station in Stirling. From there they caught a train to Glasgow.

'Ye'll stay wi' yer daddy an' me, o' course,' Mary said. 'We'll be happy tae huv ye, hen. We're aw glad tae huv ye back. There's a big family party waitin' tae welcome ye. Yer daddy an' Tommy an' Liz an' the weans – Liz has been that good wi' wee Chrissie. Ye've nae idea – a born mammy, that yin. Marilyn's there as well. An' yer Aunty Bec an' Uncle Willie an' Sandra. Oh, an' Mrs McKay, Mrs Dooley an' the two auld bachelors will be there as well. Aw the neighbours wanted tae welcome ye home tae Killearn Street, hen.'

It was kind of them, she knew, and she said so. But she couldn't shake off her confusion. She knew she was being silly but she didn't yet feel able to cope with parties or celebrations. Or even kindness. She tried to put on a brave face, however. She thanked everyone and drank wine with them and tried to laugh. Her eyes kept wandering wistfully over to Christine playing happily with her cousins and not in the slightest interested in her. Christine had been impatient with Kate's hug and kiss and pushed her away. A squabble about what toy belonged to whom was of much more urgency and importance.

'And what are you going to do now, Kate?' Aunty Bec asked. 'Jobs are awfully hard to come by these days. And you've no qualifications, have you, dear?'

'I'll survive.'

'Of course, you're lucky you've got a good daddy who's earning good money. I'm sure he hasn't minded paying for your wee girl's keep all this time but you'll not want to be a financial burden on him, will you, dear?'

'I'll find a way to make money.'

'Oh well, as long as it's an honest way, Kate. We don't want you landing back in Cornton Vale again, dear.'

Damn her, Kate thought. I'll show her!

There was still the money in the bank. Thank God. There was still the money in the bank. She told no one. She paid her mother nothing for keeping Christine. She didn't feel guilty about that. She didn't care. The money in the bank was her survival kit. If it had been possible she would have hugged it to her chest. She would have kissed it and caressed it like some crazy miser.

She wouldn't dip into it to pay for her own keep either. She'd get a job. Her living expenses, for the time being, would come off her wages. She haunted the Job Centre. Meticulously she studied the Situations Vacant columns in the newspapers and even managed a few interviews. She was willing to take any kind of work but would have preferred work in a kitchen or a restaurant. But all the publicity had made it obvious that no such establishment wanted to employ an ex-inmate of Cornton Vale. Eventually she had been grateful when she'd been asked to come for an interview to a lady called Mrs Fordyce in Newton Mearns, who wanted a cleaner. Mrs Fordyce looked as if she'd just stepped out of a beauty parlour and had never soiled her beautifully manicured hands cleaning a teaspoon. Her home was a white-painted bungalow and Kate thought it would be easily cleaned. She'd be willing and able, however, to scrub and polish a three-storeyed mansion given the chance. Mrs Fordyce, however, like all the other prospective employers, recognised Kate from the photographs that had been splashed all over the newspapers. She'd also seen her on television, filmed outside the prison, surrounded by a welcoming party of cheering women.

'I didn't realise,' For a moment Mrs Fordyce became slightly flustered, 'that you were *Kate* Brodie. When you said Mrs Brodie over the phone . . . It's a common enough name.'

'Yes, it is.' Kate knew what was coming and began to feel panic-stricken. Was she never going to be allowed to work again?

'I'm sorry,' Mrs Fordyce said dismissively, 'I don't think you'll be suitable.'

'May I ask why not? I'm young and strong and I assure you I'd keep this house spotless.'

Mrs Fordyce retreated into absentminded dignity. She glanced at her watch.

'I've other people to see. So, if you don't mind . . .'

Oh, but Kate did mind. She felt like shouting her objections in the woman's exquisitely made-up face. She wanted to create huge waves in Mrs Fordyce's no doubt smooth, safe and well-run life. It was only with difficulty that Kate managed to restrain her bitter tongue. Every interview had been the same. Not that she got many. She wrote dozens of letters applying for jobs only to get either no reply at all, or a brief note saying the position had been filled.

Then one day she was doing some shopping for her mother in Saracen Street when she noticed a card in the window of Granger's off-licence. It was for a counter assistant. She went in and, to her astonishment and delight, she got the job. The reason she was taken on was not very flattering but as her mother said, 'Beggars can't be choosers.'

The off-licence owner, Sam Granger, had welcomed her with open arms.

'I need someone capable of murder in here. I've been broken into, held up at gunpoint, had my window smashed that many times, I've had to have thick Perspex put in. And even that's a problem because people are scoring it with coins and carving their names on it. The fly buggers lean up against the window all innocent looking and all the time they're doing it sneaky-like. You can't see through the Perspex now. I'll have to get it renewed. Bloody workmen are never away from this place. They're making a fortune off me.'

Kate didn't feel in the slightest nervous. She was too grateful to get the job and, more importantly, the weekly wage packet. It meant she could afford to put Christine in a day nursery. She was increasingly worried about leaving her with her mother. Mary had definitely developed a drink problem. She vehemently denied it, of course, and admittedly she could go for weeks without a drink, except for the usual weekend whisky when she went to the pub with George. But she had regular bouts of heavy drinking. The effect it had on her was to make her retreat on to the settee and lie curled up complaining of one of her 'bilious bouts' that gave her 'one hell of a heid'.

Kate had become adept at searching out her mother's hiding places for her bottles, even the one where Mary had dangled the whisky bottle on a string outside the kitchen window. Sometimes, Kate emptied the whisky down the sink or the lavatory pan. Sometimes she refilled the bottle with cold tea. Once her mother was in the grip of one of her 'bilious bouts', Kate believed she couldn't tell the difference.

It was also good to get out of the house for a few hours every day. Once, she'd plucked up courage to go back to Byshott Street to see Budd, only to discover that he'd long gone. Nobody knew where.

'Och, it's ages ago now' one of the neighbours told her. 'While you were banged up. Just gave up the house and disappeared.'

Another said, 'I think he's got a relation down south. Or was it somebody he used to work with? Anyway, I remember, oh years back, him and his wife talking about somebody down south. That's probably where he's gone. Poor auld Budd,' the woman added. 'You can say what you like, but Pete was his only son.'

Kate had no wish to say anything, so she returned to Killearn Street, struggling to banish her father-in-law from her mind. Dwelling on the past would do nobody any good, she decided. She must concentrate on the present. That meant her work at Sam Granger's off-licence. Sam had been right about the workmen. There were always some of them around banging and battering and sawing. There was an empty flat upstairs and burglars kept breaking from there

161

through the ceiling of the shop. A joiner had had to reinforce the floor of the flat, and the ceiling of the shop. Now he had to keep coming to mend it and try to make the reinforcement even stronger. While he was there, Sam asked him to have a look at the window shutter. When Sam pulled it down, the noise brought everyone running out of their houses thinking the off-licence was shutting early. Kate was overwhelmed with the unexpected stampede of customers.

'What a carry-on,' she gasped to Sam afterwards. 'And look who's coming in now.' She'd got her eye on a man with earphones who arrived several times every day to exchange a pocketful of tenpence coins for a pound note. This man, obviously high on drugs, swaggered about all day outside the shop, pushing into people and demanding tenpence. She'd never seen him without the earphones. They seemed glued to his head.

'The till's overflowing with tenpences,' Kate complained.

'Give him the note,' Sam told her. 'I hate to think what he'd do to you if you refused, hen.'

The man never said anything and never stopped his bouncy swagger even when he was standing in the one spot. Kate supposed he must be keeping time to the music belting continuously and loudly into his ears. He just tossed down the coins and picked up the note which she practically threw at him. Then he went bouncing, swaggering, shaking and twitching out again.

Sam said, 'I admire your nerve, hen. There's a lot of your spunky wee mum in you. But one of these days that guy'll twig that in your own quiet way, you're being cheeky to him.'

'I'll tell you one thing, Sam. I wished my mother's dog had been alive yesterday when that other idiot was frightening the joiner. I would have enjoyed setting Rajah on him.'

While the joiner, a pleasant young lad called Andy, had been replacing the Perspex window, a man had been swaggering back and forwards in front of the shop brandishing a knife. Andy, sweating with fear, had got the job done as quickly as he could before nipping thankfully back into the safety of his van. Then the man, before Andy's distressed gaze, slowly and deliberately scored right across the new window with the knife.

Every day on her lunch break or any other break, Kate hurried into the next close and up the stairs to check on Granny McWhirter. Mary, and Tommy and Liz, all took turns of looking in as well. They could see though that Granny McWhirter needed to go into care. The decision could no longer be put off. Mary said,

'Ah would've taken her but what wi' Kate an' wee Chrissie stayin' wi' me, there isnae room. Anyway, it wouldnae be fair on ma man.'

Granny had become incontinent. She'd also taken to wandering and had twice fallen down the stairs. They made the decision and Granny was carted off to a nursing home in Springburn. Kate felt sad, but kept her spirits up as best she could. Her dreams and her ambitions had never deserted her. She still wasn't sure exactly how they would materialise but she clung tenaciously to them nevertheless. She was horrified when Mary said,

'Ah'm that glad ye've got settled, hen. That's you in a good job fur life now.'

For life? In Sam Granger's off-licence. No way! No harm to Sam. She liked him. She even liked the job and often had to laugh at the good-natured banter of many of the customers. But she was destined for bigger and better things. She knew it. Then, as if in answer to her desperate prayers, a small shop fell vacant a few doors away from the off-licence. She immediately applied for the tenancy and got it.

'Are ye mad?' Mary cried out when she heard. 'Huv ye gone aff yer heid? Whit in heaven's name're ye gonnae dae in an empty shop?'

Kate had thought about that. Not long before, she'd made a cake for Christine's fourth birthday. She'd fashioned it in the shape of Christine's favourite doll – even down to the last detail of the checked dress and hair-clip in the yellow iced hair. There had been a party and when Christine's friends' mothers saw the cake, they had been filled with astonishment and admiration. One of them had asked if Kate could make a fancy cake for her little boy's birthday.

'I'll pay you for it, of course,' the woman had assured her. Kate had made the little boy's cake a replica of his favourite spaceship toy. From that party she'd had another three orders for her 'speciality cakes'.

That's what she'd sell in the shop. Perhaps once she was established she could also make some of her Scottish dishes that had been so enjoyed by the family. She'd always felt that Scottish food was very much underrated. There was, she believed, something of a snobbish element in cooking. Most of the kudos went to French chefs. Now Italians and other nationalities were getting a reputation. Scottish food rarely got a look-in anywhere.

She kept on the off-licence job as long as she could and scrubbed and cleaned the wee shop in her so-called spare time. With Tommy's help she painted it as well. Above the window she'd painted the word GALLACHER'S in large gold letters. It was in honour of Joe. Anyway, she no longer had the slightest wish to be known as Brodie. She changed her name back to Gallacher. She put an advert in the local paper about the shop and what she was going to sell in it. She gave up her job and spent every hour for a few days baking cakes in the shape of plump red-coated Santas, of sleighs, of reindeer, of fairies, of Thomas the Tank Engine, of puppies, of kittens, of footballs, of racing cars, even of a pint of beer. One or two had the shape of numbers. One had the shape of a key for a twenty-first birthday. And all were colourful and delicious-tasting. Orders poured in.

Within weeks she had to employ an assistant. She took on one younger woman who'd demonstrated outside the jail and with whom she'd kept in touch the most regularly.

Within months, she had to employ another two. Delighted, they referred to the 'sisterhood'.

'That's what the sisterhood is for,' they said. 'To help one another.'

There had been a bit of a hassle from the baker's shop a few doors along. Recently she had even been threatened.

'Let anyone try, we'll be ready,' the girls said. They took the threats as a challenge. Almost welcomed them. So did Kate. She was on her way and nobody – but *nobody* – was going to stop her.

Chapter Twenty-Six

She began experimenting at home with a few Scottish recipes. Her mother helped her. Mary just laughed and shook her head, however, at Kate's dream of getting a much bigger shop.

'Perhaps in the city centre, Mammy, where I would have room to combine both the cake and the Scottish recipe sides of the business.'

She had seen a shop that catered mostly for tourists. They sold tartan-packed items like black bun, shortbread, tinned haggis and Edinburgh rock.

On enquiry, she'd discovered that the owner had similar shops in Edinburgh and towns further north and in the Highlands. For several days, Kate haunted the Glasgow shop. She also visited the premises in Edinburgh. One Sunday she took the train to see the shop in Inverness. The shops were all called Caledonia and in each one Kate bought something, admired everything and chatted to the girl assistants. She discovered that the owner, a Mr Cameron, didn't make any of the cakes, biscuits, sweets or any of the expensively and attractively packaged products.

'Oh no,' one of the girls laughed as if the vision of Mr Cameron baking or cooking was terribly funny, 'he's a businessman. He's got the agency for the firms who make these things. He's the commercial outlet for all the products.'

Kate visited a factory shop of one of the firms and bought a pot of raspberry jam at eighty-five pence. She saw the same pot in a delicatessen in Dundee at one pound ten pence. Later she compared the same pot in the Glasgow Caledonia shop. It was selling there at one pound sixty-five. She reckoned Cameron would get it at trade price for maybe forty-five pence. The size of Cameron's mark-up shocked her. She traced another product he'd bought for ten pounds and was selling for thirty pounds. The actual ingredients for the jam would cost even less than the forty-five pence and quickly Kate calculated that she could sell jam much cheaper than Caledonia and still make a good profit. The difference was she *cared* about food and the enjoyment it could give people. She wanted to give not only good value, but excellent-quality natural products. She hated the way food was being adulterated with chemicals and dyes and additives and E-numbers. Artificial sweeteners were being used more and more in sweets and confectionery, for instance, just because they were cheaper than sugar. Everybody seemed to be chasing a fast buck these days. All right, she wanted to make money too, but her love of cooking and her genuine interest in all aspects of food made her determined to make money by creating a new market. She would have more ethical values. She would concentrate all her efforts on being more creative, producing wholesome, unadulterated as well as genuine Scottish products.

There were lots of Scottish regional dishes that Caledonia obviously didn't know or care about. Delicious pashka for instance, rich with cream and glacé fruits and nuts. She could even think of more original cakes and shortbread. How about rich Easter bread, plum cake, Pitcaithly bannocks and Yetholm bannocks? Or toasted oat and raisin muffins?

She kept hopefully looking for a suitable shop. The few that did come on to the market, however, were for sale and she couldn't afford to buy. Or the occasional one she found to rent was too expensive. Eventually, to her great joy, good central premises came on the market – and at a reasonable rent. It was her big chance. The shop was everything she had been looking for and praying for. It was smack in the middle of busy Argyle Street, double-windowed and with a huge back area.

There was one disadvantage that Tommy and her mother and father were quick to point out and one that she had to admit to herself could be a problem. The premises were right next door to Caledonia, the Glasgow shop she'd been observing for so long. Not to mention questioning the assistants.

Tommy, who had taken the big step and given up his safe job in the mini-market to work for her now, was acutely worried. A timid wee soul, was Tommy. Always had been.

'I know it's a good deal as far as rent and size and all that is concerned, Kate.' He'd fixed an anxious gaze on his sister's face. 'But whoever owns Caledonia isn't going to be happy about you muscling in with the same kind of products right next door. That's putting it mildly.'

Kate shrugged.

'There's nothing anybody can do about it. It's a free country.'

Nevertheless, she braced herself for trouble.

First of all though, she needed a bank loan to equip the place properly and build up a bigger stock. That meant employing more women, buying in more materials, ordering packaging and other necessities. She made an appointment to see the bank manager, confident that there would be no problem. After all, she had long ago shown herself to be a good customer. Every penny Joe had paid her had gone into her account. All right, she'd had to draw on that when she'd started in business. But still ... She was now a successful businesswoman. She'd already proved herself. She was a very good bet.

She soon discovered that she had overlooked one important drawback. She was a woman. At least that was what she suspected the reason for the refusal was. She was not only a woman, but a young woman. And she was what was referred to nowadays as a 'one parent family'. She did her best to put her case in confident, practical terms to Mr Craigie, the bank manager, but he was having none of it. She couldn't believe that he had any good reason for turning her down. She remained calm and polite but she stared at the man's narrow bespectacled face and thought, 'You stupid macho pig. I'll show you!'

She went straight to Tommy and persuaded him to apply for a loan. Tommy was very nervous at first. She had quite a long job to talk him into it and assure him, swear to him on the Bible, that she would take full responsibility for the repayments. She would also make it very much worth his while. She promised him practically everything under the sun – except a partnership in the business. The business was hers and hers alone.

At last Tommy agreed to apply for the loan – and he got it.

'What did I tell you?' Kate said to her mother. 'I was discriminated against because I'm a woman.'

'Och well, ye mustnae forget, hen, that ye've got a record. Ye've been in prison. Whereas Tommy has held down a good regular job for years an' never been in any trouble.'

'What's that got to do with the present situation?'

'Ah dinnae know, hen. Ah'm jist sayin' that maybe Tommy seemed more dependable.'

'To make money you take risks, Mammy.'

'Well, hen, ah must give ye credit fur that. Ye're no' frightened tae take risks. Takin' on a big shop like this fur wan, an' it next door tae Caledonia. Ye've got an awfae nerve, that's aw ah can say. Ah'm terrified out ma wits.'

'Forget about Caledonia. Everything we make and Gallacher's sells will be a hundred times better and more original than anything Caledonia has to offer. We've no need to worry. I'm sure of it, Mammy. We're a couple of geniuses, you and I.'

Mary laughed.

'Ye're an awfae lassie.'

'And your mammy before you. Granny McWhirter's a great cook as well.'

'Och well, poor soul, she wouldnae know how to boil an egg nowadays. She's away wi' the fairies aw thegether. Last time I went in tae see her she didnae know me from Adam.

She's kept in bed now as well an' she was always one to be active. Ah dinnae think she'll last much longer.'

'I was feeling guilty about not being in to see her for a while but if she's not recognising anybody . . .'

'Och aye, ah know, hen, but ah wish ye'd take a wee bit time off tae go in, jist in case . . . Ye're no' doin' yersel' any good working every hour that God gives. Ah mean, ye're no' even giving' that much time tae wee Chrissie, are ye?'

Kate flushed.

'She's not being neglected.'

'Well, maybe no' . . . but still . . .'

'She loves being round at Stoneyhurst Street and playing with Tommy's kids. And Liz doesn't mind calling for her . . .'

'Ah know that. That's no' what ah'm sayin'. Wan o' these days, the wean'll be thinkin' her Aunty Liz is her mammy if ye're no' careful. That's whit – '

'How can you say things like that?' Kate cried out. 'What would you rather I do? Sit at home all day and collect unemployment money? I'm trying my hardest to make enough money so that she'll have a better life . . .'

'Aw right, aw right, keep yer hair on! Jist forget ah spoke.'

Her mother took another of her drinking bouts around that time. There hadn't been one for a while and Kate had thought there wouldn't be any more. Not that she ever looked drunk. She just curled up on the settee and went to sleep. Although Kate on this occasion detected that her mother was muttering under her breath.

'What's that you're saying, Mammy?'

'Ah'm jist sayin' ye're a pain in the arse.'

'You're drunk.'

'Drunk? Drunk?' Her mother peered round and tried unsuccessfully to raise herself in a dignified manner. 'Ah swear by aw that's holy, never a drop has touched ma lips.'

No, because it goes straight from the bottle down your throat, Kate thought, but refrained from saying the words. Instead she asked,

'Will I make you a cup of tea?'

'Aye. OK, hen. An' gie's a couple o' aspirins wi' it. Ah've got wan hell o' a heid.'

Kate made a point that evening of reading Christine an extra story before putting her to bed. She also took more time to listen to the little girl's chatter about all the excitement she'd enjoyed at Uncle Tommy and Aunty Liz's house. Then she kissed her and tucked her in.

Christine is perfectly happy, she thought. Perfectly happy and well cared for. Mammy talks such nonsense at times.

Then she went through to the kitchen and was soon applying total concentration to the important job on hand.

Chapter Twenty-Seven

It turned out that the big new shop was the saving of her mother. Despite her earlier fears and misgivings, Mary became so intrigued and excited about the expansion of the business into the heart of the city that she hadn't had one of her 'bilious bouts' or 'wan hell o' a heid' for ages. More and more, Kate roped her into helping. Kate had her dress up in a white coat and cap and put her to work alongside white-coated girls in the back shop. Marilyn was now serving in the front shop and loving every minute of it.

'But remember, you're the supervisor, Mammy,' Kate told Mary. 'You make sure my recipes and my way of doing things are strictly carried out.'

She'd wanted to include her father in the business but he had appeared somewhat unhappy and confused at the suggestion.

'Oh, I don't think so, Kate,' he said. 'I wouldn't want to let my customers down. And the Provident has always been good to me.'

She could understand it. The Provident Society had been his life. He'd known nothing else since he'd left school and had always been proud of his job and his standing in the local community.

It was unfortunate in a way, Kate thought, that now her mother was working full time in Gallacher's in the city, she couldn't always be at her father's beck and call. More often than not, when George came home in the middle of the day, it was to an empty house and no hot meal (now called lunch) ready and waiting on the table. Her mother hadn't time to dash home to Possilpark to see to him and then back to work in Argyle Street again for the rest of the afternoon. Eventually, Mary made up sandwiches the night before and left them with a flask of tea for his lunch next day. (George had never even boiled a kettle in his life.)

But what with making the evening meal (now called dinner) and seeing to the housework, she had no time and was too tired anyway, to clean his shoes and press his suit as she usually did. Kate had Christine to attend to after she'd collected her from school. She'd the shop books to keep up to date and new recipes to plan and to test. She'd also experimented with and tested new recipes in her mother's kitchen. They'd started by concentrating on the speciality cake side. Then introduced some Scottish regional cakes, biscuits and shortbreads. Not the more widely known common or garden type sold in Caledonia, and most bakeries and superstores, but the original and wide variety of something that had a long and distinguished ancestry as a 'speciality item of flour confectionery'.

Gallacher's offered festive shortbread decorated and flavoured with caraway seeds, preserved lemon, orange peel and walnuts. One was known as the Pitcaithly bannock and another recipe with crystallised ginger as the Yetholm bannock. Even Gallacher's 'ordinary' shortbread was shaped into large round bannocks or rectangles; not cut neatly into squares or wedges, but broken into uneven chunks for serving. The more genteel 'petticoat tails' of the nineteenth century were also made.

All sorts of textures were produced – gritty shortbread, fine but crunchy, and smooth 'melting' texture, to mention but a few.

As far as her father was concerned, Kate couldn't feel too much sympathy. She had developed a deep bitterness against men in general, but she tried not to let it intrude into her feelings for her father.

'It's time Daddy learned to see to himself a bit more. I've always thought it was ridiculous the way you did absolutely everything for him, fussed over him as if he was a helpless child. It wasn't good for him, Mammy.'

'Och well, he wis the breadwinner, Kate. He deserved a

bit o' attention when he wis workin' hard aw day tae keep a roof over oor heids.'

He couldn't claim to be the breadwinner any more. Not that he ever did. It was Mary who had verbally staked his claim. He was no longer the only one in the family. Mary worked harder than him and did longer hours. Baking in a busy kitchen, constantly heated by large ovens, was no light or easy task. Especially tricky was studying and carrying out all the recipes that Kate kept digging up from ancient cookery books and journals and God knows where else. Kate was often at the shop baking-tables herself, of course, but it was mostly to continue experiments with a recipe that she'd already done at home before passing it on to her mother, and from her to the other girls. Now she took on a young confectioner who did the fancy icing and marzipan motifs for the cakes. She had turned down all the male applicants for the job, preferring another spunky, independent young woman called Betsy who belonged to the militant group. They'd started to sell packaged marzipan motifs with which people could decorate their own cakes.

They'd been steaming ahead for six months, working night and day in their enthusiastic response to their surprising success when the first sign of trouble was detected on the horizon.

Kate and Mary had been working nights making marmalade in the house. Mary made her own recipe she'd been using for a lifetime. Kate experimented with one that came originally from 'The Young Ladies' School of Arts' in 1766. The marmalades were topped by a tablespoonful of rum, brandy or whisky before being sealed by tartan lids. The Gallacher label had on it a picture of a Highlander with claymore and shield held high in a defiant gesture of triumph. It was now the logo on all the Gallacher products. The marmalades were an immediate sell-out.

Aunty Bec and Uncle Willie didn't know what to make of it all. They came to dinner one evening to a chaotic house.

On top of the sideboard was a tureen of fish broth, another of mince and herb doughballs, and a big bowl of junket.

'Everyone just help yourselves,' Kate called out as, pink-faced with the heat from her mother's small kitchen, she came in carrying a pile of plates. 'There's cutlery on the table.'

Bec cast a shocked eye at the bundle of forks, knives and spoons that Mary had carelessly dumped on the table.

'I suppose,' she told Willie in the car afterwards, 'we were lucky there was a tablecloth. Although it didn't look in the least crisp or fresh. That tablecloth had been used before. Probably for every meal they've had this week. And see that – junket, she called it. It was just curds and whey only she'd flung rose petals over it. Did she actually expect us to eat them?'

Willie said, 'They might have had greenfly. And what about poor George?'

'I know. Wasn't it terrible? I've never seen my brother in such a neglected state. Or so down in the mouth. His whole house, his whole life, it seems, has been taken over by that girl. Even Tommy is under that girl's thumb. And Mary as well. I never thought much of that skyscraper of a hairstyle Mary always had, but at least it showed she took some time and trouble with herself. Now, the way she's just twisted it back into a bun . . .' Bec rolled her eyes. 'What do you make of it? She was hardly even wearing any make-up. Probably just didn't have the time, with slaving for that girl.'

'It's wicked,' Willie agreed. 'She looks like a right poor wee soul. There's nothing of her.'

'Of course, she was never what you'd call tall,' Bec reminded him. 'And she's still as impertinent . . . Boasting about that girl too. And her as proud as punch. After all she's done to disgrace the family. I'm telling you, Willie, pride goes before a fall and that girl is heading for a fall, all right.'

'Aye,' Willie agreed with equal satisfaction, 'you're right there, Bec.'

Bec had told Mary and Kate that she had been in the Edinburgh branch of Caledonia and while chatting to the manageress there, had discovered that the owner of the chain of Caledonia stores had been, for the past six months, travelling abroad to put out feelers about overseas market possibilities. The managers and manageresses of the various stores had kept the owner up to date with what was going on back home. The Glasgow manageress had been nervous at first about mentioning that Gallacher's had opened up in competition next door. She'd hoped, indeed at first felt sure, that Gallacher's would fail, but at last had been forced to report the truth. Gallacher's was a runaway success and the sales of the Glasgow Caledonia had fallen sharply. The owner was flying home that very week. 'To,' as the Edinburgh manageress had said, 'deal with the matter'.

Mary had looked anxious at the news but, as Bec confided in Willie, 'Not that girl. She'd brazen anything out, her. Remember how hard-faced she looked in the court. If you ask me, I think she intimidated that jury with that defiant stare of hers. By rights she ought to have got life for what she did. Not,' Bec hastily added, 'that I'd want to see her put away in Cornton Vale for the rest of her days. You know me, Willie. I'm a good Christian woman and wouldn't do a living soul a bad turn. But I just don't know what to make of it. Do you, Willie?'

Willie did not.

'All I know is,' Willie sighed, 'she was asking for trouble opening that shop where she did.'

'That girl,' Bec said, 'thinks she can get away with murder.'

The aptness of this cliché suddenly occurred to both Willie and Bec. They gave each other a wide-eyed, meaningful look.

Chapter Twenty-Eight

'What the hell do you think you're doing?'

'I'm arranging a display of a new product.'

Kate turned and raised a questioning brow at the man who'd shattered the quietness. It was early and she was alone. Tommy and Marilyn were on their coffee break.

'I take it you're Kate Gallacher, the owner of this place.'

'And you are?'

'Gavin Cameron. I own Caledonia.'

'Ah.'

Kate put the finishing touches to the display. She'd had posters and display boards made of the Highlander logo and one of these was the centrepiece of this particular display. The Black Watch tartan of the Highlander's kilt matched that of the deep wall to wall carpet she'd had laid in the front shop. The display was set on a rich swathe of blue velvet.

'Is that all you've got to say?' Cameron demanded. 'By God, you're a cool one.'

In actual fact, she was panicking inside, desperately praying for coolness. She had prepared herself for this confrontation since the day Aunty Bec had dropped her bombshell. Or she thought she had prepared herself. Now, faced with the fury in this man's eyes, she felt frightened, then angry at herself. No man was going to be allowed to frighten her or intimidate her ever again. Especially someone who oozed maleness and had the height, bulk and menace of a heavyweight boxer. Kate noted with dislike his cleft chin, his blue-black hair, his five o'clock shadow. Once she'd admired dark-haired, tanned men. Not any more. She had a fleeting thought that he was the type who would admire baby-faced, coquettish and very feminine Marilyn.

'What am I supposed to say?' she asked, not just coolly, but insolently. 'I run a business. It's a free market. That means competition. You surely can't object to that.'

He looked as if he was itching to strike her. She'd seen that look before. Only, thank God, this man, unlike Pete, had no claim on her. No excuse could be made by anyone that if the man assaulted her, it was 'only a domestic'.

'I certainly do bloody object,' he said. 'Fair competition is one thing. Spying on my business, then opening one of your own next door. *Next door,*' he repeated, as if hardly able to credit his own words. 'And copying my products,' he was almost choking with rage. 'That's another bloody thing altogether.'

'I have not copied your products.' She nearly added, They're not your products anyway. You're just the middleman. You don't make anything except money. But she thought better of it.

'Don't give me that,' he said. 'Cakes, shortbread, to mention just a few Scottish lines. Now you're into preserves!'

'My cakes and shortbreads, all my recipes, are quite different from what Caledonia sells, including the preserves. They're all original, regional dishes. Or recipes my mother and I have made at home, tried out on the family, and then packaged for the shop. We've worked night and day . . .'

'That's only too obvious. But I'm warning you, you're not going to get away with this.'

'What do you propose to do?' she asked. 'Lasso my customers and drag them into your shop?'

She really did think he was going to strike her then. But suddenly the shutters went down on his dark eyes. His stare became ice-cold and expressionless.

'No, I don't think that will be necessary. You'll hear from me again.'

With that he strode from the shop. The front door made such a crash behind him, Kate thought for a moment he'd shattered the glass. Miraculously, the door remained in one piece.

She went through to the back shop and poured herself a cup of tea from the giant pot used for the staff.

'Whit's up wi' you?' Mary asked. 'Ye look as if ye've seen a ghost.'

'No.' Kate was annoyed that she appeared in any way upset. 'Only the Caledonia owner.'

She was more angry than upset now. She'd had enough of being frightened and unhappy to last her a lifetime. She wanted absolutely nothing to do with men, any kind of men, in any circumstances. At first, when she'd come out of prison, she'd joined with the female militants in their rabble-rousing, placard-wielding protests about another woman being jailed after killing an abusive partner. But soon she'd flinched from the shouting and the outward demonstrations of emotion. She felt embarrassed and painfully self-conscious. Eventually, she'd decided it wasn't her way. What she had to do, and wanted to do, was throw herself heart and soul into her business. But she was still grateful to the women who had supported her when she needed them. She did what she could in return by attending their meetings (and supplying cakes and biscuits for their tea), writing letters to the prison and to MPs. And she shared with the women a bitterness against men.

I'll show them, she kept thinking. I'll show them.

If Caledonia could open up shops in Pitlochry, Crieff and Edinburgh, then so could Gallacher's. Anything any man could do, she could do better. She did what she could for abused women but only in her own private way. For a start, she determined to help her old friend, Dorothy McKinlay – or McGurk, as she had been since marrying her useless junkie of a man, to get free of him. She had no intention of giving Dorothy any handouts of money but she did arrange a place for her in a women's refuge. She also offered her a job with a good wage. Kate was conscientiously careful with money and never wasted a penny. To pay her employees decent wages, however, she considered an investment. To be good to employees was good business. That's what she believed.

Dorothy had been difficult. Stupid really. But Kate could understand how she felt and so continued to be not only determined, but patient. Dorothy had been worn down and abused so much, she no longer believed she could manage on her own, in a refuge or anywhere else.

'You'll not be on your own,' Kate assured her. 'There'll be other women in the refuge to support you. And you've always got me. Once you're away from Stoneyhurst Street, I'll help you look for a place of your own. You can get your wee girls into a nursery until they're ready for school. That won't be long now. And you'll have a good job in Gallacher's.'

'I know, Kate. And I appreciate everything you're wanting to do for me, but . . .' Dorothy looked like a shaky old woman. Kate thought it was wicked how a man could destroy not only a woman's body, but her spirit, her whole being. 'But it's the whippets . . .'

Kate clung valiantly to her patience although she felt like battering Dorothy herself. 'To hell with the dogs, Dorothy. Let Charlie worry about them. They're his whippets.'

'And there's the cat as well . . .'

'Dorothy!'

'Well, it used to belong to my mother and it's like one of the family.'

'Take it with you then, if you must.' Kate put up a warning hand. 'And don't you dare say, What if she doesn't want to go?'

'You were fond of Rajah, remember.' Dorothy's lips began to tremble. 'You were upset when he was killed.'

'I'm not asking you to kill Dinkie. Only to give her a change of address, for God's sake. You're only making excuses, Dorothy. You're frightened to stay and you're frightened to leave. I know how you feel, believe me.'

'No, you don't.'

'I can see how frightened you are.'

'All right, I'm frightened. But it's not as simple as you think.'

'You're unhappy. You're miserable. You're ill. You need to leave. It's the only sensible thing to do. He's killing you, Dorothy. But before he manages it, you might end up killing him.'

'Oh no, I could never do that. I'm not as hard as you, Kate. I'm sorry,' she added hastily, 'I didn't mean to offend you. What I meant was – you've always been stronger than me. You see, I . . . I feel if only Charlie could get help. He's not a bad man. It's not him, it's the drugs. He's always sorry. He's so sorry. I still feel for him, you see. I mean, it was all so different at first. If only – '

'Oh Dorothy,' Kate interrupted, 'wake up. Stop kidding yourself. Nothing's going to change. You owe it not only to yourself but to your children to leave that man and start a new life.'

Dorothy looked trapped in her misery. Her eyes roamed wretchedly, uncertainly about.

'Oh, I don't know, Kate.'

'Well, I do. And I'm not giving up until I get you out of there.'

'You've always been stronger than me,' Dorothy repeated helplessly.

'You can be strong too if you just give yourself a chance. OK, I was luckier than you. I had my mammy and my daddy and my brothers. You had nobody. You could have had me long ago, but you wouldn't let me near you.'

'Oh, it wasn't that I didn't want to see you, Kate. Oh, how I longed for the old days when you and I . . . We used to have such good laughs, didn't we?'

'We would have helped and supported each other, Dorothy.'

'I was ashamed. I didn't want you to see . . . Especially when Charlie was . . . He acts like a crazy man when he's "high", as he calls it. But he's not a bad man. It was losing his good job that started it. He tried but he couldn't get anything else. And he kind of lost hope. That's when he got into the heroin. It made him forget. It's an escape, you see. He can't face . . .'

'So he leaves you to face everything on your own. Charming!'

This conversation had taken place in Kate's office off the corridor that led into the back shop, while Dorothy's children were being entertained and fed biscuits by Mary and the bakery girls.

'He just got depressed, Kate. He couldn't cope. And I couldn't cope either. I can understand it. He's not a bad man.'

'Will you stop saying that? Anybody with half an eye can see that Charlie McGurk is a lily-livered, snivelling weakling. He steals to get money to feed his self-indulgent habit after he's spent even his own children's allowance. We've all seen him take it off you before you're hardly outside the post office door. He doesn't care if you and the twins starve. Why should you care about him? He's scum!'

Dorothy burst into tears. 'You can be awful cruel, Kate.'

'*Me* cruel? That's a laugh. He leads you a life of misery for years and just about kills you and the kids. And he's not a bad man? I try to help you and I'm cruel? Don't be daft.'

'I don't know why I came here today.'

'Because you're desperate. And I put a note through your letterbox pleading with you to call at the shop.'

'I know you mean well, Kate. But it's too late. I mean, I just can't cope. I don't know where to start. I sometimes can't get myself and the twins dressed in the morning, never mind organise us all to move house. Half the time the twins dress themselves and find me something to put on. I'm . . . I'm . . . losing my mind . . .'

'No, you're not,' Kate said firmly. 'In a couple of days you'll be due your post office money and Charlie will disappear for the rest of the day, right?'

Helplessly Dorothy nodded her head.

'Right. While Charlie's gone, I'll come to your house,

pack your case and get you out of there. Then I'll have a taxi to take you to the refuge and once you've settled in, you'll start work here. You can start in the bakehouse in the back. Mammy'll show you what to do. You'll be doing me a favour, Dorothy. Business is booming. I need all the help I can get.'

'Oh no, Kate,' Dorothy sobbed. 'Please, you don't realise, you don't understand . . .'

'Pull yourself together for the children's sake. Here's some tissues. Mop your face. And take this powder compact and lipstick. It'll boost your morale. Remember how we used to say that? You were a great looker in those days, Dorothy. I know it seems a lifetime ago. But it's only a few years. You can be a great looker again. What do you bet?'

'Please don't do this, Kate. I don't want you to come to the house. I can't cope with any of this. You don't understand.'

'Dorothy, you're like a bloomin' parrot, the way you keep repeating yourself. And let me tell you something. You obviously don't understand me. My mother always used to say there was a stubborn bit about me and it's true. You're going to find out, Dorothy, just how stubborn I can be.'

Chapter Twenty-Nine

Kate had never seen anything like it. Even the first time she'd set eyes on Budd's house was nothing to this. No wonder Dorothy was ashamed. She had said she couldn't cope, hadn't been able to cope for years. Kate looked at the house in Stoneyhurst Street and thought – too true!

'My God!' she gasped.

Dorothy burst into tears again.

'You shouldn't have come. I didn't want you to come. You're bullying me, Kate. You're taking advantage, you've no right.'

'I know.' Kate stood inside the front door, arms akimbo. 'And I'm going to bully you some more. Go and find a suitcase.'

'I don't think . . .'

'Right now! Don't say another bloody word.'

Kate thanked God the dogs and the cat were shut in the kitchen. She could hear them barking and miaowing and scratching. She also thanked God she'd had the foresight to drop the twin girls off at Killearn Street with her mother. She'd caught up with a bedraggled Dorothy and the children in Saracen Street when Dorothy was on her way home from the post office. After practically tearing the children from Dorothy's grasp, she'd left them happily playing with Christine.

They'd have to have a bath and have their hair washed and probably deloused before going to the refuge. So would Dorothy. There were surely limits to what even a place like a refuge would put up with.

Standing in the narrow, windowless lobby, Kate itched to get stuck into the place and bring cleanliness and order to it. She controlled the urge. Instead, she wove a path as best she could through the dog shit, the cat pee and the mountains of empty food cans, packets, old newspapers, and she dare not think what else.

The living room was no better. Absolutely every inch of every surface was chock-a-block, was covered with something. Unopened and opened packets of food, cans of beer, dirty dishes, dirty syringes and needles. Kate shut the door. She picked her way through to the bedroom. Dorothy was sitting on the edge of the bed as if in a daze.

'Shite!' Kate said out loud. She opened the wardrobe. There was a suitcase at the bottom of it. After rummaging about she found some of the children's clothes and flung them into the case. A coat of Dorothy's went the same way. After a search round the room, she found some shoes under the bed.

'Come on. That'll do.' She fastened the case, heaved it up and turned to her friend. 'Come on, I said.'

'But Kate, what about Dinkie?'

Kate dumped the case down and put a hand to her brow for a moment. Then she said, 'Wait there.'

Back in the lobby, she opened the kitchen door just enough to let the cat shoot out. This wasn't easy because of the whippets hurling themselves hysterically against the door. Returning to the bedroom she lifted the suitcase. Dorothy was miserably nursing the cat in her arms.

'Now, come on,' Kate said.

'Oh Kate . . .'

'Never mind the Oh Kate.'

With her free hand, Kate grabbed Dorothy's arm. Suddenly it occurred to her how like her mother she sounded. It was a sobering thought but there wasn't time to dwell on it. Charlie McGurk might appear at any moment, stoned out of his mind.

'It's no use,' Dorothy said.

'Oh, shut up and get moving.'

Kate dragged her bodily and none too gently from the house.

By the time they got round to Killearn Street, Mary had already bathed Dorothy's little girls. They were sitting squeaky clean and grinning, with hair plastered wetly to their scalps. Each was clutching one of Christine's soft toys. They were also, Kate noticed, wearing clean pairs of bibbed denims and Mickey Mouse T-shirts.

'Doon the stairs,' Mary answered Kate's unspoken question. 'Mrs McKay keeps changes o' clothes in her house fur when her grand-weans visit. But the weans huv long since grown oot o' these.'

'Right,' Kate said. 'Put Dinkie down. I'll give it to Mrs Dooley downstairs to look after until we get you a place of your own. You go through and have a bath, Dorothy. You can change into some of my clothes. I'll hand them in to you.'

'I keep telling her, Mrs Gallacher,' Dorothy sobbed as Kate forced the cat from her arms, 'I don't want to leave Charlie. He needs me.'

'All Charlie needs is his next fix of heroin,' Kate told her.

Mary said, 'There's nae use crossing her, hen, once she's made up her mind. Dinnae worry aboot Dinkie. She'll have plenty pals doon the stairs with Mrs Dooley. Away an' huv a nice bath. That'll make ye feel better.'

As Dorothy trailed broken-heartedly from the room, Kate called after her, 'And wash your hair.' Then she turned to Mary:

'I'm going to report that place to the Sanitary. You should have seen the state of it. It beggars belief.'

'They'd huv tae clear oot everybody in that close. As far as ah know, they're aw junkies up there. Ah wish oor Tommy could get away from Stoneyhurst Street. It's his weans ah worry aboot.'

'His close is all right, isn't it? I thought he and Liz had quite good neighbours.'

'Och aye. There's lots o' decent folk like oorsels. There's too many Charlie McGurks, though, that's the trouble. Why dae the polis no' round them aw up, that's whit ah'd like tae know. Ah mean, it's no' legal, is it? Aw that injectin' an' snortin' or whatever they call it.'

Kate shook her head.

'It beats me.'

Talking of drugs reminded her of Pete, his expensive suits, his flashy silk shirts and ties, his jewellery. It was men like him, and the drug barons who employed him, who should be rounded up, banged up and, most important of all, their money and the luxuries the drugs provided should immediately be confiscated. Their profits should then be used to help alleviate the suffering they had caused. She didn't voice her thoughts. She never spoke of Pete, seldom thought of him and never with regret at what she'd done. The blessed relief of being free of him was too wonderful. Her mind and heart kept overflowing with gratitude. She had a life! Hallelujah!

'I'd better look out some clothes for her.' Kate glanced at her watch. 'The quicker she's safely into that refuge, the better. Charlie won't be able to find her there. Anyway, we said we'd try some jam tonight, remember? The marmalade's been so successful. I've already ordered labels for the jam.'

'My God, Kate, ye're quick aff the mark. We huvnae made the stuff yet. Whit if it disnae turn oot as good? Strawberry especially can be awfae tricky.'

'Stop worrying, Mammy. Your jam's always lovely.'

'Ah huvnae made strawberry fur years. It can turn oot runny if ye're no' careful.'

'That doesn't matter.'

'Whit dae ye mean – it disnae matter. Jam hus tae set.'

'I thought we'd try what used to be called eating jam.'

'Whit the hell's that supposed to be?'

'It's one of these old recipes . . .'

Mary groaned.

'Ah dinnae know where ye dig them aw up.'

'It's a quick and easy recipe and it makes a runny, strawberry-flavoured syrup with whole berries in it. It just needs strawberries, lemons and sugar.'

'Who'd want a runny jam an' whit fur?'

'Lots of things. Served as a pudding with thick cream or as a sauce with hot pancakes, for instance.'

Mary shook her head.

'Naw, ah dinnae think that'll take, hen. Jam's fur spreading on bread.'

'I've a great recipe for berries with bread. You soak the bread in the berry syrup – strawberries and raspberries . . .'

'Aw shut up. Away an' see tae that poor soul through there. She's probably drowned hersel' by now.'

Kate went through to the bedroom to look out some underwear, a pair of jeans and a denim shirt for Dorothy. She hesitated over a quilted and hooded anorak that she was rather fond of. Then she thought, what the hell! Dorothy's need was greater than hers. Anyway, it was time she bought something new for herself. Every penny she'd spent so far was for the business. She never even went to the hairdresser's any more. She washed her hair herself and just tied it back.

She knocked on the bathroom door.

'Dorothy, are you all right?'

There was a faint reply of 'What do you think?'

This cheered Kate. Bitterness was better than helpless sobbing. It showed a bit of spunk. Maybe not quite the right kind, but still . . .

'I've left you some clothes outside the door. Put them on. Just leave the stuff you've taken off. They can go in Mammy's washing machine. And hurry up,' she added. 'I'm going to phone for a taxi.'

But she had to return to shout through again: 'Dorothy, I'll break this door down if necessary.' Kate rattled violently at the handle. 'Do you hear me, Dorothy?'

'Oh, all right!'

At last Kate managed to hustle her friend and the two little girls down the stairs from her mother's top flat. Mary called after them, 'Good luck, Dorothy, hen', then went through to give them a wave from her front-room window before the black taxi drove them off.

George arrived in the house a few minutes later.

'Was that Dorothy McGurk with Kate? I passed them on the stairs.'

'Aye.' Mary sighed. 'The poor lassie disnae know whether she's comin' or goin'. Kate's yanked her away frae her man. Only he disnae know it yet. She's takin' her tae some refuge place.'

'Charlie's not going to like that. I wish Kate wouldn't interfere in other folk's lives. She's been a different person since she came out of prison. She drives everybody and everything before her. She used to be so quiet and easygoing.'

'Deep, though. An' a bit o' a loner. Dorothy wis the only pal Kate ever had. No, Kate wis always a bit different, George. Huv ye ever known a wee girl that wis always cookin' an' messin' aboot in a kitchen instead o' playin' wi' dollies? Kate wis always more interested in pancakes than prams. When ah look back now, it disnae seem natural.'

The mention of food spurred George to ask,

'I don't suppose there's any dinner ready?'

'Oh God! See wi' havin' Dorothy's weans as well as wee Chrissie, an' then Kate came in wi' Dorothy an' the bloody cat . . .'

'Oh, never mind,' George said, defeated. 'I'll go out to the pub.' They had quite decent pies and they were very generous with their beans.

'Oh, would ye, George? That bathroom's a right mess an' ah'll have tae get aw them dirty clothes in the machine before they stink the place oot.' She gave herself a vigorous scratch. 'Ah'd better huv a bath masel'. Them McGurk weans must've been movin' wi' fleas.'

George heaved himself to his feet. He could have done without going out again. He'd been trailing the streets all day and his feet were killing him. His legs weren't much better. It had taken him all his time to climb the stairs. Gone were the days when his wife welcomed him home with a dram, then rushed to fetch his slippers. Gone were the days when the house sparkled like a new pin, the table covered by a crisp white cloth and a cordon bleu meal was served to him. Gone were the days he'd relax with his pipe for the rest of the evening and watch television.

Long gone.

The living room where he used to watch television was now awash with materials that kept overflowing from the kitchen. Half the time now, Mary and Kate actually used the living-room table for working on. Now they'd moved his television into the bedroom but there wasn't enough room there for his comfortable armchair. He'd either to sit on the edge of the bed or get undressed and go to bed. He didn't seem to have any life at all any more.

'Nae need tae hurry back,' Mary called after him. 'Kate wants us tae get intae aw sorts o' fancy jams now.'

He could just see the house crammed with jam jars.

George felt so tired and depressed, he could have wept.

The refuge was a Victorian villa in Pollokshields hidden from the road by a bank of mature trees. Other residents of the quiet, tree-lined street strongly objected to this house – or indeed any house in their neighbourhood – being used as a refuge. They had been concerned that the steady stream of bedraggled women coming and going and the large numbers of scruffy young children would lower the tone of the area. Too bad, Kate thought. A pity they hadn't more to bother them.

Inside the house, a ghost of a woman led Kate and Dorothy and the twins through a hall covered with worn brown linoleum. They reached a shabby office where a much more substantial female was sitting writing at a desk.

'It's them,' Kate told the woman. 'Dorothy McGurk and her girls, Rosemary and Eileen. I explained over the phone. I'm Kate Gallacher.'

'Oh yes.' The woman put down her pen, edged her plump body from behind the desk and bore down on them, hand outstretched. 'I'm Helen Rogers. Welcome to Shields House. You'll be all right here.'

'She's worn to a frazzle,' Kate said.

'I am not.' Dorothy sounded on the verge of tears again.

'Never mind,' Helen Rogers soothed. 'We'll go and have a cup of tea, shall we? Then I'll introduce you to the rest.'

She patted each twin on the head. 'There's lots of boys and girls here for you to play with.'

Kate said, 'Do you mind if I rush off? I've an awful lot to do tonight.'

'Not at all. On you go. Your friend will be fine.'

'I'll pop in and see you tomorrow, Dorothy,' Kate assured her tragic-eyed friend. 'Stop worrying, you're going to be all right.'

'It's Charlie I'm worried about. This is enough to kill him. He'll go completely to bits on his own.'

Let him, Kate wanted to say. Let him. Instead she murmured quietly, 'He'll be all right, Dorothy. I promise. I'll get our Tommy to look in on him.'

'Oh, will you, Kate?'

'I promise,' Kate repeated, at the same time thinking, I hope the bastard rots in hell.

Chapter Thirty

Kate decided to introduce more Glasgow and Clydeside recipes. Glasgow toffee, Glasgow punch, het pint, apple frushie. She had a double-glass-doored fridge installed and displayed in it cartons of Glasgow broth and Glasgow tripe. She had meetings with a packaging firm and ordered various forms of packaging: it wasn't as expensive looking as Caledonia's, but at least it looked interesting with the defiant Highlander logo.

From Glasgow recipes she quickly branched out into Edinburgh tart, stoved howtowdie, Holyrood pudding and barley pudding. Then for the north-east of Scotland, neep bree, skirlie and Aberdeen preserved apples. There were so many wonderful, unusual and delicious regional recipes, it amazed her that no one had cashed in on them before. Even within the bakery line, there were hosts of cakes and biscuits that no other commercial establishment seemed to have tackled. Fatty cutties, sour skous, Orkney broonies and bride's Bonn-a bridal cake that by tradition was broken over the bride's head as she entered her new house for the first time as a married woman.

Instead of the tins of haggis that Caledonia stocked, Kate had the bright idea of making haggis into dainty balls that could be speared with cocktail sticks. They turned out to be a great favourite for parties and receptions.

It took Charlie McGurk months to find out that Kate had anything to do with the disappearance of his wife and children. It had been years since he'd met Kate – before his marriage to Dorothy, in fact. He'd long since forgotten all about her. He'd questioned, pestered, bullied everyone in the street and beyond about who'd seen his family leave and who, if anyone, had been with them. Half the time the people he spoke to were in the same dream world of crazed deprivation as himself. They neither knew nor cared.

Eventually he'd heard a man in a pub talking about Kate Brodie and how she was bombing ahead in a big shop in Argyle Street.

'Remember her,' the man said. 'Not a bad looker – long hair and legs up to her oxters.'

Charlie had shaken his head.

'Och, ye must do,' the man insisted. 'She used to be pals with your Dorothy. Gallacher, she was then. Kate Gallacher. A right hard case. She murdered her man and got away with it. Or as good as. She only spent a couple of years in Cornton Vale.'

'Gallacher. Her from Killearn Street?'

'That's the one.'

He'd gone straight to Killearn Street from the pub and had battered and kicked at the Gallachers' top-floor flat. But nobody had been in. That night he'd broken into a house in Maryhill and struck lucky. He'd found more than enough to get himself a fix. He'd meant to go back to Killearn Street but after he'd gratefully injected, he'd forgotten all about the Gallachers. He hadn't a care in the world. Not even about Dorothy and the girls.

The next day, however, he was ready to commit murder. Again he went to the house. Again he found no one in. Next stop was the post office where he demanded a look at the Yellow Pages. From the outside the post office appeared like a wartime concrete bunker: no windows, no signs, no posters, not even a postbox. Only graffiti covered the concrete. Inside was equally bleak and desecrated. No Yellow Pages had been left out for customers to steal or vandalise. His request for 'a look' was refused. He bawled out that if they didn't hand over the fuckin' Yellow Pages, he'd tear the place to bits and kick their fuckin' heads in. It was decided that hanging on to the Yellow Pages wasn't worth all that bother.

A quick flick through found him the big advert for Gallacher's and the address. He abandoned the book and raced outside to Saracen Street. There he leapt on to a bus that took him into town. In Argyle Street, he had no trouble finding Gallacher's.

Kate was in her office working at her desk when she heard the commotion in the front shop.

'Where is she?' a man bawled. Then Tommy's nervous, 'Who? Who do you mean?'

'Who do you think, you stupit wee cunt? Fuckin' Kate Gallacher.'

He must have grabbed Tommy because Kate heard Marilyn give a terrified scream.

Kate knew of course it must be Charlie McGurk. She lifted the phone and was just about to dial 999 when McGurk burst into the office. He was a gaunt little man, thin as a skeleton, with eyes straining wildly out from his skull.

Kate fixed him with an icy stare.

'Who are you?' she asked. 'And what on earth do you want? If you have a complaint about any of our products, please calm yourself and tell me about it. You'll find I'll – '

'Ye know who ah am an' whit ah'm daein' here. Dinnae act it, ye hard-faced cunt. Where's ma wife an' weans?'

'I'm sorry. I don't know what you're talking about.'

She hoped Tommy would go through to the back shop to use the phone there to summon the police. Although the chances were he wouldn't have the nerve. And the girls in the back shop would have the radio on and would have heard nothing. She certainly had no hope of Tommy coming into the office to rescue her, and Marilyn had probably run screaming out to the street by now.

She made another attempt to dial but McGurk knocked the phone from the desk.

'See you! If ye dinnae tell me where ma wife an' weans are right now, ye'll be as deid as yer man. Ah'll give ye five seconds.'

He'd reached the count of three when Gavin Cameron strode into the room.

'An unsatisfied customer?' he said sarcastically.

'Don't you fuckin' start,' McGurk shouted but there was a broken edge to his voice now. It was obvious he couldn't tackle this man who was about twice the height and width of him.

'You are . . .?' Cameron said with a polite raise of his brows, 'Mr?'

'Ah'm Charlie McGurk an' that hard-faced murdering bitch hus broken up ma marriage an' hidden ma wife an' weans away somewhere. She's capable of anythin'. Even murder. That's the wan that murdered her man.'

'I know. And you have my sympathy, Charlie. But what makes you think Miss Gallacher had anything to do with the disappearance of your family?'

'Before we were married, she used to be Dorothy's pal.'

'But that's ridiculous. Be reasonable, man. Just because she used to know your wife years ago doesn't mean she had anything to do with it. Be honest. Isn't it much more likely that problems between you and your wife have led her to leave of her own accord? She'll be in some women's refuge somewhere, I'd stake my life on it. It happens all the time these days. Come on, I've got a bottle of good malt whisky next door. Let me give you a drink. It'll at least help calm you down.'

To Kate's embarrassment, McGurk burst into tears. She had always known he must be a weakling but now she really despised him for it.

'Ah know ah huvnae been aw that ah should be at times, but ah always thought we . . . you know . . . we were OK thegether. Ah've never believed for a minute ma Dorothy would desert me. It's been a terrible shock.'

'Yes, I can understand that. Come on. The whisky will help steady you.'

Cameron looked over at Kate before ushering the weeping man from the office. In his dark glance, brief though it was, she saw that he despised her, just as much as she despised Charlie McGurk.

He believes I did it, she thought. Well, so what? She didn't care a damn what Gavin Cameron thought. But it annoyed her just the same. She wanted to explain to him about how awful Dorothy's life was with Charlie and how, in fact, she'd done Dorothy a very big favour. She had absolutely no doubts about what she'd done. Nor had she the slightest regret.

Marilyn came breathlessly into the office.

'Wasn't he wonderful?'

'Who?'

'Mr Cameron, of course. I panicked, Kate. I was sure that awful man was going to kill us all . . .'

'Don't be silly, Marilyn.'

'He was so violent and his awful language . . . I just flew.'

'You didn't go next door, did you?' Kate groaned.

'Not exactly. But Mr Cameron heard me screaming and came out right away. Wasn't it lucky for us he was in his Glasgow shop! He's so often at his other places. I told him an awful man was going to kill you . . .'

'Oh, Marilyn, for goodness sake – Charlie McGurk? That pathetic excuse for a man?'

'I don't know how you keep so calm. Honestly, I don't. I feel quite faint. I shudder to think what might have happened if that lovely Mr Cameron hadn't come to our rescue. And none of us thought to say one kind word to him while he was here. Or show even one tiny bit of gratitude. I'm going to pop next door right now and thank him.'

'You'll do no such thing,' Kate snapped. 'Go through to the back and make a pot of tea. Take one of your tranquillisers.'

Marilyn pouted.

'You sound as if you don't even like him.'

'I don't.'

'But he's so gorgeous.'

'Marilyn, you think anything in trousers is gorgeous these days. It's time you got married again. You obviously need a man. I don't.'

Marilyn looked shocked. Tears filled her eyes.

'That's an awful thing to say. I've never looked at another man since I lost Joe. How can you be so cruel?'

'I didn't mean to be cruel, Marilyn. I was just stating a fact. I know you loved Joe but he's been dead a while. There's nothing wrong with you being interested in someone else now. Good luck to you. Away and make the tea. We all could be doing with a cup.'

Marilyn wandered off snivelling and wiping at her eyes. Kate picked up the phone, dialled the packaging company and placed an order for soup cartons.

She wanted to ask Marilyn if she could have one of her tranquilliser tablets. Pride prevented her.

'Damn,' she said out loud. He even knew about the murder. But of course why shouldn't he? Everyone else did. She had a sudden longing to explain the circumstances of the killing. At the same time she told herself angrily that she'd absolutely no need to explain anything to Gavin Cameron. It didn't matter in the slightest what he thought of her.

'Damn,' she said again. She closed her eyes, and leaned her brow forward on her palm.

Chapter Thirty-One

Gavin Cameron was more furious with himself than anyone else. He wasn't stupid. He knew exactly why the recent incident with Kate Gallacher had made him feel not just furious, but emotionally shattered. He was going to get a grip of himself. But it wasn't easy. He had no doubt whatever, of course, that the woman had interfered in McGurk's marriage, dominated the wife, and hustled her away somewhere. And it wouldn't be all for the wife's good either. No matter what she told her. He knew Kate Gallacher's type. He knew the type so well. He had always shut the past from his mind. He considered it not only stupid, useless and a complete waste of time, but a weakness, to keep dwelling on what had happened in his earlier years. Or at least to allow it to affect his present thinking and behaviour. For the most part, he was able to focus determinedly on the present and the future. Only occasionally, when he came across women like Kate Gallacher, did a crack open up in his mental armour and memories come rushing in. He had to struggle with them until he found some sort of balance again. He did this by getting away from the business and the city.

On this occasion, he threw his haversack in his Calibra, along with his hiking boots and other gear, including binoculars. He drove to the head of Loch Fyne and booked in for the night at a small hotel on the lochside. It had only a few bedrooms and at this time of year they were usually empty. In a couple of months' time, there might be some people like himself who enjoyed the peace and beauty of the countryside. They would arrive to spend Christmas and perhaps New Year and to savour not only the glorious scenery, but also the delicious food that was served in the bar and in the small dining room.

There were always a few locals in the bar, of course. But only a few. Quiet-spoken, pipe-smoking countrymen usually.

The place had darkly polished wood and smelled of the loch that lapped yards from the front door, and the dense pine woods at the back. It was so quiet he could hear the grandfather clock tick-tock over in the shadowy corner of the bar.

He turned up the collar of his sheepskin jacket and took his dram outside. He sat hunched on the low wall overlooking the loch. A full moon silvered the water and he could hear the wind gently rustling and whispering in the trees. He began to feel slightly better. Not happier, but calmer in his mind. He had a perfectly logical reason for disliking domineering, ruthless types of women like Kate Gallacher. As a child he'd suffered at the hands of just such a woman. But it wasn't so much his own suffering that could so deeply distress him. It was the suffering that his mother must have endured.

His mother had been such a lovely woman. He could even recall her perfume. It filled his nostrils now, blotting out the salt tang of the loch and the sweet smell of the pine woods. He must have only been a toddler when she'd first developed multiple sclerosis, but he could still remember her at her most active. He remembered her laughing with him and running with him in her arms. He couldn't recall why she was running with him. Only the warmth and the energy and the joy of her.

He remembered too the warm smell and the silky softness of her hair. He could see the worried concern on his father's face when she began to slow down, when her limbs weakened, when she developed a slight tremble. He didn't know at the time what the diagnosis had been. He only saw that his father had become concerned and even closer and more loving than he'd been before. His father had gone away a lot on business and it had only been his mother and himself. Now his father stayed at home more and the three of them were together. His mother had worried about his father neglecting the business. She was in a wheelchair now and often they'd go out together, his father pushing the chair and Gavin walking beside it. She worried about Gavin not going out to play enough with other boys.

'I don't want you to grow up a loner, Gavin. Never mind me. You go out and play football or rugby with your wee schoolfriends. I'm all right. Even when Daddy's at work, I've got Nurse Flora to look after me. I'm all right,' she kept assuring him. But of course he knew that she wasn't all right. She was changing, deteriorating before his eyes. Everything was changing. His father said he was relying more and more on his secretary, Nicola Dawson. He didn't know what he'd do without her. Young though he was, Gavin noticed how often this woman's name cropped up in his father's conversation and felt uneasy.

Then she began to appear at the house. There was always some reason or excuse: papers to sign, some urgent matter that could only be discussed in person. She was always very neat and efficient with her straight dark glossy hair, smart navy or black tailored suits, white blouses and perfectly manicured hands. She was charming, not only to his mother but to him. Gavin was a great believer now in the instinct for truth that a child can possess. He knew, despite her smiles and apparent interest in what his favourite lessons were at school and what sweets he liked best, that there was a falseness about her. It wasn't him she was wanting to impress. It was his father. It wasn't long before his father made her a partner in the business. Or at least she'd been given a sizeable portion of shares.

Then his father started travelling about on business again. Nicky went with him. There was no secret about it. She'd even said to his mother, 'I told Andrew you would understand, Jean. I can't be expected to cope with everything on my own. There are times when he must be there to do his share when there are so many overseas clients. And you're perfectly all right, aren't you, darling?'

His mother had smiled and said, 'Of course.'

It was around that time that Gavin started to hate Nicola Dawson. His mother's eyes were constantly sad now. He could see her withdraw into herself as if trying to cope with her vulnerability, trying to protect herself from hurt.

She was visibly shrunken, a pathetic little figure in her wheelchair, but still the most beautiful woman in the world to her son. She could no longer hold a book and so he read to her every evening. She told him in her sad, gentle way that she felt guilty keeping him in when he ought to be out playing with his friends.

'You're not keeping me in,' he protested. 'I *want* to read to you.'

And it was the truth. He'd never regretted one moment he'd ever spent with her.

While she was having a nap, he'd work out as best he could in the small gym his father had equipped in the basement of the house. His father used to work out regularly there. But not any more. He was hardly ever in the house. Or as often as not, when he was, Nicola Dawson was there too.

Gavin sweated on the treadmill and tried to lift weights just to prove to his mother that she didn't need to worry about him. He was well and fit despite not running around outside kicking a ball about with the other young lads. He played hard at school. That was enough.

His mind always stalled at this point. What exactly had happened to make his mother take her final decision? He didn't know. Down through the years, it had tormented him. She had a cold that day and was confined to bed. Had she been depressed because she felt this might be the beginning of longer spells in bed? Or had there been some last straw? Some particular incident? And had it something to do with Nicola Dawson? He could not prove anything, even to himself. Nonetheless he felt it in his bones.

It had been summer. He'd been on holiday from school. It had been decided that his father and Nicola would take him and Harry, the son of a friend of his father's, to Crieff for the day.

'We've a couple of business appointments there, Jean,' his father explained. 'Some clients to meet. So while Nicky and I are busy, the boys can make full use of the facilities. There's a pool, a gym, horse riding, go-karts and God knows what else in the Hydro. It'll do Gavin good. He's been hanging around at home far too much.'

'Yes, I know,' Jean said, then turned to him. To this day he could still see her sweet smile. 'You go, darling. I want you to go and have a wonderful time.'

He had opened his mouth to protest but she'd added, 'Please. For my sake.'

And so he'd gone.

Gavin had been waiting in the hall with Harry and talking about go-kart racing when he noticed Nicola Dawson come out of his mother's room. It was just to the left of the landing at the top of the stairs. His father had been getting the car from the garage. Anxiety or suspicion must have registered on his face because Nicola Dawson had laughed and said,

'She's fine. I was just checking she was all right and saying goodbye.'

But what else had she said? Over and over again, he'd asked himself that. She had said more than just an innocent goodbye. She'd said something that had tipped his mother over the edge. He felt sure of it.

He had not said goodbye to his mother. Not properly.

In Crieff he'd thoroughly enjoyed the day. He and Harry had competed in the pool and raced in the go-karts. They'd also tried to race on horseback. But the horses, as if well versed in the foolish recklessness of boys, had refused to go any faster than a leisurely trot.

It was only on the journey to Crieff, and back home that evening, that Gavin noticed the intimate looks between his father and Nicola Dawson, and the way she kept touching him.

Then the nightmare. The arrival home. The distraught

202

nurse. She'd been down in the kitchen having her supper when it happened.

'I had settled Mrs Cameron down for the night. I thought she was sleeping before I even left the bedroom. I went up to check her just a few minutes ago and found her lying on the bathroom floor.'

Nicola Dawson immediately took charge.

'Have you phoned the doctor yet?'

'No, I've only just found her. I tried to – '

'Not in front of the boy,' Nicola Dawson interrupted. 'Gavin, you go through to the sitting room. Do as you're told,' she added sharply. 'Nurse, phone for the doctor. Use this phone. Andrew, we'd better go upstairs and see what's happened.'

It was only later, at his mother's funeral, that he heard in snatches of hushed conversation that his mother had committed suicide. She'd struggled out of bed, somehow crawled and dragged herself to the adjoining bathroom, and hauled herself up to reach his father's razor, with which she'd hacked at her wrists. He couldn't bear to think of the dreadful struggle she must have had to get from her bed to the bathroom.

His poor mother. It was too terrible. And what had been her agony of mind? He couldn't bear it.

In an indecently short time, his father and Nicola Dawson were married. Gavin was thirteen years of age and had grown to hate both of them. Although his hatred towards his father frittered away and pity took its place after a few years.

Nicola Dawson was efficient and ruthless all right. Soon she was running the business, overruling his father at every turn. He could see it now, how she undermined him, how stressed he became. His heart attack had been inevitable. The funeral of her husband was barely over when Nicola Dawson got rid of her stepson. He didn't become stressed, didn't die. She didn't order him to leave his house. She just made it impossible for him to stay. It wasn't a home any more.

However, his father had not, thank God, allowed himself to be totally dominated to the extent of cutting his son out of his will. That was something Nicola Dawson hadn't known about. Her face had hardened to hide her fury when the will was read. Perhaps his father had lied to her, had promised his shares would go to her. That was obviously what she'd expected.

But they'd gone to him.

And he had made good use of them. By God, he had. One way or another, by fair means and foul, he'd acquired in time enough of the shares of the others on the board to control the business. He'd got her out. He'd ruined her by being even more ruthless than she was. He'd never regretted one turn or twist of the knife.

He'd do it all over again, with equal vehemence and without a single regret.

Chapter Thirty-Two

'I wonder what's up with Bec?' It was Sunday and Mary and Kate were going for a bus to take them to Queen's Park. The invitation had not been for Sunday lunch. Not that Sunday lunch invitations came that often but they had been extended occasionally in the past. This time there had been an urgent phone call from Uncle Willie asking if they'd come *after* lunch on Sunday.

'Poor Bec's in such a state she's fit for nothing.'

'How? Whit's up wi' her?' Mary had asked.

'Just come. It's an emergency. She needs your help.'

Mary had asked George to accompany them but he'd said he'd work to do and just to go on their own. Kate noticed her father was always either working or in the pub these days. He was hardly ever in the house.

It had been decided in view of Aunty Bec's unknown emergency that it would be better to leave Christine with Liz and Tommy. Anyway, it was a terrible day. It was pelting with rain, and so windy that Mary and Kate had to abandon their umbrellas. They got to the bus stop and stood shivering and straining their heads to see if any buses were appearing on the horizon. On a Sunday, buses were always few and far between. Nevertheless, they seemed to be waiting an unusually long time.

'Aw we need is a puncture an' a wean throwin' up in the back an' it'd be jist like oor holidays.'

They'd once hired a car and gone on holiday to Butlin's with Tommy, Liz and the children. It had been a memorable occasion.

'Is it no' high time,' Mary went on, 'that ye got yersel' a car?'

'Maybe.'

'There's nae reason why no'. Ye're jist bein' mean.'

'I'm not mean with you or anybody else in the family, am I? And I pay good wages.'

'Ah know, bit ye're mean wi' yersel', hen. An' why? That's whit ah'd like tae know. Dinnae try tae kid me that ye're short o' a bob or two.'

Kate could have said, Money makes me feel secure. Spending it makes me feel painfully anxious. But she knew her mother wouldn't understand. She hardly understood her feelings herself. Instead she murmured,

'I suppose it would be a good business investment, and more convenient for me getting around. But I've been thinking of a van first, Mammy.'.

'Ye've *got* a van.'

'I know. Tommy did a good job converting Joe's van. But I need two on the road now. A good custom-made one with the logo professionally done on it.'

'Whit on earth are ye gonnae dae wi' two?'

'Well, I know we've been managing all right delivering orders for private parties and special occasions, but I thought if I could get outlets in other shops. In other towns, I mean. That's what I'm hoping to aim for.'

A bus arrived at last. The platform was high and Mary had a struggle to heave herself up on to it.

'Who the hell designed these buses?' she shouted at the driver.

The driver eyed her.

'Somebody who made a better job of it than the one that designed your legs.'

'Cheeky bugger,' Mary said.

Kate dropped coins into the box and took the tickets from the machine.

'On you go, Mammy.'

'Any seats up the stair?' Mary wanted to know.

'Aye,' the driver said, 'but there's a bum on every one o' them.'

'Is that no' terrible – the cheek ye've tae pit up wi' on buses? It's high time ye got a car.'

'All right, Mammy. Just sit down, for goodness sake.'

It was always the same when she went out with her mother. Her mother either got into conversation with perfect strangers during which she related her whole life's history. Or, to Kate's acute embarrassment, she confided the most intimate details of the entire family. Or she had head-on confrontations. Also with perfect strangers.

The last time they'd been on a bus together, it had stopped at traffic lights and remained standing after the lights turned to green. Mary had jabbed the emergency bell. The driver scrambled furiously from his cabin, glared down the bus and shouted, 'Who rang that emergency bell?'

'Ah did,' Mary shouted back. 'Ah thought ye must be takin' root.'

'There's a bloody big van stuck in front of me. I couldn't move.'

'Aye well, aw right then.'

As the driver made to get back into his seat, he said, 'Don't you dare touch that bell again.'

Mary stuck out a defiant chin. 'Ah will if ah want.'

Kate was always having to smooth over such altercations or apologise for her mother.

'It must be something pretty bad,' Kate said, her thoughts returning to the invitation to Queen's Park. It wasn't so much an invitation really, as a desperate plea. 'I would have thought that Uncle Willie and Aunty Bec would rather die than ask help from the likes of us – never mind admit that something had gone wrong with them. What was it Uncle Willie said again?'

'Poor Bec's in such a state, she's fit for nothing. It's an emergency. She needs your help. That was his exact words. Maybe Bec's got the flu.'

'I shouldn't think so. No, Uncle Willie would want to look after her.'

'Well, we'll know soon enough, hen.'

They got off the bus at the top of Victoria Road, facing the park gates. The trees were violently agitating in the wind. Round the corner in Queen's Drive, because of the bluster, they had to shut their umbrellas. Mary's had been in danger of whisking her off her feet like an ancient Mary Poppins.

Kate pressed a button next to the name Murray and leaned close. A voice in her ear crackled:

'Is that you, Mary?'

'It's Kate, Uncle Willie, but Mammy's here as well.'

'Come away up.'

There was a grinding sound and Kate pushed open the door. The Murrays lived 'one up'.

'The best place,' Aunty Bec always boasted. 'Not too low or too high. Just nice. And such a perfect view of everything that goes on in the park.'

Inside the close there was a church-like silence. Even Mary's voice dropped to a whisper. The religious atmosphere was heightened by the crimson, royal blue and gold glass window on the landing.

Uncle Willie had the door open and was ready and impatiently waiting for them while they were still climbing the stairs.

'Whit's up wi' Bec?' Mary asked as soon as she'd set foot in the house.

'Come on through. She's in the lounge.'

Mary had in time followed the Murray example and changed to 'lunch' and 'dinner', and even 'sitting room' instead of the more common 'front room'. She drew the line at 'lounge', however.

'She's not in bed then?'

Looking a mixture of tragedy and harassment, Willie led them through the big square hall (another term Mary could not bring herself to adopt. The lobby would always be the lobby in Possilpark.)

Bec was reclining on the sofa like a beached whale.

Kate said, 'Daddy sends his apologies, Aunty Bec.'

Bec nodded. 'Tell him not to worry. There's nothing he could do.'

'Whit could he no' dae,' Mary queried. 'Whit's yer problem, Bec?'

'It's not me. It's Sandra.'

'Sandra?' Kate echoed.

'She's got in with bad company,' Willie explained. 'She's not herself at all these days. She's normally such a bright, happy girl and keen on her studies. Recently she's gone all moody and sullen. She's even been bad-tempered with her mother.'

Sandra? Kate thought. The perfect one?

Bec's eyes filled with tears.

'Sandra's always been too innocent and trusting for her own good. These people have talked her into taking drugs. The last time she was here, I found . . .' Bec choked on the words, 'a syringe in her room. We tried to talk to her, didn't we, Willie? But she won't listen to me or Willie and we just don't speak the same language as these people. They think they're something but they're just awful, aren't they, Willie?'

'Terrible!'

'I thought you'd be able to do something, Kate. You know about these things.'

'I don't know anything about drugs,' Kate protested.

'And the incredible thing is,' Bec went on, 'they're all from the university. We couldn't believe it at first, could we, Willie?'

'Unbelievable.'

'University students! What's the world coming to? It's the one place we thought our Sandra would be safe. Didn't we, Willie?'

'In Edinburgh.'

Mary said, 'Ah'm sorry tae hear aboot this an' ah know how ye must feel. Bit ah cannae see whit me or Kate can dae tae help ye.'

Bec heaved herself with some difficulty into a sitting position.

'Go and talk to her, Kate. Please! Your Uncle Willie and me are so worried and upset. You could have a word as well, Mary. Tell her how you felt when Kate got into trouble and how it nearly killed you.'

'It did nothin' o' the kind,' Mary said indignantly. 'Anyway, as Kate said, she wisnae intae drugs.' After a moment's hesitation, she sighed. 'Aw right, ah'll try ma best tae talk tae her if ye really think it might help. An' so will Kate.'

'But Mammy . . .'

'Shut up. Ye'll dae whit ye're telt.'

Kate rolled her eyes. Anybody would think, to hear her mother talk, that she was still a child. It was infuriating.

'Where is she the now?' Mary asked.

'Willie?' Bec sank back again. Willie passed over a piece of paper to Mary.

'That's the address of the flat she's moved into. It belongs to a couple of very odd people.'

Bec said, 'It's the drugs, Mary. I never thought – I mean, in Possilpark as it is now, yes. But fancy people like that in the university.'

'In Edinburgh!' Willie said, and Mary tutted,

'Fancy!'

But her sarcasm was lost on Willie and Bec.

Chapter Thirty-Three

Mary and Kate were persuaded to go straight to Edinburgh that very day.

'It only takes forty minutes in the train,' Bec pointed out. 'Forty-five at most. And Willie'll drive you to the station, won't you, Willie?'

'You've time to catch the three o'clock.'

'And Sunday is the only day you don't work,' Bec said.

This wasn't true. They didn't work in the shop but they did work at home on Sundays.

'Aw right,' Mary said. 'But ah'm no' promisin' any magic results, hen.'

'She'll listen to you and Kate.'

As Kate remarked afterwards in the train, 'I don't know why Aunty Bec kept saying that. Sandra's never listened to either of us before.'

'This time she'll listen tae ma fist.'

'You wouldn't!'

'You jist watch me.'

'No, Mammy, you mustn't. It was one thing battering me but she could have you up for assault if you raise your hand to her.'

'She'll no' be fit tae dae anythin' once ah'm finished wi' her. An' ah never battered you. Ah jist boxed yer ears a couple o' times when ye deserved it.'

Kate cast her eyes heavenwards.

'A couple of times? And it wasn't just my ears. Or even just my eyes. I've obviously got a better memory than you.'

'Aye, well, you jist watch yersel' or ye'll get wan in the eye right now.'

They found the flat not far from the university. It was in an old and run-down tenement building that looked as if it was in the process of being refurbished. Scaffolding with planks across it laced the outside and darkened the entry to the narrow close.

'Up the stair,' Bec said. Mary led the way, her high heels making a determined clicking on the worn grey stone. 'This place must be ancient. It's got that old fusty kind o' smell. Probably rotten damp.'

She clattered the letterbox of a door that had three names written on a piece of cardboard.

'Wan's a man. Dae ye see that?'

Kate saw it.

The door was eventually opened by a crop-haired girl with an earring through her nose. But she had a very proper voice.

'Yes? What do you want?'

'Ah want tae see ma niece, Sandra Murray.'

'Just a moment and I'll see if – '

'Get oot ma road.' Mary pushed the girl impatiently aside and entered the lobby. Kate followed.

'Would ye look at this lobby. Ye couldnae swing a cat in here. It wouldnae see where it wis goin' for a start.'

'Here, just a moment,' the girl protested, and then in a louder voice, 'Nigel!'

A young man appeared from a room nearby. He had long dreadlocks and was wearing a purple kaftan. Sandra could be seen behind him.

'Have we a problem?' Nigel asked, also in what Mary later referred to as 'a right toffee-nosed' voice.

'Aye, you huv but ah huvnae.'

Kate got into the room before her mother.

'Sandra,' she said. 'Your mother and father are terribly worried and upset.'

Sandra shrugged.

'Too bad.'

Quick as a flash, Mary's fist shot out and made Sandra's nose suddenly explode with blood. Sandra howled, and stumbled about like a blind woman, groping for tissues and for her spectacles, which had leapt from her face with the impact of the blow.

'Ah'll "too bad" ye. Dinnae you dare talk aboot yer good mammy an' daddy like that, ye stupit, spoiled, selfish wee brat. It's high time ye grew up.'

'Nigel,' Sandra spluttered.

'Now look here . . .' Nigel began but Mary interrupted: 'See her?' She pointed at Kate. 'She's as big as you an' she's already kilt wan man. She's gonnae make mincemeat o' you any minute now, son.'

'My God, Nigel, that's the one.' A bell had obviously rung in the cropped head of the girl. 'She stabbed her husband to death. For goodness sake, just leave them to it. It's none of our business.'

'Yes, you're right. Let's get out of here.'

And they went, shouting as they did so, 'We'll be in the pub, Sandra.'

Kate was furious.

'Don't you ever do that to me again.'

'Aw, shut up,' Mary said, then grabbed Sandra by the front of her jersey. 'Ye're comin' back tae Glasgow wi' us an' ye'd better no' give me any more o' yer cheek.'

'You can't – ' Sandra began, but was given such a blow on the side of the head that she reeled backwards and sideways, then bumped down into a sitting position on the floor. There was an ominous crunch. Sandra wailed broken-heartedly, 'My spectacles!'

'Mammy!' Kate protested. 'Stop this at once.' She struggled to hoist Sandra to her feet.

'My spectacles!' Sandra wailed again.

'You'll get wan as well if ye're no' careful,' Mary warned Kate. 'Neither o' us huv time tae waste wi' this stupit cow.' Then to Sandra, 'You're comin' home wi' us right now an' if ah hear any more o' this drug nonsense an' you skivin' off yer studies, ah'll come tae that uni if need be an' batter the livin' daylights out o' ye. If ye cannae behave yersel' away from home, then ye'll just huv tae travel tae the uni every day from Glasgow, until ye can. Now get yer belongin's gathered an' pit yer coat on. We've a train tae catch.'

'I can't see a thing without my spectacles.'

Sandra looked dazed but, holding a bunch of tissues against her nose, she allowed herself to. be led by Kate through to the bedroom. They managed, Mary and Kate between them, to get Sandra's bag packed, her nose stopped bleeding, and her cleaned up before hustling her off to Waverley Station and the Glasgow train.

'I can't see a thing.'

'Aw, shut up,' Mary said. 'Ye'll just huv tae get new specs. It's no' the end o' the world.'

Once back in the flat in Queen's Park and after Sandra had been given a rapturous welcome, Mary said,

'Now listen tae me, Bec, an' you too, Willie. Ah reckon Sandra needs a bit o' help wi' her wee drug problem. An' the silly cow's broken her glasses. So ye'd better make an appointment fur her tae see a doctor an' an optician right away. OK?'

'Absolutely,' Willie said.

'And she's no' got long tae dae at the uni so she'd be mair able tae pit aw her attention tae her studies if she stayed here till she passes her exams. After that, she can stay in a flat if she wants. She'll maybe have grown up enough by then tae be able tae look after hersel'. OK?'

'Absolutely.'

'We won't forget this, Mary,' Bec said, her eyes swimming. 'My mother always said you were a good soul at heart and she was right.'

'Aye, OK. Well, if ye've any mair trouble jist let me know an' ah'll be over here like a shot tae sort Sandra out.' She turned to Sandra.

'Ah want you tae remember that, hen. An' tae know that next time ah'll no' be sae easy on ye. You'd better believe that.'

They left Sandra weeping against her mother's ample

bosom and Uncle Willie patting her comfortingly on the head.

'Fancy you telling that man, and talking about me like that. I was absolutely mortified.' Kate couldn't get over it.

'Och, everybody knows. Wasn't it in all the papers at the time. An' on the telly. An' on the wireless. Ye gave us a right showin' up. Talk aboot bein' mortified!'

Kate resisted the urge to press her case further. It never served any useful purpose to argue with her mother.

Instead, once they returned to Killearn Street and had a cup of tea and something to eat, they got stuck into the jam making again.

'Ah wonder where yer daddy's gone,' Mary said at last. 'He'll be needin' his dinner.'

'I expect he's had something to eat in the pub. He's not a child, Mammy. He can look after himself.'

Just then, the doorbell went.

'He'll huv forgotten his key. Yer daddy's gettin' awfae absentminded these days.'

But it was Liz delivering Christine.

'Hello, darling.' Kate greeted the little girl with a hug and a kiss. 'I was beginning to think you'd gone to bed with your wee cousins at Aunty Liz's house.'

'She wanted to,' Liz laughed. 'She likes the company. But I said her mammy would be missing her.'

'See!' Christine said. 'I told you she wouldn't. She's busy making her jam.'

Kate was taken aback.

'Of course I missed you, darling. I always miss you. It's just that Mummy has to work to make enough money for us both.'

Christine sighed. It was a sigh too old for her years. Then she turned and went through to her bedroom.

'Night, night,' Liz called. 'See you tomorrow.'

'Night, night, Aunty Liz.'

Worriedly, Kate followed Christine through to the bedroom. But she still heard Liz say 'She's such an old-fashioned wee soul,' Liz confided. 'Many a good laugh we have at her. We all dote on her. Tommy and I couldn't be more fond of that wee girl if she was one of our own.'

Chapter Thirty-Four

Kate had gone to the food exhibition in the Scottish Exhibition, Concert and Conference Centre with her mother and father, and Tommy. They'd bought tickets there for the Food Industry dinner that was to be held in the banqueting hall of the City Chambers. She'd got tickets for Marilyn and two of the staff as well.

'Marilyn'll love that,' Mary said. 'Ye know how the lassie loves gettin' dressed up.'

Liz didn't want to go and insisted she'd rather stay at home and look after the children. Kate had got the two staff tickets for a special treat. They'd put the names of the bakers, the cooks and the confectionery girls into a hat and the first two names drawn out by Tommy were to have the tickets. A great cheer had gone up when the winners were found to be Josie McBeth and Davina Conway, two of the women belonging to the Militant Feminist Group.

Josie and Davina had grabbed Tommy and joyously danced around with him. He was thankful when he managed to escape to his own territory in the front shop. He was often tormented and harassed by the girls if he ventured through to the big cavern of the back, or in the early mornings when the girls arrived and trooped through the front. One of them had actually groped him in the groin in the passing. Another time one of them had nipped his bum. Their continual bawdy and sexual comments and suggestions were also hard to bear.

As he'd often said to Liz and she'd echoed his sentiments,

'I don't know what women are coming to these days. It's terrible the way they carry on.'

He had been too ashamed and embarrassed to make an issue of the girls' behaviour and complain to Kate; and he certainly wouldn't complain to his mother. He could hear the cries of 'Mummy's boy' that would follow him thereafter. All the same, it was sexual harassment, and he shouldn't have to put up with it. He could just imagine the fuss and commotion there would be if it was happening the other way around – he'd be arrested, fined or put in prison. They'd force him out of his job with their raging and rampaging, and media publicity.

They'd also demand compensation. But sexual harassment was sexual harassment, and the same treatment should be meted out to all perpetrators, whether they were male or female. This had obviously never occurred to these girls.

Tommy had been looking forward to the posh dinner in the City Chambers. He'd never been in the banqueting hall before. He feared however that his evening would be spoiled by Josie and Davina. He could only hope that because Kate would be present, and Kate after all was their boss, they would behave themselves. Kate would be, even in such a social situation, very much in charge. She would also be well-mannered and composed. Hopefully her employees would follow her example.

The City Chambers was an ornate and imposing building opened in 1888 by Queen Victoria. It was situated on the eastern side of George Square in the centre of the city. On the site had once been the town house belonging to the Alexanders of Ballochmyle. It was to the daughter of this house, Wilhemina Alexander, that Robert Burns had addressed his song, 'The Bonnie Lass o' Ballochmyle'.

Tommy always derived pleasure in thinking that the statue of Robert Burns was the most democratic of all the statues in the square. Unlike the others, it had been built from the money of ordinary people who wanted to see a statue of their poet: more than forty thousand had contributed the shilling subscription. The statue had been unveiled on the poet's birthday on 25 January. For the occasion, the societies and trades of the city had gathered in Glasgow Green and marched in procession to George Square. Some thirty thousand were waiting for them. No other statue in George Square, including the one of Sir Walter Scott on its pillar high above all the others, had had such a reception.

Tommy gazed at the Burns statue with awe and reverence as well as affection every time he passed it. He and his mother, father, Marilyn and Kate met Josie and Davina outside the entrance to the building. He groaned inside at the sight of the girls. They were beginning to look like men. Josie had short cropped hair. Davina had her head shaved and an artificial yellow down covered her skull. Both had confident swaggers. Josie was dressed in a black velvet trouser suit, white shirt and black satin bow-tie. Davina also wore trousers. Her jacket was cream-coloured. She too had a bow-tie but it was purple. It made a horrible clash with her garish yellow scalp.

At least Marilyn looked feminine in her clingy pale blue satin dress that showed her shapely figure off to full advantage. Kate looked very sophisticated in her black low-cut dress and gold and black choker high round her neck. Over the dress, she'd slung a shimmering gold lamé jacket.

Inside the building all was resplendent with Italian marble. His father said,

'This entrance hall was built to the plan of a Roman temple of long ago. See that ceiling and those domes? That's Venetian mosaic and it was made up of half-inch cubes, every one put in by hand.'

There were gasps of admiration. George was more like his old self, tall and distinguished in his hired dinner jacket, white stiff front and black bow-tie. His thick bristle of hair had been Brylcreemed down and his moustache neatly trimmed. Tommy thought he'd lost a bit of weight though. His mother had taken a lot of trouble with her hair. He'd noticed recently that quite a few grey streaks were showing but she must have dyed them because tonight her hair was all glorious red, a startling contrast to her green dress.

The banqueting hall was up a staircase of staggering proportions. In a reception salon milling with guests and waitresses bearing trays of drinks, lists of names and table numbers were displayed. Kate took charge.

'You get some wine while I go and see where we've to sit.'

In a few minutes she'd returned.

'Damnation!'

'What's up?' her mother asked.

'Gavin Cameron is one of the people at our table.'

'Ooh!' Marilyn caught a giggle against her palm. Kate gave her a reproving look.

'There's nothing funny about that, Marilyn. We're supposed to be here to enjoy ourselves and I don't think he'll be very good company.'

'Och well,' Mary said, 'he's no' the only other wan at the table, is he?'

'No,' Kate grudgingly agreed.

'Well, just ignore him if you cannae stand him.'

'I think he's gorgeous.' Marilyn acquired a dreamy look. 'I don't care what you think of him, Kate.'

'We're not *his* favourite people, Marilyn. That shop next door has lost a lot of business because of us.'

Josie downed her drink and immediately picked up another from the tray of a waitress who happened to be passing.

'I don't care a damn what he thinks. I'm here for the big nosh-up.'

Just then a man in a scarlet tailcoat and white gloves called out above the babble of voices:

'Ladies and gentlemen, dinner is served. Will you please make your way through to the banqueting hall.'

As they entered the magnificent banqueting hall with its sparkling chandeliers, Davina cried out, 'What a place!'

The richly coloured murals all around showed the progress of the city but it was the glorious ceiling paintings that caught George's eye.

'Isn't that really mind-boggling? I'd love to have gone to Florence and seen all the art and sculptures there.'

'Ah never knew ye wanted tae dae that,' Mary said.

George sighed.

'It used to be a dream of mine.'

'Why did ye no' say? We could've gone there instead o' Blackpool wan year.'

'Mary, you've never even liked going to the Kelvingrove Art Galleries.'

'Och, but ye could've wandered roon the Galleries, while ah stretched masel' oot on the beach. We still could huv oor holidays there. Maybe no' this summer wi' aw the work we've got lined up, but next year. OK?'

He sighed and Tommy felt sorry for his father. He'd never thought of him having dreams of faraway places. Possilpark was his world, his territory, and he had always lorded over it with pride. Only recently Kate had been talking about them all moving to a bigger house – to some place posh like Bearsden – and his father had looked quite panic-stricken. He'd said he couldn't leave his customers, his pals, his local. Once Gentleman George was a happy man. Now there was a sad, anxious look in his eyes. It made Tommy feel uneasy.

There were some people already seated at table number nine when Kate found it, three men and two women. One of the men was Gavin Cameron. He and the other men rose slightly until Kate, her mother and the girls had settled in their seats. Marilyn was obviously delighted to find her name on a card next to Cameron's. They all made the necessary introductions. Soon everyone was enjoying the food and relaxed in pleasant conversation.

Nevertheless, Kate was glad she was at the opposite side of the table from Cameron. She couldn't deny that he looked very handsome in his dinner jacket, the white of his shirt front accentuating the tan of his skin. But she'd no wish for an unpleasant confrontation to spoil the evening. A couple of times he'd flashed a dark glance across at her. There was unmistakable dislike in his eyes. She'd seen that look before but now she experienced a shock that disturbed her. Sometimes they all engaged in general conversation.

But more often than not, Marilyn had Cameron's whole attention.

Mary had been laughing about how they didn't know 'where tae put oorsel's in the house these days for bakin' an' cookin' an' jam makin'. Sittin' here at our leisure the night is a great treat for us. Oor table back in the house is that cluttered wi' jam jars an' God knows aw whit we've tae eat standin' up. Half the time, we've tae balance plates on oor han's like bloomin' jugglers!'

This was an exaggeration but Kate let it pass. However, she was beginning to worry about the amount of wine her mother was drinking. But Mary was obviously enjoying herself and so Kate tried to relax and keep smiling.

In the ladies' room after the dinner a shiny-eyed Marilyn announced that Gavin Cameron was seeing her home.

'He seems to fancy me. Who would have believed it?'

I would, Kate thought with a sudden bitterness that surprised her. I knew you were exactly the type he'd go for.

Chapter Thirty-Five

'Look, we're obliged to call and tell you that an allegation has been made – '

'What?' Kate stared at the man. 'Are you from the CID?'

'I'm an environmental health officer from the Council.'

'I don't understand. What allegation?'

'You are the owner of the specialist food shop called Gallacher's in Argyle Street?'

'Yes, but it's all legal and above board. It's registered with the local authorities as a food business.'

'Can I come in?'

'Why?'

'I want to inspect your kitchen.'

Kate could hardly believe her ears.

'Here?'

'Yes. If you refuse, I'll be forced to take steps to make an entry.'

'What's this all about? Who made an allegation of what?'

'I'm not at liberty to mention any names.'

Just then her mother came through the lobby to see what was going on.

'Is somethin' up, hen?'

Kate kept her attention fixed on the man but she said, 'Could you credit it, Mammy. Somebody has reported us to the Council.'

'Eh? Whit fur?'

'Something about your kitchen. He wants to inspect it.'

'Ma kitchen!'

'Yes, here and now.'

'Whit a bloody cheek. Ah'm insultit.'

'You'd better come in.' Kate stood aside and allowed the man to enter. 'The kitchen's through there.'

'Who wis it?' Mary asked. 'Jist let me get ma hands on them.'

'He's not saying but I can make a good guess. At the dinner in the City Chambers you were talking about us making jam and cooking at home, remember?'

'Oh aye . . . but surely . . .'

'Who was the only person at the table who'd want us shut down?'

'No' that Mr Cameron?'

'Of course, it must have been him. Who else could it have been?'

'An' here wis me thinkin' ye were bein' too hard on the man. He wis that nice tae me, chatting away quite the thing. The two-faced bastard!'

'Don't worry, it'll be all right.'

She went through to the kitchen.

'Look here, Mr . . .?'

'Johnston.'

'Mr Johnston, there's been a misunderstanding. What happens here is that my mother and I experiment with different recipes on a small scale and when we get it right, we then transfer the recipes, I repeat, the *recipes* – worked out in bigger quantities – to our business. The actual food we experiment with here is just eaten by the family. Either by us here or by my brother Tommy and his family. Sometimes we hand something in for a treat to a couple of the old bachelor neighbours. And to old Mrs Dooley in the bottom flat. There's no crime in that, is there?'

'No, no. It's only if you were selling food in your business that was cooked in these premises.'

'Well then . . .'

Mr Johnston was very pleasant and reasonable, and explained the legal situation in detail. He even stayed for a friendly chat, a cup of tea and a scone spread with their homemade jam. In fact, he enjoyed three scones and two cups of tea and seemed quite reluctant to leave in the end.

'Nice man,' Mary said after he'd gone and she'd given

him a cheery wave from the front-room window. 'But fancy that Cameron man doin' a sneaky thing like that. If he wisnae sae big ah'd black his eye fur him. But ah'd need a ladder tae reach it.'

'Just leave him to me, Mammy. My tongue will reach him all right. I'll take great pleasure in letting him know what I think of him.'

She went next door to Caledonia the very next morning, only to be told that Mr Cameron wasn't there. He was up north at one of his food gift shops.

Returning to Gallacher's, she said to Tommy and Marilyn, 'Isn't that damnable, he's up north at one of his other shops and they don't know when he'll be back.'

She hadn't yet had the chance to explain to either Tommy or Marilyn.

'Cameron? What do you want him for?' Tommy said.

'I'll explain in a minute. I've a telephone call to make first.'

She went through to her office and dialled the Inverness number the Caledonia girl had given her. She couldn't wait another minute to vent her fury on Cameron. She got through on the phone to him within seconds.

'Kate Gallacher here. I just want you to know what a despicable creep I think you are. The inspector from the Environmental Health Department wouldn't give me a name but I knew it could only be you who reported us. Well, I'm very glad to be able to tell you that your nasty underhand little ploy didn't work.'

'Are you quite finished?' The deep voice was smooth, tightly controlled.

'Yes, I don't have any desire to chat with you. As I say, I only phoned to tell you what a slime-ball I think you are.'

With that, and without giving him a chance to reply, she hung up. She was satisfied but shaken. So shaken that she forgot her promise to return to the front shop and explain to Tommy and Marilyn. She just sat trying to take deep, calming breaths. Then she went through to the back to help her mother and the girls. She always forgot all her worries and troubles once she got into a kitchen and started to cook. It wasn't until the coffee break, when Marilyn came through to the back, that Cameron's name was mentioned.

'You said you were going to tell us why you went next door to see Mr Cameron.' Marilyn settled down on a stool to enjoy her mug of coffee.

'Oh that?' Kate shrugged. 'It's been dealt with. I phoned him and told him what a creep and slime-ball he was.'

Marilyn was shocked.

'Kate! How could you? Why should you say such awful things? I just don't understand you.'

Kate told her about what had happened the previous evening.

'But why should you think it was him?'

'He was the only one who knew about us cooking and making jam at home.'

'Of course he wasn't,' Marilyn said indignantly. 'Really, Kate, you're terrible at times.'

'What do you mean – of course he wasn't?'

'Lots of customers know for a start. I always chat to the customers and only the other day that awful Mrs Soames-Petrie was in. You know, that hoity-toity woman who wears such expensive-looking hats. I've told you about her before. The one who said we should have a chair for customers to sit on and you put a chair out there after that.'

Kate's heart began to palpitate. She felt sick.

'You told her? Why should you tell her such a thing, Marilyn?'

'Well, I didn't actually tell her. She was sitting there waiting to be served like the Queen Mother, only not as pleasant looking. I was serving another customer and chatting to her. This customer was saying how she just loved our marmalades and jams and I said, as I've said before to other customers, that you and your mammy made the preserves first of all in your wee kitchen in Killearn Street in Possilpark. I remember that toffee-nosed one butting in on that occasion, repeating in a horrified voice, "Possilpark!" as if it was the name of a sewer or something. You should have seen her face.'

'Oh God! You think it could have been her?'

Marilyn said, 'Well, it's just as likely to be her, in fact *more* likely, I'd say, than Gavin Cameron.'

'But he's the only one who'd benefit if we were shut down. Why should Mrs Soames-Petrie report us?'

'Because she's a nasty woman, that's all.'

'No, it must have been him,' Kate said.

'Now hang on there, hen.' Her mother entered the conversation. 'I think maybe ye were a wee bit hasty.'

'He's a businessman, Mammy, and he's furious at us being here. He warned me right at the beginning that he was going to do something about it. The very first time I met him. Remember, Marilyn, you were there, weren't you? Remember how angry he was?'

Marilyn shook her head.

'Kate, you're just not wanting to face the truth. You've made a mistake, I'm sure of it. You'll have to apologise to Gavin.'

Gavin, was it now? Kate thought bitterly. He was trying to undermine her, even by trying to get her family on his side.

'No way! I meant every word I said. And you can tell him that, Marilyn, the next time you see him. You will, no doubt, be going out with him again?'

Marilyn flushed.

'As a matter of fact, I am. I don't see any reason why I shouldn't.'

'No, you wouldn't. You've always been a bit naive.'

And stupid, she thought as she turned away and went back to shut herself in her office room.

Chapter Thirty-Six

A really nasty piece of work, Cameron thought, as he replaced the receiver. He felt annoyed that she should think him capable of playing such a dirty trick. He had every intention of getting her off his back – and that meant getting her out of the shop next door to his Glasgow branch of Caledonia. If he had wanted to report her to the Environmental Health people, however, he wouldn't have made any secret about it. As it was, he had other plans. He remembered when he'd leased his Glasgow shop and the lease had been terminated, the premises had been put up for sale on the open market. The shop next door was on the books of the same factor and he'd learned by a few discreet enquiries that it wouldn't be long until the same procedures would happen with the Gallacher's premises. The lease had just about run out. The Gallacher woman would be notified and the premises would be open to offers, exactly as his had been. He had topped all other offers for the Caledonia premises and he'd do the same with the Gallacher's place. He didn't care what price the Gallacher woman offered, he'd top it. By God, he was looking forward to that. And it would all be perfectly legal and above board.

He would then extend his premises and create one big food gift shop in Argyle Street like his northern branch. He would see that Marilyn for one would not be out of a job. She was a very attractive girl and an asset behind any counter. They had been out a couple of times, once for a meal and on another occasion to the theatre. He had found her company uncomplicated and relaxing. Normally he never knew where he stood with young women. He had been out with girls who sported short tight skirts and low necklines and who'd clung to his arm walking along the street and wiggled close against his body while dancing with him at nightclubs. They'd invited him into their flats for coffee but afterwards, when he'd tried to come on to them, they'd slapped his face and gone all indignant and said things like, 'How dare you spoil our friendship?' A few of course had jumped him and dragged him to their beds the moment he'd set foot in their flats. But a man never knew nowadays what signals women were giving, or if they were giving any at all.

Marilyn was a sweet girl. He admired the way she spoke about her late husband. She'd obviously loved and admired him and been a totally devoted and loyal wife. She was a good listener too, and before he knew it, he was telling her about his mother. He even managed to tell her of his mother's terrible death.

'Oh Gavin . . .' Marilyn put her hand over his. 'I'm so sorry. It must have been dreadful for you.'

'It's a long time ago now. I was only a boy at the time.' He hesitated, then managed to confess, 'But I haven't completely got over it yet. Maybe I never will.'

'I know exactly how you feel. I can't imagine me ever completely getting over Joe. He had such a violent end for such a gentle, caring person. My gentle giant, I used to call him.'

He held her hand and she gazed at him with gratitude in her eyes.

'I've never told anyone that before. People don't take me seriously, you see. They think I'm just a silly, empty-headed person.'

'You're not silly, Marilyn. You're a beautiful, intelligent woman.'

The 'intelligent' bit was maybe going too far but he felt sorry for her. At the same time, she wasn't exactly stupid. He just wished she wouldn't pout so much and flutter her eyelashes and wiggle her bum while she walked like Marilyn Monroe. He could never be sure if it was natural to her or if she was adopting affectations and forever trying to appear like her namesake. He suspected it was all an act. When she was being serious, like when she was talking to him about her husband, she forgot her silly affectations. That way, she was, to him at least, much more attractive.

He phoned her when he returned to Glasgow and they went out for a drink. It was then she brought up the subject of the environmental health officer's visit to Killearn Street.

'Tell me the truth, Gavin. Did you report Kate?'

'No, damn it, I didn't.'

'I just wanted to hear you say it,' Marilyn soothed. 'I told Kate at the time that I *knew* it wasn't you. But she wouldn't listen.'

'You surprise me,' Cameron said sarcastically.

'I told her it was more likely to be my fault. In an indirect way, you understand. I chat a lot to the customers and I remember saying about Kate making things at home in Possilpark. Most of our customers are terribly nice but one nasty, snobby woman was shocked, I remember. I think it was her. Next time I saw that woman I made it clear to her that the things Kate makes at home, she keeps at home for the family. It's just – she likes to experiment so much with recipes. The environmental health man was awfully nice about it.'

'It hasn't occurred to her, I suppose, that she owes me an apology.'

'I told her that too, but she was so convinced that it must be you.' Marilyn smiled, widened her eyes and fluttered her lashes. 'Please accept my apology for her.'

'Let's change the subject,' Cameron said abruptly. 'I'm having another drink. How about you?'

The letter came as a terrible shock. Kate had been so busy she'd actually forgotten about the lease. Time had flown so quickly, she could hardly believe it. The premises were being put on the market for sale. That was one big problem. Most of the profit she'd made had been ploughed back into the business. She'd had new ovens installed, another big display freezer, another food mixer. She'd engaged the best signwriter in Glasgow to paint the Gallacher's sign in large gold letters above the shop. On the rich polished wood panel on one side of the big window was written, also in gold, 'Gallacher's make only genuine Scottish products free from any chemicals and additives. Gallacher's believe in good wholesome food.'

Her bank balance was admittedly more healthy than it had been when she'd first started in Argyle Street. It was not healthy enough, however, to raise the sum that no doubt would be required to purchase the place. She'd have to go to the bank manager again. Surely this time there would be no difficulty in getting a loan. The business was a huge success. She could show him the books to prove it. She knew the asking price: the problem would be if someone, or more than likely more than one person, started bidding and upped the price. She became frightened. She wondered if Cameron would want the premises. Then immediately she told herself not to be a fool. *Of course* he'd want the premises. Even if it was just to get her out. No doubt he'd have plenty of money in the bank to top any offer she made. And he would. She *knew* he would because he was a businessman and she was a businesswoman. She would do exactly the same thing if *his* shop came on the market.

Even if there had been no personal animosity between them, it would still be too good a business opportunity to miss. She sat with the letter shaking so much between her fingers that it dropped and fluttered to the floor at her feet.

'Whit's up?' Mary asked. 'Has somebody died or somethin'? Ye've gone as white as a sheet.'

'Read that.'

Mary picked up the letter. After a minute she said, 'Whit are ye gonnae dae?'

'He'll try and ruin me.'

'You mean Cameron, I suppose?'

'Who else?'

'Look, hen, Marilyn swears ye were wrong about him

231

before an' the chances are ye're bein' wrong about him again. There's an awfae stubborn bit about you. Once ye get an idea into that heid of yours, there's just no budgin' it.'

'Mammy, you don't get to where he is in business without being businesslike, not to mention ruthless. He's not going to pass up an opportunity like this. He'd be crazy if he did. I wouldn't.'

Mary stared at Kate, then shook her head.

'Naw, ah dinnae believe ye would. Sometimes ah worry about you, Kate.'

'Well, there's certainly a lot to worry about now.'

'Ah don't mean this business about the shop. Ah mean jist you. Maybe this is aw for the best.'

'Are you crazy?' Kate said, angry now. 'If I lose my business, all that I . . . we've all slaved for for years?'

'Well, maybe it would give ye the chance tae settle down like ordinary folk, meet a nice man, huv a nice wee home o' yer own. Be happy.'

'I *am* happy. At least I was until that horrible, macho man appeared on the scene. I hate the bastard. I hate him even more than I hated Pete.'

'Oh aye?'

'What's that tone of voice supposed to mean?'

'Well, ye cannae murder this yin. Wan could look like an accident. Two would be chancin' yer luck.'

'That's a horrible thing to say.'

'It wis a horrible thing tae dae, hen. Ah stood by ye at the time, as ye well know, but take ma advice – it's time ye got a grip o' yersel'. Stop aw this hatin'. Gettin' yersel' aw worked up again is no' gonnae dae ye wan bit o' good.'

'I'm not all worked up,' Kate said, her voice quiet now.

'Ah'm no' stupit, hen. Ah can see whit's in yer eyes.'

Kate immediately lowered her eyes.

'I'm in danger of losing my business, Mammy. You know how I love it. I truly enjoy it. It's my life.'

'Whit are ye gonnae dae?'

'I don't know. But I'll tell you one thing, Mammy, I'm not going to be beat.'

Chapter Thirty-Seven

It was like fucking a cushion. Marilyn was docile, pliant, yielding, everything except passionate. It amazed him how such a sexy-looking curvaceous woman could be so lacking in fire. She wanted to please him. He could see that. She would have allowed him to screw her inside out. That's the only way she knew. Just to lie there with a half-smile on her full rosebud lips, and be obliging. She even told him there was no need for him to bother about a condom. She'd taken the pill.

She made him a cup of coffee afterwards, her pink satin dressing-gown doing nothing to hide the voluptuous curves of her body. It clung round the shape of her nipples, accentuating them.

The small kitchen was claustrophobic. He was too big for it. And there was too much clutter. The bedroom had been even worse. The floor was strewn with Marilyn's shoes. The two chairs and the bed were draped with a colourful selection of clothes. The dressing table was covered with a layer of dust – or was it face powder? Boxes and tubes of make-up littered its surface, along with necklaces, earrings and bangles.

Marilyn cleared a place on the kitchen table.

'Sorry about all this. I didn't get time yesterday morning and I just had sandwiches in the shop at lunchtime. I meant to clear the place in the evening. But what with meeting you . . . It's not easy at any time to keep up with things when you're working full time.'

He agreed. Although his own large airy flat in the West End had never been allowed to get into such a state. He had a woman come in every day to hoover, polish and attend to the washing and ironing. Nevertheless, she had never had to face such an untidy mess. He was as methodical and well organised at home as he was at work. He always put his clothes away in drawers or in the wardrobe. He kept his newspapers and the *Radio Times* in a stand at the side of his favourite chair. His personal mail was stored in a file on a shelf in the room where he had his desk, his computer, and rows of books on shelves that reached to the ceiling. The room looked on to the Botanic Gardens, a quiet part at the back. It gave him a sense of calmness and peace to sit at his desk and gaze out at the lush greenery.

There was no calmness here. There was a sink at the kitchen window and when he leaned across it to look out, he saw an equally cluttered back green with overflowing bins and dogs rooting about. Children were chasing each other and yelling at the pitch of their voices. When he had been small, his mother had taken him to Sunday School. A quietness had reigned in their big villa and all around it. It had seemed as if the whole world was at peace. In the afternoons, if the weather was good, his father used to take them a run in his car. They'd go perhaps to the foot of the Campsies, park the car and then have a walk up the hills. He remembered the picnics and the wonderful view of the whole of Glasgow nestling in a valley surrounded by hills. Happy days.

Before Nicola Dawson came along.

'Let's take our coffee through to the front room.' Marilyn fluttered her eyelashes at him. Her eyes were shining. She was obviously having a whale of a time. 'You'll get a more comfortable seat there.'

Was he on top of the world along with Marilyn? Most men would be if they'd spent the night with such a beautiful woman. But he was a hard man to please. It had been pleasant. He liked the girl. Now, though, all he wanted was to get away somewhere on his own. Even just back to his cool, spacious, orderly flat. He seldom saw any of his neighbours. Most were from either the BBC or the university. Broadcasting House and the university dominated the area.

Students populated many of the houses which had been converted into smaller flats and bedsits to rent. But in the Crescent, the flats had been bought by professors and lecturers. Or by TV producers, directors and researchers.

Marilyn's front room, as she called it, looked on to the busy Saracen Street. Even on Sunday, it was noisy. Groups of unhealthy-looking youths were hanging about at the Cross, obviously buying drugs. Groups of girls too: some of them could still be of school age. It was hard to tell when their faces were plastered with paint.

'It's a lovely day,' Marilyn said breathlessly. 'I'd love to go for a run somewhere, wouldn't you?' She looked as eager as a puppy. If she'd had a tail, it would be wagging. He hesitated, then thought, What the hell. It was the least he could do to please her in return for her generous-hearted efforts to please him.

'All right,' he agreed. 'Get dressed and we'll drive out to the country somewhere. We could have lunch or afternoon tea if you like. Or both.'

She laughed with delight and clapped her hands.

'Oh thank you, Gavin. I haven't been out of the city for ages. Not even with Joe. Sunday was his busiest day on the van, you see. It must have been before we were married ... the last time ... I think we went a sail down the Clyde to Rothesay.'

She ran over and planted a brief kiss on him before darting away to dress. He could hear her singing in the bedroom. She took an age, every now and again appearing at the door to affect a pose and give a twirl and ask what he thought. He only needed to pause for a second to send her flying away again to try something else.

What he thought was she hadn't one item of clothing or footwear that was remotely suitable for a day in the country. No sensible shoes and trousers and skirts for easy walking. Nothing but high heels, short tight skirts and figure-hugging dresses. The next time she appeared he immediately said she looked wonderful. She did, but not for what he thought of as a day in the country.

However, she was so happy and excited, he had to laugh along with her. It was like taking a child out for a special treat. And she was so appreciative, so grateful. He quite enjoyed it in the end. She'd tucked into the meal in the small hotel with eye-rolling, lip-smacking pleasure. Later she took off her high-heeled sandals and gambolled about on the grass by the lochside and even paddled into the icy water with screams of joy.

She'd asked him to stay the night again once they'd returned to the flat.

'No, I'm sorry, Marilyn. I've some paperwork to attend to at home before a meeting early tomorrow with my solicitor.'

Her arm coiled round his neck.

'Stay for a little while then.' Her full lips pouted. 'Please!'

He stayed for an hour or two and they made love again.

Even though it had been a pleasant day and he'd enjoyed it, he was relieved to walk into the quietness of his flat and renew his own individual identity. He could breathe here, feel free. He poured a double whisky, switched on the hi-fi and stretched out on his comfortable easy chair to listen to Vivaldi.

The Gallacher woman should have had the factor's letter by now. If not, any day now. Soon his problems in that area would be over once and for all. Everything was organised. Or would be after the meeting with his solicitor tomorrow.

He felt a glow of satisfaction. He raised his glass to himself. An old Scots toast came unbidden to his mind. He smiled with amusement at the memory of it.

'Here's tae us, Wha's like us, No' many an' they're aw deid!'

Chapter Thirty-Eight

Kate knew that Cameron was the middleman. He was the agent for most of the big, well-known firms who made the Scottish products that he sold in his Caledonia food gift shops and emporiums. That's what gave her the idea. First of all, she wasted no time in renting a unit in an industrial estate on the riverside.

At the same time, she put in a bid for the Argyle Street shop – as high as she could afford. As high, that is, as the loan the bank had agreed to give her. Very charming they were this time. She had neither forgotten nor forgiven, however, the way they had turned her down when she was desperate to start the Argyle Street business. But just as she expected, her bid was topped. She didn't need to be told who the highest bidder was.

She still had a month's grace before having to hand over the premises and she determined to strip the place of everything she could. Even the new ovens she'd had installed were going to be dismantled and taken over to the industrial estate. For the moment it was business as usual. She travelled up to the food fair at Aviemore to set up her stall and display her products. As usual, she stayed overnight so that she could attend the Gala Ball in the hotel into which all the businesspeople were booked.

She was not surprised to see Cameron at the fair and at the ball. She managed to avoid speaking to him at the fair. Fortunately, her stall was always mobbed by other people and she was saved from the temptation of getting into verbal conflict with him. Nor did Marilyn have the chance to flirt with him. Tommy had driven them both up in the van. Kate had taken Marilyn with her to help at the stall. She wished, as usual, she could have taken Christine but knew she wouldn't have enough time or opportunity to look after her. Marilyn was besotted with Cameron. Even Mary got fed up with her romantic ravings.

'Will ye shut up aboot that man,' Mary had bawled at Marilyn eventually. 'We're aw sick tae death listenin' tae ye. As if it's no' bad enough him bein' the ruination of us aw, without havin' ye witterin' on aboot how wonderful he is.'

'He's not ruining us. He's promised to keep my job on for a start.'

'Oh aye. An' whit did ye huv tae dae fur that, hen? Let me guess. Open yer legs an' – '

'You're just being horrible,' Marilyn cried out. 'I'm in love with Gavin and what we do together is our own business.'

'Oh aye? An' good business if ye can get it, eh?'

'Both you and Kate have been nagging at me for ages to get a boyfriend. And now when I do, you're horrible to me.' Tears widened the baby-blue eyes. 'I can't help falling in love with Gavin. But if you *really* don't want me to see him again . . .'

Mary sighed. 'Naebody's wantin' tae spoil anythin' fur ye, hen. But fur God's sake, will ye jist shut up aboot him.'

At the ball in Aviemore, when Kate saw Cameron's big figure approaching, she'd naturally thought he was coming to ask Marilyn to dance. Marilyn was preening herself as if she thought so too.

'Oh, isn't he *handsome*, Kate?' she whispered excitedly. 'Sexy too. So *sexy*!'

No one was more surprised than Kate when he asked her. Before she could gather her wits together to refuse, he'd taken a firm grip of her elbow and had led her on to the dance floor.

'I don't want to dance with you,' she managed. But she was already in his arms and they were moving around to a smoochy Nat King Cole number.

'Well, to be honest,' he said, 'I didn't particularly want to dance with you but it seemed the nearest I could get to being able to talk to you on your own. I did try to see you on the stall. And earlier today in the hotel. You seem to have been purposely avoiding me.'

'That's right.'

'But we've things to negotiate if I'm taking over the shop.'

'If?'

'All right, when.'

'I'll be moving out on the date I'm supposed to. I'll be taking with me everything that's movable that I bought and had originally installed in the shop. Food freezers, for instance. I got more or less a bare shell when I moved in. That's what you'll get when you move in. There's nothing else we need to talk about.'

'I might continue the employment of some of your staff.'

'That won't be necessary. I shall be continuing to employ them myself.'

'How can you do that?'

'That's none of your business.'

'You know, you could be quite an attractive woman if you weren't so hard-faced and insolent.'

She tried to break away from him and leave him standing in the middle of the floor. But his grip tightened on her and she couldn't free herself.

'Let go of me,' she hissed furiously but quietly. There was nothing she'd hate more than being involved in a scene that would draw unwarranted attention to herself.

'The dance isn't over yet.'

'I told you, I don't want to dance with you. And what's more, I don't care what you think of me.'

He shrugged.

'Well, at least I'm more polite than you. If I remember correctly, you called me a creep and a slime-ball.'

She flushed and became even more furious, but at herself this time.

'I didn't report you, by the way.'

'So you say.'

She felt terrible because, at that moment, she believed him. It was a struggle to keep her mouth clamped shut.

She'd be damned first before she'd apologise. Anyway, she argued with herself, how could he be telling the truth after what he'd done about the shop? One way or another, he'd made up his mind to ruin her. When one way hadn't worked, he'd tried the other. The trouble was, it was difficult to think straight when he was holding her. It had been years since she'd been this close to any man's body and she felt stirrings of a passionate need that was almost painful.

From then on he only danced with Marilyn. Kate slipped away unnoticed to her room. There she sat for the rest of the evening, hugging herself, fighting to come to terms with the unexpected turmoil of her emotions.

By the time they were ready to leave next morning, she was her normal cool self.

She had her plans well under way by the next time she saw him. He'd come in with a couple of workmen to give instructions to them about the work he wanted done and to allow them to take measurements.

'Why can't this wait until I move out?' she'd asked him, thinking what a bloody cheek he had.

'The workmen got their dates mixed up. But if you want to be that awkward . . .'

'Oh, very well,' she'd grudgingly agreed. And he'd gone through to the back. From her office she could hear a bevy of wolf-whistles and the ribald comments from the girls. She strode through to confront them.

'That's enough. I don't want to hear another sound. Anyone who does make another sound will be out that door. Get on with your work.'

She'd stood like a jailer making sure that her orders were obeyed. She noticed Cameron glancing over at her with what looked like amusement glimmering in his eyes and she felt herself flushing again. But she was rooted to the spot, knowing that if she did turn her back on the girls, bedlam would immediately be let loose again. They might even try to grope the man. Her flush deepened at the thought. Even her eyes felt on fire. Only recently she'd had to speak to them about sexually harassing Tommy. Not that Tommy had complained. That's why she'd never said anything before. She'd taken it for granted that it would be different with men. They'd probably enjoy it, she'd thought. Then one day when Liz had come round to Killearn Street to deliver Christine, she'd said,

'Look here, Kate. I must speak to you. Tommy would be angry at me if he knew because it's so awkward and embarrassing for him but I have to say something.'

'About what?'

'These girls you've got working at the tables, they're making Tommy's life an absolute hell. He's not going to be able to take it much longer. He's getting to dread going to his work every day. It's affecting his health. He's not eating as well as he used to and he's not sleeping either. It's not fair, Kate. As Tommy says, if it was the other way around and he'd made girl employees suffer like this, he'd be locked up behind bars by now.'

Kate was both shocked and ashamed.

'I'm sorry, Liz. I didn't realise. I mean that Tommy felt like this.'

'How's he supposed to feel? You'll have to do something, Kate.'

'I'll speak to the girls first thing tomorrow.'

And she had. But it had not been easy. They had laughed at first. Then they'd claimed that he'd not only encouraged them, but had enjoyed it.

It occurred to Kate then that she'd read about cases where men had put forward the very same argument. It was true what Liz had said. She had to admit it to herself.

It *wasn't* fair. It also occurred to her that some women were not only trying to be like men, but trying to ape the worst in men. Freedom was one thing. She believed in that. She believed in equal opportunities at work and equal pay for doing the same job as a man. But what did these girls think they were about?

She couldn't look at Gavin Cameron again. She felt not only confused and angry now, but ashamed.

Chapter Thirty-Nine

She dressed in her best and went round every supermarket in Glasgow and beyond. She took samples of her Scottish regional products and piles of attractively designed material she'd had printed about them. The pamphlets, booklets, brochures and recipe cards not only described each product and recipe, but also explained Gallacher's ethical values concerning food and food production. She smooth-talked every manager for miles around. But behind the chat was her genuine and sincere belief in what she was doing.

She built up more orders and faster even than she'd hoped and dreamed about. Tommy delivered without delay. Once they had moved into the unit in the industrial estate she had to invest in more cooking facilities and take on more girls. As she said to her mother,

'I wish I could have seen Cameron's face when he discovered Gallacher's products filling the windows and shelves of all the supermarkets. I've a good mind to call in at Caledonia in Argyle Street just to say "Hello, and how are *you* getting on?"'

'Don't you dare,' Mary said. 'That's jist bein' rotten.'

'*Me* being rotten? Mammy, for all he knew, when he bought my shop, I was going to be out of business altogether. Finished!'

'Aye well, he didnae know *you*, hen, did he?'

'No, he did not. He's done us a big favour in actual fact. That's what I'd like to tell him.'

'Listen, hen. What do ye bet he knows aboot every step ye've taken from Marilyn. He winnae need tae huv looked in supermarkets.'

'I'd just like to have told him to his face though.'

'Ye'll dae no such thing to the poor soul.'

'The poor soul? Mammy, are you into your dotage or what? He's a very wealthy and successful businessman. He's got shops all over the place.'

'Dae ye want a punch in the face? Ah'll soon show ye if ah'm in ma dotage or no'.'

'All right. All right. I'm sorry. How's Marilyn getting on these days, by the way? I haven't had a chance to speak to her recently with me being out and around so much. But last time I saw her she looked a bit peaky. I don't think she's happy working at the tables.'

'Ah think she's got a bun in the oven.'

'Cameron?'

'Well, she's no been goin' around wi' anybody else as far as ah know.'

'I think I'd better have a talk with her and find out exactly what's going on. I'll go round to Saracen Street right now.'

Mary shook her head.

'By God, ye dinnae believe in lettin' the grass grow under yer feet. She might no' even be in.'

'I need to talk to her and you know how difficult it is at the unit.'

'Well, you jist be nice tae the lassie.'

'Have I ever been anything else?'

'Dinnae you take that cheeky tone tae me, ma girl. Ah'll no' warn ye again.'

Kate rolled her eyes in exasperation but escaped from the room and the house as quickly as possible. She remembered, as she walked along Saracen Street, that it was Saturday night and the chances were that Marilyn would indeed be out. Probably wining and dining somewhere in town with Cameron. As she went in the close and climbed the shadowy stairs, she also remembered with some vividness her determination to move the family from Possilpark to some villa in Pollokshields perhaps. Marilyn could have come with them because she still felt like family. No doubt, however, Marilyn had other plans and dreams – a villa of her own probably, in which she'd live happily ever after with her 'wonderful' Gavin and their child.

She rang the doorbell and heard Marilyn's footsteps running eagerly along the lobby. She thinks it's her precious lover, Kate thought. She must be expecting him. Suddenly she wished she hadn't come. She certainly wouldn't wait long in the circumstances.

Marilyn swung the door open, her face alight with a joyous expectancy that immediately extinguished when she saw Kate.

'I won't stay long,' Kate apologised. 'I only want a quick word.'

'Come in.' Marilyn turned and drooped back into the living room. Kate came to the point right away.

'Marilyn, are you pregnant?'

Tears welled up in Marilyn's eyes as she nodded.

'Wait a minute . . .' Kate said. 'I came to clarify the situation. I mean to find out when you'd be leaving Gallacher's to get married or whatever . . . Don't tell me . . .'

'He doesn't want to marry me, Kate. He's abandoned me. We're not even going out any more. I feel absolutely terrible. I just can't believe he'd do such a thing. I keep thinking . . . When I heard the doorbell just now . . .'

Her face contorted and she began to howl and cry in the completely uninhibited way of a young child.

'I did warn you about him, Marilyn.'

'Oh, what did you know about him?'

'Enough not to trust him.'

'What am I going to do?'

'Don't worry, Mammy and I will see you all right. You won't be short of money for a start.'

'He was such a nice big man, just like Joe. And he's got more money than you and your mammy put together. I went down on my knees, Kate. I pleaded with him.'

Oh God! Kate squirmed inside. The very idea appalled as well as embarrassed her. She would rather die than plead with a man for anything or for any reason.

'Marilyn, have you no pride? For goodness sake, get a grip of yourself. He's nothing like Joe, except maybe in size. And I can't believe you're a gold-digger. You've been foolish, that's all. Now, do you want this baby? You could have an abortion.'

'You can be so heartless, Kate. I couldn't kill a baby. Joe and I always wanted a family. I love babies.'

'All right, have the baby then. But first get some courage in you, Marilyn. If this man doesn't want you now because you're pregnant, then he's not worth having. Make a life for yourself. But know that you're not alone. We're still family.'

Marilyn took some tissues from a box and dabbed her eyes dry.

'It's such a disappointment.'

'I know. But you'll get over it. Do you feel able to keep on working for a while or what?'

'I suppose. For as long as I can. I like the company of all the girls. They sometimes tease me but they don't mean any harm. We often have a good laugh.'

'OK. But if at any time you don't feel able, just let me know.'

Suddenly Marilyn flung her arms round Kate's neck and pressed her face against Kate's.

'Thank you, Kate. I do love you.'

'OK, OK.' Kate disentangled the clinging arms. 'Are you all right here just now? Do you want to come to stay in Killearn Street for a wee while?' she asked.

'No, it would be too much of a crush. I'll just relax in a nice scented bath and then watch the telly and eat some chocolates. I'm going to be brave like you and try to look on the bright side. After all, there's lots of other lovely men in the world.'

Men! Kate thought in exasperation. That's all Marilyn ever bothered about. Happiness to her obviously meant one thing.

She returned to Killearn Street, suddenly depressed to

247

the point of tears. She didn't know why. She just wanted to hide in a corner and cry her eyes out. Yet Marilyn would be all right. The family would see that she was. So why the hell was she feeling so devastated? After all, hadn't she known what Gavin Cameron was like? He probably had been using poor silly Marilyn all along just to get information out of her about what was going on at Gallacher's. Then dumped her when she was of no more use and therefore interest to him. He would know all there was to know about Gallacher's by now and no doubt would be furious that his plan to get rid of her as competition hadn't worked. On the contrary.

Nevertheless, she had to admit to herself, she had been feeling deeply upset and disappointed from the moment her mother had told her that she thought Marilyn was pregnant. Even before that. In fact from the first time she'd learned that Marilyn and Cameron had gone out together. As she trudged along Saracen Street, she had a sudden vision of Cameron's big muscular body. She remembered how it felt to have his arms around her. She remembered the glimmer in his eyes and how it had sparked off a chemical reaction in her. She felt so angry at herself, she began to tremble. Would she never have enough sense? She felt attracted to the man. That was the truth of it. Bloody fool that she was! Hadn't she learned her lesson with one cruel, selfish, domineering man? Once Pete Brodie had made her heart race and her spine tingle. She had allowed her heart and her passions to get the better of her then. It had brought her nothing but misery and bloody murder.

Never again. This time she'd get a firm grip of herself. Her step quickened. Her eyes and her mouth set hard.

Never, never again.

Chapter Forty

Kate hesitated about going to the food industry dinner. A high-ranking member of the government was to be the after-dinner speaker and she wanted to attend. She was always quick to grasp any opportunity of making contacts, of keeping her finger on the pulse and up to date on everything that was going on in the food industry. The only reason she hesitated was the fact that Cameron would be there. It had become obvious that he too never missed an opportunity. Then she thought, damn it, why should he keep me back from anything. And so she went.

The dinner was held in the Trades House in Glassford Street. Built by Robert Adam in 1794, apart from the cathedral it was the oldest building in Glasgow still used for its original purpose. It was the house and meeting place of fourteen incorporated trades of Glasgow.

Kate had never set foot in the place before and she was impressed by the elaborate carving and stained-glass windows. She had persuaded Tommy to accompany her but had not invited anyone else from the staff. They climbed the main staircase, and walked through the ornate doorway into the banqueting hall. It was panelled in Spanish mahogany but what interested Kate was a silk frieze which had been made in Belgium and showed the fourteen different crafts at work.

'I'm just beginning to realise,' Tommy said, 'how many beautiful buildings Glasgow has. I've seen the outsides often enough but I never imagined that they could be anything like this inside.'

'I've heard they do wonderful dinners as well,' Kate told him.

He rubbed his hands and grinned. 'I've been saving my appetite all day.'

There was no sign of Cameron. Kate had taken a quick, surreptitious glance around as soon as she arrived, but didn't want it to appear as if she was looking for him, or wanted to see him. She just wanted to know if he was there, she told herself, so that she would be prepared. Forewarned was forearmed. When they found their table Kate was not prepared to see Cameron's name on the card next to hers. Tommy was one side of her and Cameron was to be on the other. This couldn't just be an accident or a coincidence. She felt confused and angry. Her hand shook so much when she picked up the menu, she had to put it down again on her side plate. Before she could calm herself by getting control of her breathing, he was towering over her. She could feel the electricity from him, as he settled in the chair next to hers. He gave her a smile and a brief 'Good evening' before picking up his menu. His hands were perfectly at ease.

'How is it that from all the tables in this hall, you have been given the seat next to mine?' she said.

He glanced round at her.

'Because I arranged it.'

For a few seconds, she was speechless.

'May I ask why?' she managed coldly, although his dark stare had made chaos of every nerve in her body. This in turn made her furious with herself as well as him.

He smiled at her.

'Why do you think?'

'I have no idea. We have nothing in common except commercial rivalry.'

'I find that stimulating. Don't you?'

She didn't answer and he went on, 'I admit that parking yourself next door to Caledonia was going too far and I was having none of that. But the way you didn't go under. The way that no sooner had you lost the shop, you came up with even better ideas. That has to be admired. I take my hat off to you. You're a worthy rival.'

'Spare me the flattery.'

'It's not flattery. I mean every word.'

'Well, I'm sorry I can't compliment you in return. You may be a good businessman but the way you conduct your personal life leaves a lot to be desired.'

His smile disappeared. His eyes narrowed.

'What's that supposed to mean?'

She shrugged. 'The way you dumped Marilyn for instance. A bit irresponsible, was it not?'

'No, it was not.'

'I find that hard to believe.'

'My personal life is none of your business. And I would have thought that you would have been the last person to criticise how anyone ended a relationship.'

Kate flushed. 'It is my business when my family and I are left to bear the responsibility of your actions,' she said.

'Oh? And how is that?'

We regard Marilyn as still part of our family and we will support her in every way, including financially.'

'I see.' His voice was icy. 'Then Marilyn has not told you that I have arranged that she will lack for nothing. A monthly allowance. All expenses paid.'

Kate groaned inside but managed to appear unruffled.

'No, she didn't. All I gathered was that she was in love with you and had expected, naively I admit, to marry you. This has all been a terrible shock to her.'

'I don't know why. I never gave her one reason to think in terms of any serious commitment.'

'Not *one* reason?' Kate made a brave attempt at a sarcastic laugh.

'If you're referring to her present condition, she planned that.'

'Oh, come now . . .'

'On the very few occasions I stayed overnight with her, she assured me she was on the pill and insisted that no other protection was needed. That female is not as naive as she tries to make out. The only shock she got was when she discovered she had tried her little ploy on the wrong man. But I repeat, none of this is any of your damn business.'

With that he turned away and began a conversation with the woman seated on his other side. In a few moments, Kate heard the woman laughing.

Tommy whispered, 'Is everything all right?'

'Perfectly.' Kate's voice sounded nonchalant.

They turned their attention to the wine list. Inside, she was wishing she was dead. She didn't want to believe Cameron. Didn't believe him. Yet at the same time, knowing Marilyn, the chances were he was telling the truth.

For the rest of the evening she didn't know what she was eating or drinking. She wasn't even able to properly take in what the after-dinner speaker was saying. Her mind was trying to self-destruct, blot itself out. Her emotions were in a state of unendurable turmoil and sensitivity. She could feel the heat of Cameron's body. She could feel his presence as if a constant electric current was coming from his body into hers. She had never been so glad when an evening finished. She was so desperate to get away, she never even turned to look at him or say goodnight.

Tommy had obviously enjoyed every minute. In the taxi on the way home, he chatted happily about the food, the wine, the speaker. And every sentence he prefaced with, 'Wait till I tell Liz about . . .'

Kate could imagine the scene in his flat in Stoneyhurst Street. His plump, motherly wife would greet him with an affectionate hug and kiss. The children would be tucked up in bed and he'd drop a kiss on each of their sleeping faces. Then he'd go through to the kitchen and talk non-stop to Liz while she made a pot of tea. Liz would listen intently with her calm, loving gaze fixed on Tommy's face. They'd still be talking together as they lay in bed in each other's arms. Next day when Liz came for Christine, she was able to relate to Mary and George everything that happened at the dinner.

'She never said wan word.' Mary jerked her head in Kate's direction. 'She jist went intae wan o' her moods an' clammed up. An' here wis me dyin' tae hear aw aboot it.'

'Mr Cameron was there. Sitting right next to Kate. Tommy thinks maybe they had words.'

'Well, ah dinnae think we should blame Kate fur that. Ah'm no' very pleased at that man masel' the now. Ma tongue would've been the least he would've got from me.'

Kate felt obliged to cut in then.

'He said he'd arranged for Marilyn to have an allowance and all her expenses paid. According to him, she'd lied about being on the pill thinking he would have to marry her.'

'Och, the poor lassie. Ah can understand how she felt.'

'I can't,' Kate said. 'If it's true . . .'

'Och, it'll be true aw right. She's an awfae daft wee lassie. She needs a man. Ah've kept tellin' her she should get married again. But that's an auld trick she played. It disnae work nowadays. She ought tae huv known. She's lucky he's come up trumps wi' the cash.'

'I feel like strangling her.' The words escaped before Kate could stop them.

'Is that no' terrible?' Mary asked Liz. 'An' the poor wee lassie carryin' a wean.' Then back to Kate, 'You jist watch yer wicked tongue, m'lady.'

Kate tried to concentrate on other things. She flung herself into work. At night and at weekends, she paid more attention to Christine than she'd ever done before. The outings she suggested turned out to be somewhat fraught because Christine insisted that Aunty Liz and Aunty Dorothy and all her wee 'cousins' come too. Christine, although an only child, had become used to the noisy, crowded houses and streets of Possilpark. She didn't want to be on her own. That included, it seemed, being on her own with Kate.

Dorothy had often come to visit at Killearn Street since

she'd left the refuge. And there she'd become friendly with Liz. They had got into the habit of having Dorothy and the twins to Killearn Street for Sunday lunch. Liz and Tommy and, as often as not Marilyn, came as well. The bedsit Kate had helped Dorothy to find was far too small but she couldn't stay at the refuge for ever. There was always someone else whose need was greater or more urgent. Space was at a premium.

Then one day on her way to Sunday lunch, Dorothy bumped into Charlie.

'He looked such a poor, neglected soul,' Dorothy told Kate and the rest of the family. 'He pleaded with me to come back and promised he'd never lift his hand to me again. I told him,' she hastily added in Kate's direction, 'that he had to get help about his drug addiction before I'd go back. He's going to go to the Health Centre tomorrow first thing, Kate.'

Kate wanted to say, Don't be a fool. Charlie's never going to change. You're just going to ruin your life and your children's lives all over again. She wanted to forcibly prevent Dorothy from going. She wanted to say, You are not going to do this. I'm not going to let you. But she kept her mouth shut. She had been putting her foot in it too often recently.

'Kate,' Dorothy's voice took on an anxious, pleading tone, 'don't be angry with me. Please try to understand.'

Kate shrugged.

'I'm not angry with you. It's your life.'

And it was, of course. I must learn, Kate thought, not to try to run people's lives like I run my business. She knew what she was doing in business. She was well organised, efficient, confident, successful.

But in human relationships, it seemed, she was none of these things.

Chapter Forty-One

Kate took stock of herself. She stood naked before the wardrobe mirror in the small back bedroom she and Christine occupied in her mother's house. Christine lay sound asleep in one of the twin beds. Only Kate's bedside light was switched on but it was enough to let her see her reflection. She was in her mid-twenties. Her chestnut brown hair boasted a healthy gloss. She had good, clear skin, even features, pert little breasts, a slim waist and long, shapely legs. What was wrong with her then? There's nothing wrong with me, she told herself firmly. I've survived an abusive relationship. I've come up from nothing to create a very successful business.

Yet, why was she still here in her mother and father's house with no relationships outside of it? It was as if, since the end of her marriage, she'd shrunk back into the womb. She had spoken to her mother and father about getting another, bigger house but she'd meant for all of them. She had planned for the whole family to move with her to keep bonded together.

She struggled to be honest with herself. She wasn't here in this tiny, cramped bedroom because she lacked the money to move elsewhere. Nor had her father or even her mother shown the slightest desire to leave their own home in Possilpark. Not even for a villa in Pollokshields or a big main door flat in the West End (they'd already looked at both options) or anywhere.

'You get a place o' yer own if ye like, hen. Yer daddy and me are aw right here. Ah've that good neighbours an' friends in Possil, as you well know. An' the shops are that handy. So is Tommy an' Liz an' the weans . . .'

Kate gave a bitter, twisted smile. Here she was, supposedly

a modern, free-thinking, independent woman, and yet she was clinging to the family like a helpless limpet. She had to break away.

Another thing, while she was being so honest. Why was it she'd had no boyfriends, no sex in all the years since her marriage ended? All right, she had been concentrating one hundred per cent and more on building up her business. But still . . . She'd had offers on the way. She'd never given them a second thought. Had she been so scarred by what she'd suffered with Pete that she was afraid to take the risk of embarking on a relationship with another man?

She balked indignantly at the word – afraid. She was afraid of no man. She maybe didn't condone the lengths that the girls at the tables went to in their attitudes towards men. That was just bad behaviour. But why shouldn't she have a relationship on her own terms? She didn't need to plunge into any serious commitment and take the risk of making the same mistake she made with Pete. She could keep her independence, retain that safe distance, keep that invisible wall she'd built over the years for her protection. She was a normal healthy woman, she told herself, with normal physical needs. She ran her hand caressingly over her body. It had only been since she'd met Gavin Cameron that she had been sexually aroused. Not even with Pete at the exciting beginning of their relationship had she ever felt as strongly aroused as this.

She stared herself straight in the eye. Courage, she thought. That's what she needed. She had never been lacking in courage before and she was determined not to be lacking in it now. Two courses of action were necessary. First, she had to leave, once and for all, the warm, supportive safety of the family nest. Even her mother's sharp tongue and ready fist had acquired, with familiarity, the aura of security and safety. She knew what to expect from her mother and she had learned how to cope with it.

Men were different. A *frisson* of fear went through her but she immediately squashed it, angrily chastising herself.

Meet them on equal terms. That's what she must do as a modern, emancipated woman. After all, she'd already done exactly that in the business arena. Now she must learn to do so on a personal level. On a sexual level, to be absolutely exact.

She was sexually aroused by Gavin Cameron. So why not go for it? She wanted sex with him, so what was to stop her from having it? He wouldn't turn down the chance. Men never did turn down the chance of sex with any woman as far as she could see. She remembered only too well the bawdy conversations between Pete and his mates. Sex was just sex to men, with no emotional entanglements. Gavin Cameron had proved that with Marilyn. Marilyn was a sexy-looking woman. She'd made sex available and he'd accepted the offer, that was all. And that's how she wanted it. She was no Marilyn, angling for marriage. Indeed, even the thought of marriage was repugnant to her. She'd far, far rather go back to Cornton Vale than be condemned to spend the rest of her life tied to any man and have to suffer all the risks, the disappointments, the disillusionments that such a step might entail.

Sex, that's all she wanted. Exactly as a man would want it. And that was exactly what she was going to have. She turned away from the mirror and reached for her nightdress. But lying in bed staring through the blackness at the ceiling after she'd switched off the light, she felt her whole body throbbing with apprehension. She had to get up eventually and search about for a bottle of tranquillisers she'd once, long ago, been prescribed by the doctor. She hadn't taken them at the time, so stubbornly determined had she been not to become dependent on drugs. Instead, she had kept going under her own steam, used her own backbone, grit, strength of mind. Now, however, in the dark quiet of the night, with the effect of Cameron's muscular body, his dark knowledgeable eyes, the chemistry of him so strong in her mind, she was forced in desperation to swallow a couple of the capsules.

If she just could get a good sleep, she thought, she'd be perfectly calm, perfectly capable of dealing with any situation next day.

Once she made up her mind on any course of action, she never – as her mother would say – let the grass grow under her feet. Next day, or rather next evening, was the usual yearly gala dinner dance at the Thistle Hotel. Each business took a table and sent out invitations. Her invitations had already gone out and no doubt Cameron's had too. They obviously would not be sitting together on this occasion. But she could track him down in the ballroom. And she would. Marilyn would be there but why should she object? Or even feel hurt? After all, Marilyn hadn't even thought in terms of disloyalty when she'd gone all out for Cameron, who was obviously a dangerous competitor of Gallacher's. Even after Cameron had set about taking over Gallacher's shop, Marilyn still went her selfish, merry little way.

'So why should she keep me back. Why should I consider her feelings in this?' Kate asked herself.

Next day she splashed out and bought a slinky new dress. She hadn't planned to involve herself in any extra expense but that was before she had decided to proposition Gavin Cameron. The dress was low-cut to reveal a milky-white cleavage. Her pale skin, instead of taking on a tan, burned in the sun and so she had always avoided sunbathing. Apart from that, she found the mere idea of lazing about on some beach (or even on some sunbed) far too boring. And anyway, a creamy complexion was far more flattering against the deep burnish of her hair.

Usually at work or anywhere during the day, she wore her long hair severely tied back. For this evening, she had brushed it out so that it swung loose around her shoulders. Instead of the usual flatties she wore with trousers at work, she donned delicate high-heeled sandals. Underneath the ankle-length clinging dress, a black lace-edged silk knicker and bra set caressed the skin of her body. If knickers was the right word for the tiny wisp of silk. Even the bra was one of the briefest she'd ever seen. The black stockings were topped with lace and the suspender belt that held them up was a narrow ribbon in appearance.

She saw him as soon as she entered the ballroom. He was sitting at a small table at the opposite side talking to a middle-aged woman Kate recognised as one of the supermarkets' manageresses. She was so hyped up with what she was about to do, however, she didn't give this a second thought. She marched right over to Cameron and stood in front of him. His inborn good manners made him rise but it was with a shade of reluctance. Without wasting a moment, she looked him straight in the eye (no easy feat when he was taller than her) and said,

'Will you dance with me?'

He stared back at her with slightly narrowed eyes. Then without making any reply, he walked a few steps on to the dance floor before turning and taking her body into his arms. As they danced, neither of them said anything at first. Then Kate moved closer to him. She closed her eyes with the ecstasy of feeling his body against hers.

Eventually he said,

'Are you coming on to me?'

'Yes.'

'Why?'

'Need you ask?'

'Yes. Up till now you've talked and acted as if you've detested me.'

'I don't like your business methods. As you said, we're business rivals. That doesn't mean I don't find you sexy.'

'So everything is suddenly all right. We're not rivals any more?'

'I didn't say that. This is something quite apart. My business is my life and I intend it to continue that way.'

'So?'

'So, a little diversion, a little enjoyment now and again, when we're off duty, won't do either of us any harm. So long as we both understand that's all it is.'

She raised her chin. She looked defiantly up at him. He gazed down at her, his eyes glimmering with amusement. She had to move back a little so that he wouldn't be aware of her fast racing heart.

'I understand,' he said.

Chapter Forty-Two

After the dance, he took her back to his immaculate flat.

Kate admired the sense of order about it. A place after her own heart.

'This is the kind of flat I'd like,' she told him as she wandered nonchalantly into the hall and left him to hang up her velvet hooded cloak. She peered in through all the open doors. It looked as though the layout of his flat was of the most riveting interest in her life. In fact she was so keenly aware of him following her, she felt quite faint. Indeed she was having a hard job trying to keep panic at bay. All at once she was thinking, I must be mad. I've gone right out of my skull. This can't be happening.

'I've been thinking,' she said coolly, 'of buying a flat. I've looked at a few places. I saw a very attractive main door flat not all that far from here. I thought it would be nice to be so near to a park – for the sake of . . .' She had been going to say, 'my daughter Christine' but she never got the chance. Cameron suddenly swung her off her feet and carried her into the nearest bedroom. It was as if she had no more weight or substance than a feather. She had never felt so helpless and vulnerable. It made her feel frightened. Where was the equality of the sexes now? If she said she didn't want sex after all, he could quite easily overpower her and rape her. Pete had. On more than one occasion.

She hoped Cameron would think her obvious trembling was due to passion and not terror. But soon, as he kissed her, she felt such a surge of passion that it swept her away. There was only her deep and desperate need. Unlike Pete, he didn't rush, or hurt her. In fact he nearly drove her crazy by taking his time. He kissed her gently all over her body. She kissed him wildly in return.

Later, in the exhausted aftermath, she pulled her discarded clothes to her and said,

'I'd better go home.'

'Stay the night.'

'I can't. I haven't told my mother.' The words sounded so infantile, she hastily added, 'There's my little girl, you see. I don't like taking advantage of my mother too often. Leaving her with the responsibility.'

'Your mother was there tonight.'

'Yes.' Kate put a palm to her forehead. 'I forgot, Christine is staying overnight with my sister-in-law.'

'Relax.' He cradled her in his arms. 'Sleep with me.'

But after a moment or two she said, 'Gavin, I need to explain about what happened in my marriage – what made me finally act as I did. It wasn't something I'd planned. I didn't mean it to happen . . .'

'Ssh . . . ssh . . .' he hushed her. 'That's all in the past. You've no need to explain anything to me.' He kissed her eyes. 'Go to sleep.'

Cameron dropped her off early next morning at Killearn Street so that she could change into her working clothes and still get to work on time.

He laughed at the way she kept checking her watch.

'You're the boss, remember. You can turn up, or not turn up, any time you like.'

'That might be your philosophy, but it's not mine. If I insist on my staff being good timekeepers – and I do – then I have to show a good example.'

'I'm sure, like me, you have other commitments and appointments to keep outside your business premises. You can't always keep to their hours.'

'That's different. They understand that. But I've no outside commitments today.'

'Yes, you have. You're meeting me for lunch. A long leisurely lunch.'

Meaning, back to his flat afterwards, no doubt.

'Sorry, not today. I'll be too busy. I'm just going to send out for a sandwich. I'll be in touch.'

She had got out of the car, gone into the close and up the stairs without once looking back. She was determined to stay in control of the situation. She had to. She could really go overboard this time. It would be so easy to make a stupid, weak fool of herself all over again. More so with this man.

'You stupit cow,' her mother had once called her when she'd admitted she loved Pete and wanted to marry him. She was not going to merit that accusation twice in her lifetime.

As it was, her mother teased her good-humouredly.

'Oh aye. Is this yer new tactic tae get the better o' the opposition, hen? Or is it a case o' if ye cannae beat them, join them?'

'Leave it off, Mammy. I'm as much entitled to a bit of fun as the next person.'

'Ooh, jist a bit o' fun, wis it, eh? Come on then, tell yer mammy aw aboot it.'

'It's time I was changed and away to work.' Kate began shedding the slinky dress, forgetting about the scanty underwear.

Mary howled with laughter.

'My God, ah bet them scanties got him goin'.'

'Mammy, for goodness sake!' She grabbed a pair of denims and a denim shirt and jerked them on.

'Ah bet he wis great. A lovely big fella like that. He's more like the thing. Ah could never understand whit you saw in that ferret-faced wee runt ye married.'

Kate sighed.

'I loved him. Or thought I did.'

'Och, ye were too young tae know whit love wis between a man an' a woman. Ye were jist a wee innocent school lassie.'

'You're probably right. But don't worry, I'm not going to make that mistake again.'

263

'Ye'd huv a hard job, hen. He's deid.'

'You know what I mean. Now come on, Mammy, it's time we were at work.'

They picked up a taxi in Saracen Street.

'Ah've said it before an' ah'll say it again. Ye should huv a car. Ye take that many taxis these days, it would be cheaper.'

'Yes, I've decided to take driving lessons,' she said impulsively. She had no intention of being dependent on Gavin Cameron giving her a lift again. 'I'll buy a car. And another thing, Mammy. I think I'll go ahead and buy a flat. That main door one's been snapped up but the conversion in Kirklee Terrace was lovely as well and so near the park for Christine.'

'Now wait a minute, hen. Yer daddy an' me are no' aw that keen. The West End's maybe OK fur you. But we like Possil. Yer daddy would miss his local an' ah've always – '

'It's all right, Mammy. I meant on my own. It's time I had a place of my own.'

'Oh . . . right. That's great, hen. Dinnae get me wrong, yer daddy an' me'll miss you an' wee Chrissie but ye're quite right, hen. Ah cannae think why ye've pit up wi' that wee bedroom aw this time an' me always breathin' down yer neck.'

'I'll always be grateful to you for standing by me and then taking me in when I needed a place.'

'Och, whit else could ah dae. Ye're ma wean.'

Kate had an almost overwhelming urge to hug and kiss her mother after they'd got out of the taxi but she controlled the urge. They had never been a demonstrative, kissing kind of family. If she had kissed her mother, Mary would have pushed her roughly aside and said 'Dinnae be so bloody daft.'

Not long after she was in her office, she phoned the estate agents, discovered the Kirklee flat was still on the market, and told them she wanted to put in an offer. She had just replaced the phone when Marilyn entered the office.

'How could you, Kate?' The blue eyes filled with tears. 'I

still can hardly believe you'd do such an awful thing. I know you can be very hard and cruel at times but this – and to me. I always thought we were close. You said we were still family.'

Kate leaned back in her chair.

'I take it you're referring to my having a night's sex with Gavin Cameron?'

'You sound so cold and calculating. It's just terrible. How could you?'

'The same way as you could, I suppose. Only I'm being honest about it. I just want sex. You wanted sex and marriage. The fact that he wasn't willing to give you the marriage part has nothing to do with me, Marilyn. Your relationship with him has finished, hasn't it?'

'I'm carrying his baby.'

'Answer me honestly. Did you purposely stop taking the pill?'

'No, Kate.'

'Marilyn!' Kate groaned.

Marilyn fluttered her long lashes. 'All right, I might have forgotten to take it. It might have just slipped my mind.'

'Well,' Kate sighed. 'I guess that's as honest as we're going to get. Just count your blessings, Marilyn. You're being looked after financially, and it's true what I said, you *are* still family. You'll be looked after in every way possible. Mammy even said she'd look after the baby for you if need be.'

'I know.' It was Marilyn's turn to sigh. 'But it's not the same as having a man.'

'You're young. And the world's full of men. You'll find someone who'll be only too glad and proud of the chance to marry you.'

'Do you really think so?' Already she was drying her eyes and looking more cheerful.

'Of course. You're a real stunner, Marilyn. You've got to forget Joe. Oh, I know he'll always have a place in your heart, but he's gone, Marilyn. It's time you stopped thinking about him and talking about him and comparing other men

265

to him. You'll never get anywhere that way. That's where you've been going wrong.' Kate shrugged. 'At least, that's what I think, for what it's worth.'

'Oh Kate.' Marilyn rushed over and gave Kate a hug and a kiss. 'I do love you.'

Kate pushed her roughly aside.

'Don't be so daft!'

Chapter Forty-Three

The best thing about the flat, as far as Kate was concerned, was its huge kitchen. She loved it. It was more spacious not only than her mother's kitchen, but almost than the whole of her mother's house. Kate had a wonderful time getting it fixed up with fitted cupboards and furnished with a large table and a set of eight chairs. There was a dining room in the flat but she could see herself eating and probably entertaining family and friends to meals in her beautiful kitchen more than anywhere else. After a meal, everyone could have coffee and drinks through in the enormous sitting room at the front of the house.

Because she wanted the kitchen to be comfortable to eat in and spend so much time in, she chose a country style of décor and furnishing. As well as the pine cupboards (some with glass doors), she had a beautiful Welsh dresser hung with a set of blue and white willow crockery. There were glass jars on display full of flour and spices and long brown strands of spaghetti. There was a shiny brass kettle and a row of herbs hanging from beneath one of the shelves like a fragrant green curtain.

Kate had been so busy between work in the unit and the move, plus getting the flat to her liking, she had not contacted Cameron again. Not that she hadn't thought of him. It wasn't so bad during the day, although in the evening she was almost as busy. There was Christine to attend to. Christine had to be settled into a new school – a private school this time with a very smart uniform. Christine had gone all sulky and moody about the move to the West End at first, but she quickly made new friends at the school. The proximity of the park was a diversion. Her own room and the freedom to choose how it would be decorated and furnished helped as well.

After a couple of weeks, Cameron had contacted her. He'd been up north and now, on his return, wanted to meet her. She explained about all the work at the flat and also how she had to be in at night for Christine. Before there had always been her mother or Liz as babysitters.

'Possilpark isn't at the other end of the world,' Cameron said. 'They could still babysit. Or, we could choose not to go out. I could bring a bottle of wine and we could spend the evening in the flat.'

And the night, she thought. It was a temptation. But she didn't want Christine to wake up in the morning and see a strange man in her mother's bed. She had managed, by being so busy, to keep him either out of or just on the periphery of her consciousness. At night, however, lying in bed she had relived with painful physical longing every moment she'd lain in his arms. Now, even hearing his deep voice on the phone, she was trembling with passionate longing for his touch.

'This Saturday, Christine is going to visit her granny. I could leave her to stay there overnight. Then I'd have more time to cook dinner for you.'

'Saturday it is,' he said. 'What time?'

'Oh, about seven-ish, I suppose.'

'See you then.'

And he hung up.

She had sounded so casual. Yet she had to go and sit down for a few minutes. Her legs felt too weak to support her. This was ridiculous, she thought. And dangerous. The last thing she wanted was to lose control of herself to be dominated in any way by a man. Just when she was organising her life so well.

Marilyn had said more than once in the past, 'He's so *sexy*.' And she was so right. If I can just keep it that I enjoy occasional sex with him I'll be fine, she kept assuring herself. There's no big deal.

On Saturday morning she took Christine, somewhat reluctantly, to Possilpark. She tried to be sensible but it worried her every time she allowed Christine to become the focus of so much attention from the Gallacher clan. Yet why should she be so unhappy, jealous even, of the love and attention showered on her little girl? She kept telling herself that Christine and her happiness must come first. Since she'd lost the shop, there was no need to work on a Saturday. At first they had worked Saturday mornings at the unit but they'd discovered that most of the other places on the site shut down on the Friday night so eventually Kate decided that Gallacher's should do the same.

'Aw, there ye are, ma wee pet,' her mother greeted Christine, who skipped delightedly into the house. Kate followed her and was surprised to see Marilyn lounging back in a chair by the fire.

'You're an early visitor,' Kate said with a smile. Although if truth be told, she felt awkward with Marilyn now. She was now visibly swollen and Kate didn't like to be reminded that it was with Cameron's child. She'd rationalised it to herself and indeed to Marilyn. She knew Marilyn. She knew exactly how it had happened. But, in the circumstances of her relationship with Cameron, it was still an awkward situation.

Marilyn smiled in return. 'Oh, I got bored since I stopped work so I often pop in to see Mary.'

'Aye,' Mary laughed. 'Morning, noon an' night. But dinnae worry, ye're welcome, hen. Ye can move in aw thegither if ye like. Ah've told ye ah'll take on the wean. Nae bother.'

Kate groaned inside.

'What about your work, Mammy?'

'Och, I'm thinkin' o' packin' it in, hen. Ye dinnae need me at them tables any more. The girls know fine what they're about. Wan o' them could take over ma job nae bother.'

'We'd miss you.'

'Naw, ye wouldnae. Ye're aw goin' like the clappers. Ah'm

gettin' past runnin' in the rat race, hen. You seem to thrive on aw the biz an' competition an' aw that risky stuff. But no' me.'

'Not me either,' Marilyn said. 'I like to enjoy life.'

Kate thought, That's pretty obvious. Marilyn had opted to stop work far earlier than need be. Now she loafed about listening to her CDs, feeding her face and going to the pub (and everywhere else it seemed) with Mary and George. She'd have Mary running after her like a slave if she moved into Killearn Street. Maybe it was just a symptom of her pregnancy, of course.

Or maybe, Kate couldn't help thinking, she was just a lazy, pampered slut. Immediately she felt ashamed of the thought and said, 'You must come round one evening for a meal and see round my new flat, Marilyn. Come with Daddy and Mammy and we'll make a nice evening of it.'

Marilyn fluttered her long lashes.

'Oh thank you, Kate. I'd just love that.' Then, after a trembling smile and a little hesitation, she added, 'But I hope you'd make sure Gavin wouldn't be there. It would upset me terribly.'

'No, no, he wouldn't be there. You don't need to worry.'

'You are still seeing him, of course.'

'Yes.'

'*You'll* have no need to worry about him dumping you, Kate.'

'Oh?'

'Well, dear, it's obvious he sees in you a wonderful opportunity.'

'I don't quite follow you, Marilyn.'

But of course she did. Marilyn could be really bitchy at times in her own wide-blue-eyed, innocent way.

'He's out to take over your business, dear. Step by step. He's awfully clever, don't you think, and it's such a good way to stop any more competition. First he takes over your shop. Next he takes over you and then your whole business. These tycoon types never stop, do they? You just need to read the newspapers or listen to the news on television. There's always some take-over or other . . .'

Kate said coldly, 'You're way off beam, Marilyn. There's no question of me being taken over, as you put it, by anyone.' She glanced at her watch. 'Now if you'll excuse me, I've got to go. I've still a lot to do in the flat.' She went through to the kitchen where her mother was making a pot of tea and chatting to Christine.

'Are ye no' stayin' for a cup o' tea, hen?'

'No, I've things to do.' She hesitated. 'Mammy, I wish you wouldn't let Marilyn take advantage of you so much.'

'Here you, dinnae be sae rotten. Ma Joe would've wanted me tae take care o' her. He doted on that girl.'

Kate nodded. 'Yes, I'm sorry. Thanks for having Christine, Mammy. I'll come for her tomorrow afternoon, if that's all right.'

'Nae bother. We love havin' wee Chrissie. An' her wee cousins are comin' an' they're aw goin' tae the pictures this afternoon. Then tomorrow Aunty Bec an' Uncle Willie an' Sandra are comin' for their lunch.'

Kate kissed her daughter.

'You'll be a good girl for Granny, won't you?'

Christine sighed and rolled her eyes before turning away. Kate felt a stab of hurt. She knew the child didn't meant to be dismissive or unloving, but all the same, to let her mother go without the slightest concern or even a second look . . . Kate tried to comfort herself. She's still more used to Killearn Street and all her family and friends in Possil than the West End and me. It's understandable. She's been so much more with them than with me in the past. But things will work out, the longer she's settled in the new flat.

And her mother was right about Marilyn. The girl was pregnant and in need of as much help and support as she could get.

She was unsuccessful, however, in soothing away feelings of hurt, worry and insecurity. And thoughts of Gavin Cameron's imminent visit did nothing to ease her mind.

Chapter Forty-Four

It was all very cool at first. He hadn't even kissed her. He'd sauntered in, presented her with a bottle of wine and admired what she'd done to the flat. He liked the clean lines, the lack of fuss or clutter. The cool blue carpet and matching velvet drapes were to his taste. The elegant cream suite tempted him to sink into the cushioned luxury of it. He remarked on the paintings: 'All Scottish artists, I see.'

'Of course,' Kate said.

In the kitchen he peered into pots and said everything looked and smelled delicious. But every time their eyes met, she saw what he was really thinking. She didn't know how she was going to get through the meal.

They talked. They laughed. They ate. They drank wine. She switched on the coffee percolator, then began to clear the table.

He rose.

'Leave that.'

'It was just while I was waiting for the coffee. We could take our cups through to the sitting room.'

'All I want is to take you through to the bedroom.'

She avoided his eyes.

'Afterwards.'

'No, now.'

Before she could say any more, he'd swung her into her arms and carried her through. In the warm seductive comfort of the bedroom, and with the passionate intimacy of him, all her cool reserves, all her cold resolutions melted away.

She responded to his passion with every fibre of her being, every corner of her mind. In the fever of her response, she whispered close to him, cried out, moaned, even wept, before falling into an exhausted sleep in his arms. In the morning, she woke very early as usual. She slid carefully out of bed and went through to the bathroom where she showered and dressed. In the kitchen, she set about cooking breakfast. During the week, she made do with fruit and cereal before dashing out to work. On Sundays, she always cooked a traditional Scottish fry-up – eggs, bacon, mushrooms, sausages, tomatoes, fried potato scones. Soon she could hear Cameron moving about.

'That smells good,' he said when he came into the kitchen. 'I'm starving.'

She smiled over at his big frame now dwarfing one of her spar-backed chairs.

'Yes, you look as if you're starving.'

'You obviously know that the best way to a man's heart is through his stomach.'

'I expect you know lots of clichés.'

'I like a woman with a quick wit.'

'You just like women – period.'

Immediately she wished she'd never said it.

'What's that supposed to mean?'

She shrugged. 'You're a good-looking man.'

'Flattery will get you everywhere.' He gave her a glance as she put a plate of food in front of him. 'There's another cliché for you.'

'I like men – period. So it cuts both ways. What's wrong with that?'

He began to eat.

'Point taken.'

After the meal they had a pleasant stroll in the park. She could have invited him back for lunch, but didn't.

'I'll have to go and collect Christine soon.'

'Do you want me to give you a lift over?'

'No thanks, I've one or two things to do first.'

He walked Kate to the door of the flat and stood looking down at her in silence for a long minute. She broke the silence by quickly saying, 'See you', before turning away and disappearing inside the house. She stood, eyes closed, leaning her back against the door for a few minutes, sensing he was still standing where she'd left him. It was only with a determined effort that she moved away from the door and went through to the kitchen to have a cup of coffee. The kitchen, the whole house seemed unbearably quiet and lonely.

It became a pattern of her life to have him visit the flat every Saturday and say an abrupt goodbye to him every Sunday. And each time, instead of becoming easier, it became worse to bear.

She took panics of loneliness after every time they were together. Eventually she had to admit to herself that she loved the man and wanted to be with him all of the time. She tried to think things through and be sensible. There was surely no need to be afraid. What was there to be afraid of? Cameron was nothing like Pete, for a start. He would never bully her, dominate her or hurt her. Indeed, he'd been very kind, considerate and patient. He'd behaved like a perfect gentleman. Then what *was* she afraid of?

She turned an inward eye on herself to examine, as honestly as she could, exactly what her problem was. She shrank from opening up emotionally. She was terrified of making herself vulnerable. All she could do was peep timidly above the high wall she'd built around her emotions, and her real self. Yet had that hidden self any more reality than her everyday self, the one that everyone saw and knew?

The self that everyone knew was the self that she understood and was not ashamed of. She had suffered physically and emotionally in her marriage and she'd resolved to get over that and make a success of her life. It hadn't been easy but she had surmounted all the difficulties that had come her way.

So why couldn't she just say to Cameron, 'I love you like crazy and I want us to get married'?

The mere thought panicked her. Her mind roved about

searching for reasons. She had always been like this as far back as she could remember. In the Gallacher family any display or talk of emotion, or at least sentimental or loving emotion, had always been an embarrassment. Anger or aggression, that was all right.

Her mother had loved Joe much, much more than her. In fact her mother had been unfair to her at times, to put it mildly. As a very young child she'd known that. But even as the thought entered her head, she dismissed it in disgust as a sign of self-pity and weakness. There was far too much of this harping back to the past and blaming one's parents and one's childhood deprivations nowadays. Far better to discard it, leave it in the past where it belonged and take charge of one's life as an adult in the present. Start a new pattern.

Perhaps she hadn't managed to discard everything after all. All right, she'd learned how to protect herself right from childhood by hiding deep within herself. Unconsciously, she'd thought, 'If I can't trust my mother not to hurt me, I can't trust anybody'. There was the nub of it, she decided. She was afraid to trust. That was the pattern she had to break. Her new pattern must be to learn to trust people, beginning with Gavin Cameron.

She had never been one to hesitate once she'd made up her mind. She wanted to speak to him right away. This very minute. Unfortunately Cameron had gone abroad on business and wouldn't be back for a few weeks. She didn't even have an address at which she could contact him.

Once he'd phoned her at the flat but she'd been out and he'd left a message on her answering machine. It just said, 'Hope all goes well with you. I've something important I must talk to you about when I return to Glasgow. See you.'

She could have danced with joy and excitement. It sounded as if he might have been thinking along the same lines – about facing the fact that they loved each other, that is. Perhaps he was going to propose. Perhaps he'd bought a ring in some fancy jeweller's during his travels in America.

She wished he'd said exactly when he'd be returning. But that had been part of the unspoken bargain. They would respect each other's privacy, freedom and independence. They would never question each other's movements or interfere in each other's plans.

They had kept to this bargain so meticulously and so well. But now it was time to move on. Make another, different kind of bargain.

This time one spoken out loud and from the heart.

Chapter Forty-Five

Marilyn produced a very large baby boy. Kate was fed up hearing her mother rave on about it.

'Fourteen pounds! Fancy, the very same weight as ma Joe when he wis born. An' it's that unusual. Ah mean, most weans are half that. Seven pounds, the nurse said wis the average. But fourteen! Isn't he a corker? He's gonnae be a right big bruiser jist like ma Joe.'

Kate was tempted to remind her mother that the baby was not Joe's, but Gavin Cameron's. However, she resisted the temptation. Her mother was happy. Why spoil anything for her? She did once gasp out in exasperation,

'Mammy, you've got an obsession about size. Big doesn't necessarily mean perfect. Have you never heard the old Scots saying – Guid gear goes into sma' book?'

'Och there's nothin' tae whack a nice big man. That's whit attracted me right away tae yer daddy. There wisnae as big a man in aw Possilpark as yer daddy when ah first met him. An' he's still a fine-looking big fella.'

What really worried Kate was that Christine would feel put out by the switch of so much of her granny's attention to the baby. Marilyn had called him Joe. Kate thought this typical of her but tried not to think she'd done it for other, more selfish reasons than she claimed.

'It's in memory of our Joe,' Marilyn announced with a widening of blue eyes and a flutter of lashes.

Kate could see that to her mother, the baby was her Joe incarnate. She doted on the child, did everything for it. Marilyn was now a completely free agent. She had kept on her flat in Saracen Street and now lived between the two places. She didn't work. She obviously didn't need to with what Cameron paid her. Marilyn was living the life of Riley.

Mostly she ate in Killearn Street and brought her dirty washing to 'pop into Granny's washing machine'. She had begun to call Mary 'Granny' in honour of the baby. She was always cooing at it.

'Haven't you a wonderful granny, Joe darling?'

As indeed he had. The baby stayed with Mary all the time now. Kate felt like saying something to either her mother or Marilyn about the situation but decided against interfering. She knew she'd only have the fact thrown in her face that her mother had the full care of Christine the whole time she'd been in Cornton Vale. She was the last one who should talk about taking advantage of her mother.

At least, as far as she knew anyway, Marilyn hadn't turned up on Cameron's doorstep with the child. Kate felt a *frisson* of worry at the thought of Cameron seeing the baby. He was truly beautiful. There could be no denying that. Cameron could well feel proud of his son and want a closer connection. At least to see more of him. And that would mean seeing more of Marilyn.

There she was again, allowing fear to raise its ugly head above the battlements. She struggled to defeat it. Cameron loved her. The passion with which he made love to her surely proved it. And the way he kept coming back to her. She had sensed for some time that the self-disciplined side of conducting their relationship was becoming as much of a strain on him as it was on her. He longed to be with her all the time, just as she did with him. She knew it. Now, having been away for so long on his travels abroad, he'd had time to think things through and make up his mind to speak out. The mere idea made her feel nervous as well as happy. She treasured her freedom and independence. She had got used to all her well-organised routines in the house. She got up each morning showered, brushed her teeth, put on her day nourishing cream and patted in the gel for tightening up and preventing any puffiness or little lines around her eyes. Once dressed she went through to the kitchen to switch on the microwave for the porridge. She'd collect the morning paper which would have plopped through the letterbox earlier. *En route* she'd waken Christine for school unless it was the school holidays. Often, though, even if it was during the holidays, Christine would be away at some school camp or trip. Kate wanted her to grow up as tough and independent as herself. She put her name down for everything that was organised by the school.

After Christine left for school, Kate quickly washed the dishes and put everything away before relaxing for about ten minutes – no more – with a cup of coffee and the newspaper. Then, off to work.

She had her life perfectly planned. She had got so used to all her well-oiled routines, they had become part of herself. The strict routine in the prison had perhaps helped her to acquire this pattern of life. All the same, she'd always preferred to be efficient. She'd never liked chaos.

She couldn't imagine how she'd cope with sharing her life with a man, any man. Or even any other person, for that matter. At the same time, the acute longing to be close to Cameron for the rest of her life did not in any way diminish. Somehow she'd have to change, loosen up, compromise. Something would have to be done. Maybe it wasn't just something peculiar to her. Maybe living alone made everyone grow selfish and too fond of their little routines. Maybe this was another way of trying to feel safe and secure. It was all about creating illusions. What was needed was to tackle the deep-down motivations and realities.

She would gather all her courage around her and she'd tell Cameron exactly how she felt. They would sort everything out between them, day by day, step by step.

He was home nearly a week before he contacted her and it was arranged that he'd come to her flat the following Saturday. It was a brief telephone conversation but Kate's keyed-up sensitivities detected something different in his voice: something important was hovering in the air behind it. She felt excited again. And frightened again.

She took a great deal of care in selecting what she'd wear on Saturday. She flicked through her wardrobe of smart, tailored suits, especially her favourite trouser suits, and chose instead a moss-green wool dress that flattered her slim waist. Gold stud earrings and a couple of fine gold chains gave the outfit a bit of sparkle. She took the time off to have a blow-dry and a professional manicure in the best hairdresser's in town. Eventually she surveyed herself in the bedroom mirror with satisfaction. She looked good. Her normally pale creamy skin was prettily flushed and her eyes sparkled. She gave a twirl. She not only looked good, she looked on cloud nine of happiness.

The doorbell shattered her supreme self-confidence. She began to tremble.

Courage, she told herself, taking a slow deep breath. You've got it. You've always had it. Courage. She wanted to throw her arms around him the moment she opened the door and saw him. Before she could gather her wits, however, he had presented her with the usual bottle of wine and sauntered past her into the house. It was a white Sancerre and felt as if it had come straight from the fridge. She went through to the kitchen with it chilling her hands.

'How was your trip?' she asked in her usual cool tone of voice.

'I'll tell you all about it after dinner. First tell me all about you, and all the Glasgow gossip.'

This was their usual routine now. They talked. They laughed. They ate. They drank wine. She made the coffee and they took it through to the sitting room. Later they'd make love and she'd go to sleep in his arms.

'All right,' she smiled at him when she'd finished telling him the news. 'Now it's your turn. You said when you phoned from New York that you'd something important to tell me.'

'Oh yes. I've been putting out feelers and there's a definite commercial opportunity to be taken advantage of in America. Why don't I act as your agent there? I've so many good contacts now and they're crazy about anything Scottish. It's time your products were known outside of Scotland, Kate. You've limited your business by not – '

'This is what was so important?' she interrupted.

'Well, isn't it? America is an enormous market. It would be a wonderful opportunity. It would be a good deal for you.'

'For you, you mean. A wonderful opportunity. A good deal.' She was so disappointed, distressed, outraged, she daren't think. But still a memory of what Marilyn had once said flew unbidden into her mind. *He sees in you a wonderful opportunity. He's out to take over step by step. First he takes over your shop. Next he takes you over. Then your whole business . . .*

'No, I mean for you.' His voice had become cold.

'Listen,' she said, 'I know the kind of mark-up you take.'

'We could discuss all the details.'

'No. Let's get this clear once and for all. If I want to expand my business, whether it's to sell in America or whatever, I'll do it myself, do you hear? I'll do my own thing.'

She could see he was trying to keep his temper and at least he managed not to raise his voice as she was doing.

'You're just acting like a stubborn fool.'

'I'm maybe stubborn but I'm no fool, so don't you dare try to take me for one.'

'For God's sake, I thought I was doing you a favour. I've got the agencies for a dozen other firms and they've never had any reason to complain. Quite the contrary. What's the matter with you?'

'Did you sleep with them too? Is that your most successful *modus operandi*? Well, hard luck. It's not going to work with me.'

Temper flashed in his eyes.

'For Christ's sake! Is that really what you think?'

'You heard what I said.'

He got up.

'You're really something, do you know that? As hard-faced

a bitch as I've ever come across. No, worse. I've had more than enough of you.'

And before she knew what had happened, he was gone.

Chapter Forty-Six

To hell with him, she thought. She worked like fury. One step at a time? All right, that's what she'd do. First step, England. Harrods, Fortnum and Mason's, nothing but the best. She went immediately to a travel agent in town and booked a flight to London and a couple of nights in a hotel. She would have been ashamed to admit it to anyone, but she'd never been out of Scotland before. (She'd never even been up in an aeroplane.)

London opened up a new world to Kate. She found it incredibly exciting. Cities appealed to her much more than country areas. Loch Lomond, the Trossachs, the Highlands were all very well for a quick visit. She could enjoy a few days in the country and admire the scenery. But a few days, one week at most, was enough. After that she was bored and restless. Drug users got their 'buzz', their 'high' with heroin or whatever poison they happened to be using. She got hers by being part of a busy commercial metropolis. She felt the excitement of so many people (potential customers?) milling about. She adored all the shops and markets. There were theatres and other places of entertainment too but her priorities were all connected with business. She'd rather spend valuable time in her hotel in the evenings taking notes and planning the next day's strategies. Right away she saw she needed (and wanted) more time in London and fortunately the hotel was able to accommodate her for the full week.

She phoned her mother first of course and made sure that Christine could be looked after for the week.

'Listen, hen, we're aw fightin' tae huv the wean. Liz has won so far but even Aunty Bec's offered tae take wee Chrissie fur a night or two. Bec misses Sandra since she's gone on that VSO thing in Somalia or some weird place at the other end o' the world. Poor Bec's that worried in case Sandra gets hersel' killed.' Christine was called to the phone and Kate chatted with her and told her she'd bring her a special present from London.

On her day of arrival, Kate went to Harrods in Knightsbridge. What a thrill it was to see the size of the building and the beauty of it. She'd never seen so many windows belonging to one shop, and each window was a work of art. Kate strolled along lost in admiration. Eventually she went into the shop to reconnoitre. She had an appointment with the buyer next day but first she wanted to see the lie of the land, to observe and take note of everything that might help in her sales pitch. They obviously went in for good-quality, classy products. She came to the same conclusion when, later that day, she made a similar study of Fortnum and Mason's.

But the first thing that met her keen eye in the food hall of both establishments was some of the products for which Cameron had the agency. He'd been here before her. Well, fuck him, she thought. That wasn't going to stop her plugging her much more original and far better-quality Scottish products. She knew what was in every food recipe that came from her establishment. She could absolutely guarantee the unadulterated purity and top-class quality as well as the delicious taste of each and every article. The Highlander logo defied anyone to contradict this claim.

She had brought samples with her and piles of literature about the products including price lists which were far more competitive than anything Caledonia had to offer. After two or three days' hard sell, she got her toe in every door. She won orders; not huge orders, but it was a beginning. She was supremely confident that once people tried her products, they'd come back for more. Sales would steadily grow. Cameron's would decline. She was sure of it. She would show him!

Her excitement and adrenalin were at an all-time high.

Unfortunately, while she was in such a state, sleep was well-nigh impossible. She lay trying to blot out thoughts and sensations of being held in Cameron's arms, of feeling the hardness of his mouth on hers, and his manhood deep inside her.

By the last evening, she could bear it no longer. She sat in the hotel bar hoping against hope that one or two night-caps of whisky would help blot her out until the next day, when she was due to fly home. Instead it increased her sexual longings to an unendurable degree. All right, she thought, she was an independent, liberated woman. She wanted a man for sex so why shouldn't she have one. She glanced around the bar. Most people were in couples. There was, however, a sprinkling of single men. One in particular she knew was a resident. She'd seen him in the dining room at breakfast. He looked Scandinavian – broad shouldered but slim-built, blond, bearded and with piercing blue eyes. He was elegantly and expensively dressed. He would do very well. She met his eyes, smiled and raised her glass to him. Smiling in return he moved along the bar and came to sit beside her. 'Oh God,' she thought.

'Can I buy you another drink?' he asked.

Suddenly, she felt she needed one. She should not be doing this. Her mother would give her a black eye and worse if she knew. And quite right too.

'Thanks.' Again she smiled at the man who, if he was Scandinavian, had a surprisingly upper-class English voice.

'I'm Richard Smythe-Denby.'

Definitely not Scandinavian.

'Kate Gallacher.'

'Scottish?'

'How did you guess?'

He laughed. 'Well, apart from your lovely accent, the Gallacher gives you away.'

'Could be Irish.'

'With a Scottish burr like that?'

'And you?'

'I'm from Buckinghamshire.'

'I'm from Glasgow. I deal in high-quality Scottish food products.'

'I'm just here to do a round of galleries, concerts and shows.'

'On your own?'

'On this occasion, yes. Sometimes I prefer my own company.'

'So do I. I like to do my own thing.'

'What shows have you seen?'

'This has been a strictly business trip for me.'

'Evenings as well?'

'Yes. Tonight though, I feel like celebrating. I fly home tomorrow.'

'A bit late for the theatre.'

'I wasn't thinking about going out.' She gave him a meaningful look.

'Well.' He smiled. 'Could I help you celebrate?'

'You could try,' she said, smiling in return but wishing she could die. She was beginning to feel a little drunk. She was glad of that.

'Your place or mine?' He was still smiling.

'Oh God, this was terrible. The absolute pits.

'Mine,' Kate said. She sauntered upstairs to her bedroom with him as if she'd been picking up strange men all her life. She knew she'd regret this in the morning. She was regretting it now. In the bathroom she changed into her nightdress, a flimsy see-though garment that showed every inch of her naked body. She had a mad impulse to tell Smythe-Denby a joke about the two Glasgow women in a bus and one of them said to the other, 'Ah don't like them see-through nighties. They show ma vest.'

She controlled the impulse. It wasn't the right time for jokes. It wasn't the right time for anything. Anyway, it wasn't a joke. The Glasgow incident was real. She'd been sitting behind those women in the bus. She had a feeling, however, that somebody from Buckinghamshire with a name like

Smythe-Denby wouldn't be able to appreciate down-to-earth Glasgow humour.

He did seem to appreciate the look of her, though. She went over to the bed where he was already lying naked. This could not be happening. She got into bed and closed her eyes.

Chapter Forty-Seven

He was really very understanding when, in the morning, she felt like committing suicide. Not that she actually told him she felt suicidal. But it must have been pretty obvious that she was embarrassed, to say the least. And, as her mother would have said, she had 'Wan hell o' a heid'.

She awoke to find Smythe-Denby propped up on one elbow gazing down at her face.

'Oh God!' She'd said it out loud this time.

'No, Richard Smythe-Denby.'

She hoped she hadn't been snoring. Or even worse, dribbling. She closed her eyes again.

'This can't be happening.' She said that out loud too.

'It can and it has. Great, isn't it?'

'No. Was I very drunk?'

'I'd like to think you knew exactly what you were doing when you invited me to your bed.'

'I'd like you to know that's the first time in my life I've ever done such a thing. I mean, picked a man up. I have been married,' she added inconsequentially. She felt she was babbling and struggled to get a grip on herself.

'And where's hubby?'

She hated that word. It was so un-Scottish.

'He's dead.' She nearly added, 'I murdered him,' but decided it would be taking unfair advantage of the man to risk frightening him when he was naked. Being naked certainly made her feel vulnerable.

'I'm sorry.'

He wasn't, of course. It was just one of those polite things people said. She felt like answering with an impolite 'I'm not', but instead she told him, 'I've a plane to catch. I'd better get up and get dressed. Close your eyes.'

He laughed and didn't.

'Please,' she said angrily. 'I'm embarrassed.'

'Oh, very well.'

She flung back the bedcovers and dashed to the bathroom. There she showered and dressed as speedily as she could.

He was dressed when she returned to the room. He said, 'I'll see you to the airport.'

'No, I'd rather go on my own.'

'We must keep in touch.'

'Sorry.'

'I'm not allowing you to leave this room until you tell me your address and telephone number.'

'Don't be daft.'

'I mean it.'

'Why?'

'I want to see you again.'

'I've no plans to return to London. At least not in the near future.'

'I'll come up to Glasgow, then.'

'There's no point. I'm a very busy woman and my life's complicated enough as it is.'

'A little bit more complication isn't going to do either of us any harm.'

'Oh? And do you think your wife's going to agree with that?'

'My wife died eighteen months ago.'

'Oh, I'm sorry.' Now *she* was saying it. 'But look,' she went on in a more serious tone, 'you don't know anything about me. And believe me, there's things you wouldn't want to know. Last night was very nice. Best just to leave it that way.'

'Give me your address and telephone number.'

'You'll regret it.'

'Let me be the judge of that.'

She scribbled her home address and telephone number on the back of one of her business cards. Then she flung her things in her case and made to leave.

289

'Aren't you even going to kiss me?'

'No.'

He shook his head. 'You're a strange girl.'

'I know. Bye.'

And she was away. Flushed and flying like the wind from her guilt and embarrassment.

Once safely settled in the plane and with London receding into the far distance, she began to think more calmly. The best thing to do was just forget all about the incident and get on with her life as if nothing had happened. After all, to some of the women she knew, the women she employed for instance, what had happened would have been no big deal. They probably did it all the time. What's good for the goose is good for the gander was their motto. She still wasn't convinced though about their aggressive militant philosophy. They seemed to hate men while at the same time trying to ape all the things they hated about them. It didn't make sense to Kate and, she was beginning to realise, it was making less sense as time went on.

All right, she'd nursed a deep hatred of men for a while. It had showed in other ways. For instance, she didn't employ one male person. She'd turned down every male application for every job, even driving the vans. For this she'd got into trouble at an Industrial Tribunal. But had managed, with sob stories and excuses, to get off the hook. For a short time she'd had to take on a male employee, but he'd been given such a hard time of it he'd been glad to leave. Her brother Tommy was the only exception to her all-female rule. Maybe he was one of the reasons she had begun to doubt her feelings and actions. She couldn't hate Tommy. There was no valid reason to hate him. And he was a man. All right, she'd had reason to hate Pete. But not every man was the same as him. Some were quite nice human beings. Like Tommy. Like Richard Smythe-Denby.

Human beings. Those were the words she must remember. It was time she changed the all-female policy she had in the business. It was discriminating. And discrimination was discrimination, no matter who it was levelled against. Her brother would be pleased. Poor Tommy was far from happy at being so outnumbered. She suspected he was still being picked on and sexually harassed at times, despite her severe warnings to the staff about this on more than one occasion.

The trouble with Tommy was, he was too nice. And too timid for his own good. But the customers liked him. He was always ready with a smile and an eagerness to please and be helpful. She had him going out and around more now getting orders, which helped with his problem with the girls in the unit.

By the time she arrived back in Glasgow, Kate was totally immersed in thoughts about the business and had, to all intents and purposes, forgotten that anybody called Richard Smythe-Denby existed. She went straight to the unit to do some work in her office and to deal with any problems that might have arisen. Later she went to collect Christine and give her the present she'd brought from London.

Marilyn was at Killearn Street as usual, and greeted Kate with her usual affectionate kiss. A few minutes afterwards, while Marilyn was making a pot of tea, she said,

'Do you know, Kate, I was thinking. It isn't fair that Gavin has such a lovely son and yet is being denied the right to even see him.'

'Has he asked to see him?'

'No, not exactly. But I think it's only right that he *should* see him. Don't you?'

Kate shrugged.

'It has nothing to do with me, Marilyn.'

'You wouldn't mind, dear?'

'You must do what you think right.'

Marilyn pounced on Kate and kissed her again.

'Oh, I knew you'd understand.'

Marilyn's perfume remained to clog Kate's nostrils, making her feel sick. Or was it the idea, the fear of losing Cameron? But what was she thinking about? She already *had* lost him. She'd *wanted* to lose him. He was a cold, ruthless, calculating bastard. Who needed him?

That night, lying alone in bed, she fought to kill the idea that she did. She couldn't banish him from her mind. But she would be damned if she was going to give up trying.

When, about a week later, Smythe-Denby phoned, she was quite pleasant to him. He asked if he could come up to Glasgow to see her. She only had a few moments' hesitation before saying, 'All right.' She added, 'You're welcome to stay at my flat, but in the spare bedroom.'

'Of course,' he said.

'Have you been to Glasgow before?'

'Only passing through on my way to visit friends in the Highlands.'

'It's a much more interesting place than people think. And the people are *very* friendly.'

'I know.'

What wit! She chose to ignore it. 'I'll show you around and get tickets for a couple of shows. And there are some good exhibitions on.'

'You do go to the theatre and the galleries in Glasgow then?'

'Not really. I never have the time. But I'll make time for you.'

'I'm honoured.'

'To show you around Glasgow. I'm proud of my city. That's the only reason.'

'Of course,' he said.

Chapter Forty-Eight

It took Cameron quite some time to get over his anger at
Kate. Then he began to miss her. She was a ruthless, calculating, competitive bitch. Usually he avoided women like
that. Certainly never chose to have any kind of relationship
with them. But she'd made him an offer that he found
difficult to refuse. Now, he couldn't get her out of his mind.
He tried. He kept himself busy as long as he could. He even
steered clear of Glasgow for a while. Nothing worked.

Damn the woman, he kept thinking.

It confused him when women took the initiative in
relationships. He knew he was old-fashioned in this respect
but he didn't care. He liked to be the one who made the
first move. He looked back with longing to the days when
it was the man who invited the woman out on a date.

They insisted on equal pay. But a drinking buddy of
his, Matt Bromley, owned a bookshop and he'd said that his
female employees insisted on equal pay and he'd agreed to
pay them the same as the boys. But every time there were
boxes of books to be carried upstairs or downstairs, it was
the lads who had to do it. The girls were indignant if it
was suggested they carry anything so heavy.

'Fair enough,' Matt said. 'But why should the lads have
to do extra for the same wages as them?'

They'd both agreed that it should be equal pay for equal
work. There was a difference.

In fact men and women were different in so many ways,
not only in physical strength. And as the French said, 'Vive
la différence!'

Another thing Matt was complaining about got Cameron
mad as well. Matt had three sons, one at primary school and
twins at secondary. One day recently, a bus had been going

round all the schools. It was fitted up to demonstrate modern technology, science and computers and stuff. But only girls were taken from each class and allowed in the bus and shown everything. The boys were left sitting in the classrooms.

'It's getting bloody ridiculous,' Matt said. 'My boys are beginning to shrug and just give up hope. And it's eroding their self-confidence and sense of self-worth.'

It made Cameron think of his own son. He had made sure that the boy would always be well provided for and lack for nothing that money could buy. It was beginning to occur to him though that money wasn't everything. Maybe he should take more of an interest in the child's welfare. He had very little, if any, faith in Marilyn's ability to give serious thought to the youngster's education. Would she make sure he was encouraged to participate in sports to keep his body healthy? Would she choose the best school in which his character as well as his mind would be developed to the best of his ability?

Maybe he was being a little premature. After all, the boy could not even walk yet. But that was another thing. Would Marilyn have enough sense to enrol him into a decent nursery school?

He groaned. If it wasn't one extreme, it was the other. Marilyn had what to his mind were some of the worst in female characteristics. She was clinging, affected, babyish, totally helpless and dependent. He didn't want that either.

What *did* he bloody want? A kind of balance, he supposed. A partnership of mutual respect. Each bringing their own genuine qualities to a relationship to be valued for their own sake.

He didn't believe that either extreme – Kate or Marilyn – was for him. Yet still, he couldn't get Kate out of his head. On a recent business trip to London, he had noticed the Highlander logo in Harrods and Fortnum and Mason's. Surprisingly, he couldn't feel angry at that. On the contrary, he felt like laughing. She really was the bloody limit. He had to admire the spirit of the girl. Eventually he decided to call on her. It was no problem. Her flat was only a couple of streets away from his. He wouldn't phone her first though, in case she hung up on him. He'd go on Saturday. He'd take the usual bottle of wine. Surely she wouldn't shut the door in his face. Anyway, he wouldn't allow that. But he'd keep things at their usual cool, laid-back pace. They'd drink the wine, they'd talk, they'd laugh. And finally he'd take her to bed and make love to her. Although on the surface she was a cold calculating bitch, in bed he'd been glad to find she was truly passionate.

When Saturday came, he could hardly wait until the time when he was in the habit of arriving on her doorstep. He felt a deep satisfaction; more than that, a deep thrill at the thought of being with her again. He always felt, one way or another, stimulated by her presence.

Dead on time, he rang the bell. Kate looked flushed, even flustered.

'Oh, it's you.' A moment's hesitation. 'I suppose you'd better come in.' It was no more than he'd expected. What he didn't expect was the blond, bearded guy sitting at the kitchen table. He might have known. Yet, not for one moment had it entered his head that she'd pick up another man, especially with such speed. And she would have taken the initiative in that as she did in everything else. It seemed no time since they'd lain in each other's arms. It had seemed so right. So permanent, he realised now. What a fool he'd been. What a fool he felt now.

'Gavin Cameron, Richard Smythe-Denby.'

She had recovered her cool. He and Smythe-Denby shook hands.

'You'll stay and have a meal with us?' she said.

'No thanks. I've been out of town. I just called in to see if . . .' he said the first thing that came into his head, 'you'd had second thoughts about the agency.'

'No,' she said. Not even a sorry. He could have strangled her.

'OK.' He shrugged. He smiled. 'I'd better be on my way. I'm meeting someone. Enjoy your meal.'

He needed a drink. He drove along to Byres Road and went into the first pub he came to. Why the hell should he care who she slept with or what she did with her life? But he did. Suddenly she was both a stranger to him, and an urgently intimate, a necessary part of himself. He couldn't visualise life without her. It was crazy. He didn't want it to be like this. It must *not* be like this. What good would it do him?

He downed a couple of double whiskies without even noticing.

Without her, his life seemed suddenly empty, pointless. In his struggle to find firm common-sense ground, he remembered his son again. It gave him a focus, a way out of his emotional morass. It was time he took more responsibility for his son. He hadn't even seen the boy. He couldn't wait another day. He drove straight to Possilpark and to Marilyn's flat. There was no reply. The child would (or should) be in bed by now and if she wasn't here with it, the chances were she'd be at her mother-in-law's. He remembered that they were very close and Marilyn was a regular visitor to Killearn Street. So he went to Killearn Street. It was a right dump of a place. The outside wall and the wall inside the close were covered in graffiti. Litter flapped through from front to back. This was no place for any child of his to be brought up. Marilyn's flat in Saracen Street was no better. He was glad he'd come. He had a responsibility to his son. He rang the doorbell.

'I'll get it, Granny.' Marilyn's affected cooing voice made him cringe.

'Gosh!' Her surprise was sincere enough. But the sincerity, or at least as far as he could judge, didn't last long. 'Would you believe it, I've been trying to contact you. Come in, darling.' She raised her voice. 'Granny, you'll never guess who our unexpected visitor is!'

Granny appeared at the kitchen door, drying her hands on a tea towel.

'Who, hen?' Then seeing him, 'Gavin Cameron? Away through tae the sitting room, son. Ah've jist made a pot o' tea. Ah'll bring ye both a cup.'

In the sitting room Marilyn began stroking his arm as if he was her favourite cat.

'Sit down, Marilyn. I want to talk to you.'

'Yes, darling.'

'I'd rather you didn't call me that.'

She pouted prettily. 'I always used to.'

'I'm not here to turn the clock back so don't get any ideas like that.'

Her eyes widened. 'Well, why are you here?'

As if she didn't know. 'I want to discuss my son's future and agree access.'

'Oh, I don't know about that. After all, you did abandon us both.'

'Don't talk nonsense, Marilyn.'

She pouted again. 'Yes, you did.'

He began to think it must have been the whisky that had brought him here. He should have waited and made an appointment tomorrow with his lawyer. He'd do that. Discuss the situation with old McFarlane. Get the whole position legalised. No doubt he could use money as a lever with Marilyn. She wasn't that stupid.

How he'd ever thought her even physically attractive, he didn't know. Now he found her almost repulsive.

Then she brought the baby through. She'd obviously lifted him from his cot. He was sound asleep.

Cameron stared at the child's face. He took one of the small hands in his. Something happened to him then. He wasn't sure what. He only knew that in that moment both he, and his life, had changed for ever.

Chapter Forty-Nine

Kate decided on charcoal grilled beefsteaks with whisky and shallot butter for Smythe-Denby's meal. She made the whisky and shallot butter by beating together softened butter, finely chopped parsley, some shallots, whisky, salt and freshly milled pepper. She brushed the steaks with oil and grilled them to the required degree then spread the meat with the butter. She'd learned that Smythe-Denby liked chocolate and so she made chocolate-dipped fruit. She melted a bar of Green and Black's milk chocolate, took some strawberries, with a little bit of stem still in place, and dipped them until one side of the strawberries was covered with the chocolate. After that had set, she did the same with a bar of Green and Black's dark chocolate, dunking the other half of each strawberry.

Richard enjoyed the meal so much, she thought he was never going to stop going on about it.

'Why so surprised that I'm a good cook?' she said. 'I told you I was in the food trade.'

'I'm sure not everybody in the food trade can cook so well, if at all. Many concentrate on the business and sales side, I imagine. Is that what your friend does?'

'Cameron? He's the agent for most Scottish food products and he owns outlet shops in different parts of Scotland.'

'And he wants to take over your products?'

'Yes.'

'Is he a good businessman?'

'Yes.'

'Then why did you turn him down?'

'I don't need him.'

Smythe-Denby smiled. 'I see. You're obviously a very independent lady.'

She shrugged. 'Anything he can do, I can do better.'

'Oh! I'm beginning to feel sorry for the poor chap.'

'Why on earth should you feel sorry for him?' she heard her voice snap back. 'You don't even know the man.'

'I can imagine what formidable competition he'll have in you.'

'That's business.'

'Cut-throat, ruthless . . . Is that how you see it?'

'I didn't say that. You're fond of exercising your imagination, aren't you?'

He raised his glass to her.

'Here's success to all your ventures.'

'You haven't told me much about yourself.'

'I run my estate in Buckinghamshire.'

She had thought as much.

'Estate sound rather grand,' he went on. 'In fact, most of it was sold off by my father when he was alive. But there's still a few acres left, and the house is of historic interest. It's open to the public during weekends in summer. You'd be surprised at the amount of work and organisation that takes. We get tour bookings from Japanese parties, lots of Americans, even Russians nowadays. And I've had a couple of pop festivals in the grounds.'

Kate put the coffee pot, cream and sugar, some *petits fours* and china cups and saucers on a tray.

'Let's go through and drink our coffee in the sitting room.'

'Allow me to carry that.'

'I can manage.'

In the sitting room she could feel him watching her every move as she poured the coffee.

'You've a very pleasant flat,' he said.

'I like it.'

'You must come and visit my house.'

'I'm very busy . . .'

'So am I, but I really would like the opportunity to return your hospitality.'

'Very well. One weekend perhaps?'

'Soon I hope.'

'If you wish.'

'I do.'

After a moment's silence, Kate said, 'Why me?'

'Why you what?'

She shrugged. 'I don't know. Yes, I do. We're poles apart.'

'In what way?'

'In every way.' Why waste time, she thought. Time was too short. Life was too short.

'I don't understand,' he said.

'Let me spell it out. You seem a nice man. I like you. Because of that I feel I should be honest with you. I won't think any less of you if you don't want to see me again after tonight, after what I tell you about myself. Indeed if you want to walk out now, I'll understand.'

He laughed. 'As bad as all that? Have you committed a murder or something?'

'As a matter of fact, I have.'

His smile faded. He stared at her in stunned disbelief for a moment. 'You're joking.'

'I don't joke about murder. I come from one of the roughest districts of Glasgow. My husband dealt in drugs. I hated him for that. And a whole lot of other things. The batterings he gave me, for instance. Eventually, he went too far. I happened to have a kitchen knife in my hand and I stabbed him. I was found guilty of culpable homicide. I believe it's called manslaughter in England. I served two years of a three-year sentence.'

Another silence.

'Well, you are full of surprises.'

'Aren't I just?'

'I'm sorry, Kate.'

'You're leaving.'

'Don't be silly. Of course I'm not leaving. I'm sorry that you've suffered so much. But it explains a lot.'

'Explains a lot of what?'

'Of how you are.'

'A bit of a psychologist, are you?'

'Maybe. I think you've suffered a great deal. You've been deeply hurt, and you try to cover it up with a hard shell.'

'You'll be asking for a fee next.'

'Come here.' He put out his arms for her. For a moment she hesitated. Then she thought, What the hell, and went over to sit beside him on the settee.

He took her in his arms and kissed her deeply. Soon they were in bed together and making love. Again it was enjoyable but she found herself faking an orgasm. She felt affectionate towards him but not passionate. Maybe that was something that would develop in time. She hoped so. Yet, long after he had fallen asleep, she lay wide awake and feeling sad to the point of tears. She was thinking of Cameron. She couldn't help it. The bastard cared about nothing except his business. No doubt of course he'd enjoyed his weekly Saturday meal with the passionate 'afters'. Why shouldn't he? What man wouldn't? They were all the bloody same. Out for what they could get. No, they weren't, she argued with herself, fighting to stem her tears. She must try to stop going to such extremes. Richard was different. Even after such a short time, he seemed to genuinely care about her.

Next day, he asked her if she'd be down in London again soon. 'If so, we could meet there again. But I'd rather you came to Buckinghamshire. It's a beautiful part of the country.'

'I'm not much of a country person,' she confessed. 'I'm a city girl through and through. In fact, I've often thought that one day when I've time I'd like to do a tour of all the world's capital cities.'

'All right. We'll do it together, shall we?'

She laughed.

'We'll see. Perhaps one day.'

'It would give me a chance to give you an all-round education.'

She looked at him warily, ready to be offended.

'Education?'

'In the arts. The sculptures of Michelangelo in Florence. His ceiling in the Sistine Chapel in Rome. From what I've heard, you have sadly neglected these things in your life.'

She relaxed again. 'Oh well, it's just a question of time, you see. I'd like to but – '

'Kate, you really must get your priorities right. Everybody needs some time to relax and enjoy the really important things in life.'

It was obvious he had never needed to worry about security, or having to make money.

'OK, OK.'

To please him during the next few days she took him around the art galleries in Glasgow. And the museums. And the theatres.

'I'm impressed,' he said.

'I'm exhausted.'

'Oh, I'm sorry, Kate. I've been so selfish and thoughtless, dragging you and your little girl around from morning till night for nearly two weeks. She's beautiful, by the way, no wonder you're so proud of her.'

'She's had a wonderful time, Richard. You've been very good to her.'

'And you've been far too good to me. All the wonderful meals you've cooked, for a start. As well as trying to keep in touch with your business. Well, I'm not going to allow you to cook dinner or do another thing today, either for me or for your business. Tonight I'm taking you out for dinner. Could you get someone to babysit for Christine?'

'But it's your last night. I planned something special.'

'I appreciate that but I want you to relax and get attended to for a change. I want to pamper you and spoil you.'

It sounded a good idea.

He booked a table in One Devonshire Gardens after Kate told him she'd never been there but had heard it was really good and very near to her flat, which was handy. They soon discovered that indeed the food was wonderful. Kate was thoroughly enjoying her meal until Cameron entered the small dining room accompanied by Marilyn.

So that's how the land lay, she thought. She might have known.

The moment Marilyn caught sight of Kate, she sashayed straight over to her. She was wearing a tight satin dress and she'd obviously had her blonde head professionally brightened and curled.

'Darling Kate,' she cried. 'How wonderful to see you.' (She'd seen her only the other day.)

Kate introduced her to Richard.

'I'd just *love* it if we could make a foursome, dear.' Marilyn looked her most innocent.

Cameron said tersely, 'Marilyn, it's a private party.'

Marilyn pouted. And as he tried to drag her away, she resisted.

'But Kate and I are *friends*. There's nothing private between us.'

Kate had never been nearer to telling Marilyn to fuck off. But Richard was signalling to the waiter to set two more places. He was rising, smiling and saying, 'Yes, of course. Do join us.'

Oh God! Kate thought.

Chapter Fifty

Cameron could cheerfully have killed Marilyn. He'd been to his solicitor to find out where he stood. He'd planned everything to last detail. He'd also been gathering interesting, useful facts, learning a thing or two about Marilyn. He'd phoned and asked her if he could come and discuss, in detail, the subject of his son's future. He wished on this occasion he'd just arrived on her doorstep. It wasn't convenient, she said. The house was in a mess and anyway she'd never been out for a meal for absolutely *ages*. He already knew it was a mess but for the sake of peace, and maybe it would be easier anyway, they would speak on neutral ground. Or so he'd thought.

He'd booked at table in One Devonshire Gardens. It was bad enough to see Kate sitting there with Smythe-Denby. But for Marilyn to make such a fool of herself . . . Or was there method in her madness? Was there more than just wanting to embarrass both him and Kate? Could she be avoiding or postponing what he wanted to talk to her about? Smythe-Denby had remained perfectly relaxed. So had Marilyn. But Kate was visibly uptight. She tried to contribute to the conversation, but failed miserably. He felt anything but happy himself. While Marilyn warbled on, and flapped her lashes, she gazed adoringly at Smythe-Denby as if each and every word he uttered was an astonishing jewel.

He'd thought the night would never end. By the time he was taking Marilyn back to her dump of a flat, he was furious with her. She was a lazy slut and definitely not fit to be a mother. He told her this while she was wiggling out of her coat like a striptease artist, the invitation in her eyes.

'Look at this place. It's a bloody disgrace. You can neither keep your home decent nor take care of your child. You've dumped him on your ex-mother-in-law because you're a lazy slut.'

Marilyn's mouth was hanging open as he spoke. Then she burst into tears and sobbed,

'You're a cruel, heartless beast. I hate you.'

'I don't care a damn what you think about me. All I care about is the welfare of my son.'

'His granny loves looking after him. She insisted on looking after him. She says it's just like having her Joe all over again.'

'I've seen a copy of the birth certificate. His name is Joseph and that's what I want him to be called. And another thing. I'm applying for custody.'

'What?' Marilyn screamed incredulously. 'You can't do that!'

'Why not?'

'You're a man. They don't give custody to men.'

'I'm not "men". I'm the child's father.'

'But you're a man.'

'If the mother is proved to be not a fit and responsible person it's a different story.'

'But just because I get a bit disorganised with the housework doesn't mean – '

'Marilyn, I've been having you watched by a private detective. Two, in fact. They do shifts.'

Her mouth dropped open again. Then she managed huffily, 'Why shouldn't I have a bit of fun? I haven't been doing any harm.'

'On the nights you haven't been sleeping at Mrs Gallacher's, you've been bringing men back here.'

'Why shouldn't I have a few friends? I'm still young. I want to get married again. I don't like being on my own. So I have to get out and meet people.'

'In pubs and hotel bars? Half the time you're pissed out of your mind.'

'That's a lie!'

'Marilyn, you've taken me for a fool once. You're not

doing it again. I've photographs. I even have you on tape. By the way, you've missed your vocation. You should have been a striptease artist. That's one thing you can do well – take your clothes off.'

'You were certainly happy enough to let me take them off for you.'

'Well, I'm not happy now.'

'You'll regret talking to me like this.' Marilyn's normally pretty rosebud mouth had taken on an ugly twist. 'I'll fight you every inch of the way in court. I'll blacken your character. I'll . . .'

'What with? I'm going tomorrow to tell the bank to stop your allowance. There won't be a penny for you from next week onwards. I'll also transfer Joseph's allowance to Mrs Gallacher's name while she's still got him. She can't be very flush, to say the least, since her husband's retired.'

'You can't leave me without a penny.' Marilyn began to wail and weep again.

'Oh can't I? Just you watch me.'

'It's not fair. I've never done Joe any harm. I couldn't. I made sure he was all right with his granny.'

'She's not his granny, Marilyn. She's no blood relation to him whatsoever. And she has a drink problem.'

Marilyn's eyes widened with shocked disbelief.

'She has not! That's a terrible lie.'

'No, it isn't. Apart from Kate once confiding in me about it, I've learned from other sources. I have written statements.'

He'd had to pay for those. But it had been worth it. He had no qualms about this. After all, what they said was no more than the truth. Mrs Gallacher's problem apparently came and went. Flared up, then died down again, for weeks or months. But it was a problem nevertheless. A potential danger to a young child.

Then there was the appalling social conditions in Possilpark. It was not, he genuinely believed, the best place to bring up any child. He would employ a good nanny, and his home in the opulent West End, although a flat, had plenty of rooms and was within yards of a beautiful park. He could afford to buy an even bigger house elsewhere, with a garden. Maybe he would one day but at present there was no need. He would give the boy every care, every chance in life. And the time to start was right now, while he was still young enough to forget the Gallachers and Possilpark.

Cameron wasn't on such confident legal ground for custody as he was making out to Marilyn. He was actually staking everything on her selfishness and greed, and her inability to have any depth of feeling for the child. Now he said,

'Look, Marilyn, I just want to do my best for the boy. If you agree to give me full custody, then I'll not only continue with your allowance until you marry again, but I'll give you a lump sum now. A very generous lump sum. You could treat yourself to a wonderful holiday abroad. Go on a cruise to the Bahamas perhaps. Think of the kind of men you'd meet on a luxury cruise liner. You deserve to get out of this place and give yourself a real chance, Marilyn.'

She deserved a kick up the arse but he could see the light come on in her baby-blue eyes. Even as he spoke she was seeing herself bathed in luxury, enjoying nothing but sunshine and roses. And men. Or rather the flattery, the pandering, the petting and the good times men could give her.

'Well, as long as my dear little Joe is all right. I suppose you could afford to give him far more than poor little me. I adore him of course, and it will break my heart to give him up but I'd do anything to make sure he's well taken care of.'

She made him feel sick. He could have puked right there and then.

'Rest assured, Marilyn, you needn't worry about Joseph. He will lack for nothing. Now will you meet me tomorrow at my solicitor's . . .'

He took one of McFarlane's cards from his pocket and

scribbled a time on the back of it before handing it to her. 'We'll get everything legalised. You'll just have to sign a few papers and, of course, I'll give you the cheque. After that, you can go straight to the travel agent's. Buy some new outfits too, no doubt.'

She was shiny-eyed and flushed with excitement at the thought. She clapped her hands like a child at Christmas. She seemed to have the emotional age of a five-year-old. If that. Never a worry about leaving her son or leaving Mrs Gallacher bereft. Even he felt guilty about that. The old woman was probably not all that much more suitable than Marilyn to bring up a young child, especially in that slum where she lived. But at least she seemed genuinely fond of Joseph and had been trying to do her best for him.

Marilyn was doing her sexy wiggle again.

'Darling Gavin, stay with me tonight, why don't you?'

For one thing, he remembered that she wasn't sexy at all. For another, he would rather fuck anybody else but her.

So he managed a regretful smile. 'I'm sorry, Marilyn. I've still some paperwork to do at home. So much piles up when I'm away from my Glasgow base. You have a couple of nightcaps. Go to bed and dream of your plans for the future. The very near future. With a bit of luck you might get a booking for that cruise within days.'

'Ooh yes.' She clapped her hands again. 'I can't wait.'

He made for her door.

'I'd better go. See you tomorrow morning at McFarlane's.'

'McFarlane's?'

'The solicitor's office.'

'Oh yes.'

After he left he could hear her triumphant cry of 'Yippee' as he went down the stairs. He swore to himself that she, or any of the Gallacher clan for that matter, would never be allowed to come near his son again.

Chapter Fifty-One

'Here, hang on there. Whit dae ye think ye're at. An' who's this ye've brought?'

Cameron had come to Killearn Street with the smart uniformed Nanny Livingstone to collect the child. Mrs Gallacher had welcomed him in. It was only after he announced he'd come to collect his son that she became aggressive and confused.

Cameron groaned.

'I don't believe it! Although I might have known, I suppose, that Marilyn hasn't told you.'

'Ah hivnae seen the lassie aw week. Whit's this aw about?' Then to Nanny Livingstone, 'Take yer hands aff that wean.'

Cameron said, 'I'm really sorry about this, Mrs Gallacher. Marilyn promised to tell you. I wanted to come and have a talk with you before any action was taken but she insisted that she was the one who should do all the talking and explaining.'

'Ah dinnae know whit ye're on aboot.'

'Marilyn's gone abroad. But before she left she agreed to give up the baby. It's all been done legally and above board. I have to have full custody from now on. This is Nanny Livingstone who'll be Joseph's nurse.'

He felt truly sorry for the old woman. She had gone a sickly grey colour. She sat down with a thump as if her legs suddenly couldn't support her.

'Are you all right?' he asked.

'Aw right? Aw right? Ye're talkin' aboot stealin' ma wean!'

He wanted to abruptly point out that Joseph was not her child, but instead he managed to gentle his voice.

'I'm sorry. Truly sorry. And I must thank you for taking such good care of my son. He *is* my son, Mrs Gallacher, my

flesh and blood. He belongs with me.' He nodded to Nanny
Livingstone, who lifted the child and wrapped him in a
blanket.

'Ye cannae dae this.' Mrs Gallacher's voice rose to a
broken-hearted wail. 'Where's Marilyn? She'll no' let ye take
her wean.'

'Marilyn's gone.'

'Marilyn's gone? She cannae be gone. She wouldnae go
away an' leave her wean.'

'Mrs Gallacher, Marilyn doesn't care about the child. But
I do. You have my word that Joseph will always be loved and
taken care of.'

Mrs Gallacher seemed incapable of getting up from the
chair. But her wail gained in strength as Nanny Livingstone
and Joseph disappeared out of the door and away from the
house.

'Is there anyone I could phone or fetch to be with you.
Any of the neighbours? Your husband?'

She looked dazed. She had started to nurse herself and
repeat over and over again, 'Oh Joe. Oh Joe. Oh Joe.'

He thought she must have become completely unhinged.
He didn't know what to do for the best. He knocked at a
couple of doors on the way downstairs but there was no
reply. All he could hear was the terrible keening noise from
the top flat.

He remembered it was Saturday. Perhaps Mr Gallacher
and almost everybody else would be at the big football match
at Ibrox. He should tell the old woman's daughter. He had
no desire to turn up on Kate Gallacher's doorstep again but
he felt it might seem cowardly in the circumstances just to
phone. Nanny Livingstone had her own set of keys. The
house was all ready to receive Joseph, including a beautifully
decorated and equipped nursery. The nurse's bedsitting
room with en suite bathroom was next to the nursery.

He dropped Nanny Livingstone and Joseph off at the
house and he drove round to Kirklee Terrace to Kate's flat.
She had a car of her own now so he wouldn't need to give

her a lift back to Possilpark. Not that she would accept a lift or anything else from him. Her lover with the double-barrelled name would probably be there anyway. Cameron wondered what a guy like that would make of Killearn Street. He rang the doorbell. Kate opened the door and the moment he saw her, with her long hair tied back and strands of it straggling forward across her brightly flushed face, he felt an unexpected tightening in his chest. She was wearing a striped navy and white cook's apron over her open-necked blouse and blue jeans. A delicious smell of cooking wafted out from the kitchen.

'I've something on the cooker. You'd better come in.'

He followed her through. She switched off the gas and moved a pot. Then she turned to him, wiping her hands on her apron.

'Well? What's it to be this time? Another good business deal for Gallacher's? Or another jolly foursome with Marilyn?'

He winced at the memory of that.

'It's your mother.'

Immediately she was alert, anxious.

'What's wrong with my mother?'

'She's very upset. I think you should go to her.'

She began hastily tugging off her apron.

'Upset about what?'

'Have you got your car?'

'Yes.' She ran through to the bedroom and came back struggling into a coat. She had the car keys in her hand. 'What's happened? Where is she? Have you seen her?'

'I've just come from Killearn Street.'

They left the flat together. Outside she turned to him before getting into her car. 'Have you left Marilyn with her?'

'No, she's on her own.'

Kate flashed him a brief, puzzled look before the car shot off.

Kate ran up the stairs to the top flat and knocked on the

door. She waited impatiently and, when nobody came in response, she knocked again, this time louder and with more urgency. Still no reply. Her heart began to thump with fear. She called through the letterbox:

'Mammy, it's me. Open the door.'

She peeked into the lobby. She could almost see the silence, everything was so still and empty. She battered at the door with her fists. Then after another fruitless minute or two, she knocked at the other door on the landing. No reply there either. Anyway, Mrs Dooley in the bottom flat was the only one of the neighbours who kept her mother's spare key.

Kate dashed downstairs and thumped at Mrs Dooley's door. Only the cats miaowed in answer. Then Kate caught sight of Mrs Dooley coming shuffling into the close weighed down by two plastic shopping bags. Filled with tins of cat food, by the looks of them.

'Mrs Dooley, have you got my mammy's keys?'

'Aye, hen. They're hangin' on a nail behind ma door.'

'Can I have them please. I've forgotten mine.'

'Aye, sure.' Mrs Dooley opened the door and was immediately engulfed in cats of all shapes and sizes and colours.

'Watch you don't tramp on the kittens, hen,' she warned as Kate followed her into the house. 'Jist help yersel'.'

Kate grabbed the keys and ran back upstairs shouting, 'Thanks, Mrs Dooley.'

She found her mother in the sitting room.

'Mammy, what's wrong?'

Her mother looked defeated, old, shrunken.

'Mammy,' Kate repeated, this time giving the tiny body a shake. 'I can't help you if I don't know what's happened.'

'Ye cannae help me. Naebody can.'

'But what's happened?'

'It's ma ain fault fur gettin' too fond o' that wean. Ah should huv hud mair sense.'

'Something's happened to Joe?' Kate cried out.

Her mother sighed.

'Aye. Somethin' happened tae Joe a long time ago. But ah suppose ah never really believed ah'd lost him fur good. Ah've been a silly auld woman. Ah'm needin' ma heid looked at.'

'Has Marilyn taken the baby away? Is that it?'

'It's been such a shock – wi' wan thing an' the other. Ah've aye been that fond o' the lassie. Because Joe wis that fond o' her, ah suppose.'

'So she has taken him. Well, I wouldn't worry about that, Mammy. She'll be back with him sooner or later. Sooner, I'll bet. I can't see Marilyn taking full responsibility for the baby. She hasn't shown any sign of doing that up till now. In fact I think – '

'It wisnae her. Oh, she's gone aw right. Gone abroad it seems, an' never even a cheerio tae me or yer daddy. Him an' Tommy's at the big match so he disnae know yet. He'll be that cut up as well. He's been good tae that lassie.'

Kate was beginning to see the light. Although she could hardly believe it possible.

'Then who was it?'

'Mr Cameron came wi' a strange woman. Ah couldnae have stopped them even if ah'd been able. Ah hudnae the right, ye see. As he said, the wee fella's his son. Ah've nae claim on him at aw.'

'The bastard!' Kate cried out.

'Naw, he's no', hen. Ye've aye been too quick tae down that fella.'

'It was a terribly cruel thing to do.'

'Naw, it wisnae. He'd every right. Ah see that now. The fella wis as nice as he could be about it. He thought Marilyn had broken it tae me – paved the way, ah suppose.'

'I'll bet.'

Mary sighed.

'Ye can take that look aff yer face. Whit that fella does is none o' yer business. Ye've got a fella an' ah expect Mr Cameron's got himsel' a wee lassie. That's probably why he wants the wean. Jist you keep yer interferin' nose oot o' it.'

Kate felt offended.

'I was only thinking about you.'

'Well dinnae. Ah've come through as bad as this, an' worse, before an' ah've survived. An' ah'll survive again. Away an' make me a cup o' tea. An' put a good slug o' whisky in it,' she called after Kate.

Chapter Fifty-Two

He had the cheek to phone and ask how her mother was.

'She's all right but no thanks to you, you bastard,' Kate said.

'You're obviously back to your normal self. Fine.' With that he hung up.

She felt shaken at the sound of his voice. It took her a few minutes to calm down again. She had a long drive in front of her. It wouldn't do to set off in such an emotional state. She was upset enough about not being able to take Christine with her. Her father had pleaded with her to leave Christine with her mother. She might have resisted his pleas but then her mother had broken down and wept.

'Don't take wee Chrissie away frae me as well. No' the now, hen. Ah couldnae bear it.'

In the face of her mother's distress, Kate had swallowed her own. She'd arranged for Christine to have a week off school. Christine had been disappointed, of course, but eventually she'd accepted the promise that she would visit Richard another time.

'Soon, darling,' Kate assured her. 'I'll arrange it while I'm there.'

She drove fast, despite her efforts to calm down. It was November, cold and foggy in patches. The trees were crisply white. Except the ash trees. The sudden frost had stripped them. Masses of leaves lay under each like black carpets. Everything looked cold and black and unfriendly. She wished with all her heart she was back in Glasgow.

She tried to think of Christine rather than Cameron. She was glad she'd left her in Possilpark. It would do her good. Recently she had been reluctant to visit her granny or her Aunty Liz. In fact she didn't want to go to Possilpark for any reason. It was understandable in a way. Her friends were now her fellow pupils at her posh private school. It was the 'posh' part that Kate had begun to worry about. Christine seemed to be getting a bit snobby. Little minx. She'd have to have a good talk with her when she got back. There were lots of decent folk in Possilpark. They weren't all druggies, alkies, gangsters and vandals. And if people were unemployed, it wasn't their fault.

She seemed to have been driving for days. It was so boring. She stopped at a motorway café for a cup of tea and a sandwich. She studied her AA road map while drinking the tea and absentmindedly chewing the sandwich. Then back on the road again.

No way was she going to allow Christine, or anybody else, to look down their nose at her mother and father. Or Liz and Tommy. Or any of the family for that matter. She'd discovered that Christine had a talent for mimicry and she'd caught her on one occasion taking the mickey out of Aunty Bec and Uncle Willie – much to the hilarity of a group of her schoolfriends.

After they had gone, Kate grabbed Christine by the ear and led the howling and protesting girl into the kitchen.

'Listen, you,' she told the child, 'it's not nice to make a fool of your Aunty Bec and Uncle Willie. It's cruel and it's rude and I won't have it, do you hear?'

'It was only a bit of fun.'

'Oh yes?' (Where had she heard that before?)

'But I won't do it again. I promise.'

'Good.' She released her ear and Christine rubbed vigorously at it.

'Impersonate Mrs Thatcher all you want, but not family.'

'I can do one of her. Do you want to hear it?'

Kate had to laugh.

She must have lost her driving concentration because soon she found that one country road looked much the same as any other. Eventually, to her great relief, she spotted a sign to Denby House.

She could hardly believe her eyes when she saw it. It looked more like a castle than a house, with its battlements and towers. A waiting manservant opened the car door for her, then attended to her luggage. An elderly housekeeper smelling of lily of the valley welcomed her at the big studded door. Kate had hardly set foot inside when Richard appeared, arms outstretched to give her a hug.

'How was your journey? You must be exhausted.'

'No, I'm all right, thank you.' She gazed beyond him at the suit of armour, the stuffed heads of stags and the big empty fireplace above which was a coat of arms. Beyond it was a dark oak stairway.

'I'll show you around later,' he said. 'First I'm sure you'll be ready for a drink.'

He led her into what she later learned was the lower drawing room. There was another much larger drawing room upstairs, this one with huge windows all round. They were resplendent with embroidered Jacobean curtains that stretched from floor to ceiling and had an intricate design of birds and trees. Oriental rugs lay on the floor. An ornate clock stood in one corner. Richard went over to a glass-fronted drinks cabinet.

'G and T? Whisky? . . .'

She gazed out of the french windows on to a beautiful silver fairyland of garden as far as the eye could see. She could imagine it lush and green and rainbowed with flowers in the summer.

Suddenly she thought of her Granny McWhirter slaving half her life in the rubber factory. Struggling for the other half to bring up a family in a room and kitchen with no hot water and the toilet outside on a draughty stair. Trying to keep decent. She thought of Possilpark's bleak streets, its jobless people, some defeated by despair, others fighting defiantly against all odds. Like her mother. Like herself. For a moment Kate was overcome by a feeling of hatred and bitterness against a system which allowed people to live in such ease and comfort like this when they'd done nothing

317

to earn it. While others worked hard all their lives and died still worried about how they'd pay their next month's rent. While people lived in huge places like this with others to serve them hand and foot, other human beings at this very minute were huddled, cold, miserable and homeless, in shop doorways. She'd seen many of them in London. In Glasgow too, there was a growing problem of homelessness.

She hated the whole class of parasites who lived like this, most of whom no doubt thought themselves far above the likes of Granny McWhirter and Mary Gallacher and any other untouchables from Possilpark.

'Kate,' Richard was repeating, 'G and T or whisky, or I've sherry or . . .'

'Whisky, thank you.'

She didn't normally drink spirits but felt the need of a good dram right now.

'Do sit down. Make yourself at home.'

She sat on one of the Louis XIV chairs. At home, here? she thought, that's a laugh.

'I've told Mrs Straiton to serve afternoon tea at four o'clock. Is that all right?'

'Fine.'

She was always served afternoon tea on the stroke of four!

When he handed her the glass of whisky he bent down and kissed her.

'I'm very pleased to see you. I do hope you'll like it here.'

She gave him a small smile.

'You're very kind, Richard.'

Indeed he was. She couldn't really hate him. It wasn't his fault, she supposed, that he'd been born into this comfortable, privileged world. Anyway, at the moment at least, it didn't seem to her to be all that comfortable. The room for a start was too big and none too warm, despite the fiercely blazing fire. Kate guessed that when unlit, five or six people could stand side by side inside the fireplace. It was so high and wide.

'Sit nearer the fire,' Richard urged, as if reading her mind. 'It's too draughty over here.'

As she moved over to a chair on one side of the fire she gazed around at the glowering portraits on the walls. Richard's ancestors looked a miserable crowd. Not one smile between them. She was glad of a hot cheering cup of tea. A maid in uniform (maids in uniform in this day and age, Kate thought incredulously) entered with a trolley. She poured the tea into fine bone china cups. After tea, Richard said enthusiastically, 'I'll give you a tour of the house now. Tomorrow morning I'll show you around the estate. There's just a few acres of parkland, but I think you'll find them very attractive. Even at this time of year.'

She wondered what he regarded as 'a few' acres. But to ask might give him the wrong impression. Marilyn Gallacher would have been totally awed and impressed by size and wealth. But Kate Gallacher wasn't. No personal harm to Richard, she thought, but he hadn't worked to earn any of this. Everything he had was inherited. She most admired men who had to graft for what they had in the bank, and what they owned.

She'd had to. She knew what it was like to graft.

Before the tour of the house (indeed before they'd had tea), Kate had been shown to her room. It was a lofty-ceilinged place, dark-panelled in oak with a huge four-poster bed, heavily draped and canopied in what looked like ancient material. The suffocating cloth matched the equally heavy and ancient curtains.

The upstairs drawing room boasted a magnificent grand piano. 'Can you play?' Kate asked. Then felt stupid.

Of course he'd be able to play.

He shrugged.

'I'm a mediocre pianist. I wish I could do better.'

Later that evening he was to prove how modest he was. Kate thought him an astonishingly talented musician. He could also, it turned out, play the violin and the guitar.

What of course interested her most about the tour of

Richard's home was the stone-flagged, raftered kitchen with its huge pine table and rows of copper pans and utensils hanging on one wall. She would have liked to stay there for a while, talking to the plump and smiling cook and the shy but also smiling kitchen maids. However, Richard whisked her enthusiastically away again to show her the gun room with its twelve- and twenty-bore sporting guns and, alongside them, rifles for killing stags. Pistols lay beside boxes of ammunition. Then, she supposed, she was meant to admire (but couldn't) another room where glass cases displayed a host of stuffed birds and other large and small animals. She could not, for the life of her, understand how anyone could find pleasure in slaughtering animals, just for a bit of sport. Especially when these very people were countrymen who were supposed to have a love or appreciation of country life. She thought it repulsive and barbaric.

The tour, in fact, was making her feel more bitter and angry by the minute. This place could house all of London and Glasgow's homeless put together. Yet here was one man, *one* man, living in all this space and luxury. It was wicked!

Yet the more she got to know Richard Smythe-Denby, the more confused she became. He was such a charming man and so kind and thoughtful. Of course, she reminded herself, it would be easy enough to grow up with all these qualities, and more, in such an environment. What had he ever to be bitter, or frustrated, or aggressive, or ruthless, or depressed about?

They enjoyed an excellent dinner in the panelled dining room, its plaster ceiling ornamented with intertwined roses and thistles. The dark, polished dining table down the centre of the room, when extended, could seat twenty-six. It had a high-backed throne-like chair at each end. Kate was glad to be seated at the end of the table nearest the fire because the dining room, like most of the other rooms, was extremely cold.

'I thought,' Richard said eventually, 'that you'd like to

retire early tonight, after such a long drive. You must be tired.'

She agreed that she would like to 'retire' as he put it and he kissed her goodnight and left her outside the bedroom she'd been allocated. It was most considerate of him, she thought, not to try to sleep with her tonight. She *was* tired and she had so much to think about. It was also thoughtful of him to have made sure she was given one of the very few rooms in the castle that had an en suite bathroom. She would never have been able to find a bathroom otherwise. The place was a rabbit warren of dark corridors and staircases. Some of the latter were spiral, with ancient uncarpeted stone steps and bare stone walls feet thick.

She thanked God for that bathroom, and for the electric light. There were still parts of the castle that hadn't even that.

Once Richard had gone and the door of the vast room shut, she looked around in some dismay. Everything looked so alien, so forbidding. It was as if she had suddenly stepped back in time. She could smell age. She felt reluctant to undress in case it made her feel even more vulnerable. Which it did. She crawled beneath the blankets of the four-poster and felt as if even the drapes were threatening. Gathering all her courage and determination about her, she switched off the bedside light.

Oh God! she thought as she lay, stiff as a poker in the blackness, this is terrible.

She had never known such darkness, heard such stillness, such total silence. And she was freezing into the bargain! She'd never be able to sleep a wink all night. It was worse than being in Cornton Vale. A hundred times worse. She was bloody terrified.

She longed for the noise, the comforting familiar sounds of the Glasgow tenements. She longed for the sound of heavy footsteps plodding about in the flat above. Or the fight between husband and wife. Or the children laughing and playing. Or the baby crying through the night.

Earlier in the evening Richard had played her a CD of one of Mahler's symphonies. But now, lying stiff and saucer-eyed and alone, all she wanted to hear was her beloved tenement symphony.

Chapter Fifty-Three

Kate didn't know how she'd stuck it out for the rest of the week. Well, to be perfectly honest, she did. She had seduced Richard to sleep with her every night after that first night. (Not that he needed much seducing.) She had clung to him like a limpet day and night. She'd never clung to any man like that before in her life. She felt ashamed. But survival, by any means, had always been of first importance to her. Anyway, Richard didn't seem to mind. He told her it had been absolutely wonderful having her as a guest and she must come back very, very soon. Indeed, he'd tried to persuade her not to go home at the end of the week, but to stay over Christmas and New Year. Two months? No way!

She said she had to get back because her daughter would be missing her. (That would be the day!) He said why not send for her? She could be put on a plane in Glasgow and they could meet her and bring her to Denby House. Kate could just imagine how well Christine would fit in here. How she would love the castle. She wouldn't want to return to Glasgow. Unless it was to boast to all her friends.

'No, Christmas and New Year have always meant family gatherings for us,' Kate explained. 'My mother and father will expect us to be at their place. I'm sorry,' she added, seeing the disappointment in his face. It occurred to her then that Richard might be lonely. After all, he was a widower and had once shared his life here with his wife.

'You must miss your wife.' She had voiced her thoughts before she realised it. He looked surprised, then wistful.

'Yes, I do. Especially at this time of year. As you say, it's a time when families should be together.'

She was tempted to invite him to join the family gathering in Glasgow but it seemed so ridiculous. He wouldn't fit in, in

Possilpark, any more than she had fitted in here. Then, because he looked so much like a sad-eyed spaniel, she felt compelled to somehow explain why she wasn't issuing any invitations.

'Richard,' she began awkwardly, 'I'd invite you to join us in Glasgow . . .' Oh God, his face had lit up with such hope. 'But I really don't think you'd enjoy it.'

'Oh yes, I'm sure I would, Kate.'

'No, Richard, you wouldn't. I'm not ashamed of my background or my family but there can be no doubt that you've nothing in common with them. Apart from the fact that they live in a very deprived area, notorious for its drug users, none of them are into music or the arts. Well . . .' she hesitated, trying to be fair, 'my father enjoys going to the art galleries and he likes brass bands, especially the local Salvation Army band. And pipe bands, of course. He thinks there's nothing to beat the Glasgow Police Pipe Band.' She became aware that Richard was smiling at her. He was amused. Stuff him!

'I see that already you find my family amusing.' Her words were aimed at him like icicles. 'Well, for your information, they are the salt of the earth.'

'I believe you, darling. I'm only smiling because they sound so wonderful and I'll adore joining them for Christmas and New Year.'

Oh God!

'Well, you can't stay with them,' she said, feeling quite frustrated and grumpy. 'Your dog kennels are bigger than their house. You'll have to stay with me.'

'Oh bother!'

'Now you're laughing at me.'

'Well,' he shrugged and happily spread out his elegant hands, 'isn't life one big joke?'

Maybe to you, pal. But just you try living in Possil in a room and kitchen for a few years and see if you're still laughing at the end of that. Or have a go at working down a pit for a while. That'll soon wipe the smile off your face.

'Oh, a scream,' she said out loud. 'All right, come if you must but don't say I didn't warn you.'

And so it was fixed that he'd arrive in Glasgow the day before Christmas and leave on the 3rd of January.

'I can't afford to take any more time off work,' she explained.

She waved him goodbye from the car as he stood at the door of the castle. As the car shot off, her heart was light and full of joy.

'Glasgow here I come!'

To hell with castles, and titles, and double-barrelled names, and inherited wealth. They could keep them. Stick it all up their aristocratic backsides, for all she cared. She couldn't get back to poor old, tough old, friendly old Glasgow quick enough.

And if Richard Smythe-Denby didn't like Possilpark when he came, well sod him! He'd liked what he'd seen before but she'd only shown him the sunny side, the arty side. Next time he'd have to swallow the lot, and she didn't care if it choked him.

She was thankful, back in Glasgow, to throw herself whole-heartedly into her work. She had so much to catch up with. Admittedly, Tommy was conscientious and dependable. The business wasn't likely to fall to bits as long as he was around. She'd also a very capable manageress in Laura Braeburn. Not to mention a staff of excellent, hard-working girls and now several male van drivers, a male secretary and even a male confectioner. She'd warned the girls that if they didn't behave themselves, she'd just keep employing more men until they were completely outnumbered. In her last pep talk to the staff, she'd told them that they were all excellent at their jobs. They were all members of a team, the Galla-cher's team. She expected them to be proud of that. She wanted them to respect each other for the good, creative work they did. It didn't matter what sex they happened to be. If somebody did a good job, they deserved respect, not harassment.

It looked as if she was beginning to get through to them – male and female. Not even Tommy had made any complaints recently. According to Liz, he was very much happier and more content.

Kate decided to give all the staff a Christmas bonus. They were, needless to say, delighted. Everyone was looking forward to the Christmas and New Year holidays. Nobody more so than Kate's mother and father.

'Do you need any help, Mammy?' Kate asked.

'Listen, hen,' Mary said, 'Ah wis a better cook an' baker than you before ye were born.'

'OK,' Kate laughed. 'Can I bring something? After all, this year you'll have my friend Richard as well as me and Christine and all the rest of the family.'

'Well, if ye must, ye can bring the cake.'

Her father piped up then,

'And the wine. You know your Aunty Bec and Uncle Willie. They always like a glass of good wine with a meal. I'll supply the whisky.'

'Fine,' Kate agreed. 'That's no problem.'

'The weans are aw excited already. They've been helpin' tae decorate the tree. An' George an' Tommy are hangin' up aw the wall an' ceilin' decorations an' balloons an' things.'

'It looks lovely.'

The tree, along with the coloured paper and balloons hanging on the walls and ceiling, made the sitting room look tiny. Kate couldn't imagine how everyone would squeeze into it at Christmas. But not to worry. Then her mother announced that Marilyn was going to be there as well.

'Marilyn?' Kate squealed. 'After what she did? Mammy, have you gone out of your mind?'

'Och, ye know whit she's like. She thought she wis doin' the right thing givin' the wean to its daddy. He's that well aff an' could give the wean everythin' she couldnae. Then she wis too timid tae come an' tell me an' yer daddy. She wis that upset in case she'd hurt us.'

Kate closed her eyes in exasperation.

'Oh Mammy!'

'Less o' yer oh Mammys. Joe wouldnae huv wanted me tae cut his Marilyn aff. She'll aye be wan o' the family tae me.'

'I thought she'd gone to live abroad.'

'Naw, jist some cruise or other. A wee holiday. An' she met this sailor that worked on the boat. A nice fella, he seemed. Johnny somebody. Ma memory's gettin' like a sieve in ma auld age.'

'Are they married?'

'She said no, he wis jist her partner.'

This is all I need for a Merry Christmas and a Happy New Year, Kate thought. Fluttering eyelashes, tight dresses, wiggly bum and kiss, kiss, darling!

'An' get that sulky look aff yer face,' Mary warned. 'Ye'll be nice tae oor Marilyn, do ye hear?'

'Yes, Mammy.'

'An' you watch yer tone o' voice as well. Or ah'll ram that nasty tongue o' yours doon yer throat.'

'I never said a word,' Kate protested indignantly.

'Ah know you, m'lady. When ye're no talkin' cheeky, ye're thinkin' cheeky. Jist you watch yersel'.'

Kate sighed. She couldn't win. Not with her mother.

'Just the cake and the wine then,' she said. 'Are you sure that's all you need. How about a couple of boxes of crackers?'

'Aye, OK, well. They're awfae expensive, right enough.'

'Right,' Kate said. 'That's everything settled then.'

Mary beamed.

'Aye, we're gonnae have a great Christmas, so we are.'

Kate could just imagine it!

Chapter Fifty-Four

They were packed in like sardines. Tommy's children and Christine had to sit at a little separate table over at the window. Mary and Kate had to crush past it every time to serve the big table. Everyone, grown-ups as well as children, was wearing a silly paper hat. Kate felt embarrassed but everyone had become pie-eyed. (That wine had been stronger than she'd thought.) Corny jokes were being read out from crackers. They were all laughing themselves silly, including Richard. He was howling so much he'd be peeing himself next. In the kitchen when Mary was dishing the Christmas pudding, she remarked to Kate, 'Richard seems a nice fella. Where did ye say he came from?'

'Buckinghamshire.'

'Is that near Buckingham Palace?'

'No, of course not.'

'Keep yer hair on. Ah only asked a civil question. Whit's up wi' ye? Ye're as tight-faced as a badger's arse.'

Kate couldn't help laughing.

'That's better,' her mother said. 'Now get these plates through.'

The pudding, like the rest of the meal, was delicious. That was one thing: nobody could fault the meals that her mother produced. Kate always appreciated the fact that, in the kitchen, she could not have had a better example of excellent wholesome cooking.

Granny Gallacher was saying,

'Now you all must come to me for New Year's dinner. You too, Richard.'

Oh God!

'No, no, Mother,' Aunty Bec protested. 'You're not as

young as you used to be. It would be far too much for you, dear.'

Thank God!

'You must all come to Queen's Park. We'd love to have everybody. Wouldn't we, Willie?'

'Absolutely!'

And so it was arranged.

After the Christmas meal, there was the opening of the presents. While Richard had been chatting on the phone from Denby House and making the last-minute arrangements for his visit, he'd casually asked who all would be at the Christmas dinner. Kate had rhymed the names off to him but was taken aback when, after he arrived, he revealed he'd brought a present for each and every one of the Gallachers (and the Murrays) including Marilyn. He'd even bought a small present for Johnny, Marilyn's partner.

'For goodness sake, Richard,' Kate said, 'you shouldn't have done that. It's far too much. And you haven't even met any of them. Except Marilyn.'

'I've had so much fun already,' he said. 'Don't spoil it.'

'All right. But I must say it's very generous of you.'

And it was. Everyone was delighted with their gifts.

After the opening of the presents, there were innumerable silly games and forfeits. Richard was one of those who had to 'do a turn'. He announced that his guitar was in the boot of the car. He'd bring it up and give them a tune.

'My God, son,' Mary said, 'you were takin' a risk. It's well seen ye dinnae come from aroon' here.'

'How do you mean?' Richard looked genuinely puzzled. The innocence of the man.

'You'll be lucky if your car's aw in wan piece, never mind your guitar.'

However, by some miracle, everything was as it should be, and up came a smiling Richard again, and with his guitar all in one piece.

Everyone was thrilled with his 'turn' and sang along with him with great gusto. Then they asked him to play their favourites and he was happy to oblige. Granny Gallacher asked for 'The Old Rugged Cross' and sang the words with a quavery voice full of feeling while Richard strummed an accompaniment, following her as best he could. Aunty Bec, not to be outdone, favoured the company with a shut-eyed, chest-heaving rendition of 'Abide With Me'. To cheer everyone up again, the children volunteered some rap dancing to Richard's accompaniment.

Kate escaped to wash the dishes and clean up the kitchen. Nobody had had enough room for a piece of cake after the dinner, so now Kate cut it into dainty fingers and arranged them in a cake basket. Her mother came through.

'Oh, thanks hen. Ye've cleared everythin' up. An' made the tea. Good for you. Here, that's a great fella ye've got through there. Is it serious?'

'I don't know,' Kate said truthfully.

'How? Whit's wrang wi' him?'

'Nothing. Nothing at all.'

'Well then?'

'He lives so far away for a start.'

'It's England, no' Australia we're talkin' aboot, hen.'

'I know. But my business is here. I've worked so hard to build it up.'

'Well, maybe he'd move up here. Whit job does he dae? Wi' aw this crowd tae see tae, ah've niver had the chance tae ask him.'

'He's . . .' Kate hesitated. 'He's in entertainment. In a way,' she ended lamely. Her mother would be incapable of understanding someone not needing to work.

'Och well, that's aw right then. There's plenty pubs and clubs in Glasgow he can play his guitar in. If he's really stuck, ah've heard there's quite a fair bit of cash tae be made at the buskin'.'

Kate could imagine Richard's aristocratic ancestors birling in their graves at the mere idea.

'Just leave it be just now, Mammy,' she pleaded. 'I'm not sure if I like him enough.'

'Like him enough? That lovely fella through there?' her mother shouted incredulously. 'By God, ye'll go farther an' fare worse. *Again!*' she added with some force, pushing her beaky face forward. 'Ye've never had any sense wi' men, you. Yer taste's aw in yer mouth.'

'Ssh, ssh,' Kate pleaded. 'Away through with the cake, for pity's sake. I'll bring the tray with the tea.'

When it was time to leave, and noisy goodbyes were said. Mary shouted after Richard,

'Haste ye back, son.'

Aunty Bec and Uncle Willie reminded everybody about their 'wee soirée' the next week.

Christine fell asleep in the car on the way back to the West End. Richard had to carry her into the flat and lay her on her bed. Kate took the child's shoes off, unzipped her from her party dress and covered her with the duvet.

'That was one of the best Christmases I've ever had,' Richard said later in the kitchen. 'If not *the* best.'

'I'm glad you enjoyed it.'

'I love you,' he said unexpectedly.

'Oh Richard.'

'I do. I've just realised it.'

She tried to laugh.

'You enjoyed the party *that* much?'

'I mean it.' He came across to take her in his arms.

'Richard!' She put out a hand to ward him off. 'Forgive me, but I'm very tired. I can't think of anything else just now but getting to bed and having a good sleep.'

'Of course!' he immediately agreed. 'I'll say goodnight then.' He kissed her hand, then smiled. 'Goodnight, darling.'

'Goodnight, Richard.'

Later she tossed and turned, unable to get the problem of Richard out of her mind. Then she wondered, Why am I thinking of him as a problem? He had everything – looks, wealth, position. Most women would gladly give their right arm for him.

Contrary to what she'd said to her mother, she did like him. It was just so difficult to utter the word 'love' to her mother. What she'd meant was she didn't love Richard. At least, she didn't think she did. Although she was very fond of him. Maybe that was a more mature basis for marriage. The chances were, she suspected, that Richard was going to ask her to marry him. Nowadays, marriage seemed superfluous. So many couples were just living together as 'partners'. She thought of herself living permanently in Denby House. She remembered the lofty-ceilinged public rooms with their glowering portraits. The guns, the dead animals. The spiral stairs in dark towers, the maze of visitors' bedrooms. The Green Room, the White Room, the Brown Room, the Tartan Room, room after room after room. On the fifth floor, the maids' rooms and above that the lofts piled high with cobwebbed trunks and ancient furniture. The never-ending silent space. Except for the occasional scuttle of rats high in the towers.

She couldn't live in Denby House. Permanently or otherwise. She wouldn't care if she never set eyes on the place again. Would she care if she never saw Richard again? She tried to be honest with herself. She *was* fond of him. She quite enjoyed his company. When he left she would keenly miss him for a few hours, just as she'd miss any other good friend who came to visit. Then she'd get caught up with her work and her familiar little routines and she'd be glad she was on her own again and her life was back to normal. There was always Christine of course, but that was different.

She had once, not so very long ago, wanted to spend the rest of her life with Gavin Cameron. She had wanted it so desperately. Even now, thoughts of him could fill her with pain and longing. She could not pretend that she felt the same about Richard Smythe-Denby. She only wished she could. Richard was a far nicer, more sensitive, more considerate, far kinder man than Gavin. Richard would make such a good husband and father. She could see how well he got on with the children at the party. Christine especially was well on her way to adoring him.

Of course, Kate thought, I haven't known Richard for very long. Perhaps what I feel for him is a different, longer-lasting kind of love. Something that will grow and deepen with time. Best not to make any hasty decisions. Perhaps if she was honest with Richard about how she felt about Denby House, they could tackle the problem together. Do something about the place to cheer it up. Perhaps they could organise their lives so that they stayed for so long (just the summer months perhaps?) in Denby House and the rest of the time in Glasgow. He liked Glasgow so there might not be a problem in that.

She drifted into sleep still trying to work things out.

Chapter Fifty-Five

When Nanny Livingstone went home to Aberdeen for Christmas and New Year, Cameron felt apprehensive about being left with the complete responsibility of looking after Joseph. On the other hand, he was glad of the opportunity. Already he'd bathed him, dressed and undressed him many times under Nanny's supervision. Joseph had been off the bottle for some time now and enjoyed about as varied a diet as Cameron did himself. Everything had to be chopped up for Joseph, of course, just to be on the safe side. He was a happy little boy who laughed a lot at Cameron's efforts to entertain him. He was affectionate too, indeed a very loving and lovable child. Cameron's heart melted every time the small warm arms twined around his neck and the soft mouth pressed against his cheek. Now, when he was not out on business, Cameron devoted every moment to the boy. He had cut down on his travelling, delegating authority, and in every way organising his time so that he could spend as much of it as possible at home. Or taking Joseph for outings. Places he'd never been to since his own childhood. The zoo, the seaside regained their innocent wonder. Even his occasional sorties into the countryside took on a whole new dimension, a higher level of enjoyment.

He began taking an interest in toy shops, bringing home not only cuddly bears and comical long-limbed pink panthers but Thomas the Tank Engine and his friends and other mechanical delights.

Nanny Livingstone warned him on more than one occasion about the dangers of spoiling the child. He didn't care. He couldn't see any danger in being loved as much as possible. He loved to watch Joseph toddle about on his plump little legs. He loved the delicate stalk of his neck, the silky fair curls, the perfect features, and flawless skin, the innocent eyes.

The truth was he adored his son and he wasn't one bit ashamed or embarrassed about it. While Nanny was away and the Botanic Gardens were carpeted with snow, he wrapped Joseph up warmly in leggings, jersey, anorak, woolly hat and scarf, and took him over to the park. Joseph's eyes popped wide with wonder at his first sight of snow. Then, feeling it through his mittened hands, he squealed with delight. Cameron made him a snowman and taught him how to have a snowball fight. Joseph had become rosy-cheeked and perhaps somewhat over-excited. Eventually Cameron carried him home with the promise that they'd return the next day.

Joseph was a clever child and quick at speaking. Cameron would never forget the thrill when Joseph had first managed the word 'Daddy'. He told everybody in the Glasgow Caledonia shop about this success. They (and the staff in many of his other shops as well) knew of every 'first' that Joseph achieved. He'd also taken Joseph into the shops to proudly show him off. He suspected they shook their heads and laughed (in a kindly way) behind his back and thought him besotted with Joseph. But they too had become fond of the boy and always made a great fuss of him. Now, if he didn't bring Joseph into the shop, there were loud cries of disappointment from the staff. They wanted to know why not.

It fascinated him to think how parenthood was so different from what he'd always imagined – if he'd ever thought about it at all. From the moment he'd seen and touched Joseph, the child had meant more to him than life itself. He looked at Joseph and saw his own flesh and blood, but only the best of everything in him. Here was immortality: it gave him a worthwhile purpose in life.

He couldn't understand how Kate Gallacher could farm her child out on her mother and her sister-in-law and God all knew who else the way she did. He'd always known she was hard and cold-hearted but how could she distance herself from her own child? How could she have put herself and her ambitions so uncompromisingly first? Thinking about her, even in this detrimental way, made every nerve in his body ache. He had long since faced the fact to himself that he loved her. Despite all her faults, he loved her. But he loved his son more. In a different way. But much, much more. He would deny himself her love, even if she offered it, because he believed she would not, could not, be a warm and loving mother to his son.

Not that there would ever be any danger of Kate Gallacher's offering him anything but cold hatred. Apart from that, she had obviously set her sights on another man. He could just imagine her looking on Smythe-Denby as an important step up her ambitious ladder. Not long ago he'd come across a picture of Denby House in his AA Road Guide. The place was a tourist attraction in the summer. There had also been a potted history of the family.

This must be about as high as anybody could get, he thought. And she was going to get it. He still admired her single-mindedness, her ability to rise from nothing and claw her way to the top. He only wished he wasn't still in love with her. He had to use all his will power in the attempt to stifle his feelings. He tried to banish her from his mind, and sometimes he was successful. Sometimes he didn't think of her for days, even weeks. Then he'd see the defiant Highlander logo and she'd come rushing back to him again.

Joseph helped. He only needed to look at his son to know that in him was the future, and his own future happiness.

Just after having a magic time at Christmas with Joseph, he'd had the unexpected shock of Marilyn coming to the door.

He hadn't asked her in.

'What do you want?'

She'd pouted and fluttered her eyelashes at him – stupid cow!

'Darling, don't be like that. I just came for a little chat. Aren't you going to ask me in?'

'No.'

'But it's private. You surely don't want all your neighbours to know. Honestly, it is private, dear, and it is so important. It's about Joe.'

Reluctantly he stood aside and allowed her to enter the flat. Joseph was safely asleep in bed and he had no intention of allowing her anywhere near the nursery bedroom.

'Well?' he asked once they'd reached the sitting room.

'I was wondering,' Marilyn cooed, 'if you'd do me a little favour.'

'Oh?'

'You see, I have this lovely man. But he can't find any work here. I met him when he worked on a ship but there was a little misunderstanding and he lost his job with the company.'

'Get to the point, Marilyn.'

'Well, I thought that, well – he thought actually, that if we could get over to say, Australia, and start a new life there, it would be just lovely and solve all our problems.'

'Are you trying to tell me that you are going to marry this man?'

'I'd just love to marry him, darling, I really would.'

'What's keeping you? Oh, I get it, the allowance. Well, hard luck, Marilyn. You know our bargain and you can't say I wasn't generous. Far more than was necessary, I would have thought.'

'Yes, you were, you were. And what I thought, what we thought, was if I got married, you'd be saving pounds and pounds every month.'

'True.'

'So I thought you would be generous enough to give me another lump sum like the last time, so that Johnny and I could cover our tickets abroad and get ourselves started in our lovely new life.'

'You must think I'm a right fool. Do you know what I think, Marilyn? I know your devious, stupid little mind, you see. And I think you've already married this man and then once safely married, you spilled the beans to him. He's sent you along with this cock and bull story to try to screw me for thousands before I find out the truth.'

'Honestly, Gavin, we *do* want to go abroad and start a new life. That's the truth. Really it is.'

'I believe you. And I hope you'll manage it. But you're not getting another penny out of me. Not a lump sum. Not another month's allowance. Nothing.'

'You can't do this,' Marilyn cried, bright tears rushing to her eyes.

'I think you'd better leave now, Marilyn.'

'I'll take the baby back.'

'Out.'

'Johnny said we could take the baby back. If you don't give us what we ask.'

'Tell Johnny to go to hell.'

'Oh, don't do this, Gavin. He won't be pleased and he's got such a dreadful temper. He frightens me sometimes. When he found out . . . he called me awful names. He said I'm stupid and didn't need to get married. He said I'd thrown away all that money. I promised I'd get it back and more. I promised him.'

Gavin had hustled her to the front door.

'Hard luck. Goodbye.'

He got her out none too gently and shut the door. Then he went straight to Joseph's bedroom, bent over and kissed the peacefully sleeping child.

'You're well rid of her, son,' he said.

Chapter Fifty-Six

As she'd expected, at the end of the holiday, Richard asked her to marry him.

'I adore you, Kate, and we get on so well together. I seem to have been accepted by your family already. I was an only child and to be part of such a large family crowd is wonderful. All I need to make my happiness complete now is for you to say yes.'

Kate stared at him.

'Why so sad, darling? You do love me, don't you?' he said.

'It's not that, Richard.'

'What is it then?'

'A couple of things – most important things.'

'Tell me, please.'

'I don't want to hurt your feelings. You were so kind and hospitable when I visited your home. But . . . but it was so big and intimidating and gloomy. Well, to tell you the truth,' she said with a sudden strengthening of her voice, 'I was too terrified to sleep on my own in that big mausoleum of a room.'

He laughed uproariously.

'Is that all?'

'What do you mean, is that all? I've just said I was terrified of the place.'

He struggled to make his face serious.

'Darling, you'd soon get used to it. It's just different from this little flat, that's all.'

She had always regarded her flat as big. Not as spacious as the flat Cameron occupied. But big. Compared with Denby House of course . . .

'Honestly, you'd get used to it,' he repeated. 'And there will never be any need for you to sleep alone. You saw it at a disadvantage too. The weather was so cold and bleak. Wait until you see it in the summer. And it's busy all the time then with tourists. You'd have plenty of company all summer. Plenty of people milling cheerfully around. What's the other thing?'

'My business,' she said. 'I've spent years building it up, Richard. And I enjoy it. It's part of me, somehow. I don't want to give it up.'

'Well, I don't see why you need to give it up.'

'But I work from Glasgow.'

'Expand. Have a base near Denby House as well. Build a place on my land. There's acres of room. Have as many acres as you like. Make it a show place. Tourists could include it in their visit. They could buy your products as well as Denby souvenirs, books and postcards.' He sounded more enthusiastic by the minute. She had to laugh along with him. It did sound an exciting idea. It fired her imagination.

'It would cost an awful lot of money,' she said. 'To build from scratch like that.'

'It's only money,' he said. 'I've got oodles of the stuff.'

'Of course, it could make a fortune,' she said, seeing in her mind's eye a place like one of those show food factories up north with a shop attached. Only hers would be better. Bigger. More attractive. Better quality. More competitive.

'Say yes, darling. Make me the happiest man in the world.'

The new food factory was filling her mind and her imagination, exciting her more and more by the second. It was a proposition she couldn't bring herself to refuse.

'Oh, all right,' she said, still laughing, still seeing the wonderful business opportunity.

The wedding was arranged for the spring so that she could be in Denby in time for the summer season. She could also start plans for the new base for Gallacher's. People came from all over the world to visit the historic house and estate, Richard told her. And so her products, and the name of Gallacher, would in time be known, be famous worldwide. The thought thrilled her. This was what she'd always wanted.

Success acted on her like an aphrodisiac. The night before Richard left she hadn't needed to fake an orgasm. He planned to return a couple of days before the date of the wedding. The house opened for tourists in May and he had a lot of paperwork and bookings to see to. He had a secretary and a few locals as office staff who started full time every year after the Christmas holidays but there was a great deal to do and he had to be there to pitch in along with them.

'You get everything arranged at your end,' Richard told Kate. 'The business as well as the wedding.'

She spoke to Tommy and asked him to take over the Glasgow branch in partnership with Laura Braeburn. A generous raise in wages to both sealed the agreement. 'I'll still come up at regular intervals to check on everything,' Kate said. 'I'll really be coming up to see the family but I'll look in to visit as well. OK?'

They agreed that would be fine with them.

Kate began to visualise the new place. She drew sketches but she was no artist. She'd have to employ an architect. She'd see to that as soon as possible after the wedding. No doubt Richard would know somebody. She took notes of what had to be done, mostly in connection with the business expansion. She was almost forgetting about the wedding and what was needed to be organised for that.

'Here you,' her mother said. 'Are ye plannin' tae walk up the aisle in them denim trousers?'

'No, of course not.'

'Well, whit then? Aunty Bec's got her outfit. So has Liz an' aw the weans. Oh an' here, ye'd better invite Dorothy. It'll maybe cheer the poor soul up. Did ye hear whit happened?'

'No, I haven't seen her for ages.'

'Her man was back in the Bar L . . .'

'Surprise, surprise.' The Bar L was the Barlinnie Prison.

'Aye, but this time he topped himsel'.'

'Oh God! When?'

'Ah jist heard the other day. But apparently it wis a few weeks ago. It wis in the papers but ah missed it. Anyway, there's that many folk doin' themsel's in these days. It's no' exactly front-page news. Poor auld Charlie. No' that he wis that auld. But he looked it, didn't he?'

'I'll go and see Dorothy. She'll be better without him, of course. But you know what she was like. I still can't get over her going back to him. What a fool she was.'

'Aye well.' Her mother eyed Kate sarcastically. 'We cannae aw be as perfect as you.'

Kate decided to write a letter of condolence to Dorothy first. It might be more tactful than turning up unexpectedly at her door. In the letter she explained that she was planning to get married and leave Glasgow and she hoped they'd get together very soon. She wrote the letter that very afternoon and posted it at the Byres Road post office because she had to go to the supermarket across the road to do some shopping. Christine had invited some friends to tea and had given her a list of their favourite pizzas, cakes, biscuits and cans of Coke.

It was on her way down Byres Road that she met Gavin Cameron. He was carrying a little boy in his arms.

'Hello.' She felt awkward and embarrassed. 'This must be Joe.'

'Joseph.'

'Sorry, Joseph. He's quite the little man now.'

'Yes, he's growing fast. I've got his name down for Fettes already.'

She didn't know if he was joking or not. Fettes College was a most exclusive school in Edinburgh.

'Oh well, he's a lovely child. You must be very proud of him.'

'I am, yes.'

She noticed a stiffness, a coldness about him and his dark eyes were devoid of expression. Of course, he'd always been a cool customer and he'd never liked her. What was it he'd last called her – a ruthless, calculating bitch, was it?

'I'm getting married in the spring,' she said impulsively.

'Congratulations.'

'To Richard Smythe-Denby.'

'I'd never have guessed.'

His eyes narrowed and she saw something else in them. Memories of the naked passion they'd once shared. He might be a sarcastic bastard. But he was bloody sexy. She felt herself flush and a pulse throbbed painfully in her neck.

'Haven't you any help with Joseph?' She knew it was a silly thing to say but she had to say something to cover up the confusion he'd awakened in her.

'This is Nanny Livingstone's afternoon off. I also have a daily woman but I don't trust anyone with Joseph except the nurse.'

'I see. Well, I'd better go.'

'Goodbye.'

'Bye,' she sang out cheerily. She felt anything but cheerful. In fact she felt upset. He always had that effect on her. Damn the man! She'd been perfectly happy and in the space of a few minutes, her mind and her emotions had been thrown into complete turmoil. That look in his eyes told her that given the chance, he'd have sex with her again. Repeat performance. No strings attached. Well, hard luck. Been there. Done that.

As soon as she got back to the flat, she phoned Richard and told him she missed him. She wished he was here right now. She was hoping that he'd say, 'I'll be on the next plane.' Instead he soothed her:

'Darling, it'll only be a few weeks now and then we'll be together for good. How are all your arrangements going? Have you bought your dress? I hope you're not thinking of doing any cooking for the reception. I don't want you overtiring yourself on the big day.'

'It's only going to be a small affair. Mostly family. Is that all right? Did you want something bigger? I know you haven't any family left now, Richard, but you must send me

343

a list of friends you'd like to be there. I'll have to know about numbers soon if I've to book a hotel.'

'Oh, most people I know are either up to their eyes in it with summer visitors or they're abroad. I won't be bringing anybody.'

'Nobody at all? Are you sure?'

'Perfectly. I'll be quite happy with your friends and family.'

'All right. I'd better go now. Christine has invited some of her friends for tea.'

'I hope she'll like it here.'

'Don't worry, she'll adore it.'

'I love you, darling. Say you love me. You never actually say the words.'

'Oh, you'll just have to get used to us hard-nosed, unsentimental Glaswegians,' she laughed. 'We believe it's sissy to talk like that. Anyway, you know I do. I'll have to go. Bye now.'

She hung up. She felt guilt now as well as all the other bothersome emotions that were plaguing her.

Damnation! She went through to the bathroom and took a couple of paracetamols. At least that would help her headache.

After she attended to the tea party for the girls, she returned to the bathroom and, teeth gritted with determination, stood under an icy cold shower.

Chapter Fifty-Seven

The house looked quite respectable. When Dorothy left her in the sitting room to go and fetch the tea tray, Kate studied the place. It was a bit untidy. But clean. Not in the least the shocking tip it had been the last time she'd been here.

'I would have come earlier if I'd known,' she told Dorothy when her friend came back and started pouring out the tea. 'How long has it been now?'

'Five weeks and three days.'

'I'm so sorry, Dorothy.'

'No you're not, Kate. You never liked Charlie.'

'I never wished anything like that on him. I know how you must feel.'

Dorothy sighed.

'Poor Charlie. He tried to get off the drugs. He tried so hard. But the last time I visited him in Barlinnie, I could see he was depressed. He didn't talk much. But just before I left, he said, "It's no use, hen. I'll never manage it. You'd be better without me." I should have spoken to one of the prison officers. I should have known what he was going to do.'

'No, you shouldn't. How could you? I'm sure he'll have said things like that before, Dorothy. He did get depressed before, didn't he?'

'I know, but I keep thinking . . . if only I'd said this, if only I'd done that.'

'Och, everybody who's lost somebody close to them feels that, Dorothy. My mother said things like that after our Joe died.'

Dorothy nodded and tried to smile.

'You must be fed up with me and all my troubles, Kate. I don't know why you don't give up on me altogether.'

'You know me,' Kate laughed. 'Stubborn as a mule. I never give up on anything.'

'I hear you're getting married again.'

'You'll never guess. He's got acres of land and I'm going to have the headquarters of Gallacher's there. It's going to be custom built and have a big superstore and display area attached. People from all over the world will come and buy Gallacher's products. I've all sorts of ideas for the place. I was thinking I might even have the staff – in the shop, at least – wear Highland dress . . .'

'Kate, is it the new business you're marrying or the man?'

Kate was taken aback.

'What a daft thing to say.'

Dorothy shrugged.

'I suppose business has always come first with you. I don't know how you do it. But as long as you're happy, I suppose . . .'

'Of course I'm happy. You'll come to the wedding, I hope. It's not until the end of April.'

'Gosh, that's not so far off.'

'It's just to be a small affair. What I really would like is for you to be my bridesmaid, Dorothy.'

'What about Sandra?'

'I suppose I'll have to have her, otherwise Aunty Bec'll go all huffy. But I want you as well. You're the one I *really* want.'

'All right. If it's all that important to you.'

'Thanks, Dorothy.'

They launched into the details of the wedding arrangements then and Dorothy seemed a lot brighter by the time Kate left. She walked up Stoneyhurst Street instead of going down towards Saracen Street. Byshott Street was now being pulled down. The housing department were clearing away a lot of the old tenements. Part of Killearn Street was also disappearing. Desolate patches of earth were all that was left of some of the houses where so many people had been born and lived and died. One block stood, depressingly empty and waiting with windows and close mouth boarded up. She wondered if, one day, all of Possilpark would disappear beneath the bulldozers. It made her feel sad. She went up to her mother's to collect Christine and as she passed Mrs Dooley's door she wondered what would happen if this building was to be knocked down. The housing people would never allow her to have all her cat family in one of their nice new houses. (Kate suspected that if the housing department knew of the cats in her present home, they'd make short work of them.) It would be the death of poor old Mrs Dooley if she was bereft of her feline pals.

Indeed, Kate wondered how her mother would feel if she had to move away from her house and all her good neighbours. Everything seemed on the verge of change. Kate felt as if her whole existence, even the very ground under her feet, had become shifting sands. She suddenly felt like a child who, feeling frightened and insecure, wants to cling to its mother for comfort and to be told not to worry, that everything's all right.

In the top flat in Killearn Street, she loitered at the door after saying cheerio, longing to reach out to her mother, to cling to her, to tell her she loved her today, just as she'd always loved her all her yesterdays.

'Whit's up wi' you?' Mary said. 'Huv yer shoes glued ye tae the flair?'

Christine tugged impatiently at her arm.

'Come on, Mum.'

'All right, all right. Well, cheerio, Mammy.'

'Ye're gettin' tae sound like a bloomin' budgie. That's the third time ye've said cheerio. Fur goodness sake, away ye go. Ah'll be missin' *Coronation Street* on the telly.'

The door shut the moment Kate put her feet over the threshold. Already Christine was running down the stairs, eager to return to what she now regarded as her own home territory – the West End and the elegant Kirklee Terrace. Christine felt no affinity with Possilpark, was not in the slightest affected by it.

Kate sighed. Maybe that was a good thing. After she got

home she poured herself a stiff whisky. Then another. It didn't help. She was in a strange mood. A kind of empty limbo. She didn't know what was wrong with her. Pre-wedding nerves, probably. She'd heard or read somewhere that it was quite common to suffer all sorts of doubts and anxieties.

What doubts? What anxieties? she asked herself angrily. The anger perked her up. Made her feel more like her old spunky self. She knew what she was doing. She had the chance of a lifetime, and she was grabbing it with both hands. Gavin Cameron – eat your heart out! He said he travelled the world to get people to buy the goods he dealt in. *She* said – World, come to me!

She went to bed happy and slept the moment her head touched the pillow. Next day she bought a wedding dress. Her mother and Aunty Bec said she should get one made especially for her but she hadn't had the time for all that fuss. Anyway, there was a sale on and she managed to pick up a very nice one at a bargain price. Why waste money on something she'd only wear once? It cost a ridiculous amount as it was. She'd gone for the plainest in the shop. She had never felt right in frills and flounces, even as a wee girl. She remembered a party dress that Granny Gallacher had bought her for her birthday – her fifth or sixth maybe. Her mother forced her to wear it for the party. Loathing its every gauzy frill and flounce, she'd gone into a furious sulk and remained that way. Granny Gallacher and Aunty Bec had tried to cajole her out of her black mood and bribe her with flattering words and sweeties. Eventually her mother had boxed her ears and dragged her off to bed. There she'd lain, while the birthday party went merrily on without her. But although she was broken-hearted, she was triumphant. The dress lay discarded on the bedroom floor, never to be worn again.

The wedding dress had a simple but elegant cut and a scooped neckline. A choker of pearls would be a good idea. And maybe a plain satin-covered coronet to hold the veil.

She was content with that. She also bought white satin underwear and white satin shoes. She took her purchases back to the flat, glad that that job was over. All she could think of, all she was really looking forward to, was wearing comfortable denims and Doc Martens and trudging around Richard's estate looking for the best site for her wonderful new project.

But her mother and Aunty Bec and Liz, and even Dorothy now, started nagging at her about the other jobs she'd to do in connection with the wedding.

'Where are ye gettin' yer hair done? No, ye cannae wash it yersel' for yer weddin'. Dinnae be sae mean. Ah dinnae care if ye're up tae yer eyeballs at yer work. Dorothy, will you make an appointment fur her an' make sure she keeps it?'

'Sandra's getting her dress made, dear, but she wants to meet up with you at her dressmaker's one day very soon to see what you think before her final fitting. Also she'd like to talk to you about what the pages are going to wear and all the little girls. I think she and Liz are having a little disagreement. I really think, dear, you should be taking more interest and not leaving all this worry to our Sandra.'

'Kate, will you tell Aunty Bec and Sandra that it's your wedding, not theirs. Tommy and I are fed up with Aunty Bec and Sandra interfering and bossing everybody about. They're in their element with all this, especially now that they've found out your man's a toff and lives in a castle. They've been boasting to so many folk, your mammy said to them the other day, "Why dae ye nae hire wan o' them vans wi' loudspeakers on top an' go round aw the streets so's ye'll no' miss anybody".'

'Kate, I know you feel you have to work every day to get the place organised before you go down south but now that I'm in there helping you again, surely you can take a bit more time off. Tommy and the manageress would understand. If you don't, it's your wedding that's going to be in chaos. Not your business. And by the way, I'm getting awful fed up with your Aunty Bec and cousin Sandra bullying me all the time.'

And of course the guest list had grown by the day. Uncle Willie was even wanting to invite some of his customers.

She told Richard over the phone. He laughed.

'I can just imagine it. It'll be like that crowded, noisy, chaotic Christmas party all over again.'

Oh God!

Chapter Fifty-Eight

Cameron was sick to death of hearing about it. The girls in the Glasgow shop were afire with gossip. He'd had to tell them eventually to shut up and pay more attention to their work. But of course their work was with customers and the customers wanted to gossip about it.

'The Wedding of the Year', the newspapers had dubbed it. Journalists took all sorts of angles. 'Possilpark Girl Makes It Big', 'From Possil Tenement to Historic Castle', 'From Rags to Riches'. Some papers dragged up the murder. 'Convicted Killer Makes it from Cornton Vale to Castle.' 'How Did She Do It?' the papers asked. He could have told them. Pushiness. Brass neck. Single-mindedness. Steely determination to get what she wanted out of life.

To a certain degree, he too was like that. He didn't mind admitting it to himself. In fact he'd been very much like that. Now, having his son to think about, his priorities had changed. It was a matter of getting the balance right as well. He wanted to retain his successful business. Once it had been the be-all and end-all of his life, but now everything revolved around his son. Success in business, and the money he made from it, only mattered in so far as he could give Joseph a good life, the best education, the most secure and fulfilling future.

In a way, he felt sorry for Kate Gallacher. She had a rigid, closed mind. She was encased in an armour of ambition. Deeper emotions like love, not sexual pleasure but deep, unselfish caring love for another human being, were beyond her. She was incapable of shedding that armour.

He felt even more sorry for Richard Smythe-Denby.

Cameron was so fed up with hearing about and reading about the wedding, he was considering going abroad beforehand and taking Joseph and Nanny with him. He had plenty of business to do overseas. Not that he needed an excuse. He was perfectly free to go where and when he wanted. First, though, he would have to see what Nanny Livingstone thought about the idea. She had an elderly mother in Edinburgh who wasn't keeping too well at the moment. Maybe she wouldn't want to travel too far from the old woman. He resolved to talk to Nanny the next day. Today was her day off and only the daily help, Mrs Banks, was in the house. She was a good-natured, hard-working widow and he was lucky to have found her. She was very fond of Joseph and he of her. Cameron felt secretly ashamed that he had always refused to leave the child with Mrs Banks. He would take the day off work to be with Joseph when the nurse wasn't there.

'You don't need to stay off your work, you know,' Mrs Banks said in what he could see was a slightly hurt manner. 'I'm perfectly capable of looking after wee Joseph.'

'I know,' he'd assured her. 'Of course you are. But I feel you've enough to do with all the housework and cooking.'

'Och, what cooking do I do? I just lift the phone and order all that rubbishy stuff you want delivered. All I ever cook are pots of soup and a few puddings. And Joseph loves my soup and puddings, don't you, son?'

'Nevertheless . . . Anyway, I enjoy spending a full day every week with Joseph. But any day, if I need to leave him with you, Mrs Banks, rest assured I won't hesitate.'

He hadn't seriously thought the day would come. And such a day. Never in his worst nightmares.

It had started in a perfectly normal way. Mrs Banks had arrived, hung her coat and hat away and donned her floral wrap-around apron. Nanny had seen to breakfast and now, after a friendly chat with Joseph, Mrs Banks got stuck into washing the breakfast dishes. Nanny told Joseph to be a good boy for his daddy, said goodbye and left. He poured himself another cup of coffee and spread the *Guardian* on the kitchen table. He had changed temporarily from the *Glasgow Herald* to avoid any reminders about the wedding.

Joseph hung around Mrs Banks, enjoying his usual chatter with her. The phone in the hall rang a couple of minutes after Mrs Banks had left the kitchen to polish the brass on the front door.

He heard her answer the phone. He knew she liked this job. It made her feel important, more like a secretary. It amused him to hear the polite voice she affected. She'd turn and call out, still in her posh accent, 'Mr Cameron, a Mr Brown to speak to you, sir.'

That amused him as well. She never called him 'sir' on any other occasion. He supposed she imagined that's what posh secretaries did.

This time, however, he heard her gasp in her own voice, 'Oh no, that's terrible. I'll tell him. Yes, I've got that. Right away.'

Immediately Cameron strode through to the hall but she'd already replaced the receiver.

'You've to go to the Edinburgh shop right away. There's been a terrible fire. That was one of the assistants. She was phoning from a call box because everybody had to evacuate the shop. She seemed quite hysterical.'

'God! I'll have to go. Will you be all right with Joseph?'

'Of course. Haven't I always told you? Joseph and me will get on fine. Sure we will, son?'

He kissed the little boy and told him to be a good boy for Mrs Banks and that Daddy would try not to be too long.

'Aye, you go and don't worry,' Mrs Banks repeated. 'I'll stay as long as I have to.'

He dashed out to his car, not forgetting to wave to Joseph before driving away. Both Joseph and Mrs Banks waved back to him.

He glanced at his watch, wondering if he'd be quicker to drive to Queen Street station and catch a train from there. But he would just miss the one on the hour and would have another half-hour or more to wait. There was always the danger of delays. Trains were often late. He decided to get on to the motorway and put his foot down.

Cigarettes. He could bet that's what had caused the fire. The girls smoked like funnels at every coffee and tea break. Somebody would have left a lighted cigarette somewhere and then forgotten about it. He wasn't a smoker himself and had never been happy about this habit of his employees. They'd pleaded with him, however, and he'd listened to them.

'We'd never dream of smoking in the front where there's customers, Mr Cameron. But in the back shop and in our coffee breaks. What's the harm in that?'

Well, here was the harm in it. The shop would probably be nothing but ashes by now. He'd have lost thousands. Not to mention the fact that somebody may have been hurt.

He was getting too soft, that was the trouble – taking Joseph in so often for the girls to drool over. What on earth had he been thinking of? It had made them see a weaker side of him and they'd taken advantage, become more chatty, more familiar. For all he knew, they could have been smoking all over the place.

Well, never again. They'd had that. From now on, smoking would be forbidden in all of his premises. He'd harden up, distance himself, lay down the law, watch them like a hawk; they would have nobody to blame but themselves.

As usual, the traffic didn't help his impatient speed. In Edinburgh it was horrendous. Ignoring parking restrictions, he dumped the car in the first convenient spot he could find near the shop. There was no sign of any fire engines. When he reached the shop, there was no sign of any fire. A hollowness was making his stomach and his gut cave in. But his mind only registered the words, 'It must have been confined to the back shop.'

He strode into the shop and the assistants looked over at him in surprise. Two of them were serving customers. The other smiled and said, 'Hello, Mr Cameron. Where's Joseph today?'

He went through to the back shop. Everything was in perfect order. One of the juniors was unpacking a box of shortbread fingers. She looked up in surprise. She too smiled.

'Hello, Mr Cameron . . .'

He turned and raced into the office. Miss Anstruther, the manageress, was on the phone. He snatched the receiver from her and dialled his home number.

Mrs Banks's polite voice answered.

'Hello, this is the Cameron residence. Mrs Banks speaking.'

'Joseph!' he shouted. 'Is he all right?'

'Well . . . I . . . You should know that, Mr Cameron.' He caught the huffy note.

'What the hell do you mean, woman?'

'You sent his mother to collect him. You didn't trust me despite the fact . . .'

'You fool,' he bawled. 'You fool!'

'Oh really, Mr Cameron . . .'

'God knows where he is now and what's happening to him.'

'But she said you'd phoned her from your car phone. She knew about the fire and everything.'

'I'm going to phone the Glasgow police. Then I'm coming straight back.'

He banged down the phone. Then redialled.

Miss Anstruther was twisting at her hanky in distress.

'Oh, Mr Cameron, this is terrible. Do you think . . .?'

He raced from the shop. He daren't think.

Chapter Fifty-Nine

'Look, Daddy, it's not that I don't want your friends, or that I've anything against them,' Kate said. (She didn't even *know* her father's drinking cronies.) 'It's just that the wedding's getting out of hand. It started as a quiet family affair. Now half of Glasgow seems to be coming.'

'I don't know what you're worried about, Kate,' George said. 'After all, Richard has very generously offered to pay for the whole bang shoot.'

'It's not a question of money, Daddy. If things go on like this, I'll not know most of the guests at my own wedding. It's ridiculous. I've a good mind to phone Richard and suggest we run away by ourselves to Gretna Green.'

'Don't you dare!' her mother warned. 'Ah'll never forgive ye if ye disappoint aw oor friends an' neighbours.'

Even Mrs Dooley was coming now. Kate wouldn't be surprised if all the cats turned up as well.

'This is supposed to be my day.'

'Dinnae be sae bloody selfish.'

'Oh, great. Just great.'

'Or sarcastic either. Everybody's lookin' forward tae the weddin', so dinnae you go an' spoil it, dae ye hear me, m'lady?'

'Yes, Mammy, I hear you.'

She wondered if she would really dare run away to Gretna. She definitely wanted to. The thing was, Richard was looking forward to their wedding. He was as enthusiastic as everybody else. And to hell with the cost.

'It's going to be great fun,' he laughed. 'I can hardly wait.'

Well, they hadn't long to wait now. She would be glad when it was all over. It was driving her mad. Even the press wouldn't leave her alone. They would all be at the wedding, of course. At the moment they were concentrating on questions – endless questions – about her wedding dress and her going-away outfit. And where she'd be going on honeymoon. Actually they weren't going anywhere. Not that she wanted to. She had never had the slightest notion for lazing about on holiday. They even questioned her about her shoes. Shoes had nearly caused a split in the family. She'd bought her white satin shoes in the shop where she'd purchased her wedding dress. Uncle Willie was furious, indignant, offended. Deeply hurt.

'Here am I,' he announced dramatically, 'your uncle. One of the family. Managing the best shoe shop in Scotland.' (Uncle Willie was prone to exaggeration.) 'And you go elsewhere for the most important footwear of your life. What's Mr McGinty (the owner of the shop) going to think?'

Kate didn't care a tinker's curse what Mr McGinty thought. But for the sake of peace in the family, she abandoned the first pair of shoes, and bought a new pair from Uncle Willie.

One crisis after another blew up. Never a day passed but the family erupted in some silly bickering and argy-bargy. If it wasn't the colour of the dresses, it was the colour of the flowers. As for the food . . . Her mother had interfered so much at the hotel and changed her mind so often about the menu, had even barged into the hotel kitchen, Kate felt too embarrassed to set foot in the place again.

She lived in fear and apprehension of her mother giving one of the hotel staff a black eye and really shaming her. Her mother was still as wiry, as tough and as hard as nails as she'd ever been. If anybody in the staff was too tall for her, she'd catch them bending over or sitting down. The press would have a field day with that. Kate could just imagine the headlines:

'Tough Possilpark Granny Floors Hotel Manager'

The whole thing was becoming a shambles. Kate couldn't concentrate at work and she'd so much to think about and discuss with Tommy and the manageress prior to the move down south and how the two outlets were going to liaise.

Impulsively she phoned Richard.

'Darling!' he greeted her. 'Two phone calls in one day. What have I done to deserve this?'

'Richard, I want to run away with you to get married quietly in Gretna Green. Just the two of us. Not another soul.'

He was roaring with laughter even before she'd finished speaking. Great. Oh, just great! That's all she needed.

'I'm glad you're amused,' she said icily. 'Anything for a laugh. That's me.'

'Kate, darling,' he said, 'it's only pre-wedding nerves. Everyone suffers from pre-wedding nerves and anxieties.'

He didn't sound nervous or anxious. But then, he wasn't having to cope with the bloody circus up in Glasgow.

'Sorry I spoke.'

'Now, don't be like that.'

'Like what?'

'Don't go all sulky on me.'

'Don't you dare call me sulky, you smug, self-satisfied twit!'

He was laughing again. She could have strangled him. Did nothing ever ruffle his aristocratic feathers?

'Kate, I love you. All this will soon be over and you'll be happily settled here in Denby House.'

She sighed. 'Oh, I suppose so. But at the moment, it's pure hell.'

'Just hang on for a little while longer. Just keep thinking of being here, with me. Now, make my day. Say it!'

'Say what?' Although she knew perfectly well.

'I . . . love . . . you,' he intoned slowly.

'Oh, piss off,' she said. Then before she hung up, 'And stop laughing at me.'

Just think of being here with me, he'd said. Maybe that was the trouble, she hardly ever thought about that at all. There had been so many other things crowding for her

358

attention but, as Richard said, it wouldn't be long now. Only a few days.

She felt a *frisson* of fear. Immediately, angrily, she hardened it away. She would be damned if she'd be nervous or anxious. In actual fact, all this harassment and hard work proved she had nerves of steel and was stronger than most.

She wished Christine wasn't staying with one of her friends. She'd been invited to Patsy Freeman's birthday party and asked to stay over the weekend. At least Christine would have been somebody else in the house. She could have chatted to her, asked her about how she was getting on at school. She seemed to have made lots of friends. All in the expensive school uniform and all from well-heeled comfortable backgrounds. Giggly girls who thought they knew everything but actually knew nothing about life. Ah well, they'd probably learn soon enough.

Her thoughts wandered from Christine to Joe, or Joseph as Cameron called him. She didn't quite know what to make of that situation. Cameron had looked quite the doting daddy with the child in his arms. It was an aspect of the man she'd never seen before. She'd been furious about him snatching the boy away from her mother at the time. But as her mother had kept pointing out, he was Cameron's son. He had every right. On thinking about it in a calmer frame of mind, she came to accept that it probably had something to do with Marilyn's stupidity. All the same . . . She had never thought of him as a fatherly figure.

Thinking of Marilyn again reminded her of the Christmas dinner. Fancy Marilyn bringing her 'partner', as she called him. She could have upset her mother by doing that. Her mother, if Kate remembered correctly, had thought Marilyn's Johnny a nice fella. Kate hadn't taken to him at all. Oh, he was being terribly nice right enough, but – let's put it this way, Kate thought – I wouldn't employ him in my business. As an employer, she had developed quite a nose for sly, sticky-fingered folk. For Marilyn's sake, she hoped she was wrong. Marilyn was obviously smitten by him.

It was strange: even while she was thinking of Marilyn and her boyfriend, images of Cameron kept floating before her mind's eye. It was as if a ghostly film was unrolling before her that she didn't want to watch. She kept thinking of other things but the film continued. She even saw the very first time he'd stormed into her shop. She saw and heard again all their other confrontations. Their relaxed Saturday dinners, their passionate sessions in bed. The last time she had seen him, in Byres Road, came into clearer focus, the way his eyes narrowed, the sexual signal she'd read in them.

She sighed. Love, hate – she no longer knew what she felt about the man. Not that it mattered any more. As long as she didn't see him, she'd be all right. As long as she didn't have to look into those sexy eyes and listen to that sarcastic tongue, she'd be all right. She was tempted to phone Richard again but although twice in one day might amuse him, three times might have him beginning to think she was a bit of a fool.

Thinking of his amusement made her wonder if that's how he really regarded all her family and friends. He'd obviously never before come across what he'd once called 'ordinary working-class people'. Although she had often used the term herself, she'd bristled at him using it. To be truthful, she'd never seen anything wrong with it. She had used it with pride about herself and her background. But when Richard had used it, she'd immediately gone on the defensive.

'There's nothing *ordinary* about me or my family and friends. There's nothing to be ashamed of in hard work. My Granny McWhirter made an honest living in a rubber works. My Granny Gallacher – '

'I never said there was anything to be ashamed of,' he'd interrupted good-humouredly. 'Aren't you the touchy one!'

All right, maybe she was touchy about some things. She'd wondered if, at the party, for instance, it was a case of something different that had livened up his too easy and at times perhaps too boring life. Had he gone back to his county set and amused them with hilarious stories of working-class characters and their actions? The mere idea made her burn with fury.

Richard had once said to her,

'Kate, don't you think it could be the other way around?'

'What on earth do you mean?' she snapped at him.

'You're the one with strong class feelings, darling, not me.'

Oh yes, all very well for him to take an easygoing, good-humoured, well-balanced view of life. It surprised her how much bitterness was still buried deep inside her. She knew perfectly well that it wasn't Richard's fault that she'd been subjected to some of the worst rigours of being born and brought up in a place like Possilpark. He hadn't battered her about. Or caused her to be locked away in prison. He hadn't created the jungle which she had to claw her way through.

She tried to be fair. She was trying so hard right now it was giving her a headache.

And still she could see Cameron hovering at the back of her mind, watching her, mocking her, with his dark bullets of eyes.

Chapter Sixty

'It's not really kidnapping,' Johnny said. 'He's your own child, isn't he?'

Marilyn nodded but still looked saucer-eyed and anxious.

'Gavin thinks we're going to harm him if he doesn't pay the money. I didn't like saying that, Johnny. I wouldn't harm Joe. Gavin said – '

'Never mind what Gavin said. Do you want to live here in this dump of a place for the rest of your life? Neither of us has a job. Do you really want to exist on the dole? That means no money for all the things you're so fond of, remember. Make-up, clothes, jewellery, going out to good restaurants, clubs and pubs. Travelling. Is life on the dole in Possilpark the kind of life you want, Marilyn? If it is, we may as well pack it in and say goodbye right now. Because it's not what I want.'

'Don't talk like that, Johnny. I've done what you said. I've got Joe. I'm just frightened that we won't get the money and we'll go to jail instead. I'd never survive that. I'm not as strong as Kate Gallacher.'

'Just do exactly as I say and you'll be all right.'

'But what about Joe? We surely can't move him again. Where could we go? And what have you given him to make him sleep so much? I don't want anything bad to happen to him, Johnny. I just said what you told me, but you promised . . .'

'He's fine. He's better out for the count. He won't know anything about what's happening this way. He won't be scared. Stop worrying.'

'I suppose you're right. But how – '

'I've told you. You get the money in the plain black brief-case he's put in the left-luggage locker. Then you phone

Cameron at his house as we arranged to tell him where the kid can be collected.'

'But I still don't understand . . .'

'Christ,' he groaned, 'how many times must I go over it? You then create a diversion. You go up to somebody in the South American queue waiting for boarding passes. You say you feel ill. You faint. Then while the crowd's attention is on you, I switch cases.'

'But why must I do all that? Why don't I just meet you on the plane with the money?'

'First of all, because I know how scatty you are. You'd lose the bloody money if you had it more than a couple of minutes. You'd leave it behind in the ladies' room because you'd be so taken up with powdering your nose or fluffing up your hair. You've got a mind like a sieve, Marilyn. I wouldn't trust you with a tenpenny piece, never mind a fortune.'

Marilyn pouted.

'That's not a very nice thing to say.'

'We go on separate planes, Marilyn. Do you understand that?'

'Yes . . . but . . .'

'We're doing it this way because we've got to be one move ahead just in case Cameron has brought the police into this.'

'I told him on the phone he mustn't and he swore he wouldn't.'

'OK, but just in case. I'll get the money and then we'll meet exactly as we've arranged.'

'And Joe will be here all right for Gavin to collect?'

'Of course. *We* can't be lumbered with him, can we?'

Marilyn widened her eyes again.

'It's best that he should be with his daddy. I've always just thought of what's best for Joe. As long as nothing bad happens to him.'

'What bad can happen to him here?'

Marilyn gazed around the empty, boarded-up room. It

was at the back of the house and it was lit with a lantern-shaped torch Johnny had brought along. There was cracked and worn linoleum on the floor left by previous tenants who were now probably getting themselves into a lot of debt buying carpets to cover the floors of their new houses. Joe was lying over in one corner covered with a blanket. He looked very small and still. She went over and knelt down beside him to peer close to his face. He was breathing evenly.

'Granny's just a couple of doors along,' she said.

'Don't act daft. He can't hear you. He's sound. You'd better go.'

'I'm frightened, Johnny.'

He pulled her up into his arms.

'What's there to be afraid of? You're only getting what you're entitled to. He abandoned you, remember. He deserves to fork out and he can afford it. You've told him all you want is this one payment to help you start a new life. Then he'll never see you again. It's as simple as that. You deserve your new start. Look what you've given him. A beautiful son. No amount of money can compare with that.'

'Yes,' she said. 'You're right, Johnny. And we'll be so happy together, won't we? We'll buy a house in the sun. Somewhere near one of those beautiful beaches. I'll have a maid come in every day. One of the local people who can cook lovely meals for us. And we can just lie in the sun . . .'

'Yes, all right.' He glanced at his watch. 'You'd better go.'

'But I've not to leave until morning.'

'Marilyn, I don't want anyone to see you leaving here. Go to your flat now. Set your alarm clock. Don't forget that. Then get some sleep. In the morning, go straight to the airport.'

He kissed her deeply on the mouth. 'Just keep thinking about that lovely life in the sun.'

She nodded, then gave the figure in the corner a quick glance before slipping quietly away.

It wasn't until after she was back in the tiny flat in Saracen Street that she remembered her handbag. In the excitement she'd forgotten she'd laid it down beside the kitchen sink in the condemned Killearn Street flat. She had been in such a state she'd felt quite faint and needed a reviving glass of water. As it happened the water was turned off. So she'd had nothing to cool the heat of her anxiety.

She'd left her handbag beside the sink. In it was her precious make-up purse, her wallet with all her cash, her plane ticket and her passport.

Johnny was so right. She had a mind like a sieve. She needed someone like him to take care of her.

She sat in her untidy bedroom wondering what she should do, and when. Should she return immediately to Killearn Street and collect the handbag? Or should she get some sleep as Johnny had told her? Then she could collect the handbag early in the morning on the way to the airport. She nibbled at a thumbnail. But it would be light in the morning. Somebody might see her going round the back of the building and easing aside the board that covered the back close.

Either way, Johnny would be angry with her. She began to cry. The whole thing was too much for her to cope with. Eventually, exhausted by sobbing, she dried her eyes and went to make herself a cup of tea.

Johnny said to keep thinking of their lovely life in the sun. That's what she must do. Until she'd gone on that wonderful cruise, she'd never been outside Scotland before. She'd only been out of Glasgow a couple of times. In fact, apart from going to the dancing or the shops in town, she'd spent all of her life in Possilpark.

That cruise had opened up completely new vistas. It was magic. She had never been so happy, so excited, so absolutely ecstatic. Oh, the luxury of it all. She closed her eyes as she sipped the comforting tea. The bliss. The sheer joy of it. She felt herself purring inside at the memory.

Maybe she could slip into the flat without Johnny hearing her. He would have to get some sleep too. Probably he would be sound by now. She felt a little better, a little more sure of herself. That's what she'd do. While it was still dark.

But once she got back out on to Saracen Street again, she felt frightened. Apart from anything else there were knots of junkies loitering about at the Cross. Fancy, in the middle of the night. Did they never sleep?

She was sweating by the time she reached Killearn Street. Every few steps she looked over her shoulder to see if any of the junkies were following her. She looked back towards the Cross again before turning up Killearn Street. As far as she could see by the light of the street lamps, nobody had come after her. All the same, she began to run up the hill of Killearn Street. She was choking for breath by the time she skirted the rough patch of earth where the bulldozer had last been busy. The building that hid Johnny and Joe would be next to go. Her heart leapt in her chest. What if Johnny had made a mistake and the bulldozers worked on a Sunday? It was Sunday now.

'Don't be daft,' Johnny had said. 'Work on a building site on the Scottish Sabbath? No way.'

She leaned against the back wall, struggling to calm herself and catch her breath before slipping into the back close and then into the house.

She heard the strange noise as soon as she entered. A kind of gurgling, choking sound. She stumbled through the darkness into the room. Joe was lying on his back breathing in this loud, raspy, choking, frightening way.

'What's wrong with Joe?' Marilyn cried out.

'Shut up, you fool,' Johnny hissed. 'What are you doing back here?'

'I left my handbag. What's up with Joe?'

'I must have given him too much of the stuff. I think he's pegging out.'

'Oh my God, I'll have to get him to a doctor.'

'Don't be fuckin' daft. You get the hell out of here and do as we planned.'

'I can't leave Joe to die. You promised . . .'

'Shut up, will you. I didn't plan this to happen but it has. It needn't change anything. Cameron won't know until he finds him. By that time, we'll be gone.'

Marilyn was shaking so much she could hardly walk but somehow she managed to get over to where Joe was making such terrible sounds.

'Oh my God, I'll have to get him to a doctor!'

'Did you not hear what I said, you stupid cow. Get out of here. Don't touch him.'

But she was already struggling to lift the little boy into her arms.

'I'm sorry, Joe. I didn't mean anything bad to happen, honest I didn't. I'll get you to Granny's. She'll look after you.'

Johnny said, 'If you actually think I'm going to let you take him out of here just now, you're even more stupid than I thought you were.'

'Oh please, Johnny. I can't go on with this. Not now. I had a dream before but now it's a nightmare. I can't cope. I'm sorry. You do what you like.'

She'd only taken another few stumbling steps, just reached the room door when she felt such a blow on the back of her head that she was propelled into the blackness of the lobby. Then the blackness engulfed her.

Chapter Sixty-One

Cameron had kept the police informed. They knew about the phone call and the arrangements for delivering the money. They told him to go ahead as planned. They would be at the airport and watching Marilyn's every move.

'One of our officers will wait with you and after she phones to say where your son is, we'll pick her up,' the CID detective assured him.

'It won't be her,' Cameron said. 'It'll be her husband who's thought this out. It can't be as simple as you think. If anything, she's more likely to be the patsy in this. I know her. She's gullible.'

'We've got a description of the husband. Don't worry, we'll be on the lookout for him too. And we'll immediately check the location of the child. We won't risk anything until we know he's all right. As it is, there's a full-scale search going on.'

'If only I could do something instead of sitting here waiting.'

'It won't be long now, Mr Cameron.'

He hadn't slept a wink, hadn't even undressed or gone to bed. He'd sat all night watching the hands of the clock creep slowly round. Next day the policeman on duty during the night was relieved by two others. One made a pot of tea. He drank the cup they gave him without tasting it. When the phone rang, he pounced. But it was not Marilyn. It was a detective, to tell him that they'd arrested the husband as he boarded a plane. It was he who had collected the money. There had been no sign of Marilyn and no phone call had been made about the child's whereabouts.

'I knew it,' Cameron said. 'I knew it wouldn't just happen as Marilyn said.'

'We're questioning the man now. And we're intensifying the search. Has any place occurred to you where she might have gone?'

'I don't think she knew many places outside Possilpark. Saracen Street, Killearn Street . . . Unless of course some of the clubs and pubs in town. But she'd hardly be likely to go there. Not if she had Joseph. *If* she had him.'

He felt sick with worry.

'We've been combing the city. And we've been going door to door, questioning all her Saracen Street neighbours. We've been questioning everyone in the shops. Only one thing has turned up – just a matter of minutes ago. One of our officers has reported that somebody saw a woman hurrying along Saracen Street towards Killearn Street last night, during the night. It might not have been her. And of course, we've already been over Killearn Street and all the streets round there. But that was a couple of days ago. We'll go over them all again just in case. I'm on my way there now.'

'I'll meet you in Killearn Street,' Cameron said and hung up before he might be advised not to go.

By the time he got from the West End to Possilpark and turned his car into Killearn Street, a group of police cars had gathered and the police were holding back crowds of residents. He thought at first glance they were outside the Gallacher close. Then he saw it was a few yards further along in a boarded-up building. He parked the car and ran towards the place. A policeman tried to stop him getting near.

'I'm Cameron, the boy's father. Have you found him?'

A CID man he'd already met came over then.

'I'm sorry, Mr Cameron, I'm afraid it's bad news . . .'

Cameron pushed roughly past him and into the building. The wood blocking the front close had been removed and a uniformed policeman stood guard. Cameron tried to grapple his way past him but the detective got a grip of him.

'Mr Cameron, the boy's dead. The woman was holding him in her arms. She's been killed by a blow to the back of her head. We think she was trying to protect the child. There's nothing you can do. We're waiting for the police surgeon. You'll be able to see your son later for purposes of identification. This officer will take you home now. I'm very sorry.'

Cameron allowed himself to be led away and helped into a police car. His mind had stopped working. He forgot about his own car. He forgot about everything. He couldn't have told the policeman his address if he'd asked. But he didn't ask. He drove him straight back to the West End where a policewoman was waiting with another male policeman and Mrs Banks.

'Oh, Mr Cameron, what's happened? Have they found him yet?'

The policeman who'd brought him said to Mrs Banks,

'Is there any whisky?'

Mrs Banks nodded.

'I think you'd better bring Mr Cameron a dram.'

'Oh dear.' Mrs Banks went away muttering tearfully to herself. 'Oh dear.'

Cameron downed the whisky. It didn't make him feel any better, but he was able to say to the police, 'Thank you. I'll be all right now.'

'Is there any family or friends we could fetch to be with you?'

'No. Joseph was my only family.'

'Oh dear,' Mrs Banks whispered. Then, 'I'll stay with him.'

'No,' Cameron managed. 'Thank you, Mrs Banks. There's no need. There's nothing you can do at present. Just come tomorrow as usual.'

They all left. The house was suddenly, oppressively silent.

He stood with his back to the door, and wept.

As soon as Kate heard, she cancelled all the wedding arrangements and phoned Richard.

'Marilyn was my sister-in-law, one of the family. Oh, it's so terrible, Richard. Her little boy as well. We're all so terribly upset. I couldn't, none of us, could face wedding celebrations just now.'

'I quite understand the postponement, darling. Of course nobody could face a wedding at a time like this. Do you want me to come up for the funeral?'

'No, no, there's no point. You only met Marilyn a couple of times and you never knew the little boy. There'll be the two funerals and of course we'll be going to both of them. My poor mother. She was so fond of both Marilyn and the wee boy.'

'You must come down here afterwards for a holiday, darling. To help you recover from all the trauma.'

'I don't know. I can't think at the moment, Richard. I'll either phone or write.'

'As long as you contact me when it's all over.'

'Yes, I'll do that. I'm so sorry about the wedding plans, but what else could I do?'

'You did the right thing. Don't worry.'

Despite her distress, it did occur to Kate afterwards that Richard had not invited her mother to come with her to Denby House for a holiday. And after all, she had stressed that it was her mother who was as upset as anyone, if not more so.

Was it all right for Kate Gallacher to be seen by the county set, because Kate Gallacher was not bad looking, smartly turned out and a successful businesswoman? But would he want a tough wee broad-spoken Glasgow woman like Mary Gallacher to arrive and cause him embarrassment, give him a showing up?

Was that why he hadn't invited any friends to the wedding? Not one. Had he not the courage to let anyone see what her family and her background were like?

She'd mentioned the subject of guests from his side (or rather, the lack of them) more than once but he'd shrugged and said,

'To be honest, Kate, even when my wife was alive, we never socialised all that much. Since she died, I've either been doing the rounds of the shows in London in the winter or travelling abroad. Then in the summer I'm so busy with the house. I know plenty of people but it's only on a very casual level.'

She had been satisfied with that at the time and she tried to feel satisfied with it now. The trouble with her was that when she was unhappy or upset, she tended to get uptight and suspicious.

Richard was being very good about the wedding and after all, he must have been terribly disappointed. It was unfair of her to think badly of him, especially at a time like this.

It was such a dreadful business. Poor Marilyn. God knows how she'd got into such a mess. But at least she'd been trying to protect or help wee Joe. So everyone said.

Kate had written a letter of condolence to Cameron. It had been difficult and turned out very stiff and formal, but she felt she had to make some gesture.

Then came the awful day of the funerals. First Marilyn's. Cameron did not attend. Mary said,

'The man might huv come tae pay his last respects tae the poor lassie. After aw, she cannae harm anybody any more. Ah dinnae believe she ever harmed anybody but hersel'.'

Then the little boy's funeral. It was the first time Kate had seen Cameron since the time she'd met him in Byres Road. His appearance shocked her. He looked his usual hard-faced self. At the same time, she sensed the depth of his grief. She saw it in his eyes. He was hurting and suddenly she was not just sympathising, she was suffering an anguish of hurt along with him. She couldn't bear him to suffer alone. She couldn't take her eyes off him in the church. She wanted to comfort him, to be close to him, to tell him he wasn't alone. She loved him, she'd always loved him. But she'd never been able either to say the words or to express her feelings in any way other than sex. Why had she been like this? She had tried to analyse herself before. And where had it got her? She had never had the nerve to allow herself to

372

take the risk of trusting her whole self to another human being. Not since Pete. And had she ever trusted even him?

Sitting in the church not listening to the minister's solemn voice, her thoughts groped this way and that. Didn't trust take as much courage as taking any other risk? And she'd taken plenty. Wasn't allowing oneself to be vulnerable at times more courageous than being ruthless. What was that saying – better to have loved and lost than never to have loved at all. She loved this man. Maybe he would lash out at her, rebuff her, hurt her, even sneer at any attempt she'd make to open her heart to him.

But damn it all, she had to try.

After the funeral, she saw him get into his car and she ran towards it. She rapped at his window and he rolled it down. He stared at her.

'Gavin, I know we've often made each other angry. Maybe we're too much alike, that's the trouble. But I have to say something to you today, right now. This isn't easy for me, but it's the truth. I love you. I've always loved you. Always you. I love you. And I always will.'

He looked away. Stared straight ahead and released the handbrake.

'Gavin, if you want me, if you need me, if you love me, all you have to do is lift the phone.'

The car moved smoothly away. She watched it until it disappeared from sight.

Then she went to join her mother and the rest of the family.

'Fancy him no' havin' even a cup o' tea fur anybody.'

'Oh, men aren't so good at organising these things, Mammy. He'd be too upset.'

'Och aye, ah suppose ye're right, hen. Ah dinnae feel much like socialisin' masel'.' She noisily blew her nose. 'Ah keep thinkin' about that poor wean.'

George took her arm. 'Come on, Mary, I'll get you home.'

'I'm just going straight home as well,' Kate said.

'Christine's staying with a friend, so I think I'll just have a quiet night and go to bed early.'

Once home, however, she wandered from room to empty room, longing for Cameron to contact her but knowing he would not. Eventually, she wrote a long letter to Richard explaining as best, as kindly and as honestly as she could, why she would never marry him.

Then she undressed and fell on to the bed as if into a deep pit.

It was exactly two minutes past midnight, the start of a new day, when the phone rang and brought her soaring back to life.